Shooting Stars

Christopher Watson

AN [*e-reads*] BOOK
New York, NY

Copyright 2000 by Christopher Watson
First e-reads publication 2002
www.e-reads.com
ISBN 0-7592-5092-8

For Matthew.

Introduction

Shooting Stars is a work of fiction. Any resemblance of any of the characters, corporations or other like entities, situations, or events described in the book to any actual characters, corporations, situations or events, barring satiric or illustrative intent, is coincidental.

Many of the late 20th century historical events described in *Shooting Stars* are inventions of the author. Although actual corporations, parties and events are sometimes noted, the reader should be aware that some details may have been altered for dramatic purposes and that in so doing, no disrespect or commentary was intended nor should be inferred.

Despite the patient and generous tutorial efforts of numerous parties, the blame for any technical innacuracies in the text more astute eyes may discover falls entirely on the author's shoulders.

Acknowledgements

Solitary by character, writing inevitably becomes collaborative by necessity. Thus, thanks are due to the following people, for the reasons noted.

Tony DeMeo, Director of Information for the Princeton Plasma Physics Laboratory, arranged a tour of the impressive PPPL facility, including their groundbreaking Tokamak Fusion Test Reactor. Both Mr. DeMeo and PPPL Associate Director Dr. Dale Meade graciously gave of their time, reviewing portions of the manuscript and answering my many questions. Likewise, Dr. Gerald Kulcinski of the University of Wisconsin, Madison, allowed me to pick his brain and provided several papers on IEC fusion which proved invaluable. Few things would please me more than to have this modest work ignite greater interest in their more significant endeavors.

Jennifer Brown of the Vandenberg Air Force Base Public Affairs Department and Vandenberg historian Jeffrey Geiger both provided me with much useful information about the base, its history and capabilities.

On the morning of October 25, 1985, Paul Fayard of Carolina Sky Sports leaped out of a C-182 with me strapped to his chest, a tandem skydive which I broadcast live on the radio. That experience both marked the beginning of my two-year foray into skydiving and planted the seeds from which this book grew.

Roy Yukio Suenaka Sensei, founder of Wadokai Aikido, has been my teacher, my martial mentor and my dear friend for many years, and served in part as the model for Colonel Takeshita. Mac's warrior spirit was born of Suenaka Sensei's teachings to me and his hundreds of students. *Domo arigato gozaimasu, Sensei.*

Thanks to Barry Hill, who once again served as my human safety net for all matters digital, and to Rocky Allen, Michael Rupprecht and Irene Tiersten, who read early drafts of the book and provided much useful criticism. Thanks as well to Phil Danz at Mailboxes Etc. and the staff of the Somerset County, NJ, Public Library.

Richard Curtis honored me by agreeing to represent *Shooting Stars*, made it better with his criticism, and believed in it so much, he published it himself. He's the best, end of story, and I thank him.

Charles W. Watson served his country with distinction for two years with the U.S. Army and over twenty with the Air Force, retiring in 1978 at the rank of chief master sergeant. Betty D. Watson served by his side, expertly riding rein on three rowdy military brats and spending what had to have been a terribly hard year waiting for her husband's next letter from Vietnam. They promised long ago to support me in whatever I chose to do and they're still keeping that promise. I love you both.

My stepson, Matthew Leveton, is the man to whom this book is dedicated. I'd need the space of another to explain why.

Finally, thanks to my wife, Jackie. Living with a writer is like living with a ghost, glimpsed only in passing as he disappears upstairs for another solitary session at the keyboard, the occasional creaking board the only evidence of his existence. My love, and my thanks for understanding.

Table of Contents

Prologue

An observer from the ground would have seen nothing in the evening sky, save perhaps a glimpse of stars glittering through the occasional break in the thickening bank of cumulus clouds making its slow, stately way eastward almost a mile overhead. Even with a powerful telescope, even if the observer had known where to look, all that would have showed was a momentary impression of depthless shadow flashing across the starfield, a dead spot in the heavens. It would be missed in a blink, gone before the observer was even sure he'd seen it. It took more than keen eyes and a telescope to detect, but it was there.

And there were people looking, looking very closely indeed.

In a dark, cramped underground bunker somewhere in the Southern hemisphere, three uniformed men barely out of their teens sat before a long electronic console, their faces eerily lit by the greenish glow of the monitors they watched. Behind them another man paced, his black hair silver at the temples, coffee flesh laid over sharp cheekbones, his uniform breast heavy with ribbons. Waiting.

One of the soldiers murmured something, pointed at his screen. The colonel was instantly there, leaning over the subordinate's shoulder, peering intently at the lines of satellite data scrolling down the monitor.

Tense moments passed as the data were checked. The soldier shook his head. Chairs creaked as the tension in the room subsided. The colonel straightened, growled a command to his second standing patiently nearby and climbed the metal stair to the surface.

It was cooler outside but still humid, the evening breeze from the west carrying the loamy scent of the distant jungle and beyond, the

1

promise of rain. The colonel inhaled deeply. The wind felt good after the hours in the stale, dank air of the bunker. What faint light there was shone dully on the tall grasses of the pampas that stretched out before him, dotted with patches of low vegetation.

He rested his tired eyes on a wide gathering of scrub a hundred meters or so in front of him, a low clump of shadow. Below it was the missile, one of the very few they had left. His missile, awaiting his command to roar from its berth. Invisible from the air, invisible to any human, electronic, laser, thermal or sonic eye that sought it. Or so they had thought.

Somewhere in the dark a bird cried out, a long, plaintive note. A low rumble of thunder answered. There was a storm coming. It wouldn't be long now, nor would it make his task any easier.

The colonel lit a cigarette and looked up at the sky as he exhaled smoke. Their intelligence was good. He knew it was up there, somewhere, beyond the clouds. All he had to do was find it. Destroy it.

Before it destroyed them.

The new moon was invisible from the ground, the sun's rays blocked by the Earth. It was just as dark here, yet her seas seemed to glow with a dusty pale light of their own. *Mare Tranquillitatis* and *Mare Serentatis* dominated the eastern hemisphere, the trio of *Mare Cognitum*, *Mare Nubium* and *Mare Humorum* and the oblong *Oceanus Procellarum* staking their ancient claims in the west. Countless dark craters stood out in soft, shadowed relief against the pewter surface.

A sleek, flat shape inserted itself into the sphere, a deeper shadow bleeding from the sable of space. There were no running lights, little to interrupt its lethal lines. The belly of the craft bowed near imperceptibly fore to aft, the shallow curve disturbed only by a quartet of armaments resting patiently within their sealed recessed bays. The nose was severe, predatory, flowing smoothly to the flight deck, where it briefly angled sharply upward before continuing aft two meters. Here the lines darted upward again, another four meters, then leveled and sped parallel with the belly to the twin triangular tails fixed like canted sails above the orbital maneuvering system engine array, the trio of potent exhausts now silent. The ship's immense delta wing was almost indiscernible in profile, and extended gracefully outward from the belly, the main fuselage flowing smoothly downward to meet it.

Her finish was matte black, reflecting no light. The only adornment was a meter-long shield emblazoned on her port side just aft of the flight deck: an upright Japanese *katana*, the sword bisected by a shooting star that streaked downwards from right to left, sinister chief to dexter base. Crimson letters set along the top of the company crest read 82ND SPEC. AIRBORNE HALO CO. Beside it, another shield, bearing the twin lightning bolts and rising delta point of the Air Force Space Warfare Center.

Below the crests was the name of the craft: *D.S. REAGAN.*

The *Drop Ship Reagan* flitted across the moon and dove like a manta into the darker depths on the other side, speeding along her orbital translation towards her rendezvous with her target on the Earth below. Only a handful of people knew she was aloft. Fewer still knew her location and objective, and many more of those who knew nothing dreaded what she might bring. The *Reagan* was an orbital warfighter, the only one of her kind. The mere fact that she had been launched meant only one thing.

Tonight, someone, somewhere, was going to die.

The *Reagan* streaked past an enemy satellite, just five-thousand miles away. She could have passed half again or more as close undetected. Her electronic STEALTH cloak shielded her from even the most sophisticated satellite surveillance. At the most, she would read as a brief, inexplicable anomaly in the lines of data monitored in the enemy bunker on Earth.

The colonel knew this. He knew very well that the brief blip in the data he'd seen moments before could have been the object of his search, but one did not fire expensive surface-to-space missiles at blips. Not if one wished to remain a colonel.

There was another rumble of thunder, closer now. The colonel smoked his cigarette, gaze fixed on the clouds.

From the starboard nose verniers of the *Reagan* came tiny jets of flame, bright and silent in the airless void. The aft port verniers fired in unison and the craft began turning to starboard along her Y-axis, like a vehicle spinning slowly on ice. As she neared the end of her 180-degree rotation, the verniers extinguished and their twins port and starboard briefly flared, halting the big ship's inertia.

The *Reagan* now flew tail first along her translation. In a few moments, the massive rearward OMS engine array would ignite, slowing the ship until she matched the Earth's rotation precisely. There she would remain, seemingly motionless, just long enough to discharge her deadly cargo. Then the OMS engines would fire once more and send the craft speeding away to her re-entry coordinates. Back home.

From a single starboard nose vernier came a spurt of blue-white flame. It was tiny against the bulk of the ship, no more than an angry firecracker flash. Immediately, the *Reagan* began once more spinning along her translation, propelled by the brief explosion, the vernier venting a plume of white gas that instantly boiled away in the vacuum of space. It was a slow, lazy rotation. Outwardly, there seemed to be nothing wrong.

Inside the ship, all hell was breaking loose.

The thunder grumbled once more, a few cool drops of rain spattering on the colonel's upturned face. Lighting flared in the west, the purple bellies of the heavy clouds briefly glowing like luminaries.

He took another deep drag on his cigarette, watching the cherry flare hot orange beneath its ash covering. He focused his gaze through the blue haze of smoke as he exhaled, to the pampas beyond. For all he knew they could be out there right now, watching him, crouched low in the tall, undulating grasses, their arrival concealed by the clouds. There were rumors that they wore specially coated armor that bent the light, making them seem almost invisible, that their parachutes were a mere four cells wide so they flew to earth fast as falcons diving for prey. He didn't believe it. They were men, soldiers — no. Better than soldiers. The frightened boys he was grudgingly resigned to command were soldiers, barely. The men he hunted, that hunted him, were warriors.

He returned his attention to the present, laid his hand atop the cold metal weight of the sidearm at his hip. Whatever happened tonight, he vowed he wouldn't die alone.

From the camouflaged bunker behind him came the dull clang of hurried footsteps on the metal stair that led to the surface. He turned in time to see his second emerge from the doorway. His eyes were open wide.

The colonel dropped his cigarette to the ground and followed his second back into the bunker.

The soldiers were talking excitedly, their voices overlapping as they gesticulated. The din silenced at a barked word from the colonel. He

4

hurried over to the soldier monitoring the satellite feed and peered at the data line indicated by the boy's trembling finger. He closed his eyes, opened them and looked again. A single murmured obscenity fell from his lips.

The soldiers were watching him expectantly. He leaned forward and punched an alphanumeric code into the keypad in the center of the console, the digits displayed one-by-one in the narrow window above it, blinking in confirmation when he'd finished. The colonel stood erect and tugged at the waist of his jacket to straighten it, his eyes moving once again to the screen, checking the data a final time.

He smiled and gave the order to launch the missile.

Outside, a shrill mechanical whine cut through the thunder and rising patter of rain. The patch of vegetation concealing the missile silo parted. Light spilled from the widening opening, an expanding cone of illumination made visible by the humid air as it shone upwards like a beacon.

The silo cover came to rest with a clunk. The ground shook as steam and smoke boiled out of the opening. The nose of the missile emerged, gaining speed as the body followed, until the pampas were brilliantly lit by the angry, yellow-white fire that pushed the projectile skyward. The shadows cast by the scrub in its glaring wake rapidly lengthened as the missile roared towards its target, the noise and light fading until the pampas were dark and still once again.

Those inside the bunker were only dimly conscious of the dull receding rumble of the missile's engine. All eyes were fixed on the screens. The colonel was acutely aware of his pounding heart. He could smell the sour perspiration of his subordinates as they waited with him, hardly daring to breathe as the seconds crawled by.

Thirty seconds. Sixty. Seventy . . .

At exactly one minute and nineteen seconds after launch, a stream of new data scrolled down the screen. The colonel slammed his fist into the counter as the tiny room erupted in cheers. He pounded his grinning second on the shoulder and shouted over the noise of the celebration for him to place a call to central command. His missile had just blown that damned spaceship out of the sky.

General. It would be nice to retire a general.

Four minutes later and five-hundred miles north, a peasant farmer sighed wearily. His wife called to him from the doorway of their cottage, beckoning for him to come inside where the evening meal waited. He raised his hand in tired acknowledgment, stroking the dusty coat of his mule as he raised hopeful eyes to the sky. The radio said the desperately-needed rain would come from the southwest. He squinted in that direction but there were no clouds he could see, and the air was still. He said a silent prayer as he gazed at the evening sky, a prayer for rain.

As if in answer, a flurry of brilliant streaks suddenly appeared in the distance high overhead, over the jungle. The shooting stars flared even brighter as they fell, then winked out as suddenly as they had appeared.

The farmer considered it a good omen that he should have happened to have been looking in just the right place to see the meteors as he prayed. Perhaps his prayer would be answered after all.

He gave his mule an affectionate swat and headed inside to his supper.

Part One

One

I

Ignore the cold. Ignore the pain. Ignore the icy wind that whips down off the ridge and knifes through your *gi*. Ignore your numb, frozen fingers as they grasp the *jo*. Ignore everything but the task at hand. Move. Breathe. Survive.

But it was hard this morning, harder than usual. The nightmare always made it that way. He had lost count of how many times he'd jerked upright out of fitful sleep, his heart pounding, body draped in sweat-drenched sheets. There was a time when he had believed the nightmare's terror would fade with familiarity, that the passage of years would carry him to a day when sleep would bring nothing but itself. Nine years was long enough to wait.

Even now, his pulse resumed its frantic tattoo as his attention wavered only the fraction of a second purchased by the recollection. He cursed himself as he lost count of his *kata*, the *kata* he'd executed thousands of times. He stood still in the shin-deep snow for a full minute as punishment, the butt of the *jo* breaking the icy crust of the new snow with a soft crunch as he let the oaken staff slide through his fingers and come to rest beside his frozen foot. Eyes closed, he directed his focus inward, towards his one-point, the spot below his navel where his center of gravity was and his *ki* lived. He sucked a lungful of the frigid air through his nose, counting thirty, then slowly exhaled through his mouth on another thirty count. His breath hissed through his throat like steam, pluming in the air before him before the wind found it and snatched it away.

The frozen landscape around him faded from consciousness as he turned inward, seeking the only release he could find, release from exterior pain. It was the inner ache which now presented itself, a pain that cut through him more cruelly than the wind that buffeted his body like the surf, shaking him out of his reverie. You will find no forgiveness there, it moaned. You should know that by now.

He wearily opened his eyes, the biting cold flooding back into his consciousness with the daylight. He was freezing. He should go back inside his cabin, make a cup of coffee, make a fire. He knew what he should do. Instead, he did what he had to do.

He bowed to the gods and dropped back into *sankakutai*, the triangular stance that began each *jo kata*. His numb right foot plowed through the snow as he slid it backwards, no longer able to feel the ground. He inhaled and began the *kata* anew, counting silently as he executed each move.

Ichi: thrust forward to the midsection of the enemy.

Ni: raise the *jo* in a forward-slanting, two-handed block.

San: thrust forward to the enemy's face.

Shi: another overhead block.

Go: a right-side cut to the enemy's neck, the *jo* whistling through the air.

Roku: reverse and cut to the left.

Shichi: right-hand thrust to the rear, to the enemy's midsection.

Hachi: Spin one-hundred-eighty degrees to the right, the tip of the *jo* skimming the snow in a leg sweep, ending in another rearward thrust.

Ku: another block.

Ju: another thrust to the face . . .

He breathed steadily, exhaling on the thrusts and cuts, inhaling on the blocks. He pictured each foe before him as he fought, stern shadows in the snow, making no sound except in his imagination as they continued their relentless, untiring attack.

Every morning he began his day this way. And every day, the outcome was the same. No peace. No redemption, only the certainty of the battle. As he moved — now slowly, with the grace of a ballerina, then swiftly, like a pouncing panther, his movements a blur as the worn *jo* sliced through the air — he felt the hot breath of his demons on his neck and in his heart.

9

The *kata* was his meditation, and his penance. And so, he welcomed the cold. This, he knew, was transient, unlike the guilty ache that drove him to his daily torture. If he could not banish his demons, then he would master his punishment.

He executed the final movement of the *kata*, cutting downward before him as he shouted an explosive *kiai*, the guttural sound echoing over the frozen landscape like a cannon shot. He stood with his *jo* held before him, locked in the completion of the final move of the *kata*. The way of the warrior is in resolute acceptance of death. That's what Sensei always said, all those years ago. The true test, he now knew, was in living.

He slowly returned the *jo* to his side and forced himself to bow once again, closing the *kata*. Cannot forget *reigi*, proper etiquette. Sensei would have a fit. He stared dumbly at his left hand as he clenched it, feeling the joints of his fingers crackle with cold as he formed the fist, the ridge of purplish calluses thick on his knuckles.

Freezing. He was freezing to death. Get inside, that whisper from somewhere urged. Turn. Walk up the hill. It's only fifty yards or so. You'll be there in just a minute, inside the cabin where there's warmth and coffee and comfort. But he was having a hard time hearing the voice, the wind was so loud, whining over his head, the whine deepening into a roar that now filled the snow-covered glade . . .

He forced his stiff neck muscles to turn his head over his right shoulder, up towards the ridge behind the cabin. At first he thought it was a bird, but the shape skipping over the high horizon lacked the elegant upswept arc of an eagle's wings. The body was much too large as well, he calmly observed. It was thick, oblong, with stubby wings that swept back from the fuselage, thick cylindrical turbines that roared and then rotated downward as the craft sailed over the cabin and slowed to a thousand-foot hover almost directly over his head.

It was an aircar, sleek and steady as it floated in the sky. The last time he'd seen one this close, it was resting on the tarmac at Fort Bragg and spilling Army brass. The shock of the novelty pulled him fully into focus like a rubberband snapping back from the breaking point.

The pilot seemed to sense his scrutiny. The shining craft slipped sideways fifty yards, seeming for a moment as if it were about to topple and crash, then steadied and began its descent.

II

He shielded his eyes from the jetwash as the aircar touched down. The door opened and the interloper emerged, tugging on a pair of heavy gloves. He could see the man was young, maybe thirty, with short, curly blond hair that ruffled in the wind like springs. He wore rimless, wire-framed glasses, a heavy parka and leather loafers that disappeared into the snow as he gingerly stepped down off the aircar running board. The parka looked new.

The visitor lurched clumsily through the snow towards him, shouting over the wind and dying whine of the aircar turbines:

"Major Harrison? Major Mackinley Harrison?"

Steve Davis stopped, squinting against the wind. A little over a yard away the man stood in the snow like he was planted there, unaffected by the weather, a shoulder-high staff clasped lightly in his right hand. He peered closely at his face, the angular features camouflaged by the dark, full beard that reached almost to his chest. His hair was long, falling well past his shoulders, shot through with gray that swept back at the temples like wings; a lion's mane of hair that floated around his head in the wind. Davis could see now that he was wearing a martial arts practice uniform, the simple cotton jacket held closed by a tattered black belt tied around the waist, the long ends hanging limp. A thin gold necklace showed through the frayed open lapels of the jacket, the pendant some Asian-looking symbol which Davis didn't recognize.

Davis returned his attention to the face, tried to imagine it ten years or so younger, mid-thirties and without the beard, the hair close-cropped, the cotton jacket and pants replaced by an Army dress uniform.

He swallowed, feeling his pulse quicken. Holy cow, he'd done it. He'd found him.

"Are you Major Mackinley Harrison?"

"Who . . . " Mac's long-unused voice caught in his throat. He cleared it. "Who're you?"

"My name is Davis. Steve Davis. I work for UniCom. Universal Communications?"

He waited for Mac to be impressed, but the man only held that thousand-yard stare, seeming to look straight through Davis even as his eyes bored into him. For an instant, Davis felt a cold touch to his gut that had nothing to do with the weather.

He covered the awkward moment by fumbling off a glove and unzipping his parka. He reached inside and withdrew his UniCom photo ID, offering it like a magical trinket. Mac afforded it a momentary glance, long enough for Davis to take a final look at his features.

"It is you," he said, a smile showing as he replaced the ID and quickly zipped up against the cold. "I wasn't sure at first, what with the, you know . . . " He waved his hand around his own clean-shaven chin as he donned the glove. "Department of Defense told me where to look for you. Mister Conner pulled some strings." Again, he waited for a reaction. "Roger Conner? He's . . . "

"I know who he is."

"Been cruising around for an hour trying to spot this place," Davis continued, casting a glance around the property. "Pretty remote. Only one for fifty miles in any direction."

"Folks here like their privacy."

"Yeah," Davis ended lamely. "Guess so." He finally noticed Mac's bare feet, the toes clearly blue against the snow. He looked back up, open-mouthed. "Aren't you cold?"

"Yes."

Davis cleared his throat and plunged ahead. "He'd like to see you, Mister Conner. He'd like for you to be his guest for a few days at UniCom corporate in Research Triangle Park, North Carolina. He . . . "

Mac turned and started up the low rise to his cabin. Davis stared. "What'd I say?" Mac kept on walking as Davis' mind went into frantic overdrive. "I just came two-thousand miles to find you!" he shouted at the retreating back. "Don't you even want to know why?"

Mac spoke without turning, the words echoing sharply off the snowpack during a lull in the wind. "If it's that important, e-mail me. I get my messages in town twice a month." He kept walking.

"It's about Colonel Takeshita!"

He pronounced it incorrectly, making it four harsh syllables instead of three. It was close enough. Mac stopped, turned.

"What about Sensei?"

The cabin was small, just living quarters, kitchen and bathroom below and a sleeping loft above. Mac had built it himself, felling the trees and

12

stripping the logs, dragging them to the cabin site behind his battered Humvee, notching the timbers and erecting the cabin one log at a time using nothing more than the Hummer's winch and his own strong back. It had taken him all of a summer and part of the fall, finishing just as the leaves turned russet and the big bucks finally emerged from the deep woods, sternly patrolling their turf as their harems followed meekly behind, already pregnant with the fawns of the coming spring. His labor, his home. Something pure and honest that he could claim as his own.

He closed the cabin door behind him, unconsciously leaning the *jo* in its usual place against the wall beside the doorframe. He crossed the plank floor to the narrow stair that led to the loft, climbing the rough-hewn steps until he emerged into his bedroom, still reeling from the bombshell Davis had dropped into his ascetic existence.

The loft was as simple as the downstairs. There was a bed, a dresser bearing a single electric lamp, a small plank closet, and a scuffed aluminum footlocker resting on the floor at the bed's foot. Mac knelt in *seiza* before it, sitting on bent knees, right foot automatically crossing over his left, both beginning to flood with the pins-and-needles agony of returning sensation. He read his name, stamped on the footlocker's dull gray surface: HARRISON, MACKINLEY M., MAJ. It was followed by his serial number and a handful of Army abbreviations and obscure acronyms — 82nd SPEC. AIR. DIV., HALO CO. BRAVO SQ. The locker was the same Mac had been issued when he'd first enlisted, twenty-seven years before, the surface scarred and dented by his travels.

He flipped the latches, lifted the lid, removed the folded olive drab blanket that overlaid the contents. The dress uniform came first, ribbons and polished bars bright against the smooth fabric. He laid it carefully aside on the floor and lifted the palm-sized box that next presented itself. He hesitated a moment before opening it, stared at the golden star resting within, circled by the ring that held it affixed to the silk ribbon. He waited for something to stir inside him as he gazed at the Congressional Medal of Honor, his country's thanks for his service, his sacrifice, his valor in the face of overwhelming odds. He remembered the words well, spoken as the president had draped the medal around his neck while Mac stood at attention and Sensei watched proudly.

He snapped the lid shut. He felt nothing.

He placed the box atop his uniform and raised up the object of his search. The frame was simple, purchased at a drugstore. It was the photo beneath the glass that fanned the ash-covered embers of Mac's remembrance. Fourteen men stood proudly side-by-side, twelve clad in black and gray camouflage pressure suits, the curved Ranger insignia high on their shoulders, hovering above the upright sword and angled meteor of the company crest. They held their drop helmets tucked beneath their left arms, the dark siliplas visors presented to the camera. Sergeant's stripes stood out on the arm of the thirteenth, standing at the far left end of the line. The owner stared sternly ahead, black as night, lean-limbed and screaming career Army, the light fringe of buzz-cut hair above his ears barely visible in the photo — Dropmaster Sergeant Otis Rawlings.

Standing at the far right end of the line was a stocky Japanese-American man, his black hair slicked close to his wide, round skull, the dark eyes flashing with pride beneath their slanting epicanthic folds. Colonel Yoshi Takeshita Sensei: modern-day *samurai*, martial arts master, commanding officer of the elite U.S. Army 82nd Special Airborne HALO Company. And beside him stood a slender man barely into his thirties, his face all gawky angles, his chest stuck out so far it appeared as if it would explode, his right shoulder just touching Sensei's left. Captain Mackinley Michael Harrison, Bravo squad leader.

Ghosts now, so many of them. Mac ran his hand over the photo, pausing on Sensei's face, then clenched his fist to stop it from trembling.

Davis gunned the turbines and the craft rose smoothly into the air, wheeling into a graceful one-hundred-eighty turn as the landing skids retracted. The whine of the turbines deepened into a roar as the main thrusters kicked in, speeding the craft up and over the ridge. From the shotgun seat, Mac watched his snow-blanketed world dwindle away beneath him as the car headed south.

They stopped once outside of Rockford, Illinois, long enough to refuel, relieve themselves and grab two coffees to go. It was just turning dark when the aircar set down in front of UniCom's hangar at Raleigh-Durham International Airport. There was a company limousine waiting there, Mister Conner's personal ride. Davis recognized Joseph, Conner's chauffeur, standing placidly at the ready beside the sleek black Lincoln. Mac had exited the aircar and was standing a yard off the nose, modest duffel on the tarmac beside him, stretching.

"That him?"

Davis glanced at the man next to him, dressed in the tan coverall of a Carolina Airfreight employee, one of Conner's many holdings. He'd seen him a couple times but couldn't remember his name.

"Yup. That's him."

The worker stared, enthralled. "Wow," he murmured. "Doesn't look anything like the photos. What's he like?"

Davis had been thrilled to receive his assignment from Connor, had fantasized during his trip north about spending the return flight south getting to know his passenger, collecting a few stories to tell in the pilot's lounge. Mac Harrison, the last of the Shooting Stars, big as life in the seat next to him. He cast a baleful glance in Mac's direction.

"He's quiet. Ve-ry quiet. Didn't say a word the whole damn trip."

"You piss him off?"

"Yeah." Davis jammed his thumb hard against the validation square of the e-pad log the worker held. "I breathed."

He reluctantly dropped the aircar keys into the worker's open palm, not knowing when he'd get another chance to log time in the custom ride. Mac rounded the front of the car, carrying his duffel in his left hand, and the worker pretended to examine the port belly fan. "Joseph will take care of you from here," Davis told Mac, nodding to the waiting limo.

"He knows where Sensei is?"

"He knows where UniCom is," Davis curtly replied. "Mister Conner will take care of the rest when you arrive. Nice meeting you."

He offered his hand almost as a dare, and was surprised when Mac grasped it and gave it a single, firm tug, looking directly at him for the first time since their meeting that morning.

"You're a pretty good pilot, Davis."

Mac released Davis' hand, turned and stepped into the limo. Davis watched as Joseph closed the door, climbed behind the wheel and smoothly accelerated the car towards the exit.

"You hear that?" Davis said, watching the car drive off. "Major Mac Harrison thinks I'm a pretty good pilot."

"Wait'll he sees you drive." The worker moved off as another hooked a tractor to the front of the car to haul it into the hangar for post-flight. Davis strutted towards the pilot's lounge, donning his shades as he walked. What the hell, just one quick beer before home, with the rest of the flyboys.

III

Mac shifted his weight, squirming in the too-soft limousine seat until he found an angle that took some of the pressure off his sore back. The long trip in the aircar had transformed the chronic stiffness there into a solid band of ache. He twisted left and right, stretching the muscles. It eased some of the tension, but none of the suspicion.

He was being set up. It was obvious. He'd considered pumping Davis for information during their flight but it had been clear that one question is all it would have taken to set his eager chauffeur babbling non-stop. He'd decided Davis probably knew nothing more than he'd already revealed.

Mac closed his eyes and replayed the morning's events. It hadn't been until he had walked away that Davis had played his trump card, about Sensei's stroke. Mac again felt his stomach heave at the thought but he ignored it. If Sensei's illness had been the real reason for Conner's invitation, why not mention it first? Why send Davis at all? A simple e-mail would have discharged anyone's obligation to relay the news, though there was no such official obligation he could recall, nothing that required anyone to inform him. Of course, if he'd kept in touch . . .

He winced inwardly as he thought of how long it'd been since he'd had any contact with his former CO. He thrust the swell of guilt to the back of his mind. Plenty of time for that later. There always was.

No, the real reason for his brusque summons was as Davis first said: Roger Conner demanded an audience. Mac would discover the reason soon enough, but why would Conner bother with Sensei? His former CO was retired now, living outside Fort Bragg in Fayetteville, his last station, Mac's as well, yet Conner had kept close enough watch on him to learn of his stroke, move him from Womack Medical Center on base to his private clinic. And close enough tabs on Mac to let him know. To lure him with the news to UniCom.

Mac felt himself grow angry as the realization hit him. He'd have to see about that when he and Conner met.

Most anybody on the planet knew the name Roger Charles Conner. The wealthiest man in America, a self-made trillionaire, founder and CEO of one of the world's largest technological research conglomerates. Terra Telecom was his, the global communications network, as was Max-Q, the maker's mark stamped on over half of the world's computer display systems. Alternate energy, aerospace technology, cybernetics, lasers — UniCom's corporate empire was vast. And then, there was that base on the moon.

Conner had rocked the world when he'd first announced his intention to build Moontown. People had deemed him crazy, but to everyone's astonishment he'd made it happen, completing the first phase of the mammoth, visionary undertaking in the first decade of the new millennium. Newspapers, television, cybernets buzzed with the latest news. It had even inspired a top-ten pop song and a mercifully brief dance craze. Moontown had been the word on everyone's lips.

Then came the war.

Conner had made the bulk of his fortune as a military contractor, the Pentagon's chief go-to. UniCom had designed and built the *Reagan*, the 82nd's flagship, as well as the dropsleds she fired from her topside batteries; the narrow, missile-like gliders that carried Mac and his brothers in arms streaking into combat. His pulse quickened as it always did when he remembered the sensation — the hard kick as the sled's tiny engine fired, the jarring, instantaneous transition from weightlessness to leaden heaviness as the battery door slammed open and the engine impelled the sled from its dark, claustrophobic berth and into the vastness of space, towards the Earth below him.

It was the most beautiful thing Mac had ever seen in his life, the sudden revelation of his home planet. So many shades of blue, of green, silver-white polar caps and deep rust continents, an infinite palette of colors he doubted could be named in a lifetime. His wonder was always heightened by the brief window of time he had to appreciate it, and the fatalistic determination that burned within him, the certain knowledge that in just a few moments, someone was going to die. It might be him, or one of the other men in the phalanx of sleds that streaked through the thin first layer of atmosphere with him, through the creep of fire that now painted Mac's sled, the siliplas cowling over his head beginning to glow, the sled to shake, Mac's gauntleted hands locked on the steering levers as he lay prone in the padded interior, Nick's strained baritone briefly crackling in his helmet headset as the Greek madman began to sing . . .

"Sir?"

The car had stopped. Mac's door was open, Joseph standing discreetly to the side. They'd arrived at their destination. Mac grabbed his duffel and exited the car.

It was fully dark now, the only illumination provided by the moon and the row of ground-level lights that followed the curve of the half-circle drive that led to the UniCom building's main entrance. The greenish, mirrored glass walls of the eclectic structure sloped upwards for the first half-dozen floors, then ascended vertically for an equal span, like an inverted rectangle emerging from the top of a pyramid. A crisp breeze stirred the tall pines encircling the building, their dark swaying limbs reflected in the moonlit glass, making the building seem as if it was shifting in and out of reality from some other dimension. Mac could just make out more structures behind the main building, trees and darkness disguising the true spread of the headquarters complex.

He strode up the walkway, hearing the limousine door clunk shut behind him. The building's main doors slid open automatically at his approach.

Mac's booted feet echoed on the marble floor as he made his way across the expansive, dimly-lit lobby to the curved main desk, rising on the other side of the room in one broad, polished, unbroken arc like a volcanic cone. A lone security guard stood behind it, eyes fixed on Mac as he approached. He looked crisp. No rent-a-cops for Conner.

"Good evening, sir. Step over there, please."

The guard directed Mac towards a small black box set head-high on the desk surface, angled outward over the cone's base. Mac's soldier's mind saw beyond the aesthetics of the desk's design. The angle kept visitors from peering over the edge and kept what was behind the lip, including personnel, out of reach. Good security, well thought out.

Mac stepped forward and placed his forehead against the padded headrest of the retinal scanner the guard indicated. The scan was over in seconds. Mac straightened and waited as the guard studied something before him. After a moment his hands dipped down, reappeared with a plastic ID card bearing Mac's photo. He affixed a spring clip and handed it to Mac.

"Thank you, Major Harrison. Please wear this at all times and surrender it to me when you leave."

Mac attached the pass to his jacket breast, turning as he heard a soft chime to his left. At the far end of the lobby, burnished elevator doors were just sliding open.

"Mister Conner is expecting you," the guard said, indicating the elevator. "The car is automatic, no need to select the floor."

Mac hefted his duffel and walked to the elevator. The doors closed soundlessly. He felt a hint of pressure against the soles of his feet as the car accelerated upward. There was no floor indicator panel, just the usual controls set into a polished brass plate beside the door. Conner's private elevator, he guessed. He barely had time to register the thought before he felt the car slow and halt. After a count of one, the doors parted and he stepped out.

IV

Martha Reeves was already standing as the elevator doors opened on the far side of Conner's outer office. The occupant stepped out, moved hesitantly across the imposing room, his shadowed eyes swiftly reconnoitering his surroundings before coming to rest on her.

Martha hadn't anticipated that her first impression of Mac would be envy of his hair. It was brushed straight back from his forehead and fell past his shoulders in smooth, thick waves, dark and shot through with streaks of silver at each temple which reflected the room's soft illumination. Martha had dealt with enough retired vets during her years as Conner's aide to know most let their hair grow a few inches past regulation length, if for no other reason, she surmised, than that they could. Mac Harrison had taken this simple vanity to the extreme. He didn't care what he looked like, and so didn't care what others might think of him. He lived by his own rules. Point one.

She walked forward to greet him. Martha knew from reviewing Mac's DoD file that he was forty-five but he looked fit, his waist trim beneath his jeans and fleece-lined denim jacket. His feet glided across the floor, his weight centered low, like a woman's, not up around his chest like most men. His arms hung loosely at his sides as he walked toward her. There was alertness, readiness. Mac Harrison was a man trained for battle, his bearing testament to his deeply ingrained skills. A fighter, born and bred. Point two.

19

Lastly, Martha focused on Mac's eyes as she smiled in greeting. They were a deep brown, the pupil almost indiscernible within the dark iris. Eyes that at this moment divulged nothing, except — pain, was it? No, although there was some of that there.

Grief. That was it. Grief, and anger.

In the five seconds it took Mac and Martha to meet in the center of the office, she observed, calculated and concluded that her employer definitely had his hands full.

"Good evening, Mister Harrison. Welcome to UniCom." Her words carried a light Southern twang. Mac's hand was hard and dry, and gripped hers briefly before dropping back to his side. "I'm Martha Reeves, Mister Conner's personal assistant. Thank you for coming on such short notice."

"Mister Davis said that Sen . . . Colonel Takeshita was in a clinic near here. The Collier Clinic? I'd like to see him, please."

"Of course. Arrangements have been made."

As if on cue, a set of tall wooden doors fashioned of pale wood silently swung inward to Mac's left.

"Mister Conner will see you now. You can leave your bag with me."

Mac eyed Martha suspiciously, but her expression remained pleasantly neutral. He lowered his duffel to the floor, turned and entered the dark territory beyond the wide opening, the doors just as silently swinging shut behind him.

Yes, thought Martha as she watched Mac's retreating back. Mister Conner had his hands very full, indeed.

V

On first impression, the room seemed empty. Mac waited for his eyes to adjust to the dusky illumination as the doors closed behind him, taking the too-warm air in through his nose and deep into his lungs, as Sensei had taught him, simultaneously willing his perception to expand around him, an infinite balloon reaching into every corner of the room; letting it, and not his eyes, explore the space. Letting the feel of it wash over him, searching for the room's borders.

Searching . . .

The back of his neck tensed as he sensed it. He looked to his left, his eyes now accustomed to the faint light. The figure had his back to Mac, facing the ceiling-to-floor window that comprised the entire wall before which he stood. A middling-tall man, thin and slump-shouldered with age, silhouetted in the pale moonlight which shone in through the glass.

"Major Harrison. Join me, please."

The voice was a soft baritone growl, the words at once a request and a command. Mac walked across the room and stood beside Roger Charles Conner.

Delicate, aged hands overlaid with faint, filigree veins grasped a cane of smooth teak. The suit was pearl-gray and immaculately tailored, the necktie dark, unadorned silk. His thinning, silver hair was cut short and lay flat against the egg-shaped skull. His face was surprisingly smooth, but the liver-spotted skin displayed the dusty translucence of advanced age. Standing close, Mac could feel Conner's aloofness, the way he gathered his energy around him, a tangible barrier of studied control which enveloped him like a magnetic field. There was power there, placid for the moment, inviting his approach.

Conner allowed Mac his moment of scrutiny, his upturned gaze fixed on the waning gibbous moon that floated amongst wisps of cloud above the pines. When he judged sufficient time had passed, he spoke again.

"Imagine yourself. Thousands of years ago, on a night such as this. The moon was a goddess then, Major. Holy. Worshipped. Keeper of secrets, her waxing and waning portending man's destiny. I still believe that, after a fashion. On a night such as this, I find it difficult to accept that its sole purpose is something so prosaic as to orbit the Earth and control the tides. Surely something so, wondrous, so beautiful, must entertain a higher purpose. I think our ancestors can be forgiven their flights of fancy. Don't you agree?"

Mac found himself drawn into Conner's soliloquy as he gazed at the distant sphere. The old man's rumbling voice was deep, the pitch and relaxed Southern drawl lending it a sonorous quality that was near hypnotic.

Mac turned from the window in time to see Conner look away from him, the ghost of a smile on his lips. The older man walked to the wide curved desk to his right, leaning heavily on his cane as he moved, favoring his right hip. "You must be tired. Please, make yourself comfortable." He gingerly lowered himself into his high-backed chair, not waiting for his guest to be seated.

Mac's wariness returned as he moved away from the window. He sat in one of the rigid chairs arrayed in a semicircle before Conner's desk, a low table placed beside each, the simple furnishings almost all there was to the office's spartan decor. The upholstery sighed as Mac's weight settled into it. Conner placed his cane on his desk, the dark glassy surface uncluttered save for a telephone and a slender lamp which burned just brightly enough to say it was on. He leaned back in his seat.

"I trust your flight was pleasant even in its haste?"

"Davis said Colonel Takeshita had a stroke."

Conner's expression didn't change. "So much for niceties. Yes. Six days ago. He is resting comfortably, attended by my personal physician and the finest medical staff available, I can assure you."

"Six days? Why didn't anyone let me know before now?"

"You went to great lengths to ensure you would not be unnecessarily disturbed."

"Davis seemed to find me easily enough."

"And had he failed in his search, would you have known of Colonel Takeshita's illness? It's not exactly as if you went out of your way to remain in touch . . . "

"That's not fair!"

"It is eminently fair. I learned of the Colonel's condition because I made it my business to know, which is how I found you, despite your great efforts to the contrary. As I can see thanks will not be forthcoming, I will settle for this: you will see Colonel Takeshita —"

"Tah-kesh-tah," Mac interjected.

Conner allowed the correction hang in the air long enough to demonstrate he was willing to let it remain there all night. "My apologies. You will see Colonel, Tah-kesh-tah, for as long as you wish, after I am through with you. Is that fair?"

The statement confirmed Mac's suspicions. "You used him as an excuse to get me here."

"That is essentially correct. I doubt my personal invitation alone would have done the trick."

A confession that would have brought shame to any decent human being spilled from Conner's lips as casually as a comment on the weather. Mac had been planning to attack Conner for using Sensei, but he now saw that wasn't going to work.

"What do you want."

Conner shifted forward in his chair and took his cane in hand. "I want you, *Major* Harrison." He stressed Mac's rank, chuckled softly, unsurprised, at the lack of response. Using the cane for leverage he rose stiffly from his chair, wincing as his recalcitrant hip grudgingly accepted his weight, slowly paced the shadowed room as he orated.

"Why are you so reticent about your military career? You served with honor, sir, despite the folly of the conflict, a noble contradiction with which I am well familiar."

He looked down at the cane he clasped in his right hand. "I was twenty. Four June, 1971. You weren't even born then. 55th Red Wolf Combat Engineering Squadron. We parachuted half-an-hour north-northwest of Danang. We were supposed to build an airstrip. It was a beautiful day. I'll never know how they knew we were coming. I remember feeling something hit my hip, like a hammer. I started shooting back, couldn't see a damn thing. Wound up hanging in a tree before I passed out from blood loss. They tell me it was a miracle that I didn't bleed to death or wasn't blown to bits by the air strike we called in. Five others were. We left them behind with the rest of the expendable equipment. Never did get that airstrip built."

Conner paused, regarding his cane before he resumed his pacing. "It is as Clausewitz said. War is merely the ultimate expression of politics. Yet always it seems our ability to express ourselves outpaces our wisdom."

"You've made a pretty good living 'expressing' yourself."

Conner nodded, unfazed by the shot. "Every time you and your comrades jumped, three-quarters of what went with you bore the UniCom maker's mark or that of one of our subsidiaries. I spent billions of dollars sending thousands of men and women into battle, some younger than even I was, did my damnedest to ensure nothing I made prevented them from making it back." He gazed out of the enormous window. "You and I know too many of them never came home. And now, I spend millions trying to help those who did, just barely. I pay for treatment, rehabilitation, research, honoring their service and their sacrifice as best I can."

"Is that why you're taking care of Sensei? Because you feel guilty?"

Conner turned to face Mac from across the room, his face hidden in shadow. "There is a difference between duty and guilt, Major. I will admit to resorting to the ready convenience of money to scrub a tarnished conscience. But one thing I am not doing is running away. I don't have that luxury. I'm too big. But you . . . "

Mac listened to Conner's cane thump against the floor, watched him slowly emerge from shadow as he spoke, stalking Mac like an ancient spider leisurely contemplating how best to ensnare its prey. "You, Major Harrison, are an entirely different story." His words came in a chiding, almost sing-song cadence. "You've spent these last nine years doing your level best to deny the war, Stormcloud, everything that happened! Haven't you?"

Mac leaped up from his chair, stung by Conner's goading. "Who the hell do you think you are? What gives you the right to judge me? I've done nothing, nothing since the war but try to deal with what happened!"

"By running away? What the hell kind of a soldier are you?"

"I'm not! Not anymore! Why is that so hard for people to understand?"

But Conner was moving in closer, his cloudy blue eyes intense, zeroing in on their suddenly-exposed target. "That's right! You are more than a soldier! You-are-a-warrior! And a warrior stands fast and faces his challenges, regardless of whence they come!"

Mac stared, astonished by the audacity of the man. He was being methodically dissected, Conner's scalpel expertly flaying open his layers of defense. "What do you want from me? Okay, I survived! The *Reagan* blew to hell and for some reason, I'm still here! The only one left!"

"You sound as if you wish you weren't."

"Maybe I do wish! Everyone was calling me a, a hero, while the best friends I ever had were . . . "

He stopped, fighting to control the unfamiliar crescendo of long-suppressed emotions. Conner's voice came softly in the sudden silence.

"Finally, some truth."

Mac's anger flared hotter. He broke off their staredown, turning on his heel and heading for the doors, speaking almost to himself as he crossed the room. "I don't need this . . . "

"Obviously you do."

"Take me to see Sensei. Then take me home."

Mac arrived at the doors. They remained shut. He grasped the curved brass handles and tugged. The doors barely moved. Conner's voice crackled off their surface.

"I'm not through with you yet."

Mac stared at the polished wood a yard before him. Goddamn this man. Goddamn this world, goddamn the whole stinking, miserable . . .

Seated at her desk, Martha jumped as she heard a battering ram slam into the doors of Mister Conner's office, heard Mac's *kiai* detonate in concert to the impact. Her head snapped around in time to see the heavy oak doors shudder and give almost a full inch towards her. Doors that opened in the opposite direction, the electromagnetic lock designed to withstand a thousand pounds of concentrated pressure. Mister Conner had instructed her before Mac arrived not to disturb them but if he was in trouble, if Harrison had hurt him . . .

She reached for the slim telephone resting at the corner of her desk just as Conner's calm voice issued from the tiny speaker set into its base: "It's okay, Martha."

She withdrew her hand. She knew how Conner could be, but this was a first. Nobody had ever tried to smash their way out of his office before.

Conner released the intercom button set into the touchpad at the desk's edge — God, the man was fast! Conner had heard the report of the blow almost before his mind had registered Mac's sudden whirling motion. Had the attack been directed at himself, he'd knew be dead without having moved a muscle.

He composed his features as Mac turned, face dark with anger. "You want to go?" Conner offered. "Go. We both know I can't keep you here." He was careful to keep his voice free of patronage. "See the Colonel, then leave. I'll have Davis fly you back first thing in the morning or whenever you like, and I can assure you you'll never hear from me again. But if you stay . . . " Now he allowed a little more passion to color his words. "If you stay, and hear me out, I promise you the adventure of a lifetime!"

Conner touched another pad on the desk's surface. Mac heard a soft *click* behind him as the door lock disengaged, but he ignored it. He'd expected to turn and find Conner laughing at him but instead, he read fear in the small man's stiff posture, in the studied casualness with which he'd pressed the lock release with his bony finger.

Conner wanted something from Mac, wanted it terribly. That was the fear Mac saw. Fear that he might call Conner's bluff and walk out of the room, forever. And that gave Mac what he'd been unable to regain since leaving his Montana cabin.

Control.

He crossed back to his chair and stood, waiting. Conner didn't miss the shift in dynamic, decided to tolerate it. He spoke as he sat first, Mac following a moment later.

"I wish to discuss your military service. The 82nd Special Airborne HALO Company. A unit unique in all of military history. The Shooting Stars. A poetic name. It suited you all. Shot like missiles from your orbiting dropship, hurtling towards your Earth-bound target! Cloaked in the scorching fires of re-entry, then emerging into the darkness and bursting free from your dropsleds like moths from a cocoon!"

He leaned forward, hands resting atop his cane, his face half-shadowed in the light of the lamp to his right. "What was it like, Major Harrison? Streaking earthward through the cold, black night, the wind of your passage screaming past your helmet, the darkened Earth flattening below you, rushing up to meet you as you deploy your parachute at the last possible second, not knowing if the next few seconds would bring your death . . . !"

Like an ancient newsreel, the memories unspooled in Mac's mind. This time, he kept them at a manageable distance, knowing Conner was playing him once again. Still, something must have showed on his face.

"Yeeees," Conner purred. "I thought as much."

"Is this why you brought me here? To trade war stories?"

A fleeting wave of irritation showed in the ice blue of Conner's eyes. Gotcha, thought Mac. Conner tilted his head in Mac's direction, silently acknowledging the point. "No, Major. I brought you here because you can stomp on a junebug from two-hundred-miles up."

"What?"

"There's lots of skydivers who have more jumps than you do. Hell, I'm told there's some with over twenty-thousand. That's a lot of jumps. You don't have nearly that many. What is it, eight-hundred? Nine?"

"Something like that."

"What you do have, however," Conner continued, "is altitude. You have jumped from altitudes higher than any man or woman alive, under fire, in atmospheric conditions that any sane jumper, if you'll allow me that debatable sobriquet, would consider suicidal. And, as my battered door will attest, you appear to be in decent shape for a man your age."

"I'm not that old."

"In short, as far as I am concerned you are unquestionably the best skydiver in the world. And you are more than that."

Conner raised his head higher. "You *are* a warrior, Major. It's not a vocation, not something you can remove like a uniform and hang in a closet. It's in your flesh and in your bones. You need challenge like you need air, water. And a warrior's greatest challenge, his constant foe, always lies inside himself. And he fights it, every minute of every damn day he fights it. He doesn't run and rot in a cabin in Montana, waiting for it to just, go away."

Mac bit back an angry response. "Make your point."

"Not a point. A proposition. An undertaking beyond your wildest imaginings. And you are the only man on this Earth who can do it."

Conner was grinning now, his eyes glittering with anticipation as he neared the climax of his pitch. He leaned forward, hands clasped on the desk. Nailed Mac's attention with his eyes, savoring every word.

"Mackinley Michael Harrison. How would you like to skydive from the moon?"

VI

The Collier Research Institute was a simple, two-story building of pale brick and stucco, over two-hundred-sixty-thousand square feet of wards, laboratories and offices situated on eight wooded acres about a mile from UniCom headquarters. Though it boasted a state-of-the-art hospital wing, CRI was primarily a cybernetics research facility, named after the late Dr. Edmund Collier, a pioneer in the use of guided biofeedback coupled with neuromuscular implants to control cybernetic prostheses. Conner had drawn him into the UniCom fold with the promise of his own shop and unlimited research money, a coin which also served to purchase Collier's silence once he became aware that his patron was incorporating his research into the creation of advanced weapons interfaces. Dead for ten years, Collier's name was almost all that remained of his legacy.

"I wish you and I could have met under more agreeable circumstances," Dr. Bid said as he and Mac made their way down the silent corridor of the clinical wing. Dr. Rajiv Bid was small, Eastern Indian, a few strands of black hair carefully combed over his shining brown pate. His diction was precise, his accent lending his words a musical lilt. "Mister Takeshita is resting as well as can be expected, given his condition. We're doing everything we can to make him as comfortable as possible until it's over."

Mac stopped, his gut tightening in a cold knot. "Until what's over?"

Dr. Bid hesitated. "I'm sorry. I thought Roger had told you. The stroke was massive. He's a strong man to have held on this long. For the first few days, he showed some improvement. Then, two days ago, he had another. He's been in and out of coma ever since."

He watched Mac's eyes grow distant as the news sank in, waited a respectful moment before continuing, the words well-rehearsed: "There's always a chance he might recover. We could keep him alive indefinitely on life support, while we waited."

Dr. Bid's eyes belied his words. "You don't think he'll recover," Mac managed.

Dr. Bid shook his head. "We've done all we can. I'm sorry."

Mac struggled to keep his focus as the words sank in. Colonel Yoshi Aaron Takeshita, modern *samurai*, the peerless warrior whom neither bullets nor weight of years could bring down. The only immutable element in Mac's ragged universe.

Sensei was going to die.

Like the rest of the clinic, the ICU was painted in pale greens and blues. Any calming effect the décor was meant to produce, however, was nullified ten times over by the life-support equipment surrounding the room's single bed. Sensei lay in the midst of spaghetti-strands of wires and tubing, the only sign of life the rhythmic chirping of the cardiac monitor and the shallow heaving of his chest. The nurse seated at the bedside looked up from her magazine as the door opened, relaxed as she spied Dr. Bid following Mac into the room.

"Stay as long as you like." With a single nod to the nurse, the doctor exited, softly closing the door behind him.

Mac slowly walked the few steps to Sensei's bedside, laid his hands on the cold metal railing. He hadn't seen his mentor in years, not

28

since he'd disappeared from the world like a rock into the ocean. He remembered the night before he left. I won't be gone long, he'd said. I just need to get away for awhile. Sensei had only smiled, his dark eyes holding Mac's across the low table at which they knelt as they lifted their tiny cups of *sake* in a final toast.

Come back when you are ready, Sensei had said as they embraced. Come back when you are healed. And then he'd presented Mac with the *ki* pendant he had never removed since.

Seven years ago. It was the last time they'd spoken.

Mac gazed at the figure lying in the bed, much thinner than he remembered. It bothered him that he couldn't remember Sensei's birthday, how old he was. At least sixty-five. His dark hair was now streaked with gray and lay limp across his broad, pale forehead. The oxygen prong beneath his nostrils half-obscured the pencil-thin salt-and-pepper moustache Mac had never known him to be without. His cheeks were sunken beneath the high cheekbones, his jaw unshaven, mouth sagging open, drooping to the left. His respiration came in short, labored wheezes.

It was as if Mac were looking at a stranger. He could still see the man he'd known, still recognize the features. But the essence was absent, the palpable, preternatural awareness that always extended from Sensei now turned inward, every ounce of energy focused on maintaining his tenuous grasp on consciousness. On life.

Oh, Sensei. Where have you gone?

"Are you a friend?"

Mac startled at the nurse's question. He'd no idea how long he'd been standing at the bedside, gazing down at Sensei while his mind raced down corridors of memory: the warm-sweat smell of the *dojo*, Sensei's feather touch on his body as Mac was sent flying; listening to his stories over *sake* and *sushi* during those rare and special dinners off-base; the satisfied expression on Sensei's face whenever Mac asked a certain question, as if Takeshita had only been waiting for his student to open that door to the further teaching which lay beyond. Never did Mac think of the war when he remembered Sensei, never the weight of arms and the ceremonies of death to come. Never soldier and CO. Always something else.

The nurse regarded him with her professional mix of interest and sympathy. Mac gave the barest nod.

"We go back quite a ways."

"How do you know him?"

"He's my —"

Mac swallowed, looking down at the figure in the bed. He's my commanding officer. He's my teacher. He's my friend. He's the only person on the planet for whom I would lay down my life. This very moment I would willingly take this horrible cruel thing from him and into myself, gladly settle into my death if I could only hear him speak to me one last time.

Mac wiped the moisture from his eyes.

"He's my sensei."

Mac took Takeshita's left hand in his, careful not to disturb the intravenous tube beneath its covering of surgical tape. He rubbed his thumb across the had blue-pink calluses flowing across the huge knuckles.

Sensei's hand squeezed Mac's, a quick, hard motion.

"He moved!" Mac turned to the nurse, rifle-shot of adrenaline surging through him. "He squeezed my hand!"

"It's a spasm." Her expression was compassionate, her words forthright. "A reflex response to stimulus."

Mac barely heard her. He was focused like a laser on what he now felt. It tingled against his palm as he held Sensei's limp hand, like a low-level electrical charge; faint, but real. That low throb of energy, Sensei's *ki*.

Mac willed his pounding heart to slow. Where there was *ki*, there was life. Maybe Sensei was wandering some other plane of existence where he could be free of his pain, waiting for his final orders to move on to his next incarnation. But for now, he was here. Mac was here. And Mac knew that, on some level, Sensei was aware of his presence.

He placed his other hand atop Sensei's and closed his eyes, willing his own *ki* to connect with his mentor's. This was *ki-musubi*, the linking of *ki*, an exchange of corporeal and spiritual energy on the most fundamental level. Mac allowed himself to become lost in the effort, ignoring the physical and intellectual barriers of flesh and impossibility, ignoring time, concentrating only on the contact between Sensei's hand and his until it became at first hard to tell where one ended and the other began and then, immaterial.

From beneath lowered eyes, the nurse watched as the ragged stranger stood utterly still, his eyes closed, holding the patient's hand in both of his. He was breathing deeply, murmuring the unfamiliar word he'd used to describe his friend. Bedside prayers she'd witnessed before, enough to pay them no mind.

"Sensei . . . "

She looked up from the glossy page before her at the cardiac monitor, alerted by the quickening cadence of its steady chirping. The numbers were rising.

Mac felt the heat of his hands warm Sensei's flesh, felt the tingle in his palm increase. He breathed deeply, inhaling energy, visualized it flowing down his arm like water, into Sensei's hand, into Sensei.

The nurse stood, dropping the magazine on the chair behind her. The cardiac monitor numbers continued to climb. Now the oxygen sat level was rising. The patient was breathing more deeply, taking more oxygen into his bloodstream.

The patient was waking up.

"Sensei."

Sensei's fingers once again tightened around Mac's own. This time, there was purpose. Mac leaned in closer to hear the weak whisper:

"Mackinley."

The nurse leaned in beside Mac, disbelieving. "Mister Takeshita? Can you hear me?"

Sensei's eyes opened, focused on Mac's face. His words were slurred by the palsy that made his face droop. "You forget how to shave?"

Mac struggled between tears and laughter to speak. "I lost my razor."

The nurse looked hard at Mac, open-mouthed. "I'll be right back," she finally managed. She hurried from the room to find Dr. Bid.

Sensei inhaled more deeply, swallowing with difficulty. When he spoke again, his voice was stronger. "I am glad you came, Mackinley. I have missed you."

"I missed you too, Sensei." God, what had he done, how could he have forsaken this man who had given him so much . . .

"I'm sorry, Sensei. I'm so sorry."

"Shhh. I have been waiting for you to come back to us."

"They're all dead, Sensei. They're all gone. Everyone's gone."

"Not all. William still lives. You survive."

31

"And you." Mac squeezed Sensei's hand harder. Takeshita only smiled.

"You must not survive, Mackinley. You must live. You must heal yourself."

"I'm trying, Sensei, but it's so hard . . . "

"It is always for the strong to bear the greatest burden. Your spirit was always the strongest. Even now, it strives to bear your pain."

"I miss them, Sensei." Mac wept freely now, tears falling from his cheeks onto the sheet draped across Sensei's chest. "I miss them so much."

He relaxed his grip as Sensei's hand slowly rose, still clasped in Mac's. It came to rest over Mac's one-point.

"They still live, Mackinley. In here. In you. Now you must live for all of us."

"I don't know if I can anymore."

Sensei's eyes closed, and for one horrible moment Mac wondered if he was going. Then he felt it, a warm surge of energy flooding though his abdomen, calming him, focusing him. Even now, Sensei was sustaining him, extending his precious *ki* into Mac, silently reaffirming his love for his prodigal son.

Sensei spoke even more softly, but his voice was steady. "To face death is the way of the warrior. But to live, is harder still. Do not forget us."

"I never forgot you, Sensei! Never!"

Sensei opened his eyes and smiled once again.

"I know."

Mac felt the *ki* flowing from Sensei's palm increase, a steady thrumming vibration that now filled his entire body. The room faded, the steady hiss and ping of the life support equipment, all fading. Nothing existed now but the warmth that washed over him, through him, into his soul.

"I have much love for you, Mackinley."

The forgiveness came to Mac like the hush of a father to a child.

Sensei's eyes closed. He inhaled wearily, sighed.

"I have been waiting for you."

Only the smile remained now.

"Sensei?"

The sudden whine of the cardiac monitor jerked Mac out of his communion. The door opened, the nurse and Dr. Bid appearing. They rushed

forward, animated conversation abruptly cut off as they elbowed Mac out of their way, tearing Sensei's limp hand from his grasp.

"Sensei!"

He stumbled over the nurse's chair, his view of Takeshita blocked by the white coated bodies that bent over the bed. Oh no. Please no, not you too. No, Sensei, please —

The word was a scream. *"Sensei . . . !"*

VII

The lights were low and scarlet. The voice was granite hard, rough as steel wool.

"Count."

Clad in his dark camouflage pressure suit, Dropmaster Sergeant Otis Rawlings stood like an obsidian sculpture before his console, eyes fixed on the readouts. He spoke again into his headset:

"Status."

He paused once more, listening to the answer. Satisfied, he looked up, his eyes sweeping the dropbay.

"All right, gentlemen. Brain buckets on."

Captain Mackinley Harrison, Bravo squad leader of the 82nd Special Airborne HALO Company, lowered his drop helmet over his head. The light dimmed only slightly as the faceplate moved before his eyes. The dark siliplas filtered out high-frequency light, the blinding glare of the sun and white-hot tracer charges, not the low spectrum red of the drop bay. Mac's dropsuit automatically began pressurizing as the helmet clips slid into place with a sharp *click* around the neck ring, his respiration surging hollowly in his ears in the confined space.

He unfastened his restraints and rose from his chair, the butt of the long powergun strapped over his right shoulder pressing into his thigh. He automatically lay his hand over the main canopy ripcord handle above his right breast as he moved, guarding it against accidental deployment. There was no reserve handle to guard because there was no reserve. HALO stood for High Altitude, Low Opening. The 82nd would deploy their canopies at 1,000 feet while falling at over two-hundred miles per hour. If the main canopy failed to open, Mac wouldn't live long enough to regret his lack of back-up.

Mac let the zero-G carry him from his seat, feeling the rest of Bravo squad follow suit behind him. He was glad for the rote activity, something to occupy his mind as the time to drop drew closer. There would be plenty of time in the sled to contemplate what was waiting for them.

He pushed off the deck, floated over to the far right lower end of the sled rack, where his dropsled rested open in its cradle, the cowling held suspended above it, ready to be lowered and locked into place. It was one of six set side-by-side in the lower battery, Bravo bat. Five more rested in Alpha bat, level with his head — Alpha company was already standing at the ready, portside of the battery rack. Usually there were six sleds in each but Captain William Price, Alpha squad leader, had been turfed a month before during Operation Anvil. He was still recovering in hospital from the phosphor mine that had burned his legs off, melting the flesh below the knee down to the bone. He was fortunate to have survived, but he would never see another combat drop. It felt odd, jumping without his friend, jumping one man short, like Mac was missing a limb of his own. Lucky for him he didn't believe in omens. His job was hard enough already.

As always, he ran a quick visual inspection of the dropsled. The UniCom CDP-1000 NRGV — Non-Recoverable Re-Entry Glide Vehicle, a sleek, three-meter-long cylinder coated with layers of the dull, heat-reflecting siliplas that would protect it against the primeval fire of re-entry. The narrow foot-long communications and global positioning antenna protruded from the sled's blunt nose, the body of the sled widening to just under four feet then tapering to the rear, where the small thruster was affixed. It would blaze at launch, propelling the sled from the battery and into space, burning for ten seconds before automatic jettison. Once re-entry was complete, the stabilizers would deploy, slowing the sled prior to cowling jettison. From there, it was an easy skydive the remaining distance to the ground. All fifty miles of it. If you weren't blown to bits first.

Mac grasped the brace handle welded to the sled rack, holding his feet in contact with the deck. As always, he felt no vibration through the deckplate to mark the *Reagan's* fleet passage, knowing that it was hurtling along its orbital translation towards target rendezvous at better than 17,000 miles per hour.

He turned his eyes to the dropmaster, waiting.

Rawlings regarded them from behind his console at the fore end of the dropbay, anchored to the deck by his grip boots. His steely voice crackled in Mac's headset:

"Review. Drop in delta, spread at ten-grand, pull at one. Heavy cumulus at four grand, so keep your eyes on your altimeters. Upstairs blowing from relative east at six-zero knots, two-zero from three grand on down. Satellite recon picked up an armored division at twenty-two degrees three klicks from target, so watch for incoming.

"The missile silo's a hundred meters east of the bunker. Latest intel says they may know we're coming so keep it simple: penetrate, eliminate, download and destroy. Pickup will be waiting at the designated coordinates fifteen minutes after you turf. Fifteen-thirty, and you will walk home. Boykin takes Alpha squad, Harrison takes Bravo as usual. Questions?"

There were none. There never was.

"As always, Colonel Takeshita sends his best. Do him proud. And kick some ass for Price. Let me hear it!"

"Whuuup!" Rawlings smiled with grim satisfaction as the company bellowed their answer. The dropmaster gave a final glance to the readouts.

"D-minus two. Lock and load, gentlemen." He removed his helmet from its berth in the bulkhead behind him and lowered it over his head.

Mac moved to the side of the sled rack, quickly shifting his grip from the frame handle to one set just below his sled's cradle, grasping it with his left hand. In one smooth motion, he pushed gently off the deck and let the zero-G carry his lower body upward until it was parallel to the opening in the side of the rack. He pushed himself sideways, into the space beneath the cowling, alternately shifting his grips until he was floating motionless a foot above the sled's open interior.

Two small handles were set into the dropsled's lining, next to the steering levers. He grabbed them and tucked, feeling the parachute rig's straps briefly dig into his torso as he pulled his knees into his chest, then straightened his legs, angling them downward, his feet sliding smoothly into the rear restraint loops. Thus braced, he pulled himself into the dropsled's padded, contoured interior, belly down, resting on his elbows. The entire journey took twenty seconds.

He closed his fingers around the steering levers as he settled in. Too early for the demon. Not yet. Not just yet.

He waited until Alpha squad had counted off, called "Set," then listened as Bravo squad echoed his response. He found himself waiting for that twelfth voice to count off, Price's voice. He told himself he didn't have any worries about Tim Boykin's ability to lead Alpha squad but still, Mac couldn't shake the feeling of incomplete-ness that had dogged him since the night before.

Rawlings' steady voice pushed the feeling aside. "Stand-by for cowling."

After a few moments, the dark, oblong bowl descended, sinking into the grooved sink channel which ringed the dropsled opening. Mac listened to the dull thuds as the explosive jettison bolts shot into place, triggered and primed by the pressure of the settling canopy, sealing him into his sarcophagus. The tiny console inches before his face winked on in response: interior and exterior pressure and temperature, altitude, velocity, com status, time to drop, time to turf. Three buttons shone red beneath their clear protective coverings. One jettisoned the cowling. The second deployed the lateral and tail stabilizers. The third was the autodrop warning indicator, the button that opened the launch port and fired the sled's engine independently of the ship's circuit. Everyone called it the punch-out: if it blinked, you punched it and got the hell out. It was the final fail-safe, to be used only in the event that something happened to prevent Rawlings from launching the sleds from his console, or if the order came to abandon ship. Once the twin batteries were raised topside there was no turning back, one way only left to exit the ship. That glowing button was the 82nd's only control over their fate.

Rawlings's voice came once again: "Cowling seal confirmed. Batteries topside."

There came the soft *clunk* as the hydraulic pistons engaged. The rack shuddered once and Mac began to rise, the twin batteries borne upwards on the telescoping steel shafts. He watched as the bulkhead crawled downward, his eyes fixed just above the horizon line described by the coupling of the cowling and sled body, watching the flashes of brighter scarlet as the dropbay's load light strobed across the wall that slowly sank from view, replaced by the dark recessed square of the sealed launch port a yard before him.

The angled surface was visible only for a moment in the narrowing sliver of light from the drop bay below. The battery support plate rose the final few inches to its berth, coming to a halt with a groan and a final shudder, sealing the battery bay from the drop bay. There was no light. No sound. No sense of depth or dimension. Nothing but the pinpoint LCDs on the sled console, the rush of Mac's respiration, the pounding of his heart. Every beat shook his body like a physical blow. His breathing roared in his helmet like a forge bellows.

Now it comes. He felt in his gut the sudden clench of fear. Your demon has arrived.

He never fought the fear. He'd learned the futility of that exercise long ago. He embraced it, like a man plunging headlong into the shock of an icy lake, let it snake its raspy tentacles throughout his body, felt it transform him from mere trembling flesh into something more suited to its dour design. Mac Harrison receded from consciousness as he swam through the fear, feeling it strip away his weakness, his doubt, his fleshly infirmities, his identity. What remained as he emerged on the other side burned pure and dark and cold.

Breathe. The way of the warrior is resolute acceptance of death.

Slow your pulse. A dead man has nothing to fear.

A dead man cannot be killed.

I am a dead man.

Mac settled into his fell calm, tightening his grip on the steering levers as Rawlings' voice issued from his headset: "D minus one-oh-three. Batteries locked and sealed. Depressurizing."

The external pressure indicator on the sled console swiftly dove to zero, followed immediately by the flashing *DEPRESS OK*. The atmospheric pressure in the battery bay was now equal to that outside the ship.

"Depress complete. Stand-by to drop. D-minus one-two-three. Rendezvous to spot in fifty-eight seconds, mark."

In just over a minute, the launch port would open and the sled's thruster would engage, launching the rocket from its berth, into the light, towards the suddenly-revealed Earth.

Breathe in, out. In, out . . .

"D-minus one-one-oh. Rendezvous to spot in four-zero seconds, mark."

The sled lurched, once, pressing Mac's right shoulder into the padding — the gentlest shove, followed by a brief crackle in his headset. He wouldn't have thought anything of it except for the fact that in all of his previous drops, he'd never before felt it.

This would be the time when Captain Mark Guthrie, the *Reagan's* pilot, would have fired the ship's reaction control system verniers, the tiny nose-and tail-mounted maneuvering engines that positioned the *Reagan* for the decelerating OMS burn for target alignment. Maybe Guthrie had gotten antsy, goosed the system too hard. That would explain the sudden inertia. Nothing to worry about.

Still . . .

Mac glanced at his console chronometer. "Bravo leader to Dropmaster. D-minus one-oh-three, acknowledge."

"Dropmaster, acknowledge."

Mac's headset remained silent. He glanced at the steady green light of the com status LCD. Except that it wasn't green. It was blinking red:

COM INACTIVE

The demon's fingers squeezed. Mac fought the renewed fear, his knowledge of the *Reagan's* communications systems flashing through his mind in an instant.

There were three circuits: primary intership, battery, and COMDAT MFR, the mission flight data and cockpit recorder. Rawlings and the 82nd were tied into the first two: if primary intership was disabled, Mac should still be able to communicate with them on the battery circuit. Intership and battery both relied on ship's power to function, but BATCOM ran on a parallel circuit and was tied into a separate power cell in the forward fuselage, below the flight deck. Once clear of the *Reagan*, the company would switch to drop com. As a safety measure, it was locked out until the sleds were free of the ship, so as not to risk interference with the *Reagan's* sensitive electronic STEALTH cloak. COMDAT MFR ran on its own internal power, for the obvious reasons, recording its 'black box' data via wireless pickup from the transmitters, mics and cameras placed at strategic points within the ship.

COM INACTIVE

Mac flipped back the hinged covering with the tip of his gloved finger, held his thumb poised over the punch-out button. Maybe

Rawlings could hear him but for some reason the circuit was now only one-way. Maybe it was the same for everyone.

He watched the digital chronometer ticking off the seconds to launch, now barely a minute away. You know the time to drop, you know your mission. You have everything you need. You know what to do.

He fought to keep his voice steady: "Bravo squad, this is Bravo leader. Stand-by for manual launch on my mark. By the numbers, acknowledge." He waited, holding his breath. "Bravo squad, acknowledge."

00:59 . . . 00:58 . . . 00:57 . . .

"Alpha squad, acknowledge."

. . . 00:55 . . . 00:54 . . .

"Alpha leader, acknowledge. Boykin!"

. . . 00:51 . . . 00:50 . . . 00:49 . . .

Mac's stomach heaved. This was wrong, this was all wrong. The lurch of the ship, the static burst in his headset, now this . . .

A single bead of sweat dripped off of the tip of his nose, splattered on the inner faceplate of his helmet. It slid down the dark siliplas, bisecting his view of the chronometer, the numbers blurring beneath the moisture.

. . . 00:42 . . . 00:41 . . . 00:40 . . . 00:39 . . .

"Anyone, acknowledge!"

The demon's fist tightened, twisted. Mac's trembling thumb mashed the punch-out.

First came the shiver at his feet as the thruster ignited. He clamped down on the steering levers as the launch port hatch shot open. The kick of sudden acceleration compressed his body, shoving his boots deeper into the restraining straps as the dropsled exploded from the confines of its cradle, into the sudden, jarring expanse of open space —

Where was the Earth?

It should have been directly before him, he should have been staring straight into the blue-green sphere, but there was nothing but darkness. He sucked the warm air inside his helmet, frantic breaths fogging the faceplate. He strained to see over the lip of the dropsled, helmet thudding into the cowling overhead as he desperately craned his head left and right.

He caught a flicker of motion to port. Something moving fast, riding a pillar of flame, coming straight at him.

Mac twisted involuntarily to his right, seized with sudden panic as the deadly shape flashed by, barely a sled's length away. He squeezed his eyes shut against the blinding glare of the fire that drove it to its target. Jesus God, no. It couldn't be . . .

The sled bucked as it was engulfed in a ball of flame.

The *Reagan* exploded in a series of deep orange and blinding blue-white fires, the hellish conflagration utterly soundless. The shockwave slammed into the tiny dropsled like a tsunami, sending it tumbling wildly off-course, the still-burning thruster propelling it in ever-widening spirals. Mac watched in wide-eyed horror the crazily spinning tableaux that rushed past him: the fireball . . . the star-shot pitch of space . . . the Earth . . . the fireball . . . the stars . . . the Earth . . .

Fuel, oxygen and armaments consumed, the fireball winked out like a snuffed candle. The *Reagan* and her crew, Mac's friends.

Gone.

The sled was out of control. The thruster burned its last and obediently jettisoned, leaving the sled to continue along its last powered trajectory as if tied to the end of a whirling, suddenly-released string. The Earth was below and to the right, exactly where it shouldn't be. He was hopelessly off-course. Mac's shock-numbed mind calmly reviewed his slim chances for survival.

He wasn't worried about burning up in re-entry. The sled's siliplas skin would protect him against the most ferocious heat, as it had shielded him from the firestorm of the *Reagan's* explosion. But the sleds' entry angles were precisely calculated. Too steep, they would merely miss the target, a possibility that held its own significant hazards. The greater danger lay in too shallow an approach.

The Earth's two outermost layers of atmosphere, the exosphere and thermosphere, were the thinnest. He was in the thermosphere now, roughly two-hundred miles above the Earth's surface, the *Reagan's* standard drop altitude. The thermosphere was the hottest layer of atmosphere, absorbing the brunt of the sun's radiation, but the air molecules were so widely spaced that the heat was quickly dissipated.

The mesosphere was a different story. It was there, fifty miles or so above the Earth's surface, that the atmosphere thickened. This is where meteorites began burning in earnest, where the friction of passage through the air molecules would envelop Mac's dropsled in fire.

If he didn't enter the mesosphere at just the right angle, he would bounce off of it like a stone skipping across a pond, continuing on into space long after the sled's tiny power cell failed and he froze to death, long after his limited supply of oxygen was exhausted and he suffocated. An icy coffin, sailing forever through space.

And his approach was much too shallow.

Mac was beyond terror now, beyond feeling anything but the certainty of his death. The Earth grew larger as gravity pulled him downwards. How long before the bounce? Five minutes? Less? He glanced at his chronometer and realized only seconds had passed since he'd punched out. It wasn't even officially time to drop yet. The full irony of his situation struck him. If he'd remained onboard the *Reagan*, he'd be dead already. All he'd done by punching out was ensure himself a more leisurely demise. There was nothing he could do but wait, to die.

He stared dumbly at the console. He was wrong. There was one thing he could do.

Just take off your helmet and press the cowling jettison button. Death will be swift. The vacuum just inches beyond your head will suck the air and blood from your body in an instant. The way of the warrior is resolute acceptance of death. Let this be your final act, then. To die a warrior.

Like an automaton, Mac lifted the plastic cover from the button. He lowered his head, struggling to pull his elbows forward in the cramped space, reaching for the helmet clips.

Something hit the sled, hard. Mac's hands were knocked away from his helmet by the impact. He looked up . . .

He was surrounded by streaking meteors, some no bigger than a fist, others the size of the sled and larger. Another flashed by to starboard, barely missing the sled. Mac caught a glimpse of twisted, charred metal as it zoomed past.

He was being overtaken by the *Reagan's* debris field. The sled shuddered and dipped as yet another piece of flotsam crashed into it, glancing off the cowling over Mac's head with a jarring crunch, cracking the near-impenetrable siliplas. There was a sudden shrill beeping in his helmet: the sled was depressurizing. Mac waited for the cowling to blast open around the hairline cracks but incredibly, it held.

A soft wash of light like sunrise crept across the cowling's curve. Mac looked down.

41

The Earth filled the entirety of his vision — not to the side, but directly before him. The pummeling wreckage had altered his course, he was now heading directly towards the planet, descending in a lazy, end-over-end tumble.

The sudden realization galvanized him: he was going to live. If the cracked cowling held through re-entry. If the battering hadn't damaged the jettison circuit. If the debris' impact hadn't marred the siliplas coating and he didn't light like a torch and burn to death.

The sled began to vibrate as it encountered the outermost layers of the mesosphere. Mac clamped down on the steering levers, gritting his teeth as the first fires of re-entry blossomed around him. His helmet rattled against the barrel of his powergun as the vibration increased to a violent shaking, the rhythmic pounding just inches from his ear. He grunted with each strained breath, blinking against the sweat pouring from his face, not daring to glance upwards at the cowling. He'd know quickly enough if it gave.

The shaking grew worse, as if the sled was held by invisible jaws trying to tear it in two. Mac heard a roaring in his helmet and realized he was screaming, a defiant bellow against the primeval fury through which he passed, blotting out time, blotting out everything . . .

The flames receded. He'd made it through the fire.

The dropsled's violent oscillation faded away. Mac could feel he was still tumbling, he could hear faintly the windrush even though the sled and his helmet, but there was no sense at all now of downward movement. It was dark as pitch outside the cowling. Stormcloud was an evening drop, but the stark transition from fire to nothing further shocked his frayed nerves.

He shook his head in a futile attempt to clear the stinging sweat from his eyes and checked his altimeter. The console readouts were dead. When had he last checked them? He couldn't remember, didn't know what had caused them to fail. He prayed the rest of the sled's systems were unaffected. He couldn't read the faint glow of his wrist altimeter, but he knew from experience that his velocity had to be at or over Mach one, around a thousand feet per second. With any luck, his tumble through the mesosphere had slowed his descent, but attempting cowling jettison at his present fall rate was suicide. He'd have to slow the sled.

He said a silent prayer and pressed the stabilizer deployment button.

His helmet banged into the cowling as the sled lurched left. His weight shifted slightly forward, a sign that the craft was attempting to orient nose-down. He enjoyed a brief surge of hope as he gently pulled back on the steering levers, feeling the familiar fine vibration of the stabilizers through the pistol grips. His chest compressed as the sled began to belly out, killing his speed, but the vibration grew worse. The entire sled was rattling now like a decrepit subway car. That shouldn't be happening at all . . .

There was a sudden tearing screech from the foot of the sled, then a hollow pop like a board breaking. Mac was jostled anew inside the cramped shell as the sled tumbled again — more slowly, but still shuddering violently. The stabilizers weren't designed to be deployed flat against the force of windrush, the stress had ripped away a tail fin, perhaps a lateral stabilizer as well. There was no way now to decelerate further. Only one thing left to do.

He steeled himself and mashed the cowling jettison.

The explosive bolts detonated in unison, a hard *thunk* that resounded through the sled's body just before the windrush tore the cowling away in a furious instant. The sudden howling gale of his passage slapped him from the sled and flung him backwards into the open. Searing pain exploded in his right shin as the spinning shell glanced off of it before careening madly away, swallowed by the darkness.

Mac reflexively tucked into a protective ball, crying out as the motion elicited grinding pain from his injured leg. He lacked the time to worry about that now. He knew his fallrate was slowing even more now that he was free of the sled but if he arched, the wind resistance might very well dislocate his limbs, despite the reinforcing endoskeleton threaded throughout his pressure suit.

His breath came in strained grunts as he counted the seconds. He'd have to guess when to delta. It would have to be fast. The posture would throw him into a spin, but he'd kill the motion when he arched. He was counting on the helmet's shoulder brace to prevent his head snapping backwards in the windrush and breaking his neck, praying that the endoskeleton would lend his exhausted muscles enough support to hold the delta.

Ignoring the agony in his shin, Mac sucked a deep breath and thrust his body ramrod straight, arms pressed flat against his sides, ankles crossed to better support his injured leg. It was a futile provision:

he screamed as the increased pressure snapped the leg completely, felt the searing burn as the muscles in his lower back tore under the strain of remaining rigid as he tumbled through the freezing air, though more slowly now, the increased resistance further killing his fall rate. His eyes were squeezed so tightly shut he saw colors. Don't let go, he silently screamed against the pain. Hold on, goddammit! Hold on . . .

Gradually, Mac's tumble dissipated as he transformed from a cannonball to a missile, rocketing head-first towards the ground. His time sense was completely gone. He couldn't check his wrist altimeter without releasing the delta and without the altimeter, he had no idea whether impact was minutes away or seconds.

He forced open his eyes — there were no lights below him he could see, no moon to illuminate his way. Just blackness. If he pulled now, the opening shock could very well rip the shrouds from his risers or tear the canopy, if it didn't first snag on his feet and horseshoe, or wrap around his body like a burial shroud as he spun, or corkscrew behind him in a streamer. All three options meant death.

He needed to slow even more.

Beginning with his hands, Mac slowly released the delta, instinctively playing the planes of his body against the wind resistance, feeling his fallrate decrease. He quickly clasped his hands before his chest, then gradually extended them to his sides just below his shoulders, like the wings of the sled, keeping his elbows tucked. Gingerly, he scissored his legs open, knees bent, the pain in his broken shin distant now. He felt his body began to plane out, his head rising —

Mac convulsed as a spasm of pain ripped through his back and destroyed his careful posture. His arms flew backwards, torn away from his body. A fresh burst of fire exploded in his left shoulder as it dislocated under the sudden force.

He was sobbing with pain now, groaning through gritted teeth, unable to concentrate through the agony. He was tumbling out of control, his arms and legs flopping around him, strength now utterly sapped.

It was futile. He'd done what he could. He had nothing left.

He sucked a lungful of air and wearily opened his eyes. There was moisture on the outside of his faceplate, rivulets of water streaming upward in the windrush.

Mac stared at the water. What had Rawlings said? Something about — clouds. Heavy cumulus. Cumulus at four-thousand feet.

Four grand.

He was below four grand.

Pull, goddammit! Pull!

Summoning the very last of his strength from some deep reservoir, Mac threw his body into a desperate arch.

He willed his frozen fingers to close around the ripcord handle at his right shoulder.

He pulled, yanking the thin steel cable free.

He caught a glimpse of trees below before something reached down from the sky and snatched him by the scruff of his neck like a rag doll.

He opened his mouth to scream, and then the opening shock mercifully yanked him out of his body, away from his pain, away from all concern, the last sound he heard the distant, delicate flapping of the canopy slider, like a bird's wings working lazily over his head in the sudden silence.

Two

I

It took a few moments for Mac to realize he was awake, another to remember where he was.

He sat up in bed and rubbed his eyes. They felt like they were coated with a thin layer of glue. His head throbbed, his lower back an aching mass of tension. He winced as he sat up straighter. He felt like a broken-down car limping through the next bend, only to see more road stretching on to the horizon. He felt beat up. He felt old.

He glanced over at the window across the room to his right. Thin bars of sunlight rimmed the heavy drapes. He tugged his bare legs free from the tangled sheet and placed his feet on the floor. Slowly, he bent forward, arms dangling to either side of his knees as he allowed the weight of his upper torso to carry him downward. He breathed deeply, feeling his back muscles burn in protest as they lengthened. They had never fully healed from the damage sustained during the drop. That's how he referred to it in his mind. The drop. The last was the only one that mattered.

He'd awakened to find himself hanging fifteen feet above the jungle floor, suspended by his tangled shroud lines from a thick tree branch. The trunk was too wide to climb down even if he could have reached it, and there were no smaller branches within his grasp. He'd had but one choice. He cut through the lines and fell to the ground.

He'd awakened again after an indeterminable length of time, knocked unconscious by the impact, so sore he could barely move. His shoulder was back in place, probably the force of his graceless landing had done that. His back hurt terribly. For one sick moment, he thought he'd broken his spine. He'd learned later that he'd merely cracked a lumbar vertebrae and torn half the muscles from his shoulders to his hips. Lucky he hadn't been paralyzed, his doctors had said. As if they knew anything about luck. It had taken him over a year of daily therapy before he could consider himself healed, another year to regain his pre-drop limberness, but the pain was his forever.

Mac held the stretch as he ruminated, the pain in his back subsiding. He was used to the nightmare by now. It had started almost from the moment he'd been rescued, ten days after he'd parachuted unconscious into the dense canopy. Ten days of sweat-drenched stumbling over undulating tree roots, his grunts and cries of pain merging with the echoing screams of startled wildlife in the alien terrain through which he labored. Insects buzzed incessantly around his crudely set and splinted leg, the pain killers in his tiny medkit doing little to dull the near constant torture. Every night he cleaned the wound, gritting his teeth as he squeezed pale fluid from the gash the splinters of bone had ripped into his flesh.

The pain killers and medkit antibiotics played havoc with his empty stomach. His meager survival rations lasted two days. He ate insects and palm-broad spiders raw, licked moisture from foliage and drank the rainwater which collected at night in his upturned drop helmet. The only wildlife he saw were birds and monkeys. The former were too small to survive intact the blast of his powergun; the latter he dared not consume for fear of disease. He ate a snake, a constrictor as long as Mac was tall, stripping the flesh from the curving ribs and sucking the blood from his filthy fingers, the reptile's reward for slithering over his injured leg and destroying his precious fevered sleep.

His GPS indicator told him he was in the Brazilian Amazon, a thousand miles off-course. Brazil was still out of the conflict, at least officially, but there was no country truly neutral. He refused to activate his tracking beacon, couldn't risk the signal being intercepted by a hostile. Time and again he came close to flinging the device into the undergrowth as the days passed and his strength and resolve waned. He would not be captured. He would not give the enemy a Shooting Star to hold aloft as their final prize for having destroyed the *Reagan*. He would wrap his lips around the barrel of his powergun first. He thought of Sensei. He would be a *samurai*, accepting his twenty-first century *seppuku* for lack of a blade.

Another morning came. His meds were gone, the wound in his leg livid and festering. He fought to rise and couldn't. He lay on the spongy earth in delirium, bleary eyes focusing and unfocusing on the sun sparkling through the lush canopy high overhead, like a diver staring up at the ocean's surface from the depths into which he lazily descended as he breathed his last.

He had done his best. He had demanded of his training and his *ki* and his weary warrior's soul, and they had sustained him as best they were able. Now he could take his place with his fallen brothers and sisters. He had paid with his pain for this honorable death.

The beast bellowed, rousing him from his fever. It coughed its black stench, its rusted yellow bulk filled his vision as it rumbled to a halt at his feet.

He clawed feebly at the ground, searching for his powergun. There were voices, an incomprehensible babble. Hands on his body, lifting him gently to his feet.

His weight came down full on his broken leg. He screamed and the dark water took him.

Mac opened his eyes. He was holding the leg, fingers clamped tight over the knobby scar of the old wound. He unclenched his hands just as the knock came at the door.

"Who is it?"

"Roger Conner," was the muffled reply.

Mac located his jeans on the floor and tugged them on over his nakedness, rose and opened the door. He didn't bother checking to make sure it really was Conner; he doubted he'd ever mistake that gruff drawl.

He crossed back to the bed and sat as his guest entered. The ever-present cane was in his right hand, a windbreaker draped over his left forearm. Conner carried a folding pasteboard tray with two lidded insulated cups which he placed on the chest of drawers set against the wall opposite the bed's foot, crossed back to the door and closed it. He was dressed casually, slacks and a dark turtleneck. He lay his coat on the other end of the chest.

"You look worn out." Mac didn't bother answering. "Doctor Bid called me last night, after you'd left the clinic. I'm truly sorry." He indicated the cups. "Didn't know whether you preferred coffee or tea, so I brought both." He crossed to the window. "Hope black is okay."

Mac raised his hand indifferently. Without asking, Conner tugged open the drapes, flooding the room with bright winter sun. Mac shielded his eyes from the sudden glare as Conner squinted into the light. "It's a beautiful day. High-fifties. Warm even for here this time of year. I'm more of a night person myself, but you can't play golf at night. Can't play well, at any rate."

"If you've come here to ask me again, the answer is still no."

Conner moved a few paces to one of two chairs set by a small round table and eased himself into a seat. Mac merely sat as Conner placidly regarded him. It had been so long since Mac had seen his mentor that the previous night's visit seemed more like a dream than reality. Perhaps the loss would strike him later, when he had time to truly grieve, in private. He'd be damned if he'd do it before Conner.

Conner resumed talking. "You and he were very close, I know. He was more than just your CO." He waited a respectful moment before continuing. "I'm not going to pretend I know what you're feeling, although I did have a son. I know how I felt after he died. You never get over the loss but you get used to it, like a familiar ache in your bones when a storm blows in."

Conner's voice trailed away into a soft grumble. The old man was staring at his cane, his slender hands resting lightly atop it as it lay across his knees. Mac was struck by the image. Conner didn't look at all imposing now. He looked small. Old. For some reason, he didn't know why, Mac almost found himself feeling sorry for him.

"Yesterday I was halfway across the country," Mac muttered. He pulled his hair away from his face. "I was in control of my life. Now every time I turn around there's something else waiting to knock me off my feet again . . . "

He stopped at Conner's slow chuckle. "Fifty years ago, Chuck Yeager said he used to begin each day with the 'fighter pilot's breakfast.' A cup of coffee, two aspirin and a puke." Conner's smile waned. "We're all scared, Major Harrison —"

"How about just 'Mister?'"

Conner stared hard at him for a count of three, his expression stony. "What's happened to you?"

"I'm through having to justify my feelings to you."

"Ah." Conner studied his cane. "Of course, it's common knowledge that you're the only person who's ever lost someone because of the war." He looked back up. "They were soldiers, like you. Like you, they knew what they were getting into."

"Unlike me, they're dead."

"And you've been hauling their coffins around on your back for nine years," Conner shot back. "I've lost friends to war too, Mister Harrison, and not just Vietnam. The Gulf Wars, the Pan-Am and a whole bloody handful of forgotten conflicts in-between. Not a generation has ever walked this Earth that hasn't sent their children off to die, that hasn't asked itself why. But they didn't stop living while they tried to figure it out."

He leaned forward. "You could have died on the *Reagan*, but-you-didn't. Nine years or nine hundred will never be enough to truly understand why. If you're debating whether it's worth hanging around in the meantime, make your decision and be quick about it. Or, you can show your thanks to God for sparing you by being of some use to the living. I'm offering you that opportunity, right now. And I don't have another nine years to wait for you to make up your mind."

Mac held Conner's hard gaze, willing his anger into abeyance. He knew what Conner wanted him to do. What he didn't know, was why.

He rose and crossed to the chest of drawers, peeled the lid off of one of the cups. He raised it to his nose and sniffed, then sipped the strong, steaming coffee. "All right. Tell me why I should risk my life for you."

"Moontown, Mister Harrison. It suffers from lack of attention."

Mac paused in mid-sip. "A publicity stunt?"

"No. Well, not exactly, although publicity certainly is a part of it. How much do you know about Moontown?"

"I'd rather hear you tell me about it."

"NASA had always planned a lunar outpost," Conner began, ignoring Mac's sarcasm. "We'd have been there by the early nineteen-nineties, but by then their budget had been slashed to the point they couldn't build a slingshot to lob rocks at the moon without years of Congressional debate. The White House didn't give a damn about space. No administration really did, after Kennedy. Nixon, perhaps. Too expensive. So Congress changed their tactics, started bringing private industry into the equation. They bought Lockheed-Martin's VentureStar orbiter back in '96 and that was the beginning of the end of manned missions. By the oughts, Shuttle *Columbia* went to the Smithsonian, *Endeavour* became a bus for the space station, *Discovery* went into mothballs at Vandenberg and the rest were scrapped. Then in ought-five, things began heating up again in central Europe and the new administration began rebuilding defense, including cranking up so-called Star Wars research again."

"Peregrin," Mac provided. Peregrin had grown out of the Air Force's Space Warfare Talon program: the first generation of unmanned missile cruisers, drone spacecraft that could be maneuvered in orbit to fire at any target on the globe, then returned to Earth for maintenance and reloading.

Conner nodded. "Lockheed-Martin got that one, too, launching them out of Vandenberg with the 14th Air Force. But missiles and drones are ridiculously easy to target, and their latitude is limited. Your choices are destroy the target, or miss the target, which they do more often than not, never mind DoD's horseshit press. The Pentagon seriously considered reintroducing the neutron bomb . . . "

Mac was surprised. "I never knew that."

Conner flashed a thin smile. "Very few did. Fortunately, more ethical minds prevailed. A bomb that killed only people and left buildings and materiel intact was still too pernicious a prospect to consider, even with all those twitchy trigger fingers. It was decided that what was needed was a way to surgically introduce troops to a target area with the speed and surprise of a missile. To be able to both neutralize and control a target simultaneously. The Peregrine project, with humans. Which is where you came in." He shifted in his seat, wincing. "Would you be so good as to hand me that cup? This old flesh is particularly unwilling this morning."

Mac obligingly took the remaining cup to Conner, who removed the lid and placed it on the table as he continued: "Problem was, by then the government had near about cost-cut themselves out of the manned space flight business altogether. Lockheed-Martin had their hands full, Boeing-McDonnell was too wrapped up in commercial aviation, and no one at NASA could do it, not without major additions and modifications to their physical plant and billions in capital. The only personnel left was a handful of engineers and technicians at Canaveral and Johnson to keep the odd toy flying and handle the occasional shuttle launch, remote probe. The rest had acquired new jobs in private industry."

"Working for you?"

Conner took a sip of his tea, nodding as he swallowed. "I made sure of it. I had everything the government lacked. People, materiel. Money, and a predisposition to spend it. Of course, by then I had plans of my own. My terms were simple. I would provide the brass hats and suits with whatever they needed for their short-sighted war games, at bargain prices." He chuckled. "Hell, I undercut everyone. In exchange, they would give me the moon."

He set his cup on the table and stood, leaning heavily on his cane as he walked gingerly to the window. "Actually, I told them I'd settle for them staying the hell out of my way while I took it. Plus, I wanted unrestricted use of Vandenberg as a commercial launch facility, the authority to retrofit it to my needs, and full clearance to launch commercial orbiters whenever I saw fit."

"That's all?"

Conner tossed Mac an evil grin over his shoulder. "I was younger, cocky as hell." He shrugged. "What could they say? I was the only one left who could give them what they wanted. Oh, they screamed bloody murder. Called me a blackmailer. True, of course, but it irked them to be beaten at their own game. In the end, it all came down to money. It always does. They kicked everyone out of Vandenberg and got out of my way."

Conner reached into his pocket and withdrew a small object. "Nineteen months later, I was holding this."

He extended his hand so Mac could see. A dark, veined stone about the size of a quarter lay in his palm, the sharp angles worn smooth. "Ilmenite. Titanium-iron oxide, from the first hole my engineers drilled in *Mare Smythii*." Conner considered the small stone as he spoke. "The moon isn't made of green cheese, Mister Harrison. It's made of oxygen. LUNOX. Almost half the weight of lunar surface material, and it's pathetically easy to access. Melt it, send a charge through it, and you get liquid oxygen. Fuel. Mix that with a little nitrogen and a few other trace elements and you've got atmosphere. Grind ilmenite into sand, heat it, bubble hydrogen through it and you get water where there was none. Mix the water with sand and you've got cement, for building. There *is* life on the moon, Mister Harrison. Our lives." He closed his fingers over the stone. "In here. All in here."

"What about polar ice? Why do you need ilmenite for water?"

"Because by the time NASA's Lunar Prospector had relayed the news we were already locked into *Mare Smythii*," Conner answered sardonically. "And when you run the numbers, there's really no appreciable cost difference between mining LUNOX or dirty ice. There's advantages to an equatorial location over a polar one, as well. We were going to lease space for an astronomical research station. The Hawking Observatory. *Smythii's* a good place for a telescope."

Conner returned the ilmenite to his pocket. "When they asked me to put Moontown on hold to help with the war effort, I told them to go to hell. But, what Uncle Sam giveth, he can surely take away. So I built their toys. The *Reagan* and your dropsleds, chemical lasers, power-guns, a few other odds and ends. Made a little money, a few billion when it was all said and done. After the war was over, though, nobody was interested anymore in throwing cash at some hole-in-the-ground on the moon. Can't say I blame them, I suppose. The Pan-Am ensured there were more than enough things down here on which to expend capital. And so I'm sitting on the most expensive white elephant in human history. The world is tired, too tired even to dream, it seems."

There was genuine melancholy in Conner's voice. One moment, he'd been filled with passion. Now he seemed sad, as he had minutes earlier speaking of his son.

Mac drained his coffee and lobbed the empty cup into the trash. "So why do you need me? What's a single dropsled launch going to prove?"

Conner nodded, as if acknowledging the sagacity of Mac's question. "The biggest cost of maintaining Moontown, obviously, is transportation. It costs millions to launch a shuttle from Earth. Fuel isn't as much of a problem as it used to be. I send 'em up with half a tank as it is, turboram engines kick in after they're out of the gravity well. Refuel 'em with LUNOX at Moontown for the trip home, but it's still expensive. Flyback boosters help some, too, saves us the cost of having to fish SRBs out of the ocean and scrape off the barnacles, but there's still maintenance, turnaround time between missions, staff wages —"

"All right, shuttles won't work," Mac interrupted. He was growing tired of Conner's penchant to lecture. "What will?"

"A powergun."

"You mean . . . " Mac mimed firing a rifle. "A powergun?"

"I mean the same principle," Conner replied. Despite his irritation, for the first time since the old man's arrival Mac found himself truly intrigued. Conner sensed Mac's abrupt interest, his eyes glittering with renewed intensity as he described UniCom's failed attempts to create a lunar cargo delivery system. There were plans for LUNOX-fueled unmanned rockets, then a LUNOX-powered cannon, to propel drone canisters into Earth orbit, where they would be recovered. Cost and wasted LUNOX, Conner's most precious lunar commodity, had killed both ideas, plus the danger inherent in the latter: "One jam and you're looking at a new crater," Conner drawled. "So scratch that idea. But it led us to the solution."

He held his cane horizontally before him, the tip tilted upward. "Imagine a barrel just like the barrel of your powergun, only much longer, miles longer. The whole thing is lined with superconducting current loops; again, just like a powergun. Solar array provides the power. Instead of a frag cartridge, you shove a cargo canister in one end, juice it up, and whoosh!" He ran a finger from the cane's handle to the tip and beyond, finishing with a flourish. "Off it goes, simple as that." He lowered the cane. "Instead of orbiting, the canister re-enters atmosphere and parachutes to Earth. When you collect enough of them, you strap them to a booster and launch them into lunar orbit. You can let 'em float around up there indefinitely: with microgravity and no atmosphere, it's a simple matter to yank one down when needed."

"And you've built this, giant powergun? On the moon?"

"Mass driver," Conner corrected. "Superconducting electromagnetic mass driver, EMD for short." He snorted. "You know, almost all of these things were on someone's drawing board even before you were born. Mass drivers were theorized seventy years ago, MIT had a small-scale working model as early as 1977. Cost them three-thousand dollars to build, a pittance even then. Mag lev trains are damn near the same thing and the new wore off of them years ago. LUNOX extraction technology was old news decades ago, we used NASA's own First Lunar Outpost studies to come up with *Mare Smythii* as the site for Moontown. As I said, we could have been on the moon ages ago, if not for our myopic friends inside the beltway. But then, where would that have left me?" He raised the tip of his cane level with Mac's chest. "Where would it have left you?"

Mac pressed his palms together below his chin as if praying, touching his fingertips to his lips. "Let me get this straight. You want me to fly to the moon, climb into a dropsled and be fired down an electric cannon back to Earth? Just to prove it can be done? Why not launch an unmanned canister?"

"Because the press could give a rat's ass about an unmanned launch." Conner scowled around the blunt admission. "You're right. It is a publicity stunt. But so has been every manned launch since Gemini. How many unmanned missions can you remember, hm? But every schoolkid can recite the date Armstrong and Aldrin walked on the moon, when *Challenger* exploded, when we broke ground for Moontown. We only pay attention when there's an emotional stake in it for us, and it's tough to get all teary-eyed over a hunk of metal. We need to be able to imagine ourselves taking that journey. Sure, I can prove the mass driver works by launching a drone canister, I can paint it with the Stars and Stripes and stuff a copy of the Constitution and pictures of orphans inside and it'll still wind up a sixty-second feature at the end of the evening news. I need an event so big that the whole damn world watches, every goddamn person on the planet shouting 'What-are-we-waiting-for?'" Conner pounded the tip of his cane on the floor with each word. "Especially the people with money. I need investors. I need you."

Mac mulled over what he'd just heard. If he bought into Conner's theatrics, it made sense enough, as far as it went.

"So what's the rest of it?"

Conner arched an eyebrow. "How's that?"

"You're looking for a guinea pig," Mac flatly declared. Conner didn't object. "Say you get one. Say the mass driver works, you get your publicity. Why should anyone invest?" Mac spread his hands. "I mean, sure, there's certain things you can produce better in microgravity than down here but if there was money in that, you wouldn't be talking to me at all. I suppose if we ever send someone to Mars, you could use Moontown as a staging base, but NASA's still got the space station . . . "

"The space station is to Moontown as a treehouse is to the Taj Mahal."

"Fine," Mac continued, "but where's the payoff? All you've done so far is cut costs. So someone tosses you a few billion. How do they make it back?"

Conner leaned against the table, his eyes veiled, turned inward. Ah, thought Mac. Now we come to it. He spoke casually: "I mean, I still haven't heard a reason to get me to climb back into that dropsled."

The comment did its work, bringing Conner's focus back to the present. He stared hard at Mac before speaking.

"This doesn't leave this room."

Conner waited, poker-faced. After a few moments, Mac nodded agreement. "All right."

Still, Conner debated. Finally: "Fusion."

"Okay."

"Do you know what helium-three is?"

"I would imagine it has something to do with fusion." Mac took time to enjoy Conner's perturbed scowl before relenting, dredging up his knowledge of basic physics. "An isotope of helium."

"That's more than I knew when I first heard of it," Conner offered. "It popped up in one of the early geological surveys of *Mare Smythii*. We knew it was there before we even built Moontown. We just didn't know there was so damn much of it, over a million tons of the stuff in the top layer of the lunar regolith. Just lying there, waiting."

"For what?"

"For me." Conner eased back in his seat and assumed a professorial air. "Everyone knows what fission is. You blow apart nuclei to get power, nuclear power. But it's a messy business, dangerous, and not terribly efficient. You get tons of highly radioactive waste that'll be around long after we humans have destroyed ourselves. Fusion, on the other hand, is the opposite of fission."

He brought his hands together and clasped them. "Instead of blowing nuclei apart, you force them together to get power, and practically no waste." Conner reached for his tea. "Sounds simple, right?"

"Sure. That's why you can't turn around without bumping into a fusion reactor."

Conner sipped his beverage, making a face as he swallowed the tepid liquid. "Your sarcasm reveals your understanding. The problem with fusion is that it takes a staggering amount of energy to produce." Conner's discourse, for once, was brief. The first step in fusion was stripping atoms of their electrons, thus producing plasma, ionized gas, a process which required enormous heat energy. Fusion itself was then produced by forcing together the plasma nuclei. On the stellar scale, the tremendous gravity generated by the gigantic plasma balls called stars did the trick, forcing hydrogen atoms together to create life-sustaining heat energy and radiation.

"Now," Conner said, twisting in his chair and leaning forward, "bear with me. In the sun, fusion is basically a simple, three-step process. Two hydrogen atoms — two single protons — collide and fuse, releasing energy. One of the protons decays into a neutron, making deuterium. Next, the deuterium atom collides with another hydrogen proton and creates helium-three — two protons and one neutron — and more energy. Step three: two helium-three atoms collide, fusing into normal helium — two protons and two neutrons — while the two remaining hydrogen protons fly off and the process starts all over again. With me so far?" Mac nodded.

"Each collision creates increasingly more energy, but also requires more and more energy to produce. It's a lot easier to bang two single protons together than it is two atoms of helium-three. That's why down here, most folks start in the middle, using deuterium. For one thing, it doesn't require as much energy to initialize the process. The other reason is availability. There's enough deuterium in a bucket of ordinary seawater to equal the energy of a ton of coal, if used for fusion.

"But helium-three is a different story. There's really only two places to find it in any real quantity. The sun of course, but not all of the helium-three created by the sun is burned up in fusion. Some of it escapes, carried on the solar wind. Our atmosphere filters out any useful quantity before it reaches the Earth. But there is no atmosphere on the moon."

"All right," Mac said. "There's helium-three on the moon. You said it was impossible to use it for fusion on Earth —"

"No, I didn't say impossible," Conner interrupted, raising a finger before him. "It's difficult, but so was controlled nuclear fission, at first. We ran our first tokamak tests over thirty years ago."

"Toka-what?"

"Tokamak. It's a type of fusion reactor, a big hollow donut wrapped in electromagnets to generate the plasma containment field, although we've moved well past that now," and he waved his hand dismissively. "Plasma containment's been licked for ages, but the other problem, initializing the helium-three reaction, took us years to figure out."

"But you've done it?" Conner grinned. "What does that mean?"

"It means that you wouldn't be here if we hadn't." He leaned forward over his cane, his eyes bright with the fire of his vision. "Do you have any idea of the significance of what I'm describing to you? The profundity? Just twenty-five metric tons of helium-three would provide enough power to light every lamp and run every television and PC in the entire United States for a year. And like I said, there's a million tons of the stuff, maybe more, on the moon. That's forty-thousand years of power, about ten times that available from fossil fuels, minus the pollution. Twice what we could squeeze out of every nuclear reactor currently in operation, without the tons of radioactive waste. That makes helium-three potentially the most valuable substance in the known universe. Compared to fossil fuel costs today, just one metric ton would be worth over a two-hundred times its weight in gold, almost four-billion dollars! From a truckload of dirt!"

Mac remained silent, fascinated by the play of emotions on Conner's face. There was passion there, yes, but beneath it all, Mac now saw, was greed. Pure, simple greed.

"So that's why you need me," he flatly offered. "So you can make more money."

Conner's face hardened. "Money I've got, more than I could ever spend in my few remaining years. The profit I realize will be poured back into Moontown, into UniCom, into more research. I consider this a gift, my gift to the world, this generation and all those to come." He relaxed, settling back into his pitch. "And you are the final piece that will tie everything together."

Full realization at last dawned on Mac. "You're going to use the mass driver to ship helium-three to Earth."

Conner inclined his head in acknowledgement. "Where it will be used as fuel in the first line of UniCom IEC fusion reactors. Imagine it. America's greatest living hero, undertaking the most audacious excursion ever recorded in human history, touching down on his own two feet in front of the world press before strolling over and handing me the substance that will alter the destiny of humanity!" Conner shrugged in response to Mac's raised eyebrow. "A small canister of helium-three. An overly-dramatic touch, perhaps, but necessary. And minutes later, with the entire world watching, I will show them their future. Mass drivers launching men and women to the Earth. Fusion drive space shuttles, aircraft. Clean, efficient fusion reactors running our households, powered by lunar helium-three. No more nuclear waste, no more pollution, no more catastrophic oil slicks fouling our coastlines. And it all begins, Mister Harrison, with you." He leaned back in his chair. "It's magnificent."

"It's insane."

"You're a fine one to talk, *Major*," Conner countered. "And don't think I won't make it worth your while. In addition to the sizeable cash fee you would earn for the jump alone, which we can negotiate later, I stand ready to offer you UniCom stock and a not inconsiderable stake in all resultant fusion technologies. You can be a member of the board if you like, special consultant, or return to your home in Montana when it's all over. Frankly, I don't care. But whatever you choose to do, you'll never have to worry about money again."

"I don't worry about money now."

Conner nodded. He didn't seem surprised. "Then how about the satisfaction of knowing you've done something no one else has ever done or is likely to do again? Your name would be written with Charles Lindbergh, Sir Edmund Hillary, Neil Armstrong, Faith Alison. Mackinley Michael Harrison, the first human ever to . . . "

He stopped as Mac uncrossed his legs and lowered them over the edge of the bed. The offer wasn't without its appeal, but Mac had heard nothing in Conner's pitch that had truly excited him. Money he had. Not much, just his monthly retirement check, but it was enough to live his life the way he wanted.

And fame, like wealth, was useful only if exploited. Mac'd had quite enough of being in the public eye after the war. What he wanted was what he'd had until just twenty-four hours earlier. He wanted to return to the solitude of his cabin where there were no surprises, back to where no one wanted anything from him, nobody wanted him to be anything other than what he was now, what he had chosen to be.

He met Conner's eye. "I'm sorry. I'm not your man."

Conner smiled crookedly. "Well. I suppose that's it, then." He clambered out of his chair, speaking as he stretched. "I must admit, I anticipated your answer, although I was hoping I might be able to convince you anyway. I've already lined up a second."

It took Mac a moment to register the simple admission. "You found somebody else?"

Conner relaxed his stretch and met Mac's eye. "Surely you didn't expect me to place all of my eggs in your basket. I've had a signed contract for some time now. Quite frankly, you were an afterthought. As you pointed out last night, Colonel Takeshita's illness provided the impetus to draw you here. Not that I hadn't considered contacting you earlier, but we both know how that would have gone." He coolly considered Mac, all pretense of cordiality gone. "I would still prefer you be the one to do it, but this is going to happen, Mister Harrison. With or without you."

Mac shook his head in disbelief. Trying to keep on top of Conner's game was like navigating a minefield. Just when he felt he was standing on secure ground, another explosion went off beneath his feet. "Just like that, huh?" he said.

"Just like what?" Conner responded dispassionately. "Did you expect me to beg you? Forgive me if your refusal has as little impact on me as you seemed determined to allow my overtures to have on you."

He took a step towards Mac, halting just a yard away, his cane planted on the floor before him like a sword. "Allow me this final observation before I depart. You have a rather inflated sense of your own importance, Mister Harrison. Were you to emerge from your hermitage long enough, I think you'd discover the world pays you less mind even than you pay it. If you prefer to remain a footnote in history rather than a chapter, so be it. But do not act surprised if those who write the text fail to care."

Mac rose from the bed. He knew Conner was just getting in his licks because of his refusal but the shot angered him nonetheless. The two men faced off like *samurai* standing in *kamae*, swords drawn, waiting motionlessly for one to betray some sign of weakness that would allow the other to attack.

After a few moments, Mac sheathed his blade. "Thank you for what you did for Sensei."

Conner nodded once, recognizing the end of the duel. "You probably won't believe me, but I was honored."

He spoke as he walked to the door. "By the way, the man who will perform the jump in your stead is waiting for me at UniCom. I would appreciate it if you'd spend a little time with him. Not much, perhaps an hour or two. To answer any questions he may have, give him the benefit of your experience. Afterwards, Martha will provide you with the details of Colonel Takeshita's funeral. I've also asked Mr. Davis to give you a tour of the facility."

He paused just as he arrived at the door and turned to face Mac. "If you won't do it for me, consider it a small favor in return for seeing to your Sensei's care. I'll have a car waiting for you downstairs within the hour."

"Everything has a price with you, doesn't it?"

"Everything has a price, period, Mister Harrison." He opened the door and was gone.

II

Terence Innes stood before his office window, staring down at the street three stories below. Rivulets of moisture painted the glass, and the street was dotted with umbrellas of all sizes and colors. The Dickensian image of wintry London streets blanketed with snow came to his mind. It was largely a myth. It was wet. It was cold. It was England.

He sipped coffee from a china cup, holding the delicate pale saucer in his other hand. The idea that all Britons drank tea was another myth, about as accurate as the idea that all Americans wore cowboy hats. He'd learned that as a graduate student thirty years ago, in New Jersey. Three months after his 1991 matriculation from Cambridge, Innes had taken his physics degree and graduate program acceptance letter across the Atlantic to Princeton University. It was the only place he'd wanted to be. Shortly after his arrival, he'd found himself wearing a hardhat and radiation tag, standing awestruck in a gymnasium-sized room filled to the rafters with a mammoth labyrinth of conduit, cables, catwalks and machinery. And at the center of it all sat the squat donut of the TFTR — the Tokamak Fusion Test Reactor.

Though he was but a junior member of the famed Princeton Plasma Physics Laboratory, Innes could not have chosen a more exciting time to be there. Two years later, in December of 1993, the TFTR produced a record six million watts of power, using a fuel mixture of equal parts deuterium and tritium, a record they'd bested by over four-point-five megawatts less than a year later. Both surges lasted only a fraction of a second and took more power to achieve than was produced, but it was a stunning breakthrough. A true plasma, a star, had been created on Earth. It changed Terence Innes' life forever.

He stared at the tan coffee in his cup. On the gross level it was flavored water, but it was also hydrogen, oxygen and carbon; protons, neutrons and electrons, held together by electromagnetic force — building blocks of matter, from which everything was created and from which anything could be created. The ancient alchemists hadn't been that far off the mark. You could transform lead into gold. You just had to know what you were doing.

Innes could still remember the day UniCom's recruiters had visited the PPPL, the team still reeling from the news that the tokamak was to be mothballed. UniCom's smiling agents had wined and dined all the post-grads, served up tantalizing morsels of information concerning their own fledgling fusion research efforts, which they hinted would ultimately make the TFTR seem a steam engine by comparison. Resumes, academic transcripts and drafts of doctoral theses were requested and eagerly submitted. And then they all waited for the call.

His friends left for North Carolina and Innes packed for home. U.S. citizens only need apply — foreigners could not be trusted to keep mum. Word from the top, from Roger Conner, UniCom's autocratic, patriotic, bloody paranoid CEO. Innes was good enough; he just had the wrong accent.

Thirty years ago, and still the resentment burned. Innes' well-meaning father had attempted to console him by installing him at his side, running Innes Freight, Britain's second-largest transport company. From atoms and stars to lorries and trains. When a heart attack claimed Nigel Innes seven months later, his discomfited son inherited the lot.

One year later, Innes Freight was gone. In its place was Helios, Ltd. It was then Innes had commissioned the painting which hung over the fireplace in his office, just over his shoulder: the ancient Greek sun god driving his fiery chariot across the heavens. Innes would be the first to harness that power and bring it down to Earth, reducing UniCom and Roger Conner to mere satellites of his star.

There was a soft rapping at the door. He turned from the window. "Yes?"

His executive assistant entered, closing the door behind him. Without waiting for an invitation, he settled himself into one of two straight-backed antique chairs facing the desk. Innes took a last sip of cold coffee and placed the cup and saucer on the desk as he settled in behind it.

"The launch is set for Christmas Eve."

Innes was startled. "He's sure? Just eleven days?"

"Quite certain. Most of them have been forced to work double shifts to ensure they'll be ready in time, our man included. The first unmanned test of the mass driver is scheduled for a week from now, perhaps sooner."

"And this other man . . . "

"Boykin."

" . . . he's still the one who will perform the manned test?"

"He's scheduled to arrive there the day before launch."

"That's cutting it a bit thin, isn't it?"

"Not really. There's no practical reason for him to arrive any sooner."

Innes nodded absently. He'd expected the mass driver launch to take place well after the holidays, at the earliest. The accelerated schedule was not good news.

Sometimes it bothered Innes, his total lack of remorse when it came to corporate espionage. Early on in his race with UniCom he'd bankrolled a network of what he liked to call 'freelance researchers.' Spies was the better word. No one too important, no one who would attract undue attention, and all of them slaves to the almighty Euro. It was not easy, penetrating UniCom's daunting firewall of security, but he'd gleaned enough jigsaw pieces of information over the years to at least keep pace with Conner's breakthroughs. Or so he'd thought.

Helium-three! Of course; that damned moonbase. You could step outside the dome and scoop up the stuff in your hand. He studied the scale model of the Helios spheromak resting on the far edge of his desk. It still burned the classic deuterium-deuterium mixture, no way around that with the present design. But there was only one fusion method that could effectively burn helium-three. Inertial electrostatic containment, a process which bypassed ponderous and clumsy electromagnetic coils and instead used pulsed lasers to contain the plasma and force the nuclei together. Though the specs had been around for over half-a-century, few physicists truly believed IEC fusion was practicable. Fewer still had ever tried it.

Conner obviously had built an IEC reactor. A working reactor, one which warranted his investing billions in a delivery system to ship lunar helium-three to Earth to fuel it, billions he clearly felt confident he would recoup. What he had begun thirty years before was now only months away from full fruition.

Innes had always believed he was running neck-and-neck with Conner in the fusion contest. He realized now with sickening certitude that he'd already lost the race. And Innes was not a man who relished defeat. That much, at least, he knew he had in common with Conner.

"Something else has come up." The assistant continued without waiting for his employer to respond. "An hour ago, Conner visited a guest in a hotel near UniCom." He reached into his breast pocket as he spoke, withdrawing his thin e-pad. He touched the surface, reading. "The Omni Europa. The guest's name is Mackinley Harrison."

"Sounds familiar."

"Nine years ago, he was the sole survivor of the *Reagan* explosion."

"Ah." Innes remembered. "The paratrooper." He didn't see that it mattered.

"Of a sort, yes. He's one of only two people alive with orbital sky-diving experience. The other is confined to a wheelchair."

"Mm." Then, "Ah-h."

"Harrison has been a recluse for the last seven years," the assistant continued smoothly. "He is notorious for refusing interviews, visitors of any kind. You will recall the BBC attempted to interview him three years ago, to mark the five-year anniversary of the war's end."

"No, I don't recall."

"It was in the news for a bit. He wouldn't answer their queries, so they risked a visit to his property, unannounced. He drove them off by throwing stones at their van."

Innes snorted. "Serves them right, nosy bastards."

"Yes, sir. But given his obvious penchant for privacy, one has to wonder . . . "

" . . . what he's doing away from home," Innes finished.

"More importantly, what he's doing talking to Roger Conner."

"Yes, sir."

Innes pondered a moment. "This is not good."

"No, sir."

"Have you any indication that Harrison will replace, er . . . "

"Boykin, sir."

" . . . Boykin, for the mass driver demonstration?"

"No, sir, but it seems the only logical reason for his traveling to UniCom. And his involvement would certainly add more drama, his being a war hero and all that."

Innes leaned back in his chair and ran his fingers absently along the edge of the china saucer. "And we're still certain that Conner is planning his fusion announcement for just after the mass driver launch?"

"Yes, sir. Our man says they've increased helium-three mining and extraction the last month. He believes Boykin, or Harrison, will carry a small sample with him during the journey. Sort of a symbolic gesture."

Innes let the statement hang in the air a moment. He despised Conner's garish sense of drama. Of course, it was brilliant.

"We can't let that happen," he finally said.

"No, sir."

"Of course, we're close, but we need at least another four months before our own announcement."

"Yes, sir."

Innes swiveled his chair until it faced the window. His man had been part of Moontown's crew for just over half-a-year. Inserting him there had actually been easier than Innes had expected. But stealing secrets was one thing. What needed doing now was something else entirely. If Conner beat him to the punch, Innes would be ruined.

"That launch must not succeed," he said at last, without turning.

"No, sir."

"See to it that it doesn't. Whatever it takes."

"Yes, sir."

After a moment, Innes heard the door close softly behind him. He sat for a long time, watching the rain spatter the glass. The downpour simply refused to let up.

III

UniCom's main lobby looked very different in the daylight. The winter sun chased the shadows from its immaculate corners, glinting off of marble and polished brass and steel. There were perhaps two-dozen people there, dressed in everything from business suits to Middle Eastern robes and African *dashikis*; some obviously guests, other wearing UniCom ID's on their breasts. Mac waited his turn at the desk, patiently endured another ID check. A minute later, he stood once again in Conner's outer office.

He was alone, Martha nowhere he could see. He looked around, taking in details he'd missed or ignored the night before. Sunlight bathed the space, shining through the broad sloping skylights over his head. Dominating the center of the room was a black pedestal about six feet in diameter, rising out of the floor to just above Mac's waist and sheared off at the terminus at a shallow angle. He remembered passing it on his first visit, a low, shadowy shape he'd assumed was a table of some kind. He walked over and considered the diorama resting on the textured gray face. A steel plaque was affixed to the pedestal just below the surface: *Smythii Station Commercial Lunar Research Facility*, it read.

Mac returned his attention to the model and realized he was looking at Moontown.

A large central dome dominated the diorama. Judging from the relative size of the tiny vehicles and pressure-suited figures arranged around the structure, it had to be at least a thousand feet in diameter and four stories high, no doubt with more space beneath the surface. Tiny porthole windows glowing with pinpricks of light were set at regular intervals along the dome's curve. A smaller dome was set atop the main structure, ringed with larger windows — an observation room of some kind, or perhaps the main operations center. Thin tubular corridors ran tentacle-like from the main dome along the ground to several smaller, block-like structures of indeterminate function. Enormous solar panel arrays came close to dwarfing the base with their size, set in twin semi-circles on the surface well back from the main done, angled shallowly to catch the sun's rays. A space shuttle was positioned a few inches above the mock-up of the launch and landing pad, floating over the artful ground effect simulation as if the ship had been captured in a 3-D photograph. Mac touched it and it bobbled: magnetic suspension. Nowhere on the model, though, was anything that looked like the mass driver Conner had described. Perhaps he was keeping that a secret as well.

Mac stepped back to consider the whole. It wasn't the most artistic piece of architecture he'd ever seen, but its very existence lent it a breathtaking elegance and beauty. It was science-fiction made fact. What others had only dreamed, Conner had audaciously created.

There were people living there. People living and working on the moon.

Mac studied Conner's closed office doors, wondering if he was expected to wait to be summoned. To hell with that. He was fed up with playing the serf to Conner's kingly whims.

Mac strode over to the doors and paused, his fingers brushing the handles. He heard faint voices, male. One was clearly Conner's. The other was eerily familiar. Mac leaned in close, listening intently. He couldn't place the second voice, nor did he comprehend why it set his heart suddenly racing.

Mac grasped the levered handles, turned them, pushed open the doors. The voices stopped.

"Ah, Mister Harrison!" Conner's voice rang out. "Allow me to introduce you to someone."

Mac halted dead in his tracks. He was staring at a ghost.

IV

Conner was beaming as he rose from his chair, ignoring the stunned look on Mac's face. "Major Harrison, meet Captain James Boykin."

The pounding in Mac's chest subsided a bit. Of course. It couldn't be Tim. Like his brother, the man who stood and faced faced Mac was tall and broad and appeared as if he'd be perfectly at home sitting atop a tractor. He had the same chunky redneck features and thick, straw-colored hair but he was about twenty pounds heavier and a lot older. His eyes as they met Mac's displayed shock.

"You didn't tell me it was him." Boykin was speaking, his thick drawl tight with suppressed anger.

Conner did a slow take, first to Boykin, then to Mac. "I wasn't aware you two had met."

Wariness replaced Mac's shock. "What's going on?"

"I don't understand the question." Conner seemed perplexed. "As I said, I was hoping you might be good enough to brief Mister Boykin . . . "

"Him?" Mac interjected. "He's your back-up?"

"Back up?" Boykin's words came on the heels of Mac's. "I'm not the back-up —" He turned to Conner. "You told me I was the one."

Conner raised a hand placatingly. "Please, gentlemen. Mister Boykin is indeed the one who will perform the — goodness, I still don't quite know what to call it. The drop? The moondrop." He smiled. "I like that. Mister Boykin has been under contract with me to perform the moondrop for almost two months. Of course, he is aware, as are we all, that his experience in such undertakings is limited. In fact, he has no experience at all."

"I can do it."

"He is also aware, I'm sure," Conner continued, as if Boykin hadn't spoken, "that his contract provides me the latitude to seek out another more suited to the task, which is why I contacted Mister Harrison," and he nodded at Mac. "Purely out of concern for Mister Boykin's safety and the success of the drop, of course, though I continue to have confidence in his ability to perform."

He said it dismissively but Boykin relaxed a bit as he sensed the olive branch, glaring at Mac defiantly. "However," Conner continued, "since Mister Harrison has made it clear he has no interest in assisting us in our enterprise, I have asked him here to lend us the benefit of his unique experience." He shrugged and sat. "I've no idea where to start, so . . . " He amiably raised his open hand as he settled into his chair, beckoning his guests to begin.

"You're crazy," Mac finally managed.

"You don't think I can do it?" Boykin challenged.

"I know you can't do it."

"From where I'm standing, looks like there's only one of us has the balls to try."

"That's not the point! Don't you see what's going on here?" Mac pointed at Conner. "You think he couldn't have found somebody better if he'd wanted to?"

"Like who? You?"

Mac fought to keep his anger under control. "How many jumps do you have? A hundred? Two-hundred? How high? Ten grand, twelve? C'mon, Jimmy, there's men half our age with ten times your jumps, we both know it! So why'd he pick you?"

"I reckon 'cause you're still too chicken-shit."

Mac was heading for Boykin before he even realized it.

The other man swiftly backed away from his chair and into a defensive stance, right foot forward, his hands open and out before him.

Mac read the posture in an instant and took a deep circling step to his left, moving to the outside of Boykin's telegraphed defense, gliding in with his right forearm raised, ready to block and flash in above Boykin's guard. His left hand curved out and upwards, heading for the back of his neck . . .

"Gentlemen!"

The word rang out in the expansive office like a rifle shot. Mac and Boykin froze in place, faces a foot apart. Mac held his right-hand strike where it was, close enough to Boykin's chin to feel his hot breath on the heel of his chambered palm. Held Boykin's eye with his own, letting him know: *I had you.* He saw Boykin's face flush as the message struck home.

Conner's voice came more softly in the sudden calm. "Perhaps a postponement is in order."

Mac stepped back first, keeping his guard in place until he was clear of Boykin's offensive sphere. The two men held their staredown, refusing to grant the other the small victory of being the first to look away.

"Thank you, Mister Boykin."

Several moments passed before Boykin realized he was being dismissed. He glanced at Conner, then headed for the exit, his muttered "Fuck you" hanging in the air as he brushed past Mac. In a moment he was gone.

Conner pressed a spot on the desktop pad. The doors closed with a soft *click.*

"Well," he sighed. "That certainly didn't go the way I had hoped."

"It went exactly the way you hoped."

There was no point in pretending any longer, that was clear now to both of them. Conner smiled mirthlessly. "He does look like his brother, doesn't he? Then again, they were twins."

"You son of a bitch."

"Wouldn't be surprised if he still drinks, though he's supposedly been sober for some time now. But he's pathetically out of shape. My physicians tell me it's possible he might not withstand the G-stress of lunar launch, though quite honestly there's no way to tell until the event itself. Did you know his family has a history of heart disease? His father died of a heart attack at forty. Can you imagine? So young, just two years younger than his son is now." He shook his head sadly.

"And of course there's his lack of experience. You were close in your estimate. Two-hundred and six jumps, none higher than fifteen thousand feet. What is that, three miles, not even? And none of them even approaching the speed of a re-entering dropsled." He shrugged. "Still, he might make it —"

"You know he won't."

"I know no such thing," Conner growled, "except this." He raised a bony finger. "Eleven days from now, either you or Mister Boykin will climb into that dropsled on *Mare Smythii*. Whomever it is, I will pray for their safe return." He lowered his finger and gave a resigned smile. "In Mister Boykin's case, I'll simply have to pray a bit harder."

"Look," said Mac, tightly. "You want to hurt me, fine. You want to get even with me for saying no, fine, but don't take it out on him. You can't let him do this when you know he doesn't have a chance."

Conner frowned. "What's this? Concern for someone other than yourself? How atypical."

"Oh, stop the goddamn games, for once."

"*This-is-no-game!*"

Conner slammed his cane onto his desk as he abruptly rose, the sharp crack an accent to the words he hurled across the room. He raised the cane and leveled it at Mac like a sabre. "You are the one who cannot seem to grasp the reality of what I'm trying to do!," he thundered. "And I am tired of playing nursemaid to your martyred pride while the destiny of the whole goddamn planet waits for your answer!"

The cane was trembling. Conner lowered it and drew himself up, inhaling deeply. When he spoke again, his voice was sterile. "We both know you are the only real choice for this task, Mister Harrison. That knowledge has allowed you some small degree of control over our dealings." His arctic eyes were hard. "But that, is over. I would have preferred to have the, 'hero', of the Pan-Am do this for me, but the decorated twin brother of one of the 82nd's honored dead will do just as well. All that's important to me is that a human being make the journey, to prove the mass driver works. That a human being places that canister of helium-3 in my hands. All that's important is that the world finally pays attention and I will not let anything, or anyone, stand in my way."

He raised his cane and examined its polished curve, as aloof as a terrorist opening his coat to reveal the rifle beneath it. "Of course, it would indeed be tragic if Mister Boykin should die during the journey.

Just as his brother, your squadmate, died nine years ago, onboard the *Reagan*. Because you couldn't summon the courage to go in his place. Because you, said no."

He watched Mac's face pale as he squeezed off the final round. "I imagine it would be like having Timothy Boykin die all over again."

Mac only stared. Conner lowered his cane and checked his wristwatch. "Another engagement calls. I understand Mister Davis is running late. I trust you'll find some way to keep yourself amused until he arrives."

He emerged from behind his desk and moved as if to pass, then stopped at Mac's shoulder, each man facing the opposite direction, refusing to meet the other's eye. "You may still say no, of course," he said, softly. "But should you change your mind, my offer of this morning still stands."

Mac listened to the soft thump of the cane recede as Conner made the doors and exited.

V

He wanted to throw up. He always did right when he woke up. Something about microgravity and its effect on the stomach. You'll get used to it in a few days, maybe a week, the vets had said, but he'd never truly had. Morning sickness. And he wasn't even pregnant. It would have been funny if he hadn't felt like shit.

He rolled out of his bunk and dropped lightly to the floor five feet below. He didn't bother turning on the light in the windowless room. His two sleeping roommates were on third shift this week, with another cycle to go before they had to rise. Besides, the room was so small, he didn't need the light to navigate its confines. He could extend his arms and touch the bunks on either side of the narrow quarters. It was like living in a closet, only without the charm.

He donned his coverall and boots and stepped outside, squinting in the sudden light as he slid the door softly closed behind him. The corridor curved gently away to either side, barely wide enough to allow two people to stand abreast. He moved aside to allow a tired-looking woman to pass, mumbled a 'Good morning.' It could have been midnight for her but details like that didn't count for much in Moontown. There was only first shift, second shift, third shift and you were either on shift, or off. The lights were always bright, the air always the same temperature, always carrying that filtered, metallic tang that was worst than stink. It was like a fucking prison. Not that he knew first-hand, but it couldn't be much worse. You could escape from prison.

There was a story the vets liked to tell the newbies. The sod's name was Berkeley — first name or last, no one could remember. He had been on the first full-time crew, years ago, back when nobody bothered with psych screening. No one had known, not even Berkeley, that he was claustrophobic. Not until he'd ripped his helmet off. Outside, on the surface. They say he'd actually managed to take two joyful, bounding steps before collapsing.

In some versions of the story, one of the workers on the surface with Berkeley had thrown up in his helmet when he realized he'd stepped on one of Berkeley's eyes. The real old-timers just shook their heads when they heard that. Impossible, they'd say. The eyes would already have burst.

Berking out, that's what they called it now. It was Moontown lingo for going nuts. Berking out, doing a berkeley, going berkers, ass-over-berkers, berk-ass crazy . . .

His stomach lurched again as he looked around him. He knew exactly how the poor bastard had felt.

He loped down the corridor to the head, covering a yard with each gliding stride. It wasn't his day to shower but he was allowed a quick wash. He stuck his ration card in the slot above the tiny sink, and the bowl beneath the clear plastic splash guard filled with his morning toilet allowance. He regarded his reflection in the mirror over the sink. His dark hair, shoulder-length back home, was buzz-cut in utilitarian Moontown fashion. His face was pasty and bloated, dark circles beneath his eyes.

He looked away, tugged a thick paper towel from the dispenser and soaked it in the water, wiped his clammy face, held the cool towel on the back of his neck. It helped, a little. He stuffed the towel into the recycle chute when he'd completed his scant bath and dried off in the hot air blower as the sink emptied. The water would be recycled, too. Everything here was. They'd probably be drinking their own piss soon, if they weren't already.

He accepted a cup of hot tea from the dispenser in the Earthside mess, sipped it through the plastic lid as he crossed to a table near a window and sat, tuning out the tired grumbling of first-shifters and the chatter of the other seconds. He always felt better when he could see outside, even if it was close to pitch black. They were four days into the two-week lunar evening, where the Earth blocked the light from the sun. They wouldn't see true morning again until Christmas Eve, ten days away. Foodlights cast their harsh spill on a rover kicking up dust as it bounced across the pewter surface on its balloon tires, the driver and passenger wearing the red helmets of LUNOX techs. He watched until the rover disappeared into the dark.

He took another sip of tea. The recycled water made it taste like the air, liquid stink. It wasn't doing much to settle his stomach. There was only one prescription that would cure him, and that was to get out of this fucking place and get back home.

He'd laughed when Innes had first asked him to take the job. He liked money, true enough, and he would do and had done pretty much anything for it, short of murder. He was careful, though, not to let money sway him, and he'd told Innes that he didn't have nearly enough to get him to fly to the fucking moon.

What Innes did have was a detailed record of not only every job he'd done for Helios, but a few other clients as well. He had no idea how Innes had come by the information. All that mattered was that Innes had threatened to leak certain facts to the police. The parties involved made Innes look like a schoolteacher. They would want to know how the police came by the information. Innes would make sure they found out. And they had no scruples at all when it came to killing.

He again looked out of the window. It wasn't hard to picture Innes in a pressure suit, doing a berkeley. It would be interesting to see if his eyes really did explode before they popped out of their sockets.

He downed the rest of his tea and deposited the cup in the recycle bin. He had fifteen minutes to check his e-mail, suit up and make his duty station for the day. One of the photocells on the inner solar array needed replacing. It promised to be as exciting as hanging a picture.

Workers were allowed to send and receive mail once a week and today was his day. He'd sent his message before he'd gone to bed, an update on the mass driver test schedule and the manned launch date, but then the server had gone down and he'd been too tired to stand in line at another. If there was a message from Innes, it would keep. If there was a line there now, it would have to keep a little longer.

The one person at the console had already finishing her business when he arrived, tapping her e-pad as she loped away. He inserted his ID into the proper slot and waited for the iris scanner to confirm his identity. There was a soft chime and a cheery female voice emanating from the speaker announced, "You have two new messages!"

This was strange. Both messages were from Mavis, his ersatz lady love — Innes' code name. He even had a photo of the woman in his wallet. He had no idea who she was.

The first message was five days old, no doubt a response to last week's update. The second was just six hours old, sent less than ninety minutes after his last transmission. If the server hadn't gone down, he would have had to wait a week before reading it. Innes knew the days he accessed his mail. The message was obviously urgent.

"You okay?"

The voice startled him out of his rumination. A man was waiting behind him, dark-skinned and muscular beneath his sweat-damp tee, his coverall open to the waist. "Bad news?"

"No, just, uh, two letters, from my girlfriend. I was only expecting one."

"Then it's good news, eh?" The man grinned wolfishly.

He smiled gamely. "Right, yeah." He fished his e-pad out of his coverall thigh pocket, slid the head into the docking slot and pressed the download key.

"I've seen you around, but we've never met, I don't think," the other man offered. He stuck out his hand. "Jesus Mendoza. Everyone calls me Soos."

The server beeped, download complete. He absently shook Mendoza's hand as he reclaimed his e-pad, eager to read the messages before his shift began.

"You know how it is, with the crazy shifts," Mendoza continued. "You can be here forever and never meet everyone. English, right?"

"Yes, that's right."

"Don't get many English up here. Americans, of course, Japanese, couple of Russians, Canadians. And the Swedes seem to like it for some reason." He peered at hard at his new friend. "You sure you're okay? You look awfully pale."

"Fine. Just in a bit of a hurry. I've got to be surface in ten minutes . . . "

"Yeah, just coming off-shift myself," Mendoza said, as if he hadn't heard the overture to part company. He stepped up to the server and deftly executed the ID protocol. "I work on the mass driver. Got to be back at it in an hour, just enough time for a bite and a letter from home. What's your girlfriend's name?"

He turned around. The corridor was empty.

He ducked into the head and latched the door. That fucking idiot Mendoza. Only eight minutes now before he had to be at the airlock, almost on the other side of the ring.

He tapped in his e-pad passcode and pressed his damp thumb against the tactile verification square. He swore as the e-pad locked him out, wiped his thumb dry on his coveralls and tried it again. The sultry voice of the woman he'd never met issued from the pad's tiny speaker. He cut it off. Probably not even the same woman in the photo. He tapped in another passcode and waited impatiently the few seconds it took for for the decryption program to do its work.

What the hell kind of name was 'Soos', anyway?

He quickly scanned the first message. It was drivel, Innes thanking him for the last transmission and reminding him to let him know the instant he learned the date of the mass driver launch, which he'd already done in yesterday's transmission.

He deleted the message, tapped the pad again and waited while the second message was decoded. It was brief, just a few lines of text on the flat rectangular screen.

He felt suddenly dizzy. The pale walls of the cramped cubicle seemed to be closing in on him, his breaths came in short, shallow pants.

The e-pad slipped from his fingers. It clattered on the floor as he dropped to his knees and threw up into the toilet, oblivious to the vomit spattering in the micro-gee and clinging to his face. He knelt there and recycled his tea until there was nothing left.

He slumped against the wall next to the toilet. He sucked air through his nose, held it, exhaled deliberately. He did it again. Slowly, the ringing in his ears faded. The room steadied. Better. That was better.

The e-pad lay face-up by his feet. He pulled it within reach with his heel, stabbed his finger down on the delete key. He didn't need to read the message again. He wasn't likely to forget it.

Fucking Innes.

VI

Mac had known what was coming as soon as he'd walked in the door and seen Boykin standing there like the reincarnation of his former comrade, burned alive in the explosion of the *Reagan*. It didn't matter that it wasn't the same person. Mac knew why Boykin hated him and that only made it worse.

And Conner. Conner knew too. Mac had been prepared for his parting shot, but this . . .

Mac and Tim Boykin had been friends but they hadn't been close. Tim had viewed the military as the only way to see more of the world than the modest fifty acres of his family's tobacco farm in Leafton, an hour east of Raleigh. Jimmy Boykin had joined his brother on the spur of the moment. Although they were twins, it was obvious that he'd looked up to Tim like an older brother, following where he led.

While Tim Boykin had held a lifelong fascination with skydiving, Jimmy Boykin's choice to become a fighter pilot arose from no deeper a motivation than that it looked like a hell of a lot of fun. But instead of washing out, the farm boy had demonstrated from the start a startling aptitude for flying that bordered on extraordinary. His earning the Distinguished Flying Cross in the Pan-Am had surprised no one. Flying out of RAF Lakenheath, his wing man down, Lieutenant James Boykin had single-handedly shot down five enemy fighters before his F-120 Goshawk STEALTH fighter-bomber took a hit and he was forced to ditch in the Adriatic, where he spent three hours before rescue. He was back in the air 48 hours later. A month after, he was wearing captain's bars.

Mac could count on one hand the number of times he'd met Jimmy prior to his retirement, always at the Vandenberg DZ whenever Jimmy could get leave to visit his brother. Tim's incessant ribbing of his twin over his only drop being into the ocean had finally goaded Jimmy into learning to jump. It hadn't been long before he was doing RW with the best of them, earning his jump pilot's certification almost as an afterthought. When Tim easily threw and pinned him during a good-natured post-jump sparring match, Jimmy Boykin had commenced his study of Daito-ryu ju-jitsu as soon as he'd returned to his overseas duty station and fast-tracked to *shodan*, first-degree black belt.

Southern junkyard dog though he appeared to be, there was no attempted art of war James Boykin failed to master. While Jimmy considered his own accomplishments tame compared to his brother's place with the 82nd, it was clear to everyone, Tim included, that James Boykin was the superior soldier. Had anyone dared suggest as much to Jimmy, he would have knocked them down where they stood.

And then came Stormcloud. Timothy Boykin's death onboard the *Reagan* came close to killing his brother, the loss of his twin like the ripping out of his heart. Their paths no longer physically crossed, but the service grapevine brought news to Mac of Jimmy Boykin's swift and ignominious fall from grace.

Boykin began drinking. When the DoD Special Investigative Committee's finding on what was now dubbed the Stormcloud Incident was made public, Boykin, still in uniform, shouted whitewash to all who would listen. By that time, Mac was the Pan-Am's poster boy, put on parade by DoD as a symbol around which the flagging allied war effort rallied. The timing couldn't have been worse for Boykins's signed letter to the editor of the Raleigh *News and Observer*, calling Mac a coward, accusing him of panicking and deserting his post, leaving the others to die.

Boykin was slapped out of the sky, grounded, placed on indefinite leave. The dictum came directly from the Pentagon. One more word and Boykin was looking at a dishonorable discharge. If he was lucky.

And then came the last time Mac had seen Boykin, the last since just moments before. Nine years ago, his Medal of Honor reception. Mac still wearing the leg cast and back brace from his Stormcloud injuries, lying on the floor tasting his own blood as Jimmy bellowed at him, so drunk he could barely stand as the MP's swarmed over him . . .

Mac breathed deep, rubbed his eyes until he saw colors behind the closed lids. Boykin had managed to make it to his car. Minutes later, he'd crashed head-on into another vehicle, almost killing the driver. The civilian authorities had left Boykin in the hands of military justice, which fell swift and hard. He was court-martialed, stripped of his rank and drummed out of the Air Force.

The last Mac had heard, Boykin was working at a car wash in Durham. And now, he was here, still blaming Mac for surviving where his brother hadn't, lending form to the ghosts that had haunted Mac in the long years since Stormcloud, his guilt and regret made flesh.

This is what you did, Conner was saying. This is the face of your shame. Where will you run now?

VII

Martha was at her desk, speaking into her phone headset when Mac exited Conner's office. She afforded Mac an apologetic smile, raising a finger in a silent bid for him to wait:

"Thank you, general. Mister Conner asked me to extend his apologies for not calling you personally, but this couldn't wait . . . Yes sir, he understands the difficulty, although he did say he'd spot you a stroke a hole the next time he sees you if you could push this through . . . "

Mac wandered over the Moontown sculpture as Martha laughed politely. "I'll be certain to tell him that. Thank you very much, sir. Good-bye."

Mac turned on hearing the conversation end. "Sorry I wasn't here when you arrived," said Martha, removing the headset. "I got here just before Mister Boykin left." She raised her wristwatch to her lips and pressed an unseen button. "Tell Mister Conner he has to spot General Hale a stroke a hole their next game." The watch chirped as she lowered her hand.

"General Hale?" Mac asked. "Felix Hale at NORAD?"

"You'd be surprised who Mister Conner knows."

"Not anymore, I wouldn't."

Martha nodded thoughtfully. "Been a while since you and Boykin have seen each other."

"Would've been nice to know he was in on this."

"Would you have come this morning if you had?"

"That's not the point, is it?" Mac challenged. "It would have been the decent thing to do."

"Yeah, he's a real son of a bitch." She chuckled at the surprise on Mac's face. "Please. I've been with this company ten years, seven of them right here," and she tapped the desk. She paused, searching for the right words. "He's, under a lot of pressure right now. Try not to judge him entirely on what you've seen in just a day."

Mac wasn't about to tell her how he really felt. She didn't work for him. "He said you'd fill me in on Sensei's funeral arrangements."

"Forgive me," Martha offered, looking pained. "I only heard this morning. I'm sorry." Mac nodded brusquely. "It's tomorrow night. Mister Conner owns some land just outside Asheville."

"Why there? Why at night?"

"He doesn't tell me everything."

Mac locked eyes with her, felt her instinctively draw her attention further inward.

"I doubt that," he flatly declared.

To her credit, she didn't flinch. "I don't suppose you can be blamed for being suspicious."

She crossed out from behind her desk as she spoke, leaned back against the forward edge. Mac's eyes briefly strayed to her bare legs beneath her skirt as she crossed them at the ankles.

"Obviously he knew about your history with James Boykin," she began. If she'd noticed Mac's downward glance, she gave no sign. "Anyone who read a newspaper back then knows about it. Why he elected not to tell you Boykin was involved, I don't know. He's been contracted for the mass driver test for six months. He flys for us, actually, Carolina Airfreight, out of RDU. Mister Conner's big on hiring veterans, especially those who've, eh, had a tough time since the war."

"That why he wants to hire me?"

Martha guffawed at the sarcastic comment. Mac could see his dour mood intimidated her not at all. Maybe working for Conner for so long made her immune. He felt his anger subsiding.

"We both know why he wants you, Mac," replied Martha, smiling. "I told him he was wasting his time." She shrugged in response to Mac's quizzical expression. "I figure anyone who's gone to as much trouble as you have to disappear isn't about to let himself be paraded in front of the press all over again, no matter how good the reason."

"You think it's a good reason?"

"I do. How much has he told you?"

"He told me about fusion and helium-three, if that's what you're dancing around. I take it he hasn't told anyone else?"

"Oh, there's rumors, but nobody knows just how close we really are. The last thing he wants is to spill the beans prematurely and have some other outfit scoop us."

"What others?"

"There's a handful of serious players but only one that's anywhere near as close as we are. Helios. British outfit, headed by a Ph.D. in plasma physics named Terence Innes. They've been nipping at our heels for the last few years, using an older design. We actually caught one of our people feeding them information a few years ago."

"A spy?"

"You sound surprised. When you do business on this level corporate espionage is the rule, not the exception. The race to perfect commercial fusion makes the old U.S.-Soviet space race look like a stroll on the beach. That was just prestige. This is *money*," she purred, rubbing her thumb and fingers together. "Lots and lots of money." The UniCom design was superior to Helios' she said, but whomever announced first got the attention, and so the cash. Any resulting court battle over patents, even if UniCom won, would further delay the influx of capital. And then, it would be much too late."

Mac stayed silent, inviting her to continue. She watched him a moment as if judging his fidelity. "Moontown has been a money pit since the day it was built," she confessed. She gave him a somewhat different picture of the moonbase's current state than had Conner: half-completed structures, an overworked crew, and shareholders screaming for Conner to staunch the bleeding red ink by abandoning the base, or himself be forced out. "We've sold off a handful of subsidiary holdings the last eighteen months or so to finance this last push, but that money's all spoken for."

"If fusion is such a golden egg, why can't the stockholders wait?"

"The stockholders don't know about it."

Mac was stunned, as much by the admission as he was Conner's ability to keep his master plan a secret. Martha held Mac's eye, nodded in confirmation.

"That's right. Old Man Conner has lied to 'em all," she drawled. "All the launches, the money, he's had to tap dance like you wouldn't believe. Me, too. Too much of a risk they'd vote no, or leak the news. He's got to make the mass driver launch pay off big by way of apology. The most spectacular media event in history next to the resurrection of Christ himself. We know the IEC reactor works but if we can't afford to ship the helium-three, it's useless. Moontown *will* have to be abandoned, then. The stockholders will hang Mister Conner, if the feds don't lock him up first. One thing's for certain: UniCom won't make it into the next decade in one piece. If I had any sense at all, I'd be updating my resume."

She sought Mac's eyes, spoke more softly, urgently. "Yes, Boykin could probably do it. But Boykin's not Major Mackinley Harrison of the Shooting Stars."

The hero reference didn't chafe when she used it. "You think I'm going to say yes, don't you?"

"I'm hoping you will, Mac," Martha replied evenly, using his first name again. He decided he liked the way that sounded.

They were still looking at one another, Martha's cool composure washing over Mac's rigid control. He thought he saw a slight flush come over her features, but it was gone before he could be certain. He looked away, working his shoulders, trying to release the nagging knot of tension between his shoulder blades.

"Stiff?"

"All that flying yesterday, I guess."

Martha shifted her weight off the desk, standing. "Lie down." Mac stared as she crossed over to him. "I'm just going to adjust your back. I'm good. I do it for Mister Conner all the time."

She was standing directly in front of him now, her eyes flashing a gentle challenge. He caught a whiff of her scent now, warm and cool, like rain. Dark brunette hair, worn in a simple, practical style just above her shoulders. If she was wearing makeup other than lipstick, he couldn't tell. She had clear, light olive skin and a narrow nose set between rather small, hazel eyes which looked directly up into his, without threat or deference.

It was not her features which made Martha beautiful, but the serenity of their composition which coalesced in her calm, patient gaze. Mac had never thought of *ki* as being masculine or feminine, but he was at once acutely aware of just how long it had been since he'd been this close to a woman.

"Uh, well it's . . . " Mac cleared his throat as he felt his face go warm. "It'll probably just, work itself out if I let it . . . "

"Take off your coat," Martha softly said.

Mac obediently shrugged off his denim jacket, awkwardly switching it from hand to had as he looked around for some place to put it. He was about to dump it on the Moontown sculpture when he felt Martha politely tug it from his grasp. She crossed to her desk, laying the garment on it as she spoke: "On your stomach, arms down, head to the side."

She turned just in time to see Mac topple. She instinctively lurched forward to catch him, then checked herself as he landed on his open palms and smoothly lowered himself to the floor in a reverse push-up. Mac put his arms by his side and turned his head to look at her. He caught a fleeting twitch at the corner of her mouth as she crossed and gracefully knelt by his side, tucking her skirt in behind her knees. Mac stiffened involuntarily as he felt her touch his back.

"Just relax."

Martha's small fingers lightly played up and down Mac's spine, deftly feeling for knots of tension. Her hands were warm as she worked in silence, he felt their heat even through the fabric of his shirt. He closed his eyes and found himself drifting. He hadn't realized until that moment how much he'd missed this, the simple pleasure of being touched, how much he'd denied himself.

Martha felt Mac's back gradually loosen, his breathing become deeper as he relaxed. Fit as he appeared, the strength she felt beneath her hands surprised her. The overdeveloped muscles running along his spine were like thick rope, barely giving at all under the pressure of her fingers. His lower back was the worst, hard as a rock. Probably injured it, she thought. Muscles had a memory deeper than consciousness, guarding old hurts forever.

She let touch alone guide her as she watched Mac's face. The man before her was so different than the clean-shaven soldier in the wartime photographs. That man had seemed cocky, brash, all puffed chest and defiance, as if he walked an inch above the ground. This man was more drawn. Still proud, still a soldier, but he'd been knocked out of the sky like Icarus, the sun that melted his wings the same that consumed his former life. There were lines in his face now and maybe wisdom beneath them. But no peace.

Her hands rested motionless between his shoulders. It was more than strength she felt. There was a fine, electric tingling beneath her warm palms, a sensation she'd never before experienced. It seemed to increase as his back rose with every deep inhalation, eddies of energy riding the surf of his respiration. Her hands sank into the current as her eyes closed, her own breathing unconsciously matching itself with his . . .

She opened her eyes to find Mac's already open and focused on hers, as if he'd been studying her all along, listening to her thoughts. There was no unease in them, no questioning. Just him, looking at her.

Martha quickly rose to her knees, lifted aside the thatch of his hair. She placed the heel of each palm to either side of his spine between his shoulders and dropped her whole weight, torquing her hands as she came down. There was an explosion of hollow cracks and pops like someone stepping on a pile of walnuts as the locked vertebrae gave up the ghost.

Mac's eyes sprang open wider as relief gushed across his back and shoulders. He was vaguely aware of hearing the elevator doors open as he groaned with pleasure:

"Ohhhh! Ohh, my God . . . !"

He looked up at Martha to thank her, then turned his head and followed her gaze to the elevator. Davis stood before the closing doors, one eyebrow cocked, taking in the scene. He spoke straight-faced.

"If this is a bad time, I could come back later?"

VIII

He was a decorated war veteran, a combat paratrooper, a trained martial artist who once had killed with his bare hands. And today, Mac was convinced, he was going to buy the farm in a banana yellow sportscar.

Davis wove his ride in and out of traffic like a rabbit through underbrush. He had two speeds, flat out and full stop. Mac hung on and prayed they'd make it to the airport in one piece.

Thankfully, Davis seemed to have run out of things to say for the moment. He'd talked non-stop all through the tour of UniCom, sweeping Mac into one office and lab after another, pointedly announcing his guest as Major Mackinley Michael Harrison. The startled gazes of slow recognition, the heartfelt handshakes and 'I'm so honored to meet you's' — Mac had finally insisted Davis dispense with 'major' altogether and just call him 'Mac.' The younger man seemed mollified by the invitation to familiarity. It was clear to Mac by then what bred Davis' obsequious attitude. He knew the name of every solider in the 82nd, knew the names of the *Reagan's* crew, everything there was to know about Mac's history as well as any civilian could.

Mac had never encountered hero worship before, and to his surprise it didn't make him uncomfortable. Davis was the first person he'd met in a long time, Conner excepted, that remembered Mac wasn't alone in the drop bay, that the *Reagan* hadn't flown herself. Davis even knew that Nick Kaligolos had written a bawdy anthem for the 82nd, a nugget of information prized from a former dropsuit maintenance tech who'd worked for UniCom for a time after his Army retirement.

"I'd really like to hear it sometime," Davis had timidly admitted.

Mac wasn't even sure he remembered it.

He breathed a mental sigh of relief as RDU came into view. Davis bypassed the bumper-to-bumper traffic snaking its way towards the main terminals and parked in the private lot outside the UniCom hangar. They made their way into the terminal through a side entrance marked *Authorized Personnel Only* and slipped through the crowds, Davis leading the way. A VIP to pick up and deliver, that was all Davis had said before they'd left UniCom. He was already running late and promised to drop off Mac at the hotel on the way back to UniCom.

Mac slid his penknife back into his pocket and followed Davis from the metal detector down the concourse to the gate. "Good, we're just in time," Davis declared, halting out of breath a few yards from the ramp. As Mac watched the first passenger emerge from the doorway he realized why Davis had wanted him to come along.

He was heavier than Mac remembered, a noble paunch now poking out over his belt, but he had always been stocky. He had a lot less hair, too. His huge biceps bulged beneath the sleeves of his polo shirt as he pushed his wheelchair forward with smooth, powerful thrusts, a laptop computer resting atop the jacket lain across his thighs, which ended in stumps at the knees. He smiled thanks to the uniformed woman holding the door for him and scanned the area for whomever was supposed to meet him.

Mac stared. "Willie?"

William Price spied Mac and stopped, his mouth opening in disbelief. "Mac . . . ?"

But Mac was already moving towards him, his pace quickening. Price's face broke into a huge grin.

"Mac, you son of a bitch!"

Heads turned at the sound of Price's bellowed greeting but neither man noticed. Mac stopped just short of his old friend, unable to speak. Price's voice was husky with emotion.

"Well don't just stand there, son."

Mac knelt by the chair and the two men embraced like long-lost brothers. He closed his eyes and gave himself over to the moment, Price squeezing him so hard he thought his back would break, crushing him to him as if afraid he would disappear. He whispered in Mac's ear:

"Goddamn, I missed you, boy."

There they stayed, unmoving as the rest of the world flowed around them. Davis removed his glasses and wiped his eyes. If he didn't do another thing all day, this would be enough.

IX

Roger Conner shifted to the left in his chair, taking some of the weight off of his bad hip. The ache never went away, always defined by degrees. Normally he would take a lap or two around the spacious office to work out the stiffness but he had more pressing business just now.

He pressed the temperature touchpad control as the wafer-thin computer monitor rose up out of its hairline desktop slot. He released the control when the glowing digits beneath the desk surface read seventy-five degrees. Twenty years past, he'd been diagnosed with Reynaud's Syndrome, a not inelegant designation for poor circulation. If he was comfortable, his fingertips were blue. Warm fingers, and he was perspiring. No one could tell him God didn't have a sense of humor.

He tucked his icy digits beneath his armpits and focused on the computer monitor. The UniCom logo appeared, and a small icon blinked in the upper right-hand corner. He pressed his right thumb against it. The computer spoke.

"Voice verification, please."

"Roger Charles Conner. Hole four, dog leg right, par three."

The words *Password Accepted* appeared. The words and the logo disappeared, replaced by the main menu.

"Good evening, Mister Conner. Would you care to check your mail?"

"Yes. Private box only."

"You have eleven new messages in your private mailbox, one urgent. Would you care to read them now?"

"Identify urgent sender."

"Urgent message is from Leslie Trang, received today at three-seventeen-twenty-two PM. The message is encrypted."

Conner had been waiting for the communication. "Let me see it."

After a heartbeat pause for decryption it appeared on the screen: "Mister Conner: attached is a summary of the new security protocol we discussed la —"

"Quiet," Conner growled. The computer voice cut out in mid-word.

Conner tapped the attachment icon on the screen and scanned the revealed text. Leslie Trang was his chief of computer security; a reserved, toothpick-thin woman in her mid-fifties who breathed ones and zeroes and who had over the years rescued Conner and UniCom from innumerable potential catastrophes. Like any good employee, Trang was so efficient that Conner often forgot she was there. Every month, she reminded him with a memo summarizing the previous month's activities, including any hacker attempts. Her dispatches always read to Conner like a list of gunfighters shot down trying to call her out. He rarely now gave them more than a cursory glance.

Then, eight months earlier, Trang had sent him a rare mid-month communiqué. Someone was trying to hack UniCom's netframe.

Her use of the present tense had instantly grabbed Conner's attention. What all of the precisely documented attempts had in common was Trang's inability to catch the interloper in the act or effect a trace. As soon as she got close, the intruder would vanish like a wraith. The other shared trait was that each time, the intruder penetrated deeper into the system, avoiding every trap Trang set, bypassing every lock-out, every loop, rattle pit, code mine and firewall. Probe, retreat, regroup, probe again.

It appeared to Trang and Conner like sophisticated corporate espionage. There was no attempt at sabotage, but neither did the hacker seem to have a clear target. Secrets that a dozen competing concerns would have paid billions for, the intruder passed by without pause, including data on the IEC fusion project.

The latter circumvention cast doubt on Conner's initial hypothesis that Terence Innes and Helios were on the other side of the modem, though he didn't entirely rule out the possibility. UniCom's discovery two years earlier of a Helios spy in their midst, a custodian who'd been on UniCom's payroll for seventeen months, had resulted in a forty-three megabyte file on Innes and his company, prepared by Conner's new head of security. Conner was now well aware of Innes' personal animus and its source, and while he considered the man a fool, he was a tenacious one.

The mystery hadn't lasted long. Just a month earlier, Trang had felt confident enough to posit the intruder's apparent target: Conner's personal directory.

Conner's directory was locked tighter than any other in UniCom's netframe, ensconced within one of hundreds of dynamic virtual subnets accessible only from Trang's SYSOP station and Conner's personal computer port. Every secret Conner had was there, terabytes of highly classified data that could create or destroy fortunes and lives — most especially, Conner's own.

Access to the most sensitive of this data was restricted by a labyrinthine series of security checks and passwords known only to Conner, rufusing all but his personal access. The second tier of data was accessible with Conner's primary password, which he changed every week. It was a tedious chore but he recognized its necessity. Only he and Martha knew that password and Conner's computer port recognized her voice and thumbprint as well, for those occasions when he was away from his office on business and she needed access. There were ways of bypassing tactile and voice verification, but Trang assured him that anyone who managed would come face-to-face with Greedy.

Greedy was the zenith of computer security, a quiet little bomb Trang had written exclusively for UniCom after Innes' spy had been flushed. GRID-E — Conner had no idea what the acronym stood for

— was a virus resident in UniCom's netframe, which automatically and permanently replicated itself on every single byte of data stored there. Greedy remained dormant and virtually undetectable until an unauthorized user attempted to download UniCom data. Then, like its biological namesake, it blossomed into full virulence, ruthlessly destroying not only the downloaded data, but also the interloper's resident applications. The hacker would watch in helpless horror as his system crashed in on itself like a demolished building. Once Greedy awoke, it did not sleep until it had done its worst.

Conner trusted Greedy like he trusted its creator. Now, however, it appeared there was someone just as good as Trang, and 'just as good' might be good enough to defeat both her and her progeny. But Trang would have none of that; as always, she was one step ahead of her boss.

He digested the rest of Trang's message. Ferret, she called it. No acronym this time. The new program had but one purpose. It waited for an invasive attempt, located the breach and then scurried down the electronic tunnel to the other end, returning with the hacker's digital address in its teeth, similar to the obsolete Ping and Finger programs of Conner's youth but far superior.

Ferret and Greedy were ideal playmates; should an intruder gain access, Ferret would seek and identify while Greedy watched its back. Ferret was also was configured to alert Conner and Trang the instant any invasive attempt was detected, emitting an audible warning whether Conner's system was active or dormant.

Conner archived the message and leaned back in his chair, rubbing his eyes, worrying over what Trang had left unsaid in her message. There had been no mention of her attempting to stop the hacker cold. Trang was too meticulous to tolerate assumption, which meant she felt she couldn't stop him. All she could do was attempt to identify him.

Which meant Conner's files were still vulnerable. The hacker had his target in his sights, and Conner felt sure he wouldn't waste time browsing during his next attempt. Ferret would have but once chance to catch its quarry. And Conner wanted that snooping bastard caught.

The room was getting warmer but his fingertips were still cold. He tucked them deeper beneath his folded arms as he again pondered the biggest question on his mind:

Who was after him?

Conner accepted Innes' personal vendetta against him, but he couldn't imagine Innes bypassing UniCom fusion data. He knew from his own sources that the Helios spheromak was operational, but its design and size limited its usefulness to feeding commercial and industrial power grids and not much else. The UniCom IEC IV could handle those tasks just as well, at one-tenth the size. But unlike the spheromak, the IEC could be built smaller and still work, small enough to power aircraft, spacecraft, worksites, even individual homes and cars, one day. Innes had to know he was licked. If it was indeed he who was gunning for Conner's personal files, Conner had to assume Innes had forfeited the race, and was now seeking information that would give him some hold over Conner himself; a last-ditch attempt at victory.

Like hell, he decided. If it was access to his files Innes wanted, he would get it. Let's give Ferret a chance to work.

Conner sat up. "Show me the main directory."

"Please specify."

"My main directory, dammit."

The screen filled with a slowly-rotating three-dimensional graphic tree; root directories, branches of sub-directories and sub-sub-directories, folders, data dumps and archives. He'd forgotten how huge it was. So much information, so many potential landmines.

"Show me only those directories protected by level one security protocol."

Roughly two-thirds of the tree dissolved into the background like a watermark, the most sensitive data. Conner rapidly scanned the rest. Many of the directories, he was no longer certain what they contained. Some labels were obvious keys to their contents, while others were half-remembered acronyms and cryptic strings of numbers. It would easily take him a full day to check all the file contents and he didn't have that kind of time, nor did he trust the task to anyone else, not even Martha. There were things there she didn't need to know.

He pondered the screen, debating. What he was about to do was risky but if Greedy and Ferret were as effective as Trang swore they were, it would be worth the gamble. It was time to put out the welcome mat.

"Vox."

"Vox active."

"Tag all level two directories." The highlighted directories blinked red. "Remove remote access security protocol from tagged directories."

"Request requires tactile and voice verification."

Conner pressed his thumb once again against the icon as it reappeared. "Roger Charles Conner."

"Password."

"Hole four, dog leg right, par three."

"Remote access security protocol has been removed from tagged directories. You have five grace logins remaining on your current password. Do you wish to change it now?"

"No."

"Please re-verify."

"I said no."

"Confirmed."

It was that simple. No more bells and whistles to spook the intruder. Conner's life now lay open to anyone with a modem and a grudge. For an instant, he felt like he was in Vietnam again. Just a scared boy, dangling helplessly beneath his parachute canopy as the bullets screamed by.

He shook off the sentiment. "List access and active security for level two directories."

"User password required for access. GRID-E failsafe protection is resident in all directories and files. Ferret unauthorized remote user detection is active in all systems. Ferret audio and visual alert is active."

"Computer off."

The UniCom logo reappeared on the monitor as it re-aligned itself with the desk slot and receded silently into its berth. Conner wiped his forehead, the damp sheen of his sweat cool against his palm. He reached out for the touchpad and lowered the room temperature. Things were getting much too warm.

Two light, firm raps came at the doors. Martha.

"Come in."

She entered carrying a cup and saucer, crossed to the desk and set them down by the telephone. "I thought you might want some tea."

Conner smiled, glad for the interruption. "Now that I see it, I believe I do." He wrapped his chilled fingers around the steaming cup and raised it to his lips.

"The funeral arrangements are complete."

"Problems?"

"General Hale wasn't too keen to clear the pod drop. By the way, you said you'd spot him a stroke a hole the next time you see him."

"Bastard cheats as it is."

"He said the same about you."

"Small price to pay, I suppose. Well done." He took another sip of tea and swiveled his chair until he was looking out at the deepening winter dusk. The sky was clear. There would probably be frost in the morning.

He felt Martha stir behind him, spoke without turning. "I'm pushing it, aren't I?"

"I think so, yes."

"Too hard?"

"Maybe."

Conner swiveled his chair back around and placed the cup atop its saucer. "I can't use maybe, dear. This is too important."

Martha half-sat on the edge of the huge desk, a familiar gesture which Conner tolerated only from her. "You're asking a lot of him," she said. "It's too much, too fast. He still doesn't see any clear reason why he should help us. And he's not terribly fond of you. If you push him any harder, he'll say no just to spite you."

Conner didn't tell her Mac had already refused. "I can't use him the way he is now," he mused. "So full of self-pity. Self-righteousness."

"Grief," Martha flatly put in. "He's lost everyone who ever mattered to him."

"We've all suffered loss, Martha."

Martha ran her hand absently across the desk's polished surface. Her eyes briefly met the old man's. "I know," she finally said. "But it's still not easy."

"The burden never becomes lighter. Our shoulders grow more broad." He tapped the teacup with his fingernail and watched the ripples shimmer beneath the steam. "Or we can choose to put down the burden. Mister Harrison doesn't see that yet. He doesn't realize that he's the one who won't let it go."

"Maybe seeing Price again will help."

Conner smiled inwardly. Martha was telling him she knew the real reason he'd summoned Price. Not everyone Mac held dear had died on the *Reagan*. Conner was hoping seeing his old comrade again, even if for a funeral, might help pull Mac out of the depths of his self-pity.

"We've done what we can," Conner said. "If he says no, we're no worse off then we were before."

"It's still not too late to find someone else," Martha suggested. "We don't have to use Boykin. We could postpone the announcement, push back the drop until after the New Year."

But Conner was shaking his head. It was a prudent suggestion on the surface, but Martha didn't know Boykin's true purpose. Conner had always intended to reach out for Mac, had signed Boykin purely as insurance. He'd never intended to let him perform the drop. Yet now, he might be forced to play his bluff to the end.

"I'm still worried about Innes and Helios," he offered by way of explanation. "He's been quiet for far too long. The longer we wait, the more time he has to try something."

"What could he do, now?"

"I don't know. But we have to assume he knows what we're up to, somehow. I just can't see him allowing us to beat him without trying to hit us one final time."

"Do you suspect something?"

Conner stared at the computer monitor slot in his desk. "No. But you never can be too careful."

X

Price was leaning over remnants of the steak dinner he'd demolished, his broad face animated as he regaled Mac with yet another fishing story. This one began on the pier behind Price's Charleston digs and ended with him pulled out of his chair into the Intracoastal Waterway, fighting a wayward loggerhead turtle on the end of his straining line. He erupted into an infectious belly laugh as he finished, slapping the table hard enough to rattle the plates, not caring who heard.

Mac had to smile. Still the same 'ol Willie. Thank God some things never seemed to change.

He took a pull on his beer as Price's laughter ended in a spent sigh. "You oughta hang up that mountain man routine and come down to the Lowcountry for a while. Oysters are in season. You haven't lived 'til you've spent a night at Shuck's over a bucket of steamed selects!"

"Sounds nice."

"I'm serious, Mac. Come back with me after the funeral. I don't want another seven years to go by before I see you again."

Mac picked at the label on his bottle. "I don't know what I'm gonna do, Willie. I really don't."

Price took a swig of his beer. Three empties sat to his right on the table of the ramshackle truck stop diner booth in which they'd spent the last two hours. Davis had given Mac a UniCom cash card and the keys to a waiting company car before he'd parted company with them at the hotel, but Price had insisted they go elsewhere for their meal.

The thick dinner crowd was just starting to thin out, weary men with ball caps and heavy faces hitching up their pants as they headed for the bathroom and then back out to their rigs. A jukebox played country music, and the waitress knew when to check in and when to leave them alone. Mac had at first felt overwhelmed by all the people, but the uneasiness had worn off as he and Price fell back into their friendship.

Price was still the same gregarious man Mac remembered, the same booming voice and ready humor, often laughing uproariously at his own comments while others stared blankly. There'd been no denying he was a damn good soldier and a superb jumper, but Mac at first had found his blunt personality off-putting. Mac had tolerated him because he'd had to and avoided him when he could. When Price was named Alpha squad leader and Mac was tapped to lead Bravo, avoiding Price had no longer been an option. The first day of their new station, Price had cornered Mac and asked him point-blank if he was racist.

"No," Mac had calmly responded. "You just hurt my ears." Price had laughed until he'd had to sit down.

Working together, they'd quickly formed a tight friendship, drawn together like opposite charges. At the core of Price's affability was a deeply philosophical nature and a keen, penetrating intelligence that tested well above genius level. He was a man who felt and saw deeply, though where Mac was more likely to beat down his emotions with discipline and duty, Price preserved his sanity with laughter. The more grave the situation, the harder he laughed. He lived large and fought hard. It made him a natural leader, and his squad had loved him.

Mac was only on his second beer, but the unaccustomed drinking and seeing his old friend had brought on a thick melancholy buzz. He glanced up and found Price was looking at him, concern replacing the humor.

"You all right?"

"Just tired."

"You look tired."

"Haven't gotten much sleep the last two days."

"That's not what I mean."

The waitress appeared and cleared their plates and empties. Price declined the offer of another round without checking with Mac, asking instead for coffee. "I know how tough it's been for you," he said as the waitress departed. "How hard it was for you after it happened."

"A hero," Mac spat. "Did you know I'm a hero, Willie?"

"I know, I know . . . "

"Like I was the only one up there —"

"Nobody's forgotten the others, Mac," Price cut in gently. "I remember laying in the hospital, watching the news, hearing them read everybody's names. Thinking I ought to have been with them, I don't want to be the only one left."

"C'mon. You paid your price."

"Didn't make a damn bit of difference. Everyone I loved was dead. For a while I even thought about joining them, thought hard. Bet I'm not the only one."

Mac only sipped his beer.

"We all were heroes, Mac, before the *Reagan* went down," continued Price. "It was our job. And when the others died everyone else had to deal with it just like you and I did. Army's finest, blown out of the sky like they never existed, nothing left even to bury. Just all those names over empty graves at Arlington, yours included.

"And then, ten days later, you came back from the dead! Thirty miles on foot in the jungle with a goddamn broken leg until that logging crew found you and then the whole world knew! And we said *yes!* Take that, you mothers!" Price clenched his fist between them, his eyes on fire. "You blew him out of the fuckin' sky and he still made it! Seventeen dead men and women all came back to life, in you! And it turned the war around, Mac! We took their best shot and came back swinging, that's what it was all about!"

Mac was staring at the table, his face filled with some emotion Price couldn't identify. "Don't you see, Mac?" he pressed. "It could have been me, it could have been Nick, or Tim, or Rawlings, it could have been anybody on the *Reagan* and the same thing would have happened. Or maybe not. Maybe anybody else wouldn't have made it back. But you did! You survived for all of us!"

Mac couldn't bring himself to look his friend in the face. His face was hot, his ears ringing, the barrage of music and voices of the diner fading into a flat background roar. He felt his lips moving, heard a voice as if from a distance, a strained, hoarse whisper.

"I punched out, Willie."

Mac stared at the tabletop, at the ring of condensation around his beer glistening in the light. Price's voice was neutral.

"What are you saying?"

"I was in the rack, Rawlings was calling the count and then, he just, stopped. I started calling it, by the book, but nobody answered. There was nobody there."

Mac finally looked up, into Price's face. "I deserted them, Willie! I lost it! I survived because I left our friends to die! I don't deserve to be mentioned in the same breath with them. I should have died with them! I wish I had because I can't take this anymore . . . "

He no longer saw Price, the diner, the warm beer clutched in his hand. He felt utterly depleted, like his admission had severed an invisible string that had been the only thing holding him erect. His head sagged, the leaden weight pulling him forward until his forehead was resting on the scarred varnished tabletop, gritty crumbs biting into his flesh. All he wanted to to was remain there, sleep, awaken to find himself home, all his problems resolved. No more Conner, no more drop, no more ghosts . . .

He felt hands, heavy with thick fingers that pressed gently against his skull in benediction.

"I'm so tired, Willie," Mac whispered. "So tired."

Watching from the counter across the room, the waitress decided the coffee could wait a bit longer.

XI

Mac turned up his collar, his breath fogging in the cold as he walked away from the diner and into the wide parking lot to his left where a few trucks remained. Next to him Price pushed his chair, rubber tires crunching on the bluestone gravel.

Price halted, looked up at the sky. The stars shone like distant bright windows overhead, the waning moon a cold powder gray. He took a deep breath of the crisp air, listening to the highway traffic whir by.

"Beautiful night."

"I'm sorry, Willie."

Price shook his head. "Sorry for what? I don't believe I've ever met a single human being who enjoyed beating himself up as much as you do. Must be all those knocks you got from the Colonel in the *dojo*." He looked at Mac. "If you hadn't punched out, you'd be dead. Look at the good you did by living."

"So it doesn't matter to you."

"You punching out?"

"I mean why."

"That you got scared? Hell, I already knew that." Price shrugged in response to Mac's stare. "Only explanation for it. Felt like punching out myself every time we jumped. Hardest thing never was launch, it was waiting for it. Lying there in the dark, ass all puckered up . . . "

"Why didn't you ever say anything?"

Price leaned over and scooped a handful of gravel while he spoke, absently tossing the stones one by one across the lot. "You had enough to deal with. Didn't need me reminding you of what you already knew. I was pissed that you never came clean with me, but I figured I didn't have the right to ask."

"You had every right. They were your friends, too."

Price sighed and tossed a rock at a lamppost bordering the lot. It clanged off of the metal base a second later. "Look. Say you hadn't been on the *Reagan*. If you'd been given the knowledge that it wasn't going to make it back, and the power to decide whether to let everyone on board die or have one person survive, what would you have done?"

"I can't answer that."

"The hell you can't," Price said, dropping his arm in mid-throw. "You would have chosen to have that one person make it back and it wouldn't have mattered who or how or why, short of that decision causing everyone else to die, and that's *not* what happened with *you*.

96

Your decision to punch out didn't kill the others, that damn missile did. It's never mattered to me how or why you survived. The only person that's ever mattered to is you. I'd give almost anything to have the others here today, but I'll settle for your sorry ass." He lobbed the stone half-heartedly at Mac's feet.

"Did Sensei know too?"

Price looked thoughtful. "Never asked him. He never brought it up. But you know the Colonel, wasn't much got past him. I do know this," Price continued after a pause. "No matter how you feel about what you did, he forgave you a long time ago. So did I. I'm glad you had the chance to see him before he died."

Mac took a deep breath of the cold air. For so many years, he'd been too ashamed to admit his moment of cowardice onboard the *Reagan* to anyone. Now Price was telling him he and Sensei knew all along and what's more, it didn't matter. It sharpened his regret, knowing Price and Sensei's forgiveness had been his all along. But for the first time in a long time, he felt some of the burden lift.

"Thanks."

Price only nodded, eyes fixed on the passing traffic. Mac stuck his hands in his jacket pockets and felt the car keys. He opened his mouth to ask if Price was ready to return to hotel, but Price spoke first.

"Tell me again what you said inside. About not being able to hear anything when you were in the rack."

The question surprised Mac. "Just what I said. Rawlings was calling the count and then the com went dead."

"How long before spot did it happen?"

"Thirty seconds, maybe. Forty."

"Anything else happen around the same time?"

"No. Well . . . "

"What?"

Images from the nightmare flashed through Mac's mind. "Just before the com died, there was a, a bump. Like a shove. Pushed my shoulder into the padding."

"Which shoulder?"

"Aw hell, Willie . . . " Mac worked hard to remember. "Right. Right shoulder. Static squirt in my com about the same time. That's when it went dead, I guess."

97

Price had turned away from the road as Mac spoke. His eyes were shadowed in the light from the parking lot lamps, but Mac could feel the intensity of his gaze.

"Nothing about any of that in the official finding."

A count of five, silent save for a truck horn faint in the distance. "What do you mean?" Mac finally asked.

"Tell me you read it."

The incident finding had been released months after Mac's retirement in 2015. DoD had mailed a hard copy to his new home. He hadn't been able to get beyond the first few pages, just reading the names of the dead crew had been too much. He'd ultimately burned it in his fireplace.

Price let it slide. "The finding says you got the go for autodrop," he filled in, "so you went manual and punched out. All by the book."

Mac looked down. "That I told them, yeah."

"But it isn't true."

Mac shook his head. "No. The autodrop never flashed."

"But the rest of it *is* true? You definitely told them about the loss of comlink, the —"

"Yes! I told them everything. I don't understand why they wouldn't put that in the finding."

"Why'd the *Reagan* go down?"

The blunt query caught Mac flat-footed. "I don't understand." Price only looked at him. "You know what happened."

"I know what DoD *says* happened. SSM, blew the *Reagan* out of orbit like a clay pigeon. But she was running in STEALTH mode, S.O.P. So, the question becomes: how was she targeted?"

"Something happened to make her drop out of STEALTH long enough for —"

"That's right," Price interrupted. "*Something happened.*

What?"

"Crew error."

"DoD again."

"What else could it have been?"

Price smirked. "C'mon, Mac, you knew that crew as well as I did. They wouldn't just 'accidentally' drop out of STEALTH. Be like you or me 'accidentally' forgetting to pull on a jump. That crew was as good at their jobs as we were at ours," Price declared. "Mac, that missile was your target! We had intel that they knew you were coming, so you can be damn sure Sonny Haeggstrom had his eyes glued to TacOps, any sign we'd been lit and Guthrie woulda floored the OMS and put us on the other side of the planet. And even if he hadn't, Sonny could've launched countermeasures, targeted and blown that missile to bits in ten seconds! And yet we're supposed to believe he didn't even try? That no one had the time to make it to an escape pod, not even Rawlings? That Guthrie and Ashdown didn't even have the five seconds it took eject the flight deck?" Price frowned. "I've read every damn piece of paper and computer file I could lay my hands on. Truth is, nobody knows what really happened. Or they do, and they're not saying."

"There's no way anybody can know," Mac said. "Not without the flight recorder."

Price made a sound of disgust. "Yeah, how about that flight recorder, huh? Pieces of the *Reagan* were washing up on beaches and turning up in corn fields for years but the mission flight recorder, the one single piece of the whole damn ship built to survive if nothing else did, was never found. Four-inch nanocarb and siliplas shielding, so many pingers you could pick it up on your car radio. Take a nuclear strike to bust it open, but it just, disappeared, poof!" Price opened his hands. "Like it never existed."

Mac had been so numbed by his experience that he'd never bothered to question the official story. As he listened to Price, he began to see how illogical it all sounded.

Price was still talking. "Been doing more than fishing since I retired. Got myself a nice computer business, just me and a couple folks to reach the top shelves but I do okay. Some nights I sit and chat on the 'nets with the rest of the no-life computer geeks. Few years ago, I made friends with an amateur astronomer in Galway, on the West Irish coast. He's into asteroids, comets, always looking for new ones. Even discovered one, it's named after him. Edelman 115."

"Edelman?"

"I didn't say he was Irish, he just lives there. So one night I tell him about my old job, and he says, 'You know, a meteorite went down near here the night your ship blew up.' He gives me the coordinates. About a mile-and-a-half south-southwest of him, twenty-seven minutes after the *Reagan* went down."

Price sought Mac's eye, confirmed he hadn't lost his audience before continuing: "When he first mentioned it, I figured it was just more debris but nothing else had ever turned up so far East, most of it was recovered around the Americas. Newspapers the next day were full of stories, folks seeing this big glowing ball fall into the sea — downed fighter, missile, UFO shit, all that. It was still too early for news about the *Reagan*. The authorities said it was just a meteor, but the next morning the place is crawling with military ships, helicopters, aircars, got the water blocked off two miles in every direction. Some lame BS about radioactivity. So Edelman lugs his twelve-inch to the top of his church's bell tower, gets a nice clear shot of a *U.S. Navy salvage ship* hauling something out of the water. Something exactly the size and shape of the *Reagan's* MFR."

Mac's heart raced. "You're just guessing, Willie."

"Yeah? Since when's the Navy been interested in meteorites? I've seen the photos. I mean, it was the next *day*, Mac, just hours later! With the *Reagan's* position, figure the force of the blast, orbital translation, time of impact, it all fits!"

Mac was shaking his head, unable to fully open himself to the scenario Price was painting. "Come on, Willie! What are you saying? There's been a cover-up for nine years? The Army, the Navy, the entire Department of Defense?"

"Yeah," Price commented dryly. "That could never happen, could it? Just like they'd never lie in the incident finding about what you said."

"Okay, so what if it is the recorder? Why cover it up?"

"That's right, okay," Price jumped in. "Why?" He adroitly sketched and dismissed the possibilities. Had the MFR been damaged or the data inconclusive, there was no reason to hide the fact. If it truly was lost, if the *Reagan's* explosion had blown it into space beyond hope of recovery, still it could have been tracked until it sailed beyond the range of its transmitter; again, there was no reason not to include such a fact in the finding. The only other possibility was that the MFR had been recovered by the enemy and had such been the case, Price felt confident that DoD would have precluded that line of speculation with at least a minimal cover story incorporating one of the other omitted scenarios.

"Nowhere in the incident finding, nowhere in any document any-where is there any mention at all of any real attempt being made to find the recorder!" Price pressed home his point with righteous con-viction. "Only that it was lost in the explosion. That's one hell of an oversight, don't you think? Why leave a question that big just hanging there?"

"It was a hell of an explosion, Willie," said Mac curtly. Images of it sparked and faded in his mind. His defensive thorniness returned. "It's not impossible it was lost."

Price sensed he was treading now on holy ground. He pushed on, more gently but no less urgently. "You're not hearing me, brother. The recorder wasn't just, quote, 'lost.' They-didn't-look for it."

Mac's expression was still hard, but now Price could see he under-stood. "That's right. And that means one of two things. The investiga-tive committee should be lined up and shot for incompetence, or they didn't look for it because they already knew where it was. And because they knew, they didn't think to cover their tracks by pretend-ing to look."

Mac rubbed his face, hard-pressed to keep up. "I know it's hard, but step back and just look at it, okay?" Price coaxed. "All the omissions, everything you told them. A total communications failure less than a minute before the missile hit? A jolt to the ship so hard it shoved you into the side of the sled? It's not like there was any traffic up there. Why would they leave so many things out? Unless there's something they're trying to hide."

Mac knew the answer even as he asked the question. "Like what?"

"Like the real reason the *Reagan* went down."

And there it was. Mac stuck his hands in his pockets. He felt as if he'd just completed a marathon run. He stared up at the starry sky, into the past, imagining the *Reagan* streaking by in orbit high over their heads.

"Nine years, Mac," said Price. "Not a soul on this Earth with more of a right to know what really happened than you and me."

"I dunno, Willie. I've spent nine years burying our friends. I don't know if I can stand to dig them up and bury them all over again."

"You haven't buried them yet."

Price sighed when Mac didn't respond, breath pluming in the cold night air. "I wasn't there. If I had been, maybe I'd be dead now, too. I owe them." He stared at the stumps of his legs. "This much more, I have to pay. Maybe I'm wrong but one way or another I've got to find out, before I can bury them for good. One way or another, I've got to know."

Three

I

The office doors parted and Boykin entered. He was dressed the same as the day before, the same baggy, too-large suit, probably the only one he owned. He tried hard to look Conner in the eye, lasting about three seconds before glancing off to the side.

Conner allowed Boykin to hang a few moments. "You wished to see me about something?"

"Yessir." Boykin still didn't move from the doors. With the barest tilt of his head, Conner indicated a seat. Boykin crossed and lowered his thick frame into the chair. "Your business is your own, Mister Conner, but I wish you'd told me Harrison was involved in this."

"Why is that?"

"You said . . . we agreed that I was going to be the one to do the moondrop." Boykin paused, waiting for Conner to explain himself. That wasn't how this encounter was going to be played.

"Continue," Conner invited, voice neutral.

Boykin appeared lost for a moment. "Well sir, it uh, it seems to me that if you're set on Harrison doing it, you don't need me."

"I assume you have read your contract, Mister Boykin."

"Yessir. I know you can pick anyone you want, like I said, your business is your business. But if Harrison is going to do it, I'd just as soon not be involved."

"Are you saying you want to break your contract with me, Mister Boykin?"

"I appreciate being offered the opportunity and all, but, um . . . " He swallowed. "I'm not certain anymore that I'd be of any use to you."

Conner folded his bony hands in his lap and leaned back in his chair. "I see. You know, given your personal history, there are few people in my position who would have even considered you for something so important as this. Frankly, I would have thought you'd be more grateful."

The stinging comment did its work. Boykin flushed, but he didn't look away. "Like I said, sir, I do appreciate it —"

"Why don't we discuss what this is really all about. You hate Major Harrison."

"I won't deny that."

"Yet you feel unable to put your feelings for him aside and perform your duty? That's not what I expected from a man with your military record, Mister Boykin. You were a fine soldier and pilot until . . . well. We both know what happened."

Conner leaned forward, pleased to see Boykin unconsciously retreat further into his seat. "Your personal history with Major Harrison is of absolutely no concern to me. If he goes through with the moondrop you will still be his backup. Afterwards, you will be in the air, flying escort. As your signed contract mandates."

"If Harrison goes through with it?"

Boykin's eyes were locked on Conner's now. "If nothing occurs to prevent his participation between now and the time he departs for Moontown," Conner smoothly covered, inwardly cursing himself for the slip. "He still has to undergo the same physical examinations you did, although I am confident he will pass. My point is, Mister Boykin, that regardless of whether or not you feel 'useful', you are still a part of this. I will not release you from your contract. Is that clear?"

Boykin nodded thoughtfully, as if he was only half-listening. "In that case, sir, I quit."

"You quit?"

"Yessir. I quit."

Conner didn't bother to disguise his amusement. "Mister Boykin, I don't know what backwoods lawyer you've been consulting but I'd ask for my money back. You can't just 'quit' a contract."

"Pardon me, sir, but I believe I can quit this one," Boykin stonily countered. "My contract with you as far as the moondrop goes was executed as a rider to my employment contract with Carolina Air Freight. And that contract says I can quit with ten days notice. Today is Wednesday the fourteenth. The moondrop is scheduled for Christmas Eve, exactly ten days from this morning."

Boykin reached into his suit and withdrew a single folded sheet of paper as he rose from his chair. He moved forward and extended the paper across the desk to Conner. "This is my written resignation from my position as a pilot for Carolina Air Freight, effective December 24, 2022."

Conner took the paper from Boykin's hand automatically. If what he said was true there would be several positions open in legal by the end of the day. This lumbering redneck was about to escape through a loophole an ambulance chaser could have spotted in his sleep. Conner wasn't even sure if Boykin had a lawyer, he could have discovered his avenue of retreat on his own. In that case it was possible he'd misread the contract, but Conner couldn't take that chance. He had to do something now.

"I thank you for the opportunity to work for you, sir, for giving me a job when no one else would," Boykin was saying, his voice gravely formal. He extended his hand to shake. Conner stood and gave it a perfunctory tug. Boykin nodded and turned to go.

"It's a shame how all of this happened," Conner said.

Boykin stopped. "Yessir. It surely is."

"I mean, I would have never considered you at all if I had known you were drinking again."

Boykin's face went hard. "Who says I've been drinking? I haven't taken a drink in seven years!"

"I didn't want to believe it," Conner went on. "Your work certainly hasn't shown it. Then again, I've never really taken a good look at your employment record. How long has it been since your last blood test? I believe company policy for pilots is, what, eight random tests a year?"

"I had one during my last physical, for the —"

"To think how you managed to put your life back together, only to lose it all again because you couldn't keep from drinking on the job." Conner shook his head. "Makes it doubly tragic that I had to terminate you so close to the holidays."

Boykin's face was ashen. "I don't drink anymore!"

"I'm certain a blood test today will show otherwise," Conner coldly declared. "Absolutely certain. You were lucky to get this job, with your record. I doubt you'll be so lucky again. News travels. You know how people talk."

Boykin stared, his face florid with anger. "However, given that time is short, I'm willing to give you one last chance, Mister Boykin," Conner growled. "But you are on indefinite probation as of now. If I hear one more word out of you, if you so much as frown when you should be smiling, I'll see to it you never work as a pilot again."

He pressed the intercom button. "Martha, have someone from security escort Mister Boykin down to the infirmary for a blood test. Tell them I need the results today."

"Yes, sir," came Martha's voice.

Conner met Boykin's enraged, tight-jawed gaze. "Is there anything else, Mister Boykin?" He paused. "Mister Boykin?"

"No."

"Then our business is concluded. Good day."

Boykin walked like a zombie out of the office, leaving the doors open. Conner didn't notice. He touched the telephone speed dial for the head of his legal department, tapping the folded edge of the resignation letter on his desk as he waited for an answer.

II

Mac dropped his duffel on the hotel bed and shucked his coat. He considered a nap but the funeral was less than four hours away. Besides, all he and Price had done all day was lounge, killing time before the flight to Asheville. It almost felt as if they were back in their hooch during the war, killing time until the next drop. Neither of them had mentioned their conversation the night before, which suited Mac fine.

He unzipped the duffel and removed his dress uniform. It was all he'd brought with him, minus the clothes he was wearing and his kit. They were going to be in Asheville just the one night, long enough for the funeral. Tomorrow morning, they'd return to Raleigh. Then Mac would meet with Conner, to give him his final decision. And for the first time since his arrival, he was having doubts as to what that decision would be.

Price had done it, dumping all of Mac's buried memories out on the table, like pulling the uniform from his footlocker after all these years.

Seeing his friend had reminded Mac of the man he used to be, before Stormcloud. He'd been proud of himself then, of his calling, the company he kept. Captain Mac Harrison would have seen the moondrop just the way Conner had described it, as the adventure of a lifetime, would've accepted the challenge in an instant. Major Mac Harrison, retired war hero, couldn't even make up his goddamned mind.

He lay the uniform on the bed, took in the dark fabric of his jacket, the ribbons over the left breast, the gold oak leaves on the shoulders. He'd hardly worn them long enough to get used to them, still expected to see captain's bars there. Those he'd been proud of earning. His promotion to major, like receiving the Medal of Honor, felt like nothing more than a reward for having survived. For being chicken-shit, as Boykin's Southern eloquence had declared.

He pushed away the feelings, tired of walking that dead-end road. He should have the uniform pressed. The years in the trunk had set deep creases in the fabric. This would be the last time he wore it, and the most important. He would look sharp, like a soldier again.

He crossed to the phone, lifted the handset and dialed guest services. He should tell Willie what Conner wanted him to do. Willie was the only friend left whose judgment he trusted. Come to think of it, Willie was his only friend. Maybe he'd spend some time in Charleston after all. Be a lot warmer than Montana. He wondered if there was decent fishing to be had in December.

He pulled his mane of hair out of the way as he put the handset to his ear. He should probably get his hair trimmed while the uniform was being pressed, he thought. The beard too. Maybe there was a barber downstairs. It wouldn't feel right to wear the uniform looking like this. He had plenty of time.

III

Up the hall from Mac, Conner stood before the mirror in his hotel suite, throwing a perfect Windsor in his dark silk tie. He would have preferred to have stayed at the Biltmore House, the 120-year-old palatial estate and winery that rivaled Europe's most elegant mansions. Few were allowed the privilege of using it as accommodation but Conner's money had purchased what his commonplace lineage could not. The Biltmore had 250 rooms, and he and Beth had vowed to see them all before their lives together ended.

Then again, perhaps it was just as well he didn't stay there.

Conner and his wife had fallen in love with Asheville and the Biltmore during their honeymoon over forty years earlier. He'd met Beth Dresser after his Army discharge. She'd been teaching classes in art appreciation at North Carolina State University in Raleigh, where Conner had been in the third year of earning his business degree while Uncle Sam still felt he owed him something. She wasn't long out of graduate school herself, strawberry blonde and slender, every inch of her pale copper skin awash with freckles which Conner thought made her look exotic.

While only a few years older than his fellow students, Conner's experience in Vietnam and his cane made him feel and act like an old man, even then. Beth was one of the few people on campus who didn't openly shun him because of his service or act uneasy around him because of his disability. He began inventing reasons to tarry after class, asking some lame question about the day's lecture. He reveled in her, just being near her, like standing in a cool spring breeze. He soon dispensed with the art questions altogether, the day Beth told him to stop calling her 'Miss Dresser.' Halfway through the semester he'd finally screwed up enough courage to ask her out for dinner and was amazed when they woke up together the next morning. She gave him a B-plus in the class. He proposed the day he graduated and almost wept when she said yes.

Conner had insisted on finding a job before they were married and during that time, Beth had reawakened his shell-shocked youth. It had been she who'd taught him to accept his disability, getting him to see that walking was as good as running just as long as it was in the right direction. For their first Christmas together, she'd presented him with the teak cane he still used, hand-made to her specifications by a master craftsman in High Point and costing, Conner later discovered, almost as much as the modest engagement ring he'd given her. She had been the one who'd insisted on honeymooning in Asheville, leading her new husband by the hand through the Biltmore house, identifying the artwork and explaining the architecture and history of the estate. Years later, when Beth had long since stopped teaching to pay the bills and Conner could begin to call himself a success, he'd purchased ten acres of land in the nearby Smokies as an anniversary gift. She herself designed the second home they planned to build there.

They'd gotten as far as framing the house when Beth's ovarian cancer had been diagnosed. Conner by then could afford the best care and treatment available but the disease was too far advanced, spreading through her body like oil on water. Conner watched in desperate horror as she slipped away.

Less than five months after diagnosis, Beth was dead, leaving her husband utterly bewildered, leaving him with a five-year-old son to care for, Kevin Conner, a boy with fine blonde hair and the pale promise of freckles who would never truly know his own mother. His father had envied his ignorance.

With no time to grieve, Conner had poured his sorrow and anger like fuel into his work; a burning, inconsolable fury in which he forged UniCom and which by degrees hammered and tempered him into the Roger Conner in whose way no one dared stand. He welcomed his transformation, welcomed each new layer of emotional callus that hardened over Beth's memory. Never forgetting her and always remembering her, he learned, were two quite different things. The first bred bittersweet melancholy. The second broke his heart.

Twelve months to the day after Beth died, Conner hired a demolition crew to tear down every scrap of lumber erected on the mountain property, to dig up the foundation and fill the hole. Leave nothing, he'd ordered. Not a nail, not a splinter, not a crust of cement. Years later, he returned for the first time without his wife. It was May, and where the house had stood there now was a grassy meadow strewn with wildflowers, like the freckles on his beloved Beth's cheeks, opening to the lush valley that been his reason for choosing the site. He couldn't bring himself to sell the land, even though it was now worth a dozen times what he'd paid for it. It was the only place now where he could truly feel anything. Where he could, standing in the cool spring breeze, feel a stirring of the man he once had been.

Conner stared at his reflection. It had just occurred to him that Kevin had never been to the property. Had he even told his son about it? Surely he had. They'd stayed at the Biltmore house together, he and

Martha, the three of them. October, in time to see the change of season on the Parkway, just two months before Kevin had —

Conner stumbled away from the mirror. He banged his shin against the overstuffed chair behind him, groped light-headed until he fell into it. It felt as if there was someone sitting on his chest. He forced himself to inhale, fighting the pressure, sucking air in strained gasps.

It was minutes before he felt well enough to try standing, minutes spent taking deeper and deeper breaths against the subsiding pain in his chest, obstinately ignoring what it signified. He limped unsteadily to the bathroom, drank a glass of water, held a washcloth beneath the running spigot and wiped his clammy face. Too much stress, he told himself, too much work. Doctor Bid had been trying for years to get him to take a vacation. Not a bad idea, not at all. But later. After things settled down.

He walked more confidently back into the suite parlor. "Television on," he ordered, voice weak. The print of Van Gogh's *Starry Night* hanging next to the mirror dissolved into a head shot of a CNN anchor. Conner shakily re-combed his hair in the mirror as he listened:

" . . . was moderate on Wall Street today as the Dow Jones Industrial Average closed down seven-hundred-sixty-six points at twenty-one-thousand fifty-one shares. The modest drop was blamed on profit-taking. And early this morning, the UniCom shuttle *Kitty Hawk* lifted off from Vandenberg Air Force Base in Lompoc, California, on what was described as a routine re-supply and personnel run to Smythii Station, better known as Moontown."

Conner watched the stock footage of a shuttle roaring from the pad. It wasn't even the *Kitty Hawk*; CNN hadn't covered one of his shuttle launches in years. The footage was replaced by shots of Moontown as the anchor recited the rote spiel about how it was on the brink of fiscal collapse.

There was a tap at the door and Martha entered, dressed for the funeral, her coat over her arm. She closed the door and walked over to where she could watch the screen. Conner's phto appeared over the anchor's shoulder.

"Christ, I hate that picture," he groused. The anchor continued, quoting an unidentified source within UniCom who said Conner would soon make an announcement which would "'capture the imagination of the world and rekindle the excitement felt when plans for Moontown were first announced.' Coming up next on World Report: the debate continues over pet cloning, plus picks for Super Bowl fifty-seven when we do sports . . . "

"Television off." The silver swirls and purple returned. Conner turned to Martha. "Who's our unidentified source this week?"

"It was my turn."

"Good job."

"Thanks. Steve wrote it. He's already downstairs."

"Have him send CNN a new photo of me, will you?" Conner eased himself back into the chair. "The one they've got now makes me look like I'm about to break wind."

"The *Kitty Hawk* is scheduled to make her pass in less then two hours. We'd better be going."

Conner closed his eyes, murmuring. "You go on ahead. I'll be downstairs shortly." He opened his eyes when he felt Martha's hesitation. "My hip. Just want to give it a bit of a rest before we go mountain climbing."

She smiled. "We'll wait for you in the lobby."

The door closed. Conner sagged completely. He checked his pulse at his neck. It was steady. He took a deep breath, exhaled slowly. Not a twinge. Still, he should schedule a visit with Dr. Bid when they got back to Raleigh tomorrow. Do it himself, so Martha wouldn't worry. He was certain it was just stress but a quick once-over wouldn't hurt, just to be safe.

IV

Martha closed the door to the suite and moved down the hall, not liking what she'd seen. They all were tired, but for the first time she could recall, she'd been struck by just how old her boss looked.

Roger Conner soon would be seventy-two. When Martha had first met him, he'd seemed possessed of energy belonging to a much younger man. He was still formidable, but Kevin's death had slowed his stride more than he would ever confess, even all these years later. She still struggled with it as well, but she'd only lost her fiancée. She hadn't outlived her only child.

A door opened at the far end of the hall. She pushed aside her rumination as Price emerged, attired in his dress uniform, the pant legs neatly folded and pinned at the knees, coat draped across his lap. "I was just coming to get you," Martha called out as Price closed the door and rolled towards her.

"Good thing. Don't know how long I can stand being squeezed into this thing again." He patted his belly, which strained against the fabric of his dress jacket.

"You look very handsome."

Price grinned. "Don't start. You make me puff out any more, the buttons'll pop off." He moved across the hall to Mac's room and banged on the door. "Yo, Mac! Meter's running!"

After a few seconds, the door opened. "Well damn," Price chuckled. "Do I know you?"

The beard was gone, the hair cut short in military fashion, two streaks of silver riding just above the ears. Clean-shaven, his grave features were even more prominent, a few wrinkles newly revealed, deep valleys in his freshly-scraped cheeks. The dress uniform fit like the day he first donned it, immaculate, the creases paper-sharp.

"'Bout time you got rid of that nasty mess on your face," Price teased. "You ready to go?"

Mac stood in the doorway, coat over one arm, hat tucked beneath the other. He and Martha were staring at one another. There was a quiet nobility to Mac now, a focused calm. Martha held his eyes, feeling a stirring of that first tentative connection at UniCom the day before. She sensed that she was only now seeing the real man, stripped of that wild, protective disguise, as if the uniform he wore had at last made him complete. Major Mackinley M. Harrison, Bravo Squad leader, 82nd Special Airborne HALO Company, had returned for the funeral of his commanding officer.

Martha spoke more to cover her sudden self-consciousness. "The cars are waiting downstairs. You and Mister Price —"

"Willie," Price put in.

" . . . you and Willie'll be riding together. I won't be. I mean, I'll be riding with Mister Conner and Steve."

"That's fine," Mac agreed.

Seconds ticked by. Price looked from one to the other. He cleared his throat.

"I'll just wait for y'all downstairs."

Mac and Martha snapped out of their trance as Price turned to go. Mac closed the door to his room and the three of them moved down the hall to the elevator.

"Glad you got a real haircut, too," Price tossed over his shoulder as he led the way. "You looked like a mop."

"Least I've got it to grow."

"Don't make me get out of this chair and hurt you."

V

There was a light dusting of snow on the ground, a luminous blue-whiteness that flowed past the windows as the car purred forward. Dark pines and bare-limbed trees stood out against it in sharp relief, like the shadows of a plane on a cloud bank as they ascended into the Smokies.

The property was about an hour away, Martha had said before they'd gotten underway. She, Davis and Conner were in the limo ahead of Mac and Price. Most of their had journey passed in silence.

"You all right?"

Mac glanced over, nodded. "Yeah. You?"

"Guess I always thought he'd outlive us all. You made up your mind yet about coming back with me tomorrow?"

They rode on in silence a few moments more. Mac stared out of the window.

"There's something he wants me to do for him."

"Conner?"

"Part of the reason he brought me here. The main reason."

"Not the Colonel?"

Mac shook his head. "Sensei was an excuse."

"What are you talking about?"

"It's crazy."

"So are we."

Mac turned away from the window and looked Price in the face. "He wants me to skydive from the moon."

They stared at one another, the only sound the soft drone of tires on the road.

"That's crazy," Price finally declared.

"The short version is, there's a giant powergun there that he plans to use to shoot cargo back to Earth. He wants me to test it, show it works, get investors all excited, fresh money for Moontown."

Price blew air. "Man, haven't heard much talk about Moontown for a long time."

"Well, there you go. But get this," Mac continued, warming to the story. "Get who he's got lined up to do it if I don't. Jimmy Boykin."

Price's eyes widened. "Jimmy Boykin? Tim's brother Jimmy? Last I heard he was a professional lush."

"He's sober now. Flies for Conner, cargo hops."

"C'mon, Jimmy Boykin knows dick about HALO jumping, might as well be a whuffo. No way he's up to it."

"Yeah. Sure would be a shame if he died, too."

Price nodded agreement. Then he stopped. "Oh come on." Now Mac nodded. "No. He chose Jimmy to get to you?"

"Hell, he used Sensei to get me here," grumbled Mac sardonically. "Why not go for the buzz?"

Price shook his head in disbelief. "Lord have mercy. Some people just don't want to wait in line to get into Hell."

"I told him no," Mac said. "But that was before I saw Jimmy. Willie, if I don't do it, and he dies . . . "

"It won't be your fault," Price bluntly finished, irritation flaring. "Just like everybody else dying wasn't your fault. Jesus, Mac, why do you do this to yourself?"

"What, I'm supposed to ignore it?"

"The only reason Conner's got any hold on you at all is because you give it him."

"Willie —"

"I'm serious, Mac! Screw Jimmy Boykin and the horse he rode in on! If you're gonna do it, do it for your own reasons."

"I didn't say I was gonna do it."

"So you're not?"

"Didn't say I wasn't."

"Well that certainly clears things up."

"Hell Willie, I don't know." Mac reached for the umpteenth time to stroke his absent beard, settled for scratching his chin. "I'm supposed to let him know by tomorrow . . . "

He trailed off, watching in puzzlement as Price checked to make sure the privacy glass was up between them and the driver. He turned on the radio, tuned it until static filled the cabin. When he was done he leaned into Mac, voice low.

"For all I know there's a mic back here and Conner or the driver's listening to everything we say."

"What?"

Price moved closer. "Okay now?"

"Yeah. What —"

"Just listen. I didn't tell you last night. Ever since Edelman e-mailed me the photos he took I've been looking around, see if I could find anything to prove the flight recorder was recovered. About a year-and-a-half ago, I managed to break into a C4I LAN at DoD, one of the local access computer networks they use . . . "

Mac rolled his eyes. "I know what a LAN is, Willie."

"Fine, lis-ten! The really classified stuff's locked up tighter'n grandma's legs, but I saw enough. There's two findings on Stormcloud."

The back of Mac's neck felt suddenly warm. "What?"

"The quote 'official' finding, the one released to the public, is dated November 30, 2015. But there's another one, dated over two months earlier, September nine. Alpha coded."

Alpha protocol was both the highest order of wartime intelligence classification and a method of data encryption. In peacetime, merely viewing alpha-coded information without authorization guaranteed you would spend a substantial portion of your life in a prison cell. What DoD alpha-coded, they wished no one to know.

And there was an alpha-coded finding on Stormcloud.

"Why didn't you tell me this last night?" Mac demanded.

"You had a hard enough time with what I did tell you." Price brushed aside Mac's protest. "I didn't bother trying to read any of the files, I was lucky to get as far as I did without bringing the FBI or NSA or God knows who else down on me. But why would there be an alpha-coded finding that pre-dates the public finding by almost three months? Unless the one they released is bullshit."

The static from the radio seemed to fill Mac's head. "Did you . . . what . . . "

"Hang on, now," Price urged. "There was a truckload of files on UniCom, too. Makes sense, UniCom designed and built the *Reagan* from the ground up, the MFR included. State-of-the art stuff, all that picosec datastream scanning, only one like it back then. ComDat crews at Vandenberg loaded it, and unloaded it after every drop. And they worked for —"

"UniCom."

"That's right. Air Force flew the MFR to the Space Warfare Center at Falcon for dowloading. Once ComDat put it on that plane, their part was done. The only other time they'd be called in is if there was a problem retrieving the data."

Price was leaning in so closely now Mac could feel his breath on his cheek. "Mac, when I was inside DoD I saw half-a-dozen file headers that specifically referenced ComDat. Half-a-dozen, and who knows how many references in others! There's a one-paragraph reference to ComDat in the public finding, a single page on the flight recorder!"

"The SIC had to question ComDat, Willie! They probably questioned the contractor who made the *Reagan's* tires, for chrissake! Just because you found a couple of files doesn't mean there's a conspiracy!"

Price stared at Mac. "You said everyone had forgotten about the others but I didn't think that included you, too."

"Don't you fucking go there, Willie —"

"Fuck you, Mac!" Price hissed. "I've been busting my ass trying to find the truth! Where have you been, huh? I hacked into D-oh-fucking-D, you think I didn't have *your* e-mail address? You know how many letters I wrote to you and never sent? How many times I wanted to tell you what I'd found out? I respected your silence, me and the Colonel both, but I never dreamed you'd be fighting me on this!"

They sat in silence as the car slowed. It turned off the main road onto a narrow gravel path and made its way into the woods, the dark wall of trees closing in.

Price ran his hands over his bald pate. "I know I'm guessing about a lot of this. But at least admit I could be right."

"That's just it." Mac looked back at his friend, finally saying it. "I think you are."

"I know I am," Price insisted. "I can feel it, like I can still feel my legs sometimes. It's easy to believe there's nothing there. Just imagination, just a, ghost. A wish. But it won't go away."

He glanced out of the window. "Looks like we're almost there." He turned back to Mac. "One more thing you need to know. I gave up poking around in DoD after that one time. Those folks scare me."

"Doesn't sound like much has scared you so far."

Price chuckled. "Got more balls than brains, I think sometimes. But there's someplace else I've been looking."

Mac had already guessed. "UniCom."

Price nodded. "You know they're up to their eyeballs in this, gotta be. There's a good chance they'll have most of what DoD has, especially with ComDat being involved. Lots of places the information might be, but one place it has to be. Conner's personal directory."

"Find anything yet?"

"Its taken me this long to get close enough to take a peek. Hell, when Davis called to bring me here, I thought they'd nailed me. I've been ducking in and out of back alleys like a rat, looking for a hole in the wall, trying to sneak in. Now all of a sudden here were are, right in the man's living room, by invitation."

Mac finally saw where the conversation had been heading all along. "You're saying I should do it. You're saying I should tell him yes."

"Mac, Conner is opening the goddamn front door! Look, I don't care if you do it or not. Just tell him you will and we're inside, you and me, the last ones. With any luck, we get what we need before the jump and then screw him, tell him you've got the moon flu or something."

Mac guffawed and Price grinned, but didn't lose any of his intensity. "This is the best chance we'll ever have, Mac. For what it's worth, if I had my legs I'd be begging him to let me do it. But you're the only one who can."

The car slowed. The trees fell away beyond the window, revealing a broad blanket of glistening snow. Price reached out and killed the radio as the car rolled to a stop. The sudden silence left Mac feeling empty, but something now was scratching at the edge of his consciousness, something which disappeared when he turned his attention towards it. Something that quickened his pulse, for reasons he didn't yet understand.

"I don't know what I'm doing," he said at last, as much to the feeling as his old friend. "I've got no life anymore. I'm just, marking time."

"Waiting for what?" Price asked. "Time doesn't stop just because things don't turn out the way we want them to." He gently clapped Mac's arm. "They're all gone, my brother, and now the Colonel, too. You and me, we're gonna join them someday. What we do, what *you* do while you wait, is up to you."

He held Mac's eye as the driver opened the door. "Make it count for something."

VI

Roger Charles Conner stood at the top of the ridge, at the point where the glade began its graceful descent into the valley. He was draped in a heavy coat of dark wool, framed against the valley and the clear evening sky. Moonlight bathed the snow, the reflected light filling the clearing with pale radiance. Mac and Price were stationed a few paces back, facing Conner, while Martha and Davis watched a respectful distance away.

Conner clasped his cane in both hands before him, his head bowed as if in meditation. Mac caught a glint of light over his left breast. Pinned there was a Purple Heart and Silver Star. Mac hadn't been aware Conner had received the latter, nor would he have guessed. Risking his life for others didn't seem to be his style. Maybe Martha had been right. Maybe her boss was a better man than Mac allowed.

Conner raised his head and spoke.

"We are gathered here tonight to bid farewell to our honored dead." His soft words carried easily in the cold stillness. "Colonel Yoshi Aaron Takeshita, United States Army. A soldier. A teacher. A warrior in the most true and proud sense of the word. All of them noble vocations, and Colonel Takeshita wore each mantle with equal grace, strength, and humility. He will be missed."

He caught Martha's eye. She glanced at her watch and nodded.

Conner reached into his inner coat pocket and withdrew an envelope. "Colonel Takeshita left few instructions concerning this moment.

We have done what we could, in hopes that it will suffice. What few thoughts he had are contained here, I am told."

Conner walked forward and extended the envelope to Mac. This was unexpected. Mac had thought Conner would preside over the memorial entire. He took the envelope automatically and Conner moved to stand a few paces behind.

It was a plain white envelope, the edges worn fuzzy with age, bearing the pre-printed return address of an attorney in Fayetteville. Nothing else was written on the surface. Mac's hands trembled as he ran his finger beneath the gummed flap. It popped open easily, the glue yellowed and dry. He wondered how long the envelope had held its secret, whether Sensei had sealed it some night after he and Mac had spoken, years before.

The stationery was plain, the single paragraph upon it bearing no date or signature, but there was no mistaking the neat script that flowed across the page. Mac moved forward until he was standing where Conner had stood. Swallowing his emotions, he read Takeshita's final words.

"To my friends gathered here, I say do not grieve, for the Way of the warrior is in resolute acceptance of death. This, then, is my moment of greatest honor. Celebrate, rather than mourn, as I rejoin those who have passed before us following the Way. Live for them now, as they live now within you, and walk the Path by your side. For always they have walked beside you, as now I do, and forever will. Farewell."

Mac was unable to keep his voice from shaking as he read the last sentence. He carefully re-folded the paper. That magnificent life, distilled to just those few words. The end of it, nothing more.

He looked at the others. Conner stared stoically ahead. Davis' head was bowed. Martha met Mac's eye for a moment before she, too, looked away.

Perhaps he should say something, he thought. Maybe that's what the others were waiting for. He cleared his throat.

"I, ah . . . Colonel Takeshita was, um . . . "

His voice stumbled. So much he could say. Nothing he could describe, but there should be more. He should —

He felt a hand on his arm. Price was there, though Mac couldn't remember him moving. His friend gripped his forearm tightly, not meeting his eyes.

Mac turned. The two of them stared out across the valley.

Two-hundred and fifty-three miles overhead, the UniCom shuttle *Kitty Hawk* burned her OMS engines until she matched the Earth's rotation.

Silently, the twin clamshell cargo bay doors opened, revealing a three-yard-long glistening white cylinder. Harsh sunlight flooded the bay, the doors' shadow retreating to reveal the American flag emblazoned on the cylinder's surface and beside that, the upright katana and shooting star of the 82nd Special Airborne HALO Company.

The cargo bay doors halted. A piston extended, raising the nose of the cylinder until it was perpendicular to the shuttle. After a moment, it gracefully departed its cradle and sailed away, towards the Earth.

The cargo bay doors closed. The shuttle's engines fired briefly, propelling the *Kitty Hawk* out of orbit and towards her true destination, over two-hundred thousand miles away.

Behind her, as it entered atmosphere, the cylinder began to glow.

Mac returned Sensei's eulogy into its envelope like a treasure to its box. It was over. Nothing remaining but the long drive back to Asheville, the return flight to Raleigh in the morning. And still, he didn't know what he would tell Conner.

The feeling he'd experienced in the limo ride with Price at once returned, stronger now, immediate, clamoring for his attention. This time Mac did not chase it. He closed his eyes and opened himself to it, clearing his mind, granting the thing room to approach, to reveal itself and make its purpose known.

Maybe that's what he had been waiting for all along. A signal.

A sign . . .

"Mac!"

The word was soft, filled with wonder. Mac opened his eyes, followed Price's gaze upward, over the valley, high above the distant mountains.

A fiery streak knifed across the heavens, standing out in silver-white brilliance against the starry winter sky. Mac knew immediately what it was. The realization detonated in his heart, fueled his warrior's pride until it flared as hot and bright as the meteor. He swallowed against the sudden tightness in his throat, forced himself to speak.

"Comp'ny . . . atten-*tion!*"

As one, the 82nd Special Airborne came to full attention; warriors past and present, saluting their fallen comrade as the shooting star fell. Sensei's remains, burning ever brighter as they descended, bathing the heavens with their light as thousands unaware watched with faces uplifted in reverent wonder, some whispering wishes, some murmuring prayers. Sensei's final act of love, illuminating all one last time. Marking the Path. Showing the Way.

Losing none of its brilliance, the star winked out.

Mac, Price and Conner dropped their salutes. Mac felt cold wetness on his upturned face. Snow. Snow, from a cloudless sky.

The familiar sensation Mac had been struggling to identify filled him entirely now, and he marveled that he had not recognized it. It was *him*; his essence, what he had been before Stormcloud, what Sensei had taught him to be, what he had labored in shame to subjugate ever since. Conner had been right, during their first meeting. Mac could no longer deny it, for it was the truth. It was what he was.

Now it was over. No more talk was needed, no more debate. With his final words, spoken from his death bed and now, here, Sensei had told Mac what to do.

Conner arrived at Mac's right hand. Price was at his left. The three of them gazed out across the valley as the snow fell around them. The warrior spoke to them both.

"I'll do it."

Part Two

Four

I

"Twelve-grand and climbing, gentlemen."

Boykin's voice issued from the speaker set into the jumpcar fuse-lage. Fitzpatrick pressed the wireless talkback in his jumpsuit collar: "Roger that." He grinned at Mac and Price. "Just about wet myself when I saw you guys land in this thing. You sure do travel first class!"

Mac would've made Paul Fitzpatrick for a jumper a mile away. Owner of the Triangle Sport Parachute Center, he was maybe a few years older than Mac and a few inches shorter, hair so sun-bleached it was impossible to tell its true color. His face was deeply tanned, deep crow's feet etched by years of squinting up at the sky, searching for that billow of ripstop nylon. But it was his *ki* that gave him away, the easy self-confidence that marked any lifetime jumper, born of knowing you'd risked your life thousands of times by jumping out of a perfectly good airplane and had lived to brag about it. Mac had liked him the moment they shook hands.

Fitzpatrick had welcomed Mac and Price like family, had listened intently as Mac detailed his jump experience and what he would do a week from that morning, as if he didn't already know who Mac was. In the dropshack, framed under glass, was a collection of service insignia provided by the DZ's retired military patrons. The 82nd's was at the center. Everyone at the DZ knew who the morning's visitors were.

"Saw the press conference on TV yesterday," Fitzpatrick had said when Mac was done. "Half my folks think you're crazy, the other half say you'd be crazy not to do it."

124

"What do you think?" Mac had asked.

Fitzpatrick had grinned. "Hell, I thought you were dead."

The day of their return from Asheville had been spent in preparation for the media event, Davis and Martha executing the particulars while Mac and Price reviewed their contracts, the documents essentially stating that if either died, it wasn't UniCom's fault. Price's official capacity was special drop consultant, though he surmised Conner more likely wanted him there for the extra buzz having both of the 82nd's survivors on his team would generate. Ten times his yearly take at his Charleston shop to spy on his employer. He didn't waste time debating the ethics as he and Mac signed and pressed their thumbs against the touchboxes.

Price called his shop to announce his vacation, and Mac informed his local sheriff that a live-in UniCom security guard would be arriving the next morning to keep the inevitable visitors away from his cabin. Thus ended Thursday.

Friday morning at ten, the curtain rose on the 'UniCom Moondrop.' Davis had warned Mac that the press would come at him hard, and they had. After reading the dramatic preamble Davis had composed, Conner silently watched as Mac, perspiring beneath the new suit Conner had insisted on purchasing, was peppered with questions, Davis expertly riding rein on the media throng like a conductor before an orchestra of hyperactive musicians. Where had Mac been? Was it true he'd been in a VA mental hospital? Did the Army force him to retire after Stormcloud? Why was the drop scheduled for Christmas Eve?

Why indeed, Mac had wondered. He hadn't known the date was so imminent when he'd agreed, not that it would have made a difference, given his motivation. It was Martha who'd answered, declaring that Christmas was a time of hope, of dreams fulfilled, and the moondrop and all it presaged was Conner's gift to the world. True or not, Conner had nodded sagaciously as she'd spoken.

Significantly absent was any mention of fusion; Conner had made certain prior to the conference that no mention was to be offered, his unrelenting and eternal wrath the unmentioned punishment for disobeying. Dr. Robert Yamada, Conner's sixtyish, bespectacled chief of engineering, had nervously presented a brief tutorial limited to the mechanics of the drop, while Conner had offered only a cryptic reference during his opening statements of greater things to come, all of which hinged on the moondrop and Moontown. Again and again, he denied his lunar base was near collapse but the reporters wouldn't let it go. Was this a last-ditch attempt to make Moontown pay off? And what if it failed?

Conner had shrugged. "Well, LunarDisney has rather a nice ring to it."

The soundbite had been all over the news that evening — Mac learned later that Davis had written the line. Conner had wanted to create a stir, and he had done it. The day ended with dinner at his private club, him leading a champagne toast to their enterprise, beaming like a man living his dream.

Mac was in bed by eleven. The next morning, his training was to begin.

Mac was breathing deeply, doing his best to smooth the hard pounding of his heart as he sat on the long bench mounted along the fuselage in the aircar hold. After a cursory ground school session he'd done a handful of hop-and-pops, none higher than five-thousand-feet, the bare minimum review mandated by USPA regs because of his long layoff. The morning's work had been deeply satisfying, returning to the cold sky's welcoming embrace after so many years earthbound. It wasn't until he'd climbed into the aircar, though, that the fear had returned in earnest.

"Twenty grand," came Boykin's voice again, as if on cue. "Wind northeast at twenty knots. Jump run in sixty seconds."

"Roger that," Fitzpatrick replied. "He's good," he commented to Mac. "Where'd you meet him?"

"We fought together once."

Fitzpatrick turned to Price, and their animated conversation swiftly faded into the background of Mac's consciousness. There was a increasing whine in his ears that he'd been trying to write off to the jumpcar turbines, the confident humming of their power vibrating through the craft. They had another ten grand to go before jump run. It was still jump run, even though the car would be hovering above their upwind spot when they exited. The door would open and Mac would be staring straight down five-and-a-half miles. His first HALO jump in nine years. His first since Stormcloud.

The rig straps dug into his shoulders like a straightjacket. His bowels felt like they were an inch's shift away from loosening completely, stomach muscles yanked tight in a knot. It was worse than during the war, worse than it had ever been waiting in the frigid dark of the

Reagan's jump bay, waiting for the battery port to slam open, the thruster to ignite beneath his feet . . .

"Hey Mac!"

Fitzpatrick was staring at him. "I said we'll bomb out, do a little RW, couple turns. Just get you used to it again, then wave off at five and pull, give you a little time to fly around before we hit the peas."

Mac nodded, swallowing. "Sounds good," he managed to reply.

"Keep your eyes on your altimeter," Fitzpatrick cautioned, tapping the classic analog dial strapped atop Mac's right wrist. "Don't wait for ground rush. Got it?"

Mac nodded acknowledgement once more and Fitzpatrick turned away. Price leaned forward in his seat, peering at Mac. "You okay?" Mac forced a smile and a thumbs-up. Price regarded him a moment longer, clearly unconvinced.

Mac felt a sudden change in the jumpcar's vibration just as Boykin's voice issued from the speaker once more:

"Thirty grand, gentlemen. This is jump run."

"Roger jump run," Fitzpatrick replied. He unbelted himself from the bench, rose and indicated for Mac to do the same. "Pin check."

Mechanically, Mac freed himself and stood with his back to Fitzpatrick. He heard the Velcro flap tear open as Fitzpatrick checked Mac's main and reserve, ensuring that the restraining pins that held the canopies and spring-loaded pilot 'chutes in their bags were in place with nothing to prevent their release. He closed the flap and slapped the top of the rig, and Mac turned to Fitzpatrick and returned the favor. The jumpmaster donned his goggles from where they hung by their strap around his neck. He grinned.

"Showtime!"

Boykin played the thrusters inside the jumpcar cockpit, holding the craft level. The sky beyond the windscreen was powder blue, fading like a watercolor wash into a deeper hue the higher he looked. It had been a long time since he'd seen those colors, a long time since he'd flown anything that could bring him where he was now, although the jumpcar didn't even come close to the F-120 STEALTH fighter-bomber he'd flown during the war.

He didn't relish flying Harrison, didn't want to be anywhere near him. He'd felt like a prisoner since his last meeting with Conner.

Even now his face flushed hot as he remembered. He could still feel the cold sting of the needle sliding into his arm in the UniCom infirmary as the nurse drew his blood under the watchful eye of a beefy security guard, putting a cap on his humiliation. He'd worked goddamn hard to turn his life around, but Conner had made it clear that who he was now was irrelevant. Only what others thought he was mattered.

He relaxed his grip on the yoke and corrected a slight port drift with a nudge to the belly fan thrusters. It hadn't been until he'd settled into the jumpcar seat back at RDU that the foul mood that had been his from the moment he'd rolled out of bed that morning had retreated, replaced by a calm he hadn't felt in a long, long time. This was his turf. He was in control, and not a soul could tell him he didn't know what he was doing, that he didn't matter. Not here.

He lifted his face once more to the burning blue, as the poet pilot had named it decades before Boykin's birth. He felt his anger lift and disappear into the heavens. He was home.

Mac fought to keep focused as he pulled on his goggles and lifted his oxygen mask into place. He sucked a breath to ensure it was working, let it drop back to his neck.

Fitzpatrick was checking his AAD, the small black box affixed just below his rig's bottom-right corner, plain save for the digital readout on its face. The automatic activation device operated on barometric pressure — if it was climbing too fast when the jumper passed a preset altitude, a spring mechanism inside pulled the pin on the reserve parachute. Other than his wits, the AAD was the only lifesaving device a skydiver had. Some never used them, claiming they were too prone to misfire, but most jumpers were more concerned about what would happen if the AAD didn't fire. There was a saying: it's not the fall that kills you, it's that sudden stop at the bottom.

Fitzpatrick tapped the recessed button on the AAD's face and snapped the protective cover closed. He checked Mac's, setting it for 1,500 feet.

"Why so high?" Mac asked.

Fitzpatrick guffawed as he worked. "Maybe that's high for you but we don't do much HALO jumping here. I like all the insurance I can get." He finished and winked at Mac. "Besides, you never know when you might forget to pull."

"Forget to pull and I'll kick your ass," Price declared. Fitzpatrick sat down next to him, motioning for him to turn around. Price swiveled on the bench and backed into Fitzpatrick as the other man tugged Price's harness straps, pulling until Price was snug against his torso. He connected the four steel spring clips of his tandem jump harness to their twins on Price's, one at each shoulder and hip, calling "Hooked!" and "Saftey'd!" as he snapped each one home, Price nodding acknowledgement each time. When Fitzpatrick was done, Price was attached to him like a backpack in reverse, facing forward.

Mac grasped Fitzpatrick's hands and leaned back as the jumpmaster surged to his feet. Price dropped six inches, the top of his head just below Fitzpatrick's chin. Fitzpatrick gave a slight jump to double-check the security of the clips. "You ready?" he asked Price.

"Did I tell you I'm afraid of heights?"

"Me too," Fitzpatrick rejoined. "That's why we're wearing a parachute. When we're in the door, I'm gonna need you to cross your arms and arch when I tell you to, like we practiced on the ground. Don't release until we're under canopy and I say so. Okay?"

Price nodded. Leaning on Mac for support, Fitzpatrick shuffled over to the jump door. He stopped beside the control panel set to the door's right and keyed his com button. "Jimmy, stand by for de-pres."

"Roger de-pres," Boykin's voice answered. "Ready when you are."

They donned their oxygen masks. Fitzpatrick re-seated his goggles beneath his helmet and shouted to be heard through the rubber face-mask: "Set?" Mac nodded. He placed his hand on Price's shoulder and leaned into his ear. "Set?" Price nodded.

Fitzpatrick turned the safety key in the door panel. "Depressurizing," he said, and pressed the red button.

Mac's ears popped as the interior pressure of the hold was bled to equal the outside pressure. Open the door beforehand and they'd be blown outside by the explosive decompression. He swallowed and wiggled his jaw to relieve the ache in his ears. Fitzpatrick waited until the button stopped blinking, then turned the safety key back to locked position. "Door coming open! Guard your reserve!"

Mac grabbed the handle bolted to the left of the door and covered his reserve handle with his right hand. Fitzpatrick grasped the recessed vertical lever below the panel and pulled it downward. There was a thud, a hiss, and the door retreated into the fuselage.

The icy air hit Mac like a wall. It would be cold at this altitude even at the height of summer but now, just a few days before the official start of winter, it was well below freezing. The exposed skin on his face tightened, he felt the cold soak through the legs of his day-glo orange student jumpsuit and into his crotch. But all of it took a back seat to what Mac beheld.

"Ye-ah!" Fitzpatrick shouted. "Look at that, will ya?"

Twelve inches from Mac's toes the jumpcar deck ended, with absolutely nothing beyond except nearly six miles of straight down. There were a few scattered clouds below them, too thin and wispy for Mac to estimate their altitude. Slowly they drifted, like mist on the surface of a calm, invisible ocean. Far below that surface the ground waited; hair-fine stripes of roads, dots of dull color that were buildings, distant glints of gold that marked bodies of sun-dappled water.

The world was a lifeless, frozen tableaux, and as he beheld the eerie scene something long dormant awoke in the knot of Mac's belly. Something at once dreaded and welcome, the resurrection of a long-forgotten companion against whose arrival Mac was powerless to defend.

Now, it avowed. Before you know another day. There is something you must do.

"You ready?" Fitzpatrick barked. Mac gave him a brusque nod, not taking his eyes from the vista before him.

"In the door!" Fitzpatrick slid a step to his left until he was standing in the center of the jump door, legs splayed, hands grasping the doorframe to either side. Price was staring down, breathing deeply.

"Arch!" commanded Fitzpatrick.

"I just want to say how nice it's been knowing y'all!" Price shouted as he complied. He folded his arms across his chest, arched his body until his head was pressed into Fitzpatrick's chest.

"Last one down buys a case of beer!" Fitzpatrick let go of the doorframe, leaned forward and was gone.

Mac should have followed immediately. His right hand snapped off the AAD control cover. He held down the tiny button with the tip of his gloved finger until the device read 800 feet.

He snapped the cover back into place. It took four seconds.

He stood before the jump door and closed his eyes. Gone was the sky and the clouds. Gone was the clean light of the winter sun. There was only the blackness of space, the cold, and the predacious fear. Only now did he surrender, allowing it to course through his body unfettered like snarling dogs let slip from the leash. He trembled as they raced, clawing their way through his weakness, tearing away his inadequate flesh, feasting on his doubt.

Breathe. The way of the warrior is resolute acceptance of death.

Slow your pulse. A dead man has nothing to fear.

A dead man cannot be killed.

I am a dead man.

Major Mackinley Harrison opened his arms to the sky and stepped forward to embrace his death.

At first, Price felt nothing. There wasn't enough velocity yet to generate any real wind, so you didn't have the sense that you were falling at all. Only your gut registered what was happening, and it took every bit of Price's rusty training to hold his arch and resist his body's frantic impulse to reach out and grab at the air, like he'd seen so many novice jumpers do, reaching for something to grasp to stop the plunge but finding nothing. Right about the time your brain registered that tidy fact, your stomach made an urgent pilgrimage into your throat. Your inner ear went nuts, lacking any data with which to get a stationary fix, so the disorienting wash of dizziness was next, followed by the pins-and-needles rush of adrenaline zinging through your body as every sense, every primal offensive and defensive mechanism went into ass-over-teakettle overdrive.

The cold wind slapped your face as you began to belly out, shooting up your nose and into your sinuses; the roar of the windrush swelled in your ears like the thunder of surf; resistance massaged your body like an invisible, rippling wall. And then, you were flying.

All those sensations, in under five seconds. Price sucked a lungful of the icy air and whooped for joy. It was fucking great.

Fitzpatrick tucked his left arm into his head to balance their wind resistance, right hand pulling the pilot 'chute from the rig's belly band. He held it out to the side until the windrush tugged it free from his fingers and out of sight over and behind them. A moment later, there came the reassuring bump of drogue deployment. They bellied out like a weight suspended from a pendulum. In seconds, they attained terminal velocity, the point of zero acceleration at which their fall rate was balanced by wind resistance. They'd have roughly two minutes of freefall time, an eternity in the air, before Fitzpatrick would deploy the main, giving them a nice, easy ride the remaining three-thousand-feet or so to the ground.

Fitzpatrick glanced at his altimeter and shouted in Price's ear: "Relax!" Price uncrossed his arms and extended them into arch position, parallel and just below the jumpmaster's. Fitzpatrick laughed and whooped and Price joined in. "Out-standing, isn't it?"

"Awesome!" But for Price it was more than the view. It had begun during ground school, when he was again reminded of what he'd really lost when he'd left his legs behind on his last field of military combat. His chair gave him mobility but it could never show him the freedom he now felt, even tethered as he was to Fitzpatrick. In the few seconds since they'd bombed out of the jumpcar, the realization that had been growing since Fitzpatrick had surprised him with the offer of a tandem jump had fully crystallized. Legs were unnecessary in the sky. He could still jump. Without Fitzpatrick, without anyone. He could still fly.

He searched for Mac, eager to do some RW, to slap hands and hold them in hard grasp and celebrate together. He scanned the skies.

"Where's Mac?" he shouted. "You see Mac?"

He caught a blur of movement to his left, a bright orange flash streaking by.

"Mac!"

Mac held his arms flat against his sides, body straight, legs together as he flew. Delta position, wind resistance minimal, body angled sharply downward, flying at over two-hundred miles an hour.

The cold gale of his passage numbed him as he dropped like a missile towards the Earth. He was dimly aware of the rush of wind, the humid bath of his exhalation inside the oxygen mask. His eyes were open but nothing came to them — no light, no images save those that replayed in his head, images of darkness, and then of blinding fire . . .

Price watched Mac dwindle below him. He had written off Mac's abrupt withdrawal in the aircar to the same nervousness he'd been feeling. His moment of jubilation disintegrated, replaced by a sudden, sick realization.

"Catch him!" he shouted to Fitzpatrick.

"What?"

"Catch him!"

"We can't!"

"Cutaway!"

"No!" Fitzpatrick yelled. "Why?"

Price didn't know why. All he could do was watch as the dread grew inside him.

The fire receded. All before him was black. Behind him, the incinerated remains of the *Reagan* and her crew.

21,000 feet. 20,000 . . .

They were gone, sacrificed for him so he could live.

19,000 . . .

But he was not worthy of that sacrifice.

18,000 . . .

Not worthy of their blood.

17,000 . . .

He had traded his honor for his life. Purchased his breath with theirs, drowned out their final screams with the wailing of his own cowardice.

16,000 . . .

But now he was not afraid. Now he and his fear were one, as they should have been then.

15,000 . . .

Now it was time to be judged.

Master rigger Mike Hill stood separate from the other jumpers, squinting skyward, hand held over his eyes to shield them from the glare. He concentrated on the speeding dot below Fitzpatrick and Price. He knew who Mac was, had no doubts he knew what he was doing, but Fitzpatrick had briefed him before the jump. He knew the plan was bomb out, RW, pull at three. Maybe they'd changed their minds in the jumpcar, but it wasn't like Fitzpatrick not to radio it down. He was too careful about such things.

Another jumper sidled up next to him. A second or two passed as they watched.

"Jesus, he's burnin' it in," the jumper murmured.

14,000 . . . 13,000 . . .

The darkness was gone now, and the fear. Left behind in fluttering remnants, peeled away by the wind . . .

12,000 . . .

. . . the wind that streamed cold through him now as if his body were a sieve, purified in the crucible of his descent.

11,000 . . .

He was no longer flesh. No longer substance.

10,000 . . .

No longer living.

9,000 . . .

Only one thing now remained.

8,000 . . .

With a sigh as if falling into sleep, Mac went limp.

Price stared in horror as Mac tumbled out of control. Even if they did cut away now they'd never catch him, not in time to do anything.

"Shit!" It was Fitzpatrick. He had no idea what had happened, if Harrison had lost consciousness or only lost his mind. He glanced at his altimeter: 15,000 feet. Harrison would be down before they traveled half that distance.

Price was screaming: "Pull Mac! Pull!"

Hill felt his stomach yank tight as Mac tumbled. "Oh, Christ," gasped the other jumper. "Oh no . . . "

But Hill was already dashing to where the DZ's pickup truck was parked next to the manifest booth, vaguely aware of the handful of others racing after him.

Boykin stepped down from the aircar, keying the cockpit door closed behind him. He stroked the fuselage fondly, like a horseman with his mount. Too soon. At least he'd get to fly it back.

Someone was shouting. He turned and looked out over the DZ, to the other side. A man was running towards a pickup as if his life depended on it, two more following. Everyone else was staring straight up.

Boykin followed their gazes. A second later he too was sprinting for the truck.

3,000 . . .
The Earth spun by. Then the sky. Then the Earth.
2,500 . . .
Not the Earth. The ground.
2,000 . . .
It was no longer distant. It was all around him, trees and grass like arms and fingers thrusting up in a blur to embrace him, pulling him into its breast, claiming him.
1,500 . . .
Judging him.
1,000 . . .
Groundrush.
900 . . .
Like a detonation in the back of his brain, it came. It was not born of him, was not a buried wish nor mere instinct. It was a clear and solitary wordless command, a cannon shot in his emptied consciousness.
850.
Mac threw himself into arch.
800.
The windrush slapped his body and threw him over on his belly.
750.
Judge me.
700.
Judge me now.
650.
Something reached down from the heavens and grabbed him.

Far below was a brief billow of white. Price exhaled with relief. Mac's AAD had fired.

"What the hell . . . ?"

It was Fitzpatrick, beating Price to the comment as they both watched the reserve collapse just seconds after it inflated. It should still be open. At 1,500 feet, Mac should be under canopy for almost a minute, at least half that.

"Did he make it?"

"Can't tell," Price answered. "I think so . . . "

Fitzpatrick consulted his altimeter. "Hang on," he said and pulled the main deploy. Price waited impatiently through the hard jolt, craned his neck upwards in time to see the huge main fully inflate, the limp drogue trailing behind. Fitzpatrick was already reaching for the brakes even before the slider had fully descended. He tugged the yellow strap loops free of their Velcro bindings, two on each steering shroud. Price slid his hands into the lower handles.

"Grab the risers!" Fitzpatrick barked. Price understood instantly. He closed his hands around the thick forward straps. Together they pulled.

The canopy pitched forward, nosed downward. The two men swung backwards, pulled along behind the parachute like the tail of a majestic kite as it sped them groundward.

Boykin sat in the dirty bed of the pickup with another jumper, hands clamped onto the side as the vehicle bounced over the terrain. Mac's parachute had caught the barest gulp of air before he had disappeared behind a low hillock about fifty yards away. Whether he had survived, no one knew. Not yet.

His heart was pounding but he wasn't certain if it was from dread or joy. He really didn't know what he was feeling, and not knowing bothered him more than the thought of what they might find ahead.

The truck rounded the hillock on the right, jolting across a depression hidden beneath the tall grass before lurching to a stop. Boykin stood and looked over the top of the cab at the spot where everyone now stared.

Mac's helmet lay on the ground where he'd dropped it. His oxygen mask hung around his neck as he stood, surrounded by white nylon draped upon the grass like a picnic cloth, the shroud lines trailing from his rig. He smiled up at his company as he stripped off his gloves.

"Hey guys. Gimme a lift?"

Any answer that might have followed was cut off by the sound of a slider's flapping. Fitzpatrick and Price dropped out of the sky, releasing the risers as they turned the canopy into the wind barely a hundred feet above the ground. Together they flared, hit and rolled, stopping just twenty feet away.

Fitzpatrick had already unhooked Price before the canopy had completely settled behind them. Price was shouting even as he tore off his oxygen mask: "What the hell was that? Huh? What're you trying to do?"

Fitzpatrick was on his feet. He strode over to Mac, canopy training behind. Off came his helmet, goggles, mask, revealing his face in stages, each more angry than the last. He stopped a foot in front of Mac, but his eyes were fixed on the AAD. He grabbed it roughly and tilted the readout upwards. He dropped it, looked Mac in the eye, finger raised in Mac's face.

"I don't give a good goddamn who you are," he hissed with barely-controlled fury. "You don't pull that shit here, not at my DZ. You wanna kill yourself, do it somewhere else. You read me?"

He spun on his heel before Mac could respond, yanking the shroud lines out of the grass, gathering in the main.

No one in the truck said anything. Price was sitting in the tall grass, staring at Mac. Everyone stared at Mac. He held each one of them briefly in his gaze, finishing with Boykin, visible above the top of the cab, the only one besides Price who hadn't turned away.

"Didn't think you'd made it," was all Boykin said.

"Sorry to disappoint you." Mac turned and began collecting his canopy.

II

"This is *maguro*."

"It looks like tuna."

"Very good, that's what it is." Mac held his chopsticks over another piece. "This is *ebi*. . . "

"Shrimp, that one's obvious," said Martha.

Mac indicated each piece as he spoke. "*Saba* — that's mackerel, it's a little strong. This is good, *hamachi*, yellowtail, one of my favorites."

Martha touched a curved piece of white flesh with a purplish skin. "What's that?"

"Try it."

She raised an eyebrow, suspicious. "It's something nauseating, isn't it?" Martha lifted the *sushi* with her chopsticks and dipped it in the small dish of *shoyu* at her right, stuffed the morsel into her mouth and chewed, gingerly at first, then with relish. "'S good," she declared around the mouthful. "Little rubbery . . . What is it?"

Mac grinned. "*Tako*. Octopus."

Martha paused in mid-chew. "You're enjoying this, aren't you?"

Mac only chuckled and added more *wasabi* to his *shoyu*, stirring the potent horseradish into the dark caramel-colored soy sauce. It was the genuine article, not the pasty green mustard subsitute most *sushi* bars served. They'd been at the restaurant for about half-an-hour, cozy and absent of the raucous *hibachi* tables he loathed. He hadn't had *sushi* in years and hadn't realized how much he'd missed it. He was fast discovering just how many things he missed, not the least of which was the company of a woman.

Martha's call had been a welcome surprise. Price wasn't speaking to Mac in the wake of the incident at the DZ that afternoon. He'd considered trying to explain to Price why he'd done what he'd done but he didn't really understand it himself. All he knew was he felt more like himself now than he had since leaving Montana. Clear headed, for once. Alive. And hungry as hell.

He studied Martha across the table as she gamely struggled with the exotic cuisine. She'd called from UniCom, saying she'd been working there most of the day, catching up on tasks delayed by the week's frantic activities. She must have gone home to change before meeting at the restaurant; her attire wasn't what Mac would consider weekend office casual. She was wearing more makeup than usual, her lipstick a darker color from her customary shade, her eyes kohl-lined and dusky. Bronze diamonds which glittered in the overhead light dangled from her earlobes, and she wore a ring on nearly every finger and a tiny diamond stud in the fold of her left nostril. Her blouse was plum-colored silk, the buttons undone just shy of her cleavage. She was a very different woman from the one Mac first had met just a week before, looked as if she'd be more at home in a coffeehouse than a corporate office. Mac wondered if she noticed he was wearing the same shirt and slacks he'd worn at the press conference, the only dress clothes he owned other than his uniform. The well-worn brown leather jacket he'd borrowed from Price, ignoring his sullen friend's raised eyebrow. If he'd known Martha's preferred dress he would have stuck with his beloved jeans and denim shirts. Although he had to admit he liked the leather jacket.

"Is this why you invited me here?" Martha asked. "To eat raw mollusk?"

"They cook the octopus. And I believe you invited me."

Martha finished the mouthful as their waitress appeared and replaced the decanter of warmed *sake*. Mac tilted his head in acknowledgement: "*Domo arigato gozaimasu.*" The waitress bowed gracefully and glided away. Mac refilled Martha's tiny cup.

"Did Sensei teach you Japanese?"

"Just kind of picked it up, really. I can only speak a little." Mac refilled his own cup. "I'd be lost in Japan. Another loud, clumsy *gaijin.*"

"*Gaijin?*"

"A foreigner. Everyone's who's not Japanese is *gaijin.*"

Martha pored over the platter of *sushi*. "Ever think of going?"

"Japan?" Martha nodded. Mac shook his head. "It'd be interesting, but I've never felt like I had to go. Everything I know about Japan, the Japanese, customs, I learned from Sensei."

"But he wasn't completely Japanese."

"Been checking us out, huh?" Martha feigned mock innocence, and Mac dove into the life story of Yoshi Aaron Takeshita, only son of a family who traced their *samurai* lineage to the eleventh century, who took with him to his grave a thousand years of martial tradition. Takeshita's great-grandparents emigrated to Hawaii in 1862, his grandfather cutting sugar cane by day and teaching his ancestral *budo* at night — kendo, ju-jitsu and jodo. Sensei's father later added to the family arsenal the twentieth-century art of aikido, sprung from the hoary roots of daito-ryu ju-jitsu, and commemorated his new-found Western passion of baseball by giving his son the middle name Aaron, for Hank Aaron.

By the time of his son's birth, Kenji Takeshita was one of Hawaii's preeminent *budoka*. He immersed his son in hard martial training from the time the boy could stand so that by his late teens, Yoshi Takeshita possessed the martial skills of a man twice his age. With his grandfather he walked more philosophical paths, training in *misogi*, the meditative practice of ritual purification, as well as controlled *ibuki* breathing techniques and the esoteric discipline of *reiki*, the projection and manipulation of *ki*. Yet rather than remain in Hawaii to await the day he would take his father's place as head of the Takeshita Budo-kai, Sensei both saddened and made his father proud by enlisting in the Army, both emotions arising from that undeniable sign of his son's Americanization.

"We always talked about one day visiting Japan together," Mac finished. "After the war." He started to say more, settled for a thoughtful sip of *sake*.

"Willie calls him 'the Colonel.' You call him *sensei*. That means master, right?"

"Teacher," Mac corrected, setting his cup back on the table. "It means teacher."

Martha smiled. "You call him teacher."

"It's more than that. I mean, you would call a, a schoolteacher *sensei*, any sort of formal instructor. But with others it's, different." He looked down at the *sushi* platter. "It's hard to explain."

"A mentor," Martha offered.

"Close enough. He was the sweetest, most kind man I ever knew." Mac laughed at Martha's surprise. Anyone who'd seen nothing of Takeshita but the 82nd's official DoD press photos would not have dared approach the unsmiling, severe man staring back at them, just as it had taken Mac months to work up the courage to tarry in the *dojo* after completing two hours of hard *ukemi* with the company, dripping sweat as he panted his carefully-rehearsed question. He had wilted beneath ten full seconds of narrow-eyed scrutiny before Takeshita had ordered him onto the mat with a grunt and a jerk of his head, body-slamming his exhausted student for half-an-hour in silent answer to his query before bowing and exiting without a word.

"I stayed after all the time after that," Mac went on. "Wasn't a day that went by where I wasn't aching. Guys used to call me 'Mac-sochist'." That drew a chuckle from Martha. "But he wasn't being cruel. Just trying to see how serious I was about learning. Making me better. Any refining process hurts, Sensei used to call it 'knocking off the corners.' Wasn't long before he was teaching me privately almost every night. Before long we began talking after, sometimes going out to eat."

Mac paused, swirling his *sake* in the tiny ceramic cup. "I don't know when he stopped being 'the Colonel' and just became, Sensei. I mean, he never did stop being my CO, but . . . "

"I know," Martha put in.

"I never knew my dad. He was Air Force, died in a plane crash on a one-day TDY hop while we were stationed in Tampa. I was nine, he was always working. Mom died while I was in basic, heart attack while she was grocery shopping." He shook his head gently to stave off the inevitable 'I'm sorry.' "Sensei wasn't married, no kids. None he ever told me about, at least," Mac appended with a grin which just as quickly faded as he became once more thoughtful. "He was the only man I ever knew whom I could trust completely. No matter what he told me to do, no matter how confused or frightened it made me sometimes, I always did it. Not because sometimes it was an order. Because it was Sensei. I didn't have to worry about my trust coming back and biting me in the butt."

"I can tell you really love him."

"Wish I'd shown it more." Mac raised his eyes to find Martha's fixed on his, her dark lips pursed in a soft smile. "What?"

"Just thinking of the Bible story. The prodigal son. The only thing on earth that could drag you down here from Montana, and it was him. He had to know what that meant."

Mac swallowed against an unexpected swell of emotion. He had always fancied that he was the closest thing Sensei had to a son and had always berated himself for the notion, deeming its source his own ego. But it was not ego he felt now. It was love, and with it a full realization that he'd never before voiced.

"He was my father," Mac murmured, amazed to hear himself say the words though he knew them to be true. His mind returned to Sensei's bedside at the clinic. 'How do you know him?' the nurse had asked.

"Sensei was my teacher. He was my friend."

"I wish I'd had the chance to meet him," Martha offered into the silence that followed.

"Yeah, me too. You would have liked him. He would have liked you."

Martha lifted her chin, spying the glint of gold beneath Mac's open shirt collar. "What's that? You don't strike me as the jewelry type."

Mac lifted the chain. Suspended from the end was a delicate *kanji* wrought in gold, no larger than a fingernail. He held it out so Martha could see it better. "It's beautiful," she murmured. "What is it?"

"It's *ki*. The Japanese *kanji* for *ki*, the ideograph. It means life energy. The universal spirit, the energy inside of us all that makes us all a part of everything."

"Sounds like love."

"Yeah," Mac said, staring at the pendant. "It is, ultimately." He dropped it back beneath his shirt. "Sensei gave it to me. Before I left for Montana. Going-away present." He changed the topic, pushing aside the spark of melancholia. "Try the *hamachi*."

"That's the one you said was your favorite, right?"

"One of them. *Uni's* my favorite, really."

"What's *uni*?"

"Sea urchin roe. Looks disgusting. Tastes great. Supposed to be an aphrodisiac."

He hadn't meant for the remark to sound like a come-on. A half-dozen clumsy explanatory retreats raced through his mind but Martha only smiled.

"Ever notice how all the weird and disgusting food is always sup-posed to be an aphrodisiac?" She busied herself dipping the *hamachi* into the *shoyu* as she spoke. "Oysters, snails — probably the only way to get anyone to try them."

She placed the morsel between her lips, nodding approval as she chewed and swallowed. "Maybe Mister Conner's my *sensei*. He's taught me more than anyone I've ever known. I don't mean just busi-ness. He knows people. How they think, what makes them tick."

"Some might call that using people."

"Is that what you call it?"

She was looking directly at Mac, her expression neutral, continued when Mac didn't reply. "Yes. He uses people."

"It doesn't bother you?"

"Sometimes," Martha replied. "It's what anyone in his position does. People are just another resource, to be exploited for as long as they produce. I understand that. I accept it." She selected her next piece of *sushi* as she spoke. "I've seen a lot of people quit, some get fired, some can't get past their resentment at being used long enough to see that what he's asking of them will make them better. Like Sensei said: knocking off the corners." She briefly held Mac's eye, raising the morsel to her mouth. "Learning is a contact sport."

"So how'd you get hooked up with him?"

She finished chewing before she spoke, washing down the mouth-ful with more *sake*. She didn't drink much as a rule, just a glass of wine before bed, and the dry brew was a relaxing change. "I was engaged to his son. Kevin."

She briefly related to Mac their meeting, she not long out of college, working sales at Terra Telecom's Raleigh headquarters, UniCom's primary communications holding. A chance encounter at the end of a hellish day, a row when she found him sitting in her cubicle, not knowing she was dressing down the boss's son.

Flowers and an charmingly apologetic note delivered to her desk an hour later had led to dinner that night, and that had been that. The dizzying, headlong courtship had left her breathless, his earnest professsions of love had swept her off her feet.

"He wanted to get married right away. Quit my job, have lots of babies, look good on his arm at parties. I loved him." He knew she loved him. He had to know. "But I'd worked hard to make a life of my own. I wasn't ready for marriage on those terms. There were things I still wanted to do, while I was young enough and single enough to do them. He said he was willing to wait."

It wasn't as easy as she'd thought it'd be. A moment passed, silent save for the noise of the other diners.

"What happened?" Mac finally asked.

"We were going to his father's for Christmas Eve. Seven years ago. He'd had this woodworking shop built out behind the house where we lived. Every power tool you could imagine. I don't know what he thought he was going to make. Hardly ever had the chance to use it."

The scene flashed through her mind unbidden, the smells of it, the sounds — calling for him inside the house as she emerged from the bathroom in her robe, hearing the answering dull report of the gunshot from outside; running terrified to the shed, wet winter grass freezing against her bare feet; flinging open the door to the scent of sawdust and oil and that acrid stench of smoke she would never forget; his body slumped on the floor against the workbench, his eyes still open, the back of his skull an explosion of blood and brains . . .

She didn't realize she'd stopped talking until she felt Mac's hand atop hers. "He shot himself," she finished. "I didn't even know he owned a gun."

Despite the evenness of her voice, Mac saw in her eyes grief that the years hadn't yet buffered. "Everything he wanted out of life was his, me included. Just, not right then. Guess he got tired of waiting."

And there was the rest of it. Grief, and guilt, both emotions Mac understood intimately. "I'm sorry," he said, knowing there was nothing else he could offer.

Martha briefly squeezed Mac's fingers before withdrawing her hand. "After Kevin's funeral I couldn't deal with working for UniCom, so I quit. Cleaned out my desk, cashed in the few bucks I had in my pension, closed out my savings and ran away." She'd driven around the country, everything she owned crammed into a backpack in the rear of her Jeep. She'd remained in Los Angeles long enough to tan before heading back East, selling the Jeep in Boston for her plane ticket to Europe. England, Scotland, then over the channel to France.

The image came easily to Mac as she talked; he pictured seeing her strolling down a Parisian street, her hair lifting in the breeze. It had been long then, she said, and it was Paris where she'd impulsively gotten her nose pierced. "I learned enough French to get by but not enough to get a job. Fourteen months I'd been gone. Blew every penny I had. I was living on water soup, wondering how I was going to get home."

She shook her head, remembering. "I didn't know how he tracked me down. Called my parents, I found out later. A messenger arrived with a plane ticket, first class to RDU. He was waiting for me at the airport. Just him, not Joseph. He still drove back then, when his hip let him. A week later he called me at my folks' and asked if I would come in and give his assistant a hand for the day. Then I became the assistant to the assistant and when she got pregnant and left five months later, he gave me the job. Been there ever since."

Mac listened to the echoes of his own journey sounded by Martha's story. They were not so different, really. More alike, in fact, that he would ever have suspected, right down to their choice of vehicles.

"What do you drive now?" Martha stared, then broke into throaty laughter. "What?"

"That's the first patently male comment I've heard you make since I've known you." She feigned seriousness. "I bought another Jeep. A blue one. Six-cell automatic, solar reserve, four-wheel drive, SmartNav onboard GPS uplink, dual in-dash com ports . . . "

"All right, all right," Mac surrendered, laughing at Martha's exaggerated Southern drawl. "I just never would have guessed you'd drive a Jeep."

She grinned, idly poking her chopsticks into the mound of *wasabi*. "Makes us even. I never would have guessed you'd agree to do the moondrop. I'm glad you decided to stick around."

"You're going to have to tell me what that means."

"I was hoping you'd already figured it out."

Mac flushed, covered the awkward moment by re-filling the *sake* cups, feeling foolish for being the first to look away. He watched as Martha idly gathered a generous dollop of *wasabi* on the end of her chopsticks and stuck it in her mouth, rolling it around on her tongue. She looked up to find Mac staring at her in rapt expectation. "What?"

"That's *wasabi*."

"Yeah . . . ?" she began, then stopped cold. Her eyes shot wide open as she went rigid, sucking a long lungful of air through her nose as the potent vapors assailed her sinuses. Mac tried to stifle his laughter and failed, watched helplessly as Martha's hand pounced on her *sake* cup. She tossed back the shot and finally exhaled, eyes watering.

"God almighty! What was that?"

"Japanese horseradish. Nuclear strength."

"You could have warned me!"

"You didn't give me any time!" His laughter subsided as she dabbed at her tearing eyes with her napkin. "It really is good," he offered helpfully.

Martha guffawed and then they were both laughing. Mac refilled her cup. She raised it between them.

"Here's to Sensei, and your friends."

Mac raised his cup. "And to Kevin."

They each held the other's gaze and knew they understood one another.

III

He walked her to her blue Jeep, parked four spaces away from his UniCom sedan. He wasn't certain who stopped first, it seemed as if they slowed at some silent, mutual signal. *Sake* took one from the feet up but this woman he wouldn't debase by blaming his desire on wine. He drank her as they kissed, her mouth opening against his, felt his thirst intensify as her hands slid beneath his open jacket and sought the small of his back, pulling him against her.

The Europa was closer. He followed her Jeep, pulled in next to it, was at her door as she emerged. Their hands were less chaste as they whetted the edge of their appetite, the decision to surrender now forgone. Mac glanced at the sundries shop as they crossed the hotel lobby, read his answer in Martha's knowing shake of her head.

They said nothing as they made their way to Mac's room, did not hesitate as the door closed behind them. Their clothes fell in a pile around their feet and there they greedily took one another in the dark, open-throated moans and damp bodies moving together against the papered walls of the narrow foyer to a shuddering, gasping stop.

Their second time was longer, more deliberate, an unabashed exploration of one another atop the stripped plateau of the bed. Her skin was impossibly smooth, her language open and graceful and supple. They traded the lead with touch and murmured words, entreating and obeying in turn, she taking pleasure in his ready compliance, his tender empathy in contrast to the hard muscle of his torso as they finished with her atop him, his hands on her hips, pulling himself into her. She felt again that fine warm vibration which seemed to suffuse him, its surging intensity filling her in waves as she arched forward over his bucking body, her final cry in answer to his own.

Their third time surprised them both.

"You didn't tell me you got your navel pierced, too."

Martha rested her hand atop Mac's on her belly. "I went back, on a dare. My little secret when I'm dressed in my work clothes."

"You're not at all what I expected."

"What did you expect?"

"Someone who doesn't have a gold ring in her navel."

"I didn't expect you to be so limber. Sensei teach you that, too?"

She enjoyed his rumbling chuckle against her bare back. "We weren't that close."

She had wondered how she would feel, making love for the first time since Kevin's death, if she would feel any guilt. She wondered if Mac had similar thoughts, ending his years of penitent denial in a hotel room a thousand miles from home.

She felt his hand stir beneath hers, closed her eyes as it moved lower, opened herself to the answer.

Five

I

The first two-hundred punches always came hard. They hurt, bad enough to necessitate placing the mind elsewhere, on anything. Four punches per inhalation, four more as Mac exhaled, breaths pluming in the crisp night air, the solid metronome thud of his knuckles against the rope marking an internal tempo separate from time. Over and over he punched, settling into the rhythm. Nothing but him and the *makiwara*, his breathing and the blows as the pain in his callused knuckles slowly faded into that familiar numbness, his hard fists transformed into twin flesh hammers.

He was standing in the back yard of his new digs, a modest two-bedroom single-story in a quiet suburban neighborhood in Cary, a mile from the interstate. Conner kept the furnished home for long-term guests and consultants; swank though the Europa was, it was still a hotel. Martha had told him and Price about the offer before her departure early that morning, said they could move in Monday but neither Mac nor Price had seen any reason to wait.

Price had asked Mac over breakfast how he'd slept. Mac's evasive answer had died on his lips as he saw Price's amused smirk. Their rooms adjoined, and it seemed hotel walls were universally thin.

They'd moved in just after noon. Mac had driven around the neighborhood buying groceries and a handful of materiel from the only hardware store not closed for Sunday. As Price stowed the supplies Mac had spent an hour turning a scrap piece of two-by-six lumber and fifty feet of cotton rope into his *makiwara*, wrapping most of the rope in tight rows around the board until it overlaid about ten inches of the surface.

147

Traditional Okinawan *makiwara* were made of tightly-twisted rice straw; Sensei's had been a piece of canvas-covered tire tread nailed to a plank on the side of the base *dojo*. Mac used the rest of the rope to secure the *makiwara* to one of the pines dotting the postage stamp back yard.

It looked too new but it would do. He needed the *makiwara* now, to beat down the unfamiliar, lingering giddiness of his impassioned night with Martha. Needed its discipline to remind him of the real reason he'd agreed to stay.

It was just after dark, the shouts of children playing coming faint from a nearby home, the occasional soft crawling of tires from a passing car audible from the street in front of the house. All those lives, suspended in the moment as Mac punched, deep in his meditation. He was constant and they were only passing by. Everything, passing him by . . .

Over and over, Mac attacked. Over and over he was thrown. Sweat-drenched, he lunged at Sensei. In a blink he was airborne, tugged off of his feet as if borne on a gust of wind. He hit the mat and tumbled to his feet, pivoting instantly to find Sensei once again waiting, once again inviting him to attack.

His exhausted thighs burned as he pushed himself to his feet and staggered forward, pouring the last of his strength into his chambered his left arm to deliver a *yokomen-uchi* strike to the side of Sensei's head. In an instant Sensei was in his face, right hand slashing down atop Mac's striking wrist, left hand held against his opposite shoulder as he moved *irimi*, the entering defense, capturing Mac's *ki* while it was still focused backwards.

The *kiai* hit Mac like a steamship horn. His upper body arrested, his legs continued forward, off the mat until he was suspended in mid-air, staring past his feet at the ceiling before dropping like a bag of wet sand. He huffed as he impacted, his stiff neck too tired to keep his head from bouncing off the canvas as he took the hard fall from *kata*-otoshi.

Sensei stood over him, not winded at all. "That's all for tonight, I think."

Mac moved into *seiza* and bowed, sweat dripping from his nose as his forehead touched the mat, Sensei bowing in return. They rose. Mac snagged his towel from the corner, wiping his face and neck gratefully while Sensei removed his skirt-like *hakama*.

"You feel better now?" They were the first words he'd spoken to Mac all night other than instruction.

"*Hai*, Sensei."

"Mm. Where are the others?"

"Back at the hooch."

"Why aren't you there?"

"Too wound up, I guess."

"It's a drop," said Sensei, knowing what was really troubling his student. "Same as any other."

"Not the same, Sensei." Mac idly folded the damp towel. "Not without Willie." Price was still in hospital, recovering from the injury that had claimed his legs a month earlier. Mac had visited him practically every day since. "All the guys are feeling it. It's quiet as a church back there. Even Nick."

Nick Kaligolos considered it his duty to keep the atmosphere light the night before a drop, belting out his bawdy compositions as he strummed his guitar. Not tonight, though. When the somber mood had finally become more than Mac could bear he'd grabbed his *gi* and made for the *dojo*.

"It's still the same," Sensei gently insisted. "A drop, a punch, all the same."

He delivered a slow punch to Mac's chest. "Do not put your mind here," he said, tapping his fist with his other hand. "The blow will come, regardless of what you think, what you feel, what you expect. Do not let your *ki* become trapped by what might be. It's difficult enough to deal with what *is*," he finished, pressing his fist against Mac's chest on the last word, forcing Mac to take a step backwards to avoid losing his balance. Sensei *tsk-tsked* in mock criticism. "Besides," he continued, dropping his fist, "William will still be with you. In here," and he touched his one-point.

"I know. But it's just not the same without him." He looked his mentor in the eye, at last confessing his heart. "I'm scared. I can't get out from under it. I've been scared before but it was different. Willie was always there, we were a team, we were whole." He stopped talking, afraid that giving full voice to his fears would in some way make what he dreaded real. "I know I should be past feeling this way."

"I'd be more worried if you said you weren't scared," Sensei countered. "Absence of fear isn't courage. Doing what we must despite our fear, that's courage. *Neh?*"

Mac bowed and Sensei bowed in return. "I should be getting back," said Mac, turning away. "Get some sleep before oh-five-thirty."

"We're not finished here."

Surprised, Mac tossed the towel into the corner and obediently moved towards the center of the mat. Sensei followed and Mac waited for his instruction to attack. Instead, his teacher knelt in *seiza*, waiting. Mac knelt before him.

"What rank are you?"

"Captain Mackinley Harrison, sir." He saluted, but his mirth at the small joke vanished as he regarded Sensei's stern face. "I don't know, Sensei. You never said."

"A belt is nothing more than something to hold your *gi* jacket closed," Sensei began, gravely formal. "But my grandfather said they collect the *ki* of those who wear them, and I believe that to be true. Traditionally, all belts were white. As one studied, the dirt and sweat turned them darker. Washing them was said to wash away the *ki*. It also shrinks them," he said, and this time he allowed himself a small smile. "So we do not wash them. The darker the belt, therefore, the more experienced the student. But that's not the goal, to make a belt black, to have a black belt. It is nothing.

"As we continue to study, the black of experience wears away, to reveal once more the white of innocence." Sensei touched his own frayed belt, more gray now than black, the outer fabric worn away in strings to reveal a new layer of white below. "And the cycle continues. From student, to teacher, to student. One and the same. One life, one journey without end. Yet the *ki* grows ever stronger.

"You have never once asked me about rank, Mackinley. Your desire has been only to study and to learn. That is the way it should be. And you have learned well."

Sensei removed his belt, held it in his hands before him, the limp ends flowing across his palms and onto his thighs like a waterfall. "*Osu,*" he said, nodding to Mac's waist.

Mac moved trance-like, fumbling with the knot until his belt was off, held in his hands before him as Sensei held his own. With a deep, formal bow, Yoshi Takeshita Sensei presented his belt to Mac, the belt he had worn for over forty years. Mac accepted it reverently, exchanging it for his own. Sensei affixed Mac's belt around his waist as Mac did the same with Sensei's — no longer Sensei's. Mac's now. From master to student, student to master. The cycle was complete.

Mac tugged the knot taut and raised his head, deeply moved. They bowed, Mac touching his forehead to the mat, remaining there for several moments, hoping to convey to Sensei his gratitude, his honor and his respect, his love.

They rose at last. It seemed to Mac that he saw moisture glistening in Sensei's eyes. That was all it took. Mac blinked and felt water on his face.

"Thank you, Sensei," he croaked. "*Domo arigato gozaimasu.*"

"I have much love for you, Mackinley."

They embraced for the first time, Mac's eyes closed, cheek pressed against his father's, breathing his musk as Sensei held him tightly.

Mac stood unmoving before the *makiwara*. He didn't know when he'd stopped punching. Sensei's memory hung in his mind, pushing everything else away.

He lifted one end of the tattered belt he wore, nine years of his *ki* now intertwined with Sensei's. Mac still considered the belt to forever be Sensei's; a gift to him, priceless, but Mac would never be its owner, only its caretaker. It wasn't hard at that moment to imagine Sensei was still alive. And he was, Mac knew. *Ki* never died. Like the belt, it was only passed on.

"Hey Mac!" Price's voice floated out of the house. Mac bowed to the *makiwara* in gratitude for its lesson and headed inside.

Price was seated at a desk in the corner of the den, his computer atop it. Unbeknownst to Mac, he'd called Charleston the Friday before and instructed his staff to box it up and air freight it to him at the hotel. It had been waiting for them in its aluminum suitcase when they'd returned from the DZ.

The monitor was conventional, a 22-inch 3-D flat display on a swivel mount. So was the roll-up keypad, but the rest of Price's system was unlike any Mac had ever seen, obviously custom-built by its user. The primary drive, barely three fingers wide, busily chirped to one side, a separate coolant pump attached in back — the system ran hot. There were two smaller ancillary devices whose function Mac couldn't determine, fiber-op'ed to the primary drive. Red and amber pinlights fluttered on the front of one of them while the larger was cylindrical, with a closed circular door atop it. A lone lamp crowded into the far right corner of the desktop and the monitor's glow provided the only iillumination.

Mac sat in the desk chair to the right of Price, wiped his face with the sleeve of his *gi*. After his time outside the house felt like a sauna. "Damn, how high do you have the heat set, ninety?"

"Wah wah wah," Price mimicked, his eyes not leaving the screen. He was wearing glasses, something Mac'd never before seen him do. Age was catching up with them both. "Check it out."

Price nodded to the monitor where the animated Terra Telecom logo danced, hyperlinked menus arranged in frames around it. Mac had never seen a 3-D effect so clean, the words and images seeming to float enticingly in the air before the glass panel, begging touch. UniCom's *Max-Q* logo was stamped on the monitor frame; evidently Price wasn't above sleeping with the enemy. He flicked his right index finger, a VR thimble on the tip, pinlight glowing active. The floating display pointer obediently darted to the volume control slider. Mac heard stirring orchestral music.

"Nice, huh? Almost makes you wanna run right out and buy everything they make." Price clicked the volume off. "Terra Telecom's cybernet homepage. UniCom's got one for each of its subsidiaries, dozens of them all linked, one giant cyberspace sales pitch. Worse than Microsoft used to be."

"Who?"

Price let the topic drop, opened a small plastic case and lifted a translucent inch-diameter ball which shone gold in the light, careful to hold it by the dark ring which encircled it. Two more were nestled inside their padded cradles within the box. "Ever seen one of these?"

"On a golf course."

"Funny. Crystal ball, my friend. The latest in data storage." He moved the ball near the lamp, illuminating the amber translucence within. "Quartz and copper and gold and a bunch of other stuff. Three-thousand bucks a pop." Mac whistled. "Worth it, though. Each one of these can hold twenty times the data of the most dense storage disc with a read-write transfer rate a hundred times faster, it'll give as quick as you ask with no data degradation. My DPU clocks at 220 gigahertz and I haven't had a lock-up yet."

He placed the ball into the cylindrical ancillary drive, closing the lid atop it. Immediately, a graphic window opened on the monitor screen:

TerraTel App, ver. 2 .2

Below floated two buttons, *Run* and *Cancel*. Price moved the pointer over the *Run* button.

"Gaze into my crystal ball," he pronounced mock-dramatically. "Behold Conner's secrets!" His finger tapped against the air.

The Terra Telecom page disappeared, replaced by a wild chiaroscuro of colors and textures, images and text flashing by in furious sequence. The primary drive softly chittered as Price raptly watched the screen, his glasses reflecting the racing monitor view. "Sic 'em, baby," he murmured.

Suddenly, the screen went dark, save for a single blinking cursor in the upper left corner.

"What's that?"

"What computers look like with their clothes off." Price tapped the keypad and a businesslike screen appeared:

Universal Communications Inc.
Netframe Menu (ver. 6 .21)
Access Requires L10 Authentication
See SysOp for Registry

Mac realized he was staring at the front door to UniCom's main computer network. "Jesus, Willie. You *have* been a busy boy."

"Idle hands are the devil's tools. I'd read about secure systems like this but I'd never seen one first-hand until I tried getting in."

"Looks pretty basic to me."

Price let the comment pass unchallenged; Mac's ignorance of computers had been a source of ribbing as far back as the war. He thumbnailed the basics. They were presently looking at the front door to UniCom's netframe: like any, users connected to a network node and the server dynamically assigned an address, which remained while the network led the user by the hand to their destinations. The larger the network, the more hierarchical it was — sub-divided into smaller networks, each of which handled its own routing, to make navigation and maintenance easier.

"And that's where this gets tricky," said Price. He waggled a finger at the monitor. "Not only does each sub-net here have its own unique nodes, and not *only* do you have to negotiate a new address each time you get routed to a new sub-net, but the sub-nets *themselves* don't have fixed addresses within the main network. That's the new stuff I was talking about. G-nets. Ghost network. One second it's there, the next second it's disappeared.

"And I do mean second," Price emphasized. He again indicated the monitor, patiently displaying the UniCom netframe welcome. "We can stay here all day and that'll never go away. But the sub-nets constantly move around within the main network and unless you've got authorized business being there, when one disappears, so does your connection to it. And there's five sub-nets you've gotta get through to get to the one where Conner lives, five dynamic addresses you've got to negiotiate and re-negotiate and re-re-negotiate every second you're inside, like having links in a chain disappear at random. If you don't slap a new link in the hole right away, the chain collapses. Not to mention you've got to find it again every time it moves. And of course, each sub-net has its own password protocol, and so do all the trees and directories . . . "

Price trailed off, manipulating the pointer over a series of menu buttons, navigating confidently through each revealed screen as the crystal drive whined. "Correct me if I'm wrong," Mac put in after a time, "but this is illegal, right?"

"Only if you get caught," muttered Price.

"What's our chances of that happening?" Price didn't reply. "That bad, huh?"

After a few more moments Price sat back in his chair. "We're there."

Mac stared at the quiescent image on the monitor: the UniCom logo and a single pulsing square in the upper-right corner. "We're where?"

"If I'm right, the door to Conner's personal file directory."

"That fast? You just said it was hard." Price shot him a baleful look over the top of his glasses. "How're you gonna past the tactile verification?"

Price raised an eyebrow. "Keep using terms like that and folks are gonna think you know something. Thumbprint on the screen's no good without a digital record of it in the computer, so like everything else it's just ones and zeroes, just another password only it never changes, which actually makes it easier for nefarious sorts like me. Get it once, you don't need to do it again."

Price removed the crystal ball and replaced it in the case, removed a second and dropped it into the drive. Another access window opened on the screen:

X ver. 1 .0

"I'd just finished writing this when I got the call to come up here. Haven't had the chance to try it yet. Or the nerve." Price guffawed at Mac's worried expression. "Relax, brother. Haven't been caught yet, and I don't intend to be."

"What happens if it doesn't work?"

"Hopefully, nothing. Unless someone's watching, and that's what Rufus is for." He tapped the second ancillary drive. "My watchdog. Anyone peeks in on us, he'll kick up a fuss."

"And if he does?"

"How fast can you pack?"

"Pretty goddamn fast."

"Hold that thought." Price clicked on the *Run* button.

The monitor repeated its visual gymnastics, this time lasting only a second or two. Almost as soon as it began the search ended. A window in the center of the monitor declared *Password Accepted* then disappeared, replaced by a graphic file directory tree.

Price sagged backwards in his chair, his delighted laughter filling the room. He extended the VR thimble to Mac.

"You may kiss the ring."

Mac took the arm and hauled his friend erect. Price rubbed his hands together, clicked on the *File* icon at the top of the screen, then selected *Search* from the revealed menu. A textbox opened, the I-beam blinking patiently inside. He pulled the keypad closer. Mac spied the wireless headset perched on the desk to Price's right. "How come you don't use that?" he asked, jerking his chin towards it.

Price glanced over. "Your voiceprint still on file with DoD?"

"Ah," Mac admitted, feeling stupid: any voice commands Price might enter could be recorded and matched to his military record. Price tapped his right thumb and index finger together, deactivating the VR thimble. Carefully, he typed, *stormcloud* appearing letter by letter in the box.

"That's capitalized," Mac offered. Price ignored him. Below the textbox were two smaller boxes, labeled *Specific* and *Related*. Price reactivated the thimble, selected *Related*, clicked the *OK* button. A second a list of directories and files appeared instantly.

"Jesus," Mac breathed. Dozens of directories and files filled the screen, all of them holding some mention of Stormcloud. "You were right."

"Yeah, looks that way, doesn't it?"

"What's wrong?"

"It's too easy, too easy," Price distractedly replied, his voice betraying his suspicion. "Never gotten this far without being spotted. I mean, I'd like to be able to pat myself on the back, but . . . " He scratched his head briskly. "Ahhhh, shit."

He dropped his hands and clicked on the first file in the list. Immediately, a window opened:

Password?

Price exhaled. "Okay, now I feel better."

"You know the password?"

"Nope," Price replied. "Not my job." He waggled his fingers and the signature window of his decryption program reappeared. He clicked the *Run* button. The window was replaced by an amber graphic bar that slowly crept across the window from left to right:

Working. . . .

Long seconds crawled by as they watched, waiting for the program to do its work. "C'mon, baby, c'mon . . . ," Price murmured. "Don't make your papa look foolish . . . "

Password Accepted

Price stared. "Son of a bitch."

"It worked!"

"Yeah, it worked." Price was already removing the second crystal ball from the drive. He set it aside, swiftly lifting the third from the box and dropping it home.

"What's the matter?"

"I just have a real bad feeling about this all of a sudden. The sooner we're outta here, the better I'll feel." He was already highlighting the files and directories, working briskly. "Get 'em all, sort 'em out later . . . "

Suddenly, a high-pitched yapping filled the room, for all the world sounding like a dog's bark. Price's head jerked over to the security drive — red pinlights were flashing rapidly in concert to the bizarre alarm. At the same time a crimson message blinked in the center of the screen:

WARNING!
REMOTE SURVEILLANCE DETECTED!

"Shit!" Price typed furiously. He slammed his finger down on the *Enter* key. The alarm still blared. He tried again, his fingers a blur, then snatched the headset from the table and held it to his mouth: "Rufus, kill!"

The screen image instantly blinked out. The alarm died, leaving only the fading whine of the main drive's coolant pump. Then that was gone.

Price sagged in his chair, his head lolling back on his shoulders as he gave a long exhale. Mac took a deep breath to calm his thumping heart.

"You think they saw us?"

Price removed his glasses and tossed them with the headset onto the table, rubbing his face with his hands. "I dunno. Maybe. That's never happened before."

"I thought you said they'd detected you before . . . "

Price dropped his hands, shaking his head. "They knew I was looking around but they've never nailed me. Rufus is supposed to bark when they get close but they were right on top of me before he even saw 'em."

He slapped the arms of his chair, suddenly furious. "God-dammit! That was *it*, Mac! It was *right there!* Just another ten seconds. Son of a . . . "

He pushed away from the desk in disgust and rolled into the kitchen, leaving Mac staring at the blank monitor.

"Another few seconds, sir."

Conner watched his monitor, Leslie Trang's image in a window at the bottom right corner, her matronly face bathed in the glow of her workstation.

"Got it." She frowned. "It's local." An address and telephone number appeared on Conner's screen. "Recorded a one-point-four-six-second vox command just before termination. I'll copy it to security when I alert —"

"No," Conner said. "I'll handle this one myself."

"Yes, sir."

"Well done, Leslie. Superb work, as always."

Trang pulled a stray wisp of gray hair away from her face as she looked full into the camera at Conner. "Thank you, sir. I wouldn't mind knowing who it is . . . "

"Thank you, Leslie."

"Yes, sir. Good-night."

Trang's image winked out. Conner consulted his Rolodex, selected a number and dialed.

II

Price took another pull on his beer, careful to set the bottle well away from his hardware. He drank too much he knew, but he wasn't an alcoholic. God knows he'd tried after the accident. He couldn't bring himself to call it his wound, or his injury. Those words were used for things that would heal. His legs weren't coming back.

Price's job with the 82nd had been combat computer intelligence, CCI. He'd been one of the first in the specialty, dictated by the changing face of warfare. Working with Lieutenant Huey Quinn he could access, download and destroy most any computer system known, under fire, returning from battle with hostage data more valuable than any living, breathing POW. If he couldn't access the data, he tore open the computer and ripped out the data core like the still-beating heart of his enemy. And if he couldn't do that, he shot the damn thing, on principle. If the military handed out medals for killing computers like they did for killing human beings, Price's dress uniform would have weighed fifty pounds.

Price was the best at what he did, then. Now it was all he did. A computer couldn't wake you with a kiss in the morning, but it was always there when he got home.

He removed his glasses and rubbed his grainy eyes. He'd been puzzling it out all night, reviewing the computer's autolog of his aborted hacker session into UniCom's netframe. There was no other explanation: they had been waiting for him, had allowed him easier access to Conner's directory as bait. Once he'd ID'd his target, the autolog showed all those shifting nodal addresses he'd taken for granted had coalesced into a static pipeline down which the host had reached and grabbed him by the throat.

His faced flushed hot. It had seemed poetic irony a few hours ago, hacking UniCom from a home Conner himself owned. But he hadn't taken his usual precautions, routing his connection through a labyrinth of outside comnets. Too cocky, too intent on impressing Mac, too tantalized by the prospect of finally discovering answers. God only knew what his impudence might have cost them.

He glanced at the chronometer. It was almost one-thirty in the morning; Mac had gone to bed two hours ago. Price saved his work and powered down the system. He yawned as he thumbed off the VR thimble and stretched, joints crackling like snapped toothpicks. He took another long pull from his beer, absently setting the nearly empty bottle on the desk to his left as he searched for his glasses.

His fingers were releasing the bottle just as his mind registered that the bottom had caught the edge of the closed crystal container to his left. He lunged for the bottle as it toppled, reaching cross-body as his left hand grasped the desk's edge. He managed to prevent warm beer from drenching several thousand dollars worth of hardware but the crystal container went sliding across the desk, disappearing into the space between it and the wall.

Price cursed, wiping his beer-soaked hand on his pants. He placed the bottle well out of harm's way and pushed back, craning his neck to peer into the space where the container had fallen. He thought he could see a darker shadow there but his arm was too thick to reach in and retrieve it. He'd need Mac's help to move the desk. It would keep until morning.

He snagged the bottle and extinguished the lamp, plunging the room into darkness. He glanced over at the alarm control panel next to the front door. The tiny red light blinked, indicating the system was armed.

He stuck the bottle between his legs and tiredly headed for the kitchen to drop it off, and thence to bed.

III

He stepped out of the vehicle into the deserted street, pushing the door closed, leaving it unlocked. The small briefcase he held in his gloved hand weighed hardly anything at all. He made his way to the house, striding briskly down the street and up to the front door as if he belonged there.

He carefully slid the key into the lock. The windows had been dark for half-an-hour, but he had no way of knowing if everyone inside was asleep. He turned the key and slowly opened the door a few inches, scanning the narrow opening. The security chain wasn't engaged and there was nothing but darkness beyond, no sound. He returned the key to his coat pocket and slipped inside, keeping the knob turned as he closed the door, slowly released it. The bolt slid soundlessly home.

He located the alarm control panel, tapped in the four-digit disarm code. The blinking red pinlight turned green. Only now did he allow himself to pause. He listened, straining his ears for the slightest noise emanating from the depths of the darkened house.

Nothing.

He gently lowered the briefcase to the floor, withdrew the black stocking mask from his outer coat pocket and tugged it on over his head. It was hot inside the house, sweat was already beading on his top lip. Dressed as he was, he knew he'd soon be drenched. He wasn't planning on sticking around long enough for it to be a problem.

From the other coat pocket he withdrew the slender night vision ocular and held it to his eye, scanning the room as he took the briefcase in hand. The furnishings glowed a ghostly phosphorescent green, the ocular magnifying the pale streetlight spilling in through the front window. There was a wall to his right, a sofa and low coffee table. To his left was another wall, more furnishings. That wall flowed to what he knew from the floorplan was the hall which ran left towards the bedrooms, sharing an opening with the kitchen and dining room.

There it was. The object of his search.

He crept across the room to the desk, a single straight-backed chair to the side of it. He placed the briefcase atop it, lowering the ocular long enough to gently ease each latch back with both hands, forestalling the soft 'click' as they disengaged. From within he removed a single unlabeled computer disk.

He located the slot in the front of the computer, inserted the silvered disk and powered up the system. The monitor came to life, bathing the room with its soft glow.

There were only a half-dozen or so disks on the table, dropped amid scrawled notes. He quickly gathered all he could see and deposited the lot into the otherwise empty briefcase. The boot disk would take about twenty seconds to do its work, he'd been told, maybe less. Then he could get the hell out of there . . .

WOOF!

He jumped at the sound. It sounded exactly like a dog's bark, only it had come from the computer, loud in the dead silence. The ocular darted to his eye and he peered anxiously down the hallway. Every door he saw appeared to be closed save for the open bathroom door at the far end. He detected no movement, heard nothing. Perhaps his luck would hold after all.

He wiped sweat from his eyes with the back of his gloved hand, waiting even more impatiently for the boot cycle to run its course. God, it was hotter than hell in the house.

"Hey!"

He whirled. A man in a wheelchair emerged from the darkened hallway, clad in boxer shorts and a tee-shirt. His face was hard. "What the fuck . . . !"

The interloper was on him in an instant, firing off a right side kick to his chest. Price twisted in his chair, grunting as he caught the brunt of the force on his left shoulder. He wrapped his arms around the leg and torqued his body, was rewarded by his attacker's yelp of pain as he was thrown to the floor. He scrambled to his feet as Price called out:

"Mac! Mac!"

He slammed the briefcase closed as Price moved towards him, surprisingly fast. The desk chair toppled as he lifted the case and feinted with it. Price raised his arms to block the expected blow and instead caught the full force of a front kick with his sternum. The air left his lungs and the wheelchair toppled backwards. His attacker dashed for the front door . . .

Something crashed into his back. He sprawled face-first onto the floor, his chin abrading on the carpet. His left arm cracked against the coffee table, knocking the briefcase from his grasp.

He felt an arm snake around the left side of his neck; fast, competent, forearm seeking his carotid, going for a choke. He twisted into the limb and drove his right elbow up and behind him, felt contact, heard a grunt as the weight on his back fell away. He sprang to his feet, favoring his right leg as hot pain shot through the wrenched knee. Before him stood Mac: naked, knees bent, arms held at the ready before him — hands open, elbows in.

The intruder glanced to his right at the dark shape of the briefcase lying half-atop the coffee table. In that instant Mac was on him, flashing in to his right as he feinted with his left and his right fist drove towards his ribs. The thief dropped his left arm, blocking the blow as he slid right in a mirror stance and fired off a punch to Mac's head with his right fist. Mac spun out of the way and disengaged. The split-second ballet ended, the two men now facing each other from the exact opposite positions in which they had stood before.

"Who are you?" demanded Mac.

He panted. The briefcase was now to his left, just a foot or two away. He might be able to reach it without being attacked again but he'd still have to make it to the door. And his opponent stood in the way.

Mac watched the masked intruder drop into a low defensive stance, right side forward, narrowing his profile. His right arm was extended out before him, just above waist level, his left raised to ward against an inside attack. Whomever he was he was a trained fighter, but it was obvious all he wanted to do was get out, with whatever was in that briefcase.

Mac remained in *shizentai*, natural posture, facing forward with his arms held out loosely before him. The fault in his opponent's stance is that it made him vulnerable to an attack from his own left — he was telegraphing his response, ensuring he'd have to rely on a weaker reverse punch or kick if Mac attacked on the right side, wasting the previous time it would take for him to shift into a more workable stance.

He tossed a token handful of *ki* to his right, flicking his focus in that direction as he twitched his right wrist. The thief took the bait, reacting to the subtle feint by fading a few inches, pivoting back to his left, warding with his right against the expected attack, exposing his rear.

It was all the opening Mac needed. He moved *tenkan*, flowing forward to the outside, sliding on his left foot as he fired off a distracting *atemi* with his right hand. His opponent clumsily twisted to his right, raising his right arm in a desperate block. Mac pivoted 180-degrees to the outside, capturing the intruder's arm and leading him off-balance in a tight circle. He waited for that instant where he felt no resistance then smoothly reversed direction, clamping onto the man's right wrist and cutting it outwards to the left and down, *kote-gaeshi*. His adversary was pitched over his own right shoulder, thudding into the floor with a guttural cry of pain.

Mac reached for his foe's elbow, going for a pin, but with speed born of desperation the man spun on his back, disengaging from the lock and driving his shin into the back of Mac's left knee. Mac retained his grasp on the wrist as he fell backwards, bending his head forward protectively as his back slammed into the floor. He scrambled to maneuver the intruder's arm between his knees, thrusting his right foot beneath the other man's torso, left leg over his neck, trying for an *ude-gatame* lock against the elbow, but his adversary seemed to know what was coming. He bent his elbow and slid out from beneath the pinning leg. He rolled into Mac, rose and straddled his waist, raising his left arm to strike.

Mac yanked on the man's still-captured wrist. His foe was momentarily off-balanced, long enough for Mac to land a satisfyingly hard punch to his left eye. The man grunted and rolled off and Mac tumbled backwards over his shoulder, rising in one smooth motion, facing the sofa.

The intruder grabbed the briefcase from the coffee table as he lurched to his feet, made a reckless dash for the door. Mac lunged after him. With a wild surge of frantic energy Mac's quarry swung the briefcase back-handed, throwing everything he had into the effort.

The corner of the briefcase caught Mac a glancing blow to his left temple. He saw stars for a moment as he stumbled backwards. When his vision cleared, the door was open.

He raced outside, trying to look everywhere at once. He stopped in the middle of the street, forgetting his nakedness.

A few moments later, he thought he heard a vehicle crank, up the street to his left: internal combustion, poorly-tuned. In a few seconds the engine rattle faded away. The intruder, if it was him at the wheel, was gone.

Mac trotted back into the house. Price was sitting up, rubbing his chest and swearing softly. Mac knelt beside him. "You okay?"

"No. You get him?"

"No."

"Wonderful."

Mac righted Price's chair and helped his friend back into it. "You check the alarm before you went to bed?"

"Yeah, yeah, it was on."

"Then whoever that was had the code. And a key."

"Looks that way . . . " Price stared at the desk. "Aw, man!"

He pushed himself over to his computer, scanning the active system. Jiggling pixels of color filled the monitor, like thousands of glowing fleas. Price tapped a few keys on the keypad to no effect.

"God-dammit! He stabbed the disk release button on the tower drive and hurled the silvered circle across the room. "Sumbitch loaded a virus, trashed the whole system!" Price gritted his teeth against his anger, slapping the keypad in disgust with the tips of his fingers. "Stole my notes, too. If Rufus booting up hadn't gotten me out of bed, God knows what else he might have done."

"He get everything? All the disks, the programs?"

"Yes, he got —" Price paused, remembering. "Help me move the desk."

Mac stepped to the exposed end of the desk and pulled it away from the wall. There was a soft 'thud' as something hit the floor at the opposite end. Price pushed his chair tight against the wall and reached into the widened opening. His hand came out holding the crystal container. He opened it and checked the contents.

"No. He didn't get everything."

Mac walked to the front door and pushed it shut, re-armed the alarm. He picked up the viral disk from the floor beneath the window and crossed back to the desk, tossing the disk atop it. As he bent over to right the toppled chair his toe struck something on the floor, kicking it against the wheel of Price's carriage. He retrieved the object, holding it up so Price could see. Both of them recognized it immediately.

"Field issue," Price opined.

"Uh huh." Mac turned it over in his hand and read the UniCom maker's mark. "Can't get this at your neighborhood spy shop," he said, handing the night vision ocular to Price so he could read the etched writing.

"Well, that answers your question," Price grumbled, tossing the ocular onto the desk top. It rolled to a stop against the drive. "Conner most definitely saw us."

"Sloppy work."

"Tell that to my computer." He glanced at Mac. "You're bleeding."

Mac gingerly dabbed his temple where the briefcase had struck him. The small wound was already clotting. "He knows we're on to him," Mac said, absently wiping his red fingers on his thigh as he thought it through. "But he doesn't want anybody to know that. He hires someone to steal your stuff. He could have just as easily sicced his security on us."

"Maybe he did."

"Maybe," Mac agreed. "But I doubt they'd wear stocking masks. Even if it was his boy, Conner has to know that we'd figure out he was the one behind this. The key, the alarm code — whoever it was didn't even try to make it look like a burglary."

"Maybe he was supposed to but didn't have time."

Mac shook his head. "He would've just grabbed the computer and split, saved himself a bunch of aggravation." He sat in the chair opposite Price. The adrenaline rush of the battle was gone now, leaving him drained. "You think Conner knows what we were after?"

Price poked at the back of his battered skull, wincing as he spoke. "Assuming they were watching us at least at the very end, there's a good chance he does, yeah. We'll never get back in."

"You've still got your crystal ball things."

"But no computer. Except for my laptop, and that won't cut it."

"We'll get you another one —"

Price interrupted, irritated. "Mac, if I had a brand-new system right *now* I wouldn't get past first base! Smart money says they're already modifying their security! I would be, in their place!" His eyes were pained at his own folly. "I'll never get in again! It is *over*, man, I have blown this all to hell. Wouldn't be surprised if his goons snapped the cuffs on me this morning. Computer espionage, there's ten years to start."

Mac felt himself anger at Price's uncharacteristic self-pity. "Willie, shut up."

Price closed his mouth, glaring as Mac briskly ticked off the points on his fingers. "One: we now know for certain that Conner's got the scoop on Stormcloud. We saw the files. Two: Conner knows we know, knows we're after them, but he didn't drop the hammer on us because he needs me."

"Yeah, he needs *you*. . . "

"Three," Mac continued over Price's protestation. "He so much as gives you an ugly look, I'm gone." Price's features softened. "I don't give a shit if he keeps me in court for the rest of my life," Mac continued, less angry now. "But that's not gonna happen. He's got trillions of dollars riding on the moondrop, his whole damn company. He's not gonna risk doing anything that might piss me off. We are in this together, my brother."

Price nodded, chagrined. "Do me a favor?"

"What?"

"Put on some pants."

Mac snorted, too tired to laugh. Price slapped the arms of his chair, exhaled briskly. "All right, then. Conner leaves us alone, but we're still screwed. How're we gonna grab the files now?"

"Well, I'm no computer guru but if Conner's changing his security like you said, it stands to reason it'll only go as far as guarding against you trying again what you did last night. Fair enough?" Price nodded. "And I'll bet my retirement check he'll keep all this to himself. Like I said, he's got way more to lose than we do if the truth gets out. That gives us a little time."

"To do what?"

"To try again."

Price sighed. "Mac, with what? I told you —"

"Uh-uh," Mac countered before Price could finish. "Not like last night. And not from the outside. Today."

He smiled in response to Price's raised eyebrow. "Like you said when we started this thing. We walk in the front door."

IV

"We're almost ready, Chief."

"Roger that, Soos. Standing by."

Moontown Chief of Operations Tracy Johnson pulled the headset mic away from her mouth and stifled a yawn. She was past the point where caffeine would do any good and she'd long ago sworn off other stimulants, discovering stress to be the consummate tonic. The hottest chemical commodities on Moontown weren't amphetamines, they were sleeping pills.

She'd been up for forty-eight hours straight overseeing the final preparations for this moment, the one it had taken her crew over a year of breakneck labor to realize. She kept her eyes on the long curved monitor set into her command console, on the image of Jesus Mendoza and his assistant locking the carriage restraints around the cylindrical orbital transport vehicle, the dummy cargo canister they were loading into the mass driver tube.

Johnson tapped the touchscreen control, bringing up a wider image of the mass driver. The launch platform was a massive series of electromagnetic coils lining a precisely-machined tube, a giant electric pea shooter. It would work on any scale — acceleration was primarily a function of power, not size — and they'd built a handful of smaller test platforms before Dr. Yamada had green-lighted construction of the present apparatus which would speed Mac Harrison to Earth. Its tremendous length was necessary solely to allow for more gradual acceleration to escape velocity; anything less, and Harrison would end his journey a flesh bag of crushed bones and ruptured organs.

Mendoza stood atop the flat, treaded sled crawler as his assistant backed it away from the driver, the crawler's hydraulic lift arms sinking back into place as the vehicle returned to the drop shack. She could see the OTV and carriage were snug in their berth inside the drive tube, the hatch closed.

She swiveled her mic back into place. "Soos, confirm OTV load."

"Roger Chief. OTV locked and loaded, all clear. Ready for power-up when you are."

"Roger that. Danny, how are you set on your end?"

Inside the square, windowless power plant bunker a hundred yards from the mass driver base, Danny Osborne checked the indicators on his control lectern. Less than ten feet away, on the other side of the siliplas shield, the power plant sat, a blocky gray box of welded metal plates two yards high and four long, dominating the cramped bunker. Status indicators were set into the surface at irregular intervals. Osborne glanced at them out of habit, even though the data they displayed was relayed to him through his console.

"All systems nominal, Chief. Generator primed and ready, limiters on-line. Go for power-up on your mark."

"Roger. Stand-by for power up."

Osborne's suit helmet and gloves lay on the floor by his feet. He was breaking safety protocol by not wearing them, but it wasn't until the console before him had been shipped to Moontown that its design flaw had come to light. The controls were scaled for bare-fingered manipulation, not the sausage-thick fingers of his P-suit gauntlets. Soos had made him promise on pain of death to at least keep his helmet on but sans the gloves, it was pretty much useless in an emergency. Osborne knew he could don and lock the heavy gauntlets in eight-and-a-half seconds, another six for the helmet. He'd practiced.

"Danny, you on?"

"Roger, Chief."

"Soos?"

"Right here, Chief."

"All right, then." She took a breath, mentally crossing her fingers as she zeroed the count chronometer. "Power up in five, four, three, two, one — mark."

She released the touchpad. The chronometer began ticking upward.

The generator's bass hum slowly began climbing in pitch. Osborne kept his eyes glued to the power level indicator:

"Sequence initiated, plant is active. Output at ten-percent . . . fifteen-percent . . . twenty . . . thirty . . . "

A clot of personnel were gathered around the main viewscreen in the Earthside mess hall, the mass driver displayed from four different angles, each a successive stage of the OTV's path. No one spoke, their attention fixed on the monitor and Osborne's voice, issuing from the

PA: "Sixty-five . . . seventy-five . . . eighty . . . ninety . . . we are at full power. Repeat, full power achieved."

"Roger, Danny. Soos, stand by for . . . "

"Negative, Chief."

"Say again?"

"Power is still climbing. Five-percent above redline . . . ten-percent . . . "

Johnson's weariness fled before a surge of adrenaline. "Cause?"

Osborne ran a swift diagnostic. "Unknown. Limiters read on-line but they won't engage. Now twenty-percent above redline! Twenty-three, the damn thing won't stop . . . "

"All right, shut it down. Abort launch. Repeat, abort the launch —"

"I can't!" Osborne again threw the master switch on the console. "The breakers won't trip!" Osborne had to shout to hear his own panicked voice over the generator's deafening whine. "Power's still climbing . . . "

"Cut power to the EMD grid!" Johnson barked to a subordinate. "Get out of there, Danny, you hear me? Get out now!"

Hot orange sparks erupted from the generator, filling the bunker with smoke and the acrid stench of ozone and burning insulation. The overhead lights died, the dark pierced by the emergency light above the bunker's only door, the whirling scarlet beacon slicing the filament swirls of smoke like a searchlight through fog.

Osborne was coughing, eyes burning. He fell to his knees, fumbled for his helmet and gloves. Fifteen seconds, all he needed was fifteen seconds . . .

His groping hands bumped something, knocking it away. His helmet. He lunged after it, hands frantically slapping the cold cement. The smoke wasn't as bad near the floor but it was utterly dark, the emergency light focused too high to assist him.

He was gasping now, straining for breath. It wasn't the smoke, there wasn't much smoke, but it was becoming harder and harder to breathe.

His ears popped. He raised his eyes, squinting through the haze.

The door was opening.

Johnson listened helplessly to Osborne's increasingly labored breaths. "Danny, can you hear me?"

A low murmur of horror grew in the mess hall. All anyone could see was the views of the surface, the tranquil vista overlaid with the amplified sound of Osborne's desperate wheezing.

"Oh my God," someone murmured.

Jesus Mendoza locked his helmet into place with one hand, rammed the other against the drop shack airlock cycle control. To hell with the kid's bragging about how fast he could suit up. Osborne didn't believe the stories about Berkeley. Mendoza did. He'd been the one who'd brought the body in from the surface.

He waited impatiently for the airlock to depressurize. It wasn't the smoke that worried him. The bunker drew its power from the same grid and circuit as the mass driver generator, another bone-headed design flaw both he and Johnson had fought against tooth-and-nail. If the generator blew, the power surge could take out everything in the bunker with it. And there was a chance, slight but real, that the surge would freeze the single load bay door, locking the bunker occupants inside, a disaster if the generator caught fire. Or, it could go the other way, tripping the door circuit. And whichever one happened, if the kid didn't have his bucket on . . .

The cycle light flashed. Mendoza was outside a second later, cutting left, away from the mass driver. He cleared two yards with each hard bound across the dusty surface. Tracy would've ordered the grid power cut, relegating door control to the manual crank. If the order had come early enough, if the door was closed, Osborne might be saved, if he hadn't already asphyxiated on the smoke. Of if the door circuit hadn't tripped, or tripped before it had opened too much. Just a crack would suck the air out of the building like a pierced balloon but if Osborne was a fast as he boasted, that extra second could save his life.

He drew near the generator bunker. The door was rising.

He ran with everything he had towards the bunker.

Osborne watched his helmet skitter across the floor towards the opening before him. His fingers desperately clawed the floor, raked through the sheeting tendrils of smoke, legs kicking against the grasp of current now drawing him inexorably towards the door.

He tried to inhale, realized with an odd sense of detachment that he no longer could. His vision blurred, his suddenly too-thick tongue swelled in his mouth. He tasted the warm salt of his blood.

He thought he heard someone shouting in his headset, thought he heard his name through the excruciating ache in his ears. He felt a burning cold on his face and then something popped and suddenly he heard nothing, and now he saw nothing, and then he felt nothing.

"Danny! Danny!"

Johnson could no longer hear Osborne. She stared at the monitor, saw a pressure-suited figure bounding across the surface, away from the dropshack, disappearing out of the camera frame. She knew she should find out who it was but she was afraid to speak, afraid doing so would destroy any divine intervention that might be forthcoming, propelling the nightmare to its worst end.

"Tracy."

Johnson's hands darted to her headset. "Soos! Can you see Danny?"

Mendoza knelt just outside the bunker entrance, panting. Osborne's body lay face-down in the dirt, legs still inside the structure. One frozen hand clawed his ear, the other plowed into the gray-brown maria, wrist constricted backwards, open fingers curled. There was a rust smudge in the dust beside his head. Mendoza didn't bother turning him over.

"The surge tripped the door control. He wasn't wearing his bucket or gloves."

Johnson sat motionless. "Find his helmet." She marveled at the calm in her voice. "Put it on him before you bring him in."

Mendoza signed off. She spoke to anyone who was listening.

"I want that generator pulled apart screw by screw. I want every circuit, every processor, every switch and cable checked, and then checked again, and then *checked again!*" She turned in her chair to face the room, gave her fury its head. "I want a crash team on it now, *right fucking now!* I want to know why he died, goddammit!"

She ripped off her headset with the last word and stalked out of the room, down to the airlock to meet Mendoza.

The mess hall display winked out. Long seconds of silence were broken by someone's muttered curse. Another answered. Soon everyone was speaking, angry, shocked, trying to make sense of what had just happened. The gathering dispersed in clots of two and three into the narrow hall, leaving but one person in the room.

He continued to stare at the dark monitor. It wasn't supposed to have gone like this. The generator, yes, but not —

The room lurched. He fell to his knees, fingers clawing his stomach while he retched and the floor canted and spun around him.

Six

I

Conner angrily paced his office, stabbing the tip of his cane into the floor with every step. The overcast mid-morning sun through the glass wall made it seem like dusk in the room. Dr. Yamada stood tiredly in the center of the space, attired in his customary corduroy slacks and wrinkled lab coat, e-pad in hand. Martha knew he'd been up all night, ever since the call from Chief Johnson.

"Four days, Bobby!" Conner barked. "You told me it would work!"

"It will —"

"What the hell happened? How could your people make a mistake like this?"

"We don't know that it was them."

"What else could it have been? Aliens?"

Dr. Yamada rubbed his eyes, but Martha didn't miss the sudden bunching of his jaw muscles. He and Conner had been partners more than thirty years, when UniCom had been just the two of them building and selling mail-order modems and network servers in a retail strip mall, but she had rarely seen Yamada challenge his longtime friend. This wasn't going to be good.

"They've been working double shifts for two months," the engineer began, doing his best to keep his voice level.

"And they're being well-paid for it!"

"Not everything is about money, Roger! Tracy hasn't been home for almost two years! Or Mendoza, none of the primaries! We rush construction, cut corners, don't run as many tests, all because you say 'Now! Do it now!'"

"I thought you said it wasn't your people?"

"So what if it was?" Yamada shot back. "What are you going to do, fire them?" Conner glared but didn't reply. "We need more time!"

"You told me it was done! We were ready!"

"Well obviously we're not!" Yamada exploded. "I don't know what happened! We only ran one prelim at full power! Something could have happened then, something we would have detected if we'd had more time to run more tests! One more day could have saved that boy's life!"

"We have to be ready by Saturday."

Yamada glanced over at Martha, incredulous. He raised his arms helplessly as he looked back at Conner. "Haven't you heard anything I said? A man died, Roger! A boy, twenty-five years old! What if we have another accident, with Mister Harrison in the sled? With the 'whole world watching?'"

Conner had stopped pacing. He stared down at his cane. Yamada moved forward until they were only a foot apart. His voice was a whisper.

"Remember what happened nine years ago. Remember your son."

Martha felt the hairs on the back of her neck rise. She knew Yamada hadn't meant for her to hear the comment. She shifted in her chair, her mouth reflexively opening to speak, then caught herself as Conner raised his head and met Yamada's pleading gaze. She forced the moment out of her mind, re-focusing on the crisis at hand.

"No time to send fresh hands, Bobby. No shuttle ready even if there was."

Her calm comment broke the stalemate. Yamada was the first to look away. He let out a weary sigh. "Give them one full cycle off, all of them. Just, let them sleep, for crying out loud. Promise them time off when it's over."

Martha did some quick mental calculating. "A cycle off, paid vacation Earthside based on seniority after the New Year. Two weeks bonus pay for key personnel, one for everyone else."

"It's a bribe and they'll know it."

"Of course they will but you know what's at stake, Bobby. So do they. Make sure they know its compliments of Mister Conner, make sure Tracy tells them. Let them know nobody's forgotten about them."

They both waited. At last, Conner nodded curtly and turned away, gazing out of his window. Yamada sagged, the brief spat seeming to have consumed the last of his energy. "I'll let you know when Tracy calls," he said, turning towards the door.

"Bobby."

Yamada paused. Conner spoke again. "Don't tell anyone about this who doesn't have to know."

Yamada didn't bother responding. He plodded out of the office.

Conner remained where he was, as if carved of stone. Martha knew him well enough to know she should just leave.

"What did he mean? About Kevin?"

She thought she caught a stiffening of Conner's posture, a momentary tremor that ran the length of his spine. "Let me know if payroll gives you any trouble with the bonuses," was all he said.

The doors closed behind her. Only now did Conner allow himself a shaky breath. He steadied himself against his desk, checking his pulse at his neck.

Yamada lay sprawled on the cot in his lab. He stirred at the persistent beeping emanating from the pocket of his lab coat. It took him a groggy moment to comprehend the sound, another to register the cadence.

He clambered stiffly from the bed, squinting against the harsh light as he opened the door to the converted closet and hurried across the lab to his office. He nudged the glass door closed behind him, glanced at his watch: four hours since his meeting with Conner. The incoming message indicator flashed on his computer monitor. He plopped into his chair, pressed his thumb against the tac icon.

Johnson's face appeared on the screen. "Rise and shine, Bobby."

Yamada smiled sleepily. "How'd you know?"

"You kidding? I could hear you snoring all the way up here." Yamada watched her tired face become serious. "Are you alone?"

He glanced around the lab. A single worker labored at the far end of the space, well out of earshot. "Yes," he replied, puzzled. He watched her look down at something out of range of the camera, her arm moving as if she was manipulating a control.

"You should be seeing it now."

Johnson's image shrank to a smaller window inside a larger, unsteady image: a pair of bifurcated metal boxes on a worktable, illuminated by the bright spotlight of a hand-held camera. "You see it?"

"Yes." He recognized the mass driver generator limiters, disconnected from their usual berths.

"Notice anything unusual about them?"

Yamada scrutinized the image, tapping the screen to zoom in. "They look fine from here. Of course, I'd have to see them up close —"

"I'll save you the trouble. They look fine because they are. There's absolutely nothing wrong with the limiters. Or with the other four."

Yamada's still logy brain struggled to make sense out of what Johnson was saying. "The data leads on these two were burned in the overload," she narrated. "You can see what's left of them there at the bottom but they're still connected on three of the others and I'll bet the fourth was, too. That's why all systems read nominal during the test. But these weren't, the limiters. They were disconnected, had to be sometime during the twelve hours between the last prelim and the test this morning. I had Soos run a computer sim. The system's redundant, but you yank these two out of the chain . . . "

"Creepage," Yamada finished. "Overload on the active limiters, but it wouldn't happen until late in the cycle."

Johnson watched impassively as Yamada's face displayed the same slow realization she'd experienced when Mendoza had run the simulation for her an hour earlier.

"Bobby — we've got a saboteur up here."

II

He relaxed his grip on the leather-wrapped steering wheel, shifted his weight to ease the pressure on his hip. Conner hardly drove at all anymore, so the impulse to go for a solo ride had surprised Conner as much as it had Joseph, his chauffeur. He still kept the Mercedes, of course, as new as the day he'd had it delivered five years before. He didn't even know if his driver's license was current, just as he hadn't a clue from what source the urge to get out of the office had sprung. He only knew that he had to, or explode.

He hardly noticed the fallow, winter-brown fields passing by outside the tinted windows. A spy. There was a goddamn spy on Moontown. He didn't question Tracy Johnson's deduction: other than Jesus Mendoza, there was no one up there whose acumen he trusted more. And there was no party he suspected more than Helios.

The sabotage reeked of Innes' juvenile conception of cunning. Never content to play by degrees, he always went for the big kill. With what he'd already stolen of UniCom's work he could easily have made his nut through ancillary contracts, commercial fusion be damned. But he wanted more than success. He wanted desperately to see Conner fail.

How the saboteur had managed to slip through the vetting process was another matter, one which Conner would most definitely take up with security before the day ended. *Evidence* — that's what he needed. Something he could hold in his hand. No plot was perfect, just as no security system was impenetrable. There would be a footprint somewhere. He would find it, just as Trang had found Price.

Price had been so far off Conner's radar that he hadn't even considered him, saw no reason. In retrospect, it all fit: a computer expert, genius intellect, supremely adroit at bypassing sophisticated security. Lack of motive is what had kept him from consideration, but that motive was now crystal clear.

There had been a time when the 82nd Special Airborne's disastrous final mission and its very public repercussions had dominated Conner's every waking hour. How long it had been, since he'd afforded that stain on his conscience more than passing acknowledgement. Mac Harrison's arrival had caused him to think of it more, but that Price had so tenaciously delved into UniCom's netframe could only mean that they believed, or at least suspected, that the SIC's official finding was horseshit, that there was more to the *Reagan's* downing than had been disclosed.

How much Price actually knew of the truth was unclear. The disks recovered from the house had contained only free-standing algorithms and snippets of code which Trang had eagerly spirited away to her sanctum. Conner prayed Greedy had done its worst inside Price's system, prayed more earnestly that Price would be too shaken by the previous night's encounter to try it again. The full scope of his folly assailed him. The very bastard that has so vexed him for months, Conner had just put on his goddamn payroll.

He realized he was speeding, the needle climbing above seventy. He eased off the accelerator, slowed at a crossroads and turned left. He glanced at his watch. It was just after noon. He'd been driving aimlessly for over an hour. Time to head back, talk to Trang about transferring the Stormcloud files to a more secure locale, have his chat with security.

He braked, searching for a place to turn around. He recognized this road. He slowed to a stop in the middle of the lane, eyes fixed on the wrought iron gates beyond the passenger window. He realized that his impulse to go for a drive hadn't been random after all.

Like an automaton, he nosed the Mercedes through the cemetery entrance, tires crunching on the gravel as he slowly navigated the familiar path. He stopped, cut the engine, retrieved his cane from the passenger seat. The door clunked shut behind him and he stepped into the frigid winter air.

There was no one else there. Who would be, at noon on a Monday. He labored up the gentle slope, stopped before the two blue-gray granite markers set flush into the earth. He'd wanted something bigger, something he could see from the road, but he'd been told larger headstones were forbidden because they made mowing difficult. As if the dead cared. As if he did.

He knelt stiffly and brushed errant brown leaves from the cold stones with fingers already turning blue. There lay Beth and Kevin, the only two things he'd ever cared about more than his work. Surely you'd known that, son. You had to have known I hadn't forsaken you. But it wasn't your fault. None of it was your fault, I told you that. The blame is mine. Why couldn't you accept that? Why couldn't you believe me . . .

He collapsed back on his heels, the freezing damp earth soaking through the thin fabric of his pants. There he knelt beside his family, vision blurring, stones bleeding one into the other.

III

"Doctor Yamada!"

Yamada looked up from his work. "Mister Harrison! Hello!"

Mac strode into the lab, smiling jovially at where Yamada stood before a broad bank of man-high computer tower drives. The engineer brushed back his thinning gray locks and shook Mac's hand. Mac hadn't encountered him since the press conference, when he'd had to stifle a laugh the first time Yamada spoke. Despite his Japanese appearance and surname, his Southern twang testified to his Carolina birth.

178

"Well, this is a surprise," Yamada offered. "I never expected to see you down here."

"I probably should have called first. Not much to do today so I thought we'd drop by and check out your shop. It's not a bad time, is it?"

"No, not at all," Yamada assured him, glad of the diversion. He raised between them the e-pad he held. "I was just going over some plasma mix figures. We're about to run a reactor test." He looked over Mac's shoulder. "Where's Mister Price?"

"Hm?"

"You said 'we.' I assumed you meant Mister Price was with you."

"Oh. Uh, he was, but he had to use the mensroom. It takes him a while. You know."

"Ah. Yes, of course," Yamada solemnly replied.

Mac glanced to his left, past where the bank of drives ended. The broad wall was dominated by a wide recessed metal curtain. "What's that?"

"Ah." Yamada walked briskly to the wall and tapped a code into the panel set beside the curtain. There was a faint whirring of gears as the heavy shield rose into the ceiling, revealing a window almost as wide and tall as the curtain itself. He invited Mac over with a gesture and together they looked down into the gynmasium-sized room a story below.

"There it is," Yamada announced proudly.

He'd expected to see some sort of huge machine, like a nuclear reactor. Mac was surprised when Yamada pointed to a rather small metal globe, no more than a yard in diameter, raised chest-high off the floor on four outward-angled steel struts. The surface of the reactor was dripping with wires and cables, pierced with conduit and dotted with odd protuberances, like a mechanical porcupine. It was surrounded by consoles and boxy machines the function of which Mac had no idea. There were a handful of people in the otherwise empty room, two of whom worked on the reactor itself, mouths moving as they consulted.

"IEC Four" Yamada announced. "The world's first helium-three fusion reactor. Well, not the very first, but the first that's commercially viable."

"Awfully small."

"Isn't it? This room is where we used to house the old tokamak, which should give you some idea of how big *that* was. IEC reactors are tiny in comparison, which is largely a function of the initialization process, of course, although this one puts out more power than even the biggest tokamaks, spheromaks and stellerators currently in use . . . "

Before Mac could comment, Yamada was proudly singing the praises of his team's creation. Whereas Conner had spoken only of commercial power from fusion, Yamada's vision was broader. The amount of deadly high-energy neutrons produced by fusion was a mere fraction of that produced by conventional nuclear fission reactors and could actually be used to shorten the half-life of existing radioactive waste, without producing more of the same in the process of its creation. They could also be used to produce radioisotopes for medical applications and other research, even to detect land mines and hidden explosives. High-energy protons from fusion could do much of the same, while electromagnetic radiation produced could be used to sterilize food and equipment.

All these applications, Yamada gushed, were a direct result of the IEC reactor's miniscule size compared to other designs. Soon, he said, his team would be able to build them even smaller, compact enough to fit almost anywhere — inside a hospital radiology lab, above an airport baggage conveyor, or mounted on the nose of a military aircar as it flew over a minefield. And oh yes, it could produce power, too. Tokamaks and their kin were so massive, their only real application was the large-scale commercial production of electricity for sale to utility companies. You'd never be able to fit a tokamak inside a commercial airliner to power its engines, or mount one in the tail of a spacecraft to speed humanity to the edge of the solar system, and beyond.

"Almost thirty years, its taken us," Yamada sighed. "I never thought I'd see it in my lifetime. Just five years ago, I was almost ready to give up."

Mac had moved casually behind Yamada during his discourse until he was standing to his right, forcing the engineer to stand with his back to the lab's entrance.

"Why didn't you?"

"Oh heck, where else am I going to go?" Yamada replied. "There's nowhere else in the world where I can do the kind of work I do here, no one with the vision or the resources Roger has. Thirty years ago, my laboratory was a six-by-eight-foot storage room. Now look." His eyes shone as he fondly gazed at the reactor. "Look what we've done." He brightened, turning to Mac. "Would you like to observe the test?

From down there, you and Mister Price?" He started to turn towards the lab entrance.

"Actually, I had a few questions I was hoping you could answer," Mac put in quickly. "About the dropsled."

Yamada returned his attention to Mac. "Well, certainly. What kind of questions?"

"How about radiation shielding? The original CDP 1000s weren't designed to withstand long-range cosmic ray exposure."

Yamada looked surprised. "I had no idea you were so familiar with the mechanics of the sled."

"Well, you know, you pick it up."

"You'll only be exposed for a few days. Nothing to worry about."

"I know, but they didn't have any protection at all, just the siliplas for the heat."

"Well, we're adding extra shielding to deflect heavy and secondary particles, plus more internal thermal insulation, to protect against extreme temperature variances . . . "

Mac carefully kept his attention focused on Yamada while he lectured, nodding now and again in encouragement. He let his eyes flicker for a second, over Yamada's shoulder, just in time to see Price peek around the door jamb from the hall.

Yamada's office was small, a prefabricated cubicle large enough for a desk, chair, and a filing cabinet. The walls were opaque up to chest-level, where they were topped by a yard of glass. Price quietly rolled the desk chair out of the way, glancing over the top of the wall to make sure Mac still had Yamada's attention. He'd given him a few questions to ask — Mac's technical knowledge of the sled ended with the essentials of operation. All Price needed was a minute or two.

He swiftly examined the computer atop the work-strewn desk. It had to be here. If anyone would have one, Yamada would.

He lifted a sheaf of papers obscuring the face of the main drive. There it was, the familiar cylindrical opening.

A crystal drive.

" . . . all the way down to plus-thirty-degrees Kelvin, near absolute zero," Yamada was saying. "Of course, it'll never get that cold, heat is our main concern and the original specs are more than adequate." He paused, waiting for Mac to reply.

"Good, good. It all sounds, um, very good." Mac nodded in what he hoped was an intelligent manner. He'd caught only about half of what Yamada had said, stealing glances at Price's bald pate bobbing above the office wall like a buoy.

Yamada must have sensed his tutorial hadn't taken. "Tell you what. I've got some schematics in my office you can borrow that illustrate precisely what we've done."

He began to turn towards the office, just as Price glanced in their direction. Mac saw his eyes widen before his head plunged below the cubicle wall.

"Ahh, I have another question first."

Yamada turned back to Mac, waiting. Price's head cautiously resurfaced, eyes focused in Mac's direction. Mac saw him return to work.

"Yes?"

"Um, life support."

Yamada stared at Mac in mild confusion. "You'll *have* life support, Mister Harrison."

"Well, of course, I didn't mean that. I mean, how much? The old sleds only had enough for the drop, not even twenty minutes worth. Won't the extra life support, y'know, add more weight?"

Yamada studied the man before him. The question about shielding had been fair enough but this one bordered on inane. Harrison acted nervous, as well. Maybe the reality of the drop had finally hit him, Yamada reasoned. That must be it. He had to remember he wouldn't be the one making that trip, and Harrison wasn't a scientist. Obviously. At once, his irritation faded as he unexpectedly felt honored by the chance to be the one to set Mac's mind at ease.

"That's a very good point," Yamada thoughtfully replied. "But I can assure you, we've taken all of that into account in our calculations. You see," and he began tapping figures into his e-pad, holding it so Mac could observe, "the original sled's unloaded gross weight, including life support, was two-forty-five-point-one-eight kilograms, a little over five-hundred forty-one pounds. Of course, you were on suit oxygen during the war, which we'll use only as an emergency backup during the drop. Not that you'll need it, of course" he quickly added with a reassuring smile.

"The additional life support, and that includes not just oxygen and the CO_2 rebreather but drinking water, rations — not too appetizing, I'm afraid — plus heating and cooling, will add only about another twelve kilos or so. See, let's break it down . . . "

The decryption program made quick work of Yamada's password. Price waited anxiously while it sought Conner's. He was counting on the likelihood that Mac had been right in his supposition that the security protocols that'd nailed them the night before were set to detect only unauthorized remote access. By using Yamada's computer and password he shouldn't set off any alarms and if anyone would have close to unlimited access to UniCom's netframe, it would be Conner's chief engineer and longtime partner. The chain of logic had seemed sturdy enough that morning. If one of the links broke, he would have some serious explaining to do.

The computer beeped. Price snapped his head towards Mac and Yamada, ready to duck again, but the noise had been too faint to carry.

He returned his attention to the monitor, felt his heart race faster as he once more beheld Conner's personal directory. He entered the same search parameters as the night before, replacing the decryption ball with a blank as the tagged files and directories were displayed. With a tap to the screen the files began copying. There was more information than he'd imagined; he watched the download status bar steadily lengthen, the numerals below it ticking away the thirty-six seconds to completion. Damned if they weren't going to get away with it.

He jumped as Yamada's phone rang. He stared at it dumbly.

It rang again. He peeped over the top of the cubicle wall.

Yamada was turning towards the office.

Mac saw Price's head dive below the wall as Yamada turned towards his office, pausing in the middle of his lesson. "Um, you were saying?"

The phone rang a third time. Yamada raised his hand to Mac palm out as he backed away. "I'm sorry, I really must get that, I'll be right back . . . "

Mac watched helplessly as Yamada hurried across the lab. He started after him, determined to physically yank him away if he had to, but the engineer was already in his office. Mac held his breath as he waited for the shoe to drop, his mind already scrambling to come up with some excuse that would explain Price's trespass.

Yamada picked up the handset and began talking.

"Yamada . . . No, I had Dale bump the mix, the ratio is correct . . . "

Price blew a tiny dust tumbleweed away from his nose. He lay tightly curled on his side on the floor, behind Yamada's desk, cheek pressed into the gritty tile. With the computer and office flotsam littering its surface, the desk was just large enough to conceal the folded chair, which he held vertically up against the back of the desk with one beefy arm. He'd become very adept over the years at breaking down his custom carriage; five seconds once he was out was all it took to collapse it accordion-like into a foot-wide package. Unless Yamada looked over the back of his desk, Price knew he wouldn't be seen.

The computer was a different matter.

He peeked beneath the desk, across the lint-covered plain of the floor. Yamada's heels faced Price, meaning he was facing away from the desk with his back to the computer. Since the phone had been to the computer's left, he hadn't seen the monitor. Not yet.

"No, no, it's better that you checked. We only changed it about an hour ago, you were still checking calibration . . . "

Price listened to Yamada talk, counting seconds in his head. At any moment, the file transfer would be complete, the goddamn computer would beep, Yamada would check it, and that would be that.

C'mon, Mac. *Do something!*

Mac watched in astonishment as Yamada chatted on the phone. For whatever reason, he hadn't seen Price, but their luck couldn't hold long. He searched the lab for something, anything that he could use to attract Yamada's attention, short of shouting . . .

CLAAAANG!

Mac kicked the base of the nearest tower drive, flashed a sheepish smile as Yamada looked over. He made a show of scrutinizing a control panel, finger poised above it as if he was about to depress a control. Out of the corner of his eye he saw Yamada leaning over the telephone, hurriedly finishing his conversation as his legs were already making for the door. He hung up and dashed out of his office, striding up to Mac with his arm extended before him:

"Please, Mister Harrison, don't touch that!" He slowed his pace as Mac retreated. "It's in the process of running some extremely important calculations for the reactor test."

"Oh, sorry. I didn't touch anything, I promise." Mac glanced at the office, but Price was still out of sight. "So this is a computer, then?"

"Yes."

"It's big."

"Yes, it is."

"I don't think I've ever seen a computer this big."

"It's actually a parallel series of processors, several thousand of them. It has the power of three million of the most sophisticated home computers."

"Can you play games with it?"

Yamada stared. "No. We don't have much time for that."

Mac saw Price's head rise above the wall. He appeared to be hefting himself back into his chair. "I hate to be rude but that was the floor," Yamada said, gesturing towards the reactor. "I need to get down there."

There was a faint crash, and Mac saw Price topple out of sight. Yamada turned towards the noise. Mac reached for the panel again. "What's this do, here?"

Yamada whirled and almost slapped Mac's hand away from the panel. "That . . . ! is something you don't want to touch." He recovered his composure, forcing a smile. "Now, um, if you don't mind, I really must get downstairs. Wouldn't you like to join me?"

At last, Mac saw Price scoot out of Yamada's office and into the hall. He reached out and took Yamada's hand, pumping it vigorously. "I've taken up too much of your time already. Thanks for answering my questions. I'll see you around." He was already heading for the door as he finished, leaving Yamada watching in befuddlement.

"You're welcome. I, hope I was helpful."

"Oh, very helpful!" Mac called over his shoulder. "Good luck with the test!"

Yamada shook his head as Mac disappeared into the hall. And people said engineers were eccentric.

Mac held the door for Price as they exited the building. The employees-only side entrance emptied into a shrub-enclosed courtyard.

"You get it?"

"I got it, baby! I was right, Yamada's got access to the entire netframe. Like a walk in the park, except for forgetting to set the brakes on my chair."

"That's what that noise was?"

"Lucky I didn't pee my pants when he walked in on me."

They stopped at a stone table ringed with benches. Mac checked to ensure they were alone while Price pulled his laptop and crystal drive out of the nylon satchel hanging from the back of his chair. He placed them on the bench before him, plugged the drive into the laptop as it booted up, loading the ball into it. "This is it, man," he murmured as he tapped the keypad. "Showtime is . . . now."

Price maneuvered the pointer over the file access menu and clicked. Barely a second passed before a red warning window flashed in the middle of the flat monitor:

Warning! Virus Detected
Type: Unknown
Irrecoverable Data Loss Imminent –

Price yanked the drive cable from the laptop, lightning fast, aborting the operation. "I do not *believe* this, man!" he moaned.

"What? They get us again?"

Price gritted his teeth while he ran a fast diagnostic. "No," he finally decided. "But we dodged a big bullet. I want to meet whomever's in charge of their computer security. The files are tagged with a virus, probably the same one as last night. If I try to open them it'll eat the laptop for supper. I'm surprised the anti-virus program even detected it."

"So how come it didn't last night?"

"He used a boot disk, bypassed the start-up load sequence, gunned straight for BIOS. Wrote the laptop anti-vee myself, same one on my main system, variation of the code mine D&C in my field kit in the Pan-Am. No boot disk, though, it shoulda flashed a D&C ID, not a data loss flag, which means it's no good against whatever bug *this* is —"

"Can you get around it?" Mac interrupted. He had no idea what Price was talking about.

Price powered down the laptop, lowered the monitor. "Maybe. We've got the viral boot disk, I can throw some stuff at it, see if anything sticks." He tapped the dormant laptop. "Not with this system, though, not by itself. And not without time."

Mac looked grim. "I leave day after tomorrow."

"Ye-up." Price met Mac's eye. "You just might have to go through with this thing after all."

186

Seven

December 20, 2022
Tuesday

I

Tracy Johnson
Chief of Operations
Mare Smythii Commercial Lunar Research Facility
Universal Communications Inc.
12/20/22
  Dear Mr. and Mrs. Osborne:
  It is with profound sadness that I offer to you my condolences for the death
of your son, Daniel James Osborne. You may take what comfort there is in
knowing Danny was a well-liked and highly skilled member of the Moontown
team, and died in the diligent and expert performance of his duties . . .

Chief Johnson reviewed the note it had taken her an hour to compose, seven lines of carefully-worded platitudes. She could afford nothing more — any genuine expression of grief could be construed as an admission of liability in the inevitable lawsuit. Chances were Conner's legal weasels would further strip from the letter what little humanity it contained.

She saved the message for transmission later, swiveled in her chair and gazed out of the port behind her desk. The lunar landscape stretched dull and dusty into the coal-black nothing. They wouldn't get daylight for another four days, the day of the drop. Had it not been for Osborne's death, Yamada's promise of time off and bonus pay might have cheered her. She resented it now, knew her people would, too. She'd discharged her obligation by posting a curt e-mail to the general mailbox announcing the incentive. At least the extra cycle's rest would do everyone some good.

The door chime sounded. "Come in."

Soos entered, still dressed in his wrinkled coverall. The door slid closed behind him as he gave a single hop and let the micro-G carry his muscular frame into the chair in front of the desk, resting his heels on its edge as he settled. She'd never seen him in grip slippers, never ceased to marvel at the easy grace with which he moved in the partial weightlessness.

Jesus Mendoza was Moontown's senior tech, there almost from the beginning, more familiar with its insides and outsides than anyone. Even though he didn't carry an official administrative title, soon after Johnson's arrival he'd swiftly donned the *de facto* mantle of her second in command, wielding more real authority than anyone save herself. Johnson trusted him more than anyone else on the base.

Mendoza dropped his e-pad into his lap. "I asked his roomie to gather his things. His body's in the infirmary, in the back. We moved some shelves to hide it. Cleaned him up, vacu-sealed his P-suit, tossed in some desiccant. Should keep decay minimal until the next shuttle."

"Who'd have thought we'd need a morgue."

Mendoza let the comment pass. "There's been some talk of a memorial service. I think it's a good idea. Maybe after first shift tomorrow, delay second shift ten minutes or so, give folks time to attend."

Johnson stirred from her lethargy. "He left 'religion' blank on his application. I'll ask Latisha Chombe to arrange something nondenominational. Be the largest congregation she's had yet. Not exactly churchgoing types, are we?"

"You should say a few words, too." Johnson sighed. "Not much," Mendoza went on. "Just —"

"Fine."

She looked up at the *thunk*. A beer sat arm's length away. Mendoza was popping the seal off his own, studiously avoiding her eye, giving her space.

"Sorry," she grunted, reaching for the can. Mendoza raised his beer in acknowledgement of the offering and drank.

Johnson popped the seal on hers and took a grateful swallow. "This'll probably put me to sleep."

"That's the idea." Johnson rolled her eyes. "Don't gimme that," Mendoza warned. "I'll put you to bed myself."

"Don't tease. I'm too tired."

Mendoza took another pull on his beer. He set the can on the desk and sat up, lowering his feet and taking up the e-pad. "You ready to do this?"

"Find anything?"

Mendoza's check of the personnel roster had turned up six new bodies in the last six months. The rest of the crew had been there a year or more; he ruled them out on logic that they'd already had ample time to do make their presence known. Of the six newbies, three were UniCom techs twice-vetted by Conner's security: "I doubt *el Diablo* himself could snow those boys," Mendoza declared. "Which leaves three, all of whom applied from the outside. Renny Torgerson, Kyle Redding, and Aleksandr Tsibliyev."

Johnson called up the personnel records on her computer, Tsibliyev first. Mendoza carried his chair around the desk and sat next to her. The skinny Russian's ID photo nested within his personnel jacket on the monitor. "I think we can rule him out," she decided. "Works in materials management, sits in front of a computer all day." She tapped a link, calling up his surface roster. All personnel authorized for surface access were issued an airlock code which operated the doors; egress and return times were automatically noted on Moontown's netframe roster. "Look — hasn't been outside once except for his P-suit checkout. Not authorized. I don't think he's our guy."

"Okay, push him to the back burner, for now."

"Y'know, we're making an awfully big assumption here," mused Johnson. Their saboteur's motivation might not have been to stop the moondrop, she reasoned. It could just as well be a long-time crew member who'd been there a bit too long: "Bad food finally got to them or something." Mendoza didn't buy it. There were dozens of easier ways to jam a rod into the Moontown works without ever leaving the dome. Targeting the generator was too specific, too great a chance of getting caught.

"Point taken," Johnson admitted. She called up the next name. "Kyle Redding."

Mendoza peered at the screen. "I know him. Ran into him a couple days ago, down on D. English."

"From London," Johnson confirmed. "SysTech third, maintenance on the SPA, so he's got access to the right tools, spends his shift in a P-suit, cleared for access to the arrays. No one would suspect him if they saw him outside."

"Put him on the short list. By the way, I think he's claustro." Johnson looked surprised. "He looked a half-step from berkers when I saw him, sweating like a pig."

"What the hell's he doing up here?"

"Maybe didn't know he was claustro until he arrived. It's happened before, God knows the psych screens aren't perfect. Even if he isn't our man we oughta keep an eye on him."

"Tell his shift super, will you?"

"Gotta talk to him anyway, find out where he was during the 'accident.'" They both pulled on their beers, and Johnson called up Torgerson's packet. Mendoza shook his head. "Friggin' Swedes. I just don't get it. Maybe it's the cold."

"Swedish-American."

"Whatever. LUNOX extraction, okay, so he's cleared for surface access too, and access to tools." Mendoza studied the screen text. "One of Al Buckmore's crew. He's out on a long haul near *Talbot*. Left yesterday."

"Strike him."

"Not so fast, they could've dusted after the last prelim. That would've given our Swedish friend time to do his worst and still get to work on time. I'll check when they get back from the crater." He drained his beer and stretched, yawning. "I agree with you, the more I see these two. I don't think Tsibliyev is the one."

"If any of them are," Johnson groused, yawning in answer to Mendoza's. "Dammit, Soos, I wasn't hired to be Sherlock Holmes."

"Here's my advice, 'cause of course you're gonna ask for it," he added with an easy grin. "We get UniCom to run a check on all three ASAP, full retrovet while we poke around here. Have 'em check the ground server archive too, see if any of them have received any interesting messages the last few weeks."

"That's illegal."

"And?"

"Just thought I'd point it out."

"You don't think they read our mail, paranoid as old man Conner is about security?"

"So why didn't they catch any suspicious message? If there was one."

"Probably 'crypted, compressed, dozens of ways to do it, you know that. Hard to keep up with all the new crap out there."

Johnson finished her beer in two long pulls. She'd been right. The alcohol was making her sleepy. She'd have to retire now whether she wanted to or not, or risk passing out on the job.

She closed her eyes and stretched, enjoying the delicious feeling, and felt Mendoza's hands on her breasts, holding her from behind. She lay her hands over his, resting her cheek against his beard stubble. "You think anyone knows?"

"About us?"

"Mm."

"Does it matter?"

She touched a control on her desk, locking the door.

II

The planes were tied down, the beer cold, the fire roaring. Fitzpatrick drummed his hands on the side of the open cooler as Hill executed a near perfect handstand on a charred log just added to the blaze. He yelped and pushed off, flopping singed on the other side of the fire, wildly brushing sparks from his hair to the raucous approval of the other jumpers.

Martha sat in a sagging lawn chair next to Price on the other side of the bonfire, well back from the flames. She watched Mac, standing with Fitzpatrick on the other side, his teeth flashing in the firelight as he joined in the laughter. They'd spent all day at the DZ, Mac getting in as many jumps as he could before the next morning's departure for Vandenberg. The night before they'd spent together at her apartment, a more leisurely repeat of their first encounter. Price had kissed her cheek upon their meeting that morning, and then her hand, his tacit stamp of approval. Not that she felt she needed it, but it was nice all the same.

She shook her head in amused disbelief as the drunken Hill nearly fell into the fire while attempting a flamboyant bow. "You guys are nuts," she declared.

"Gotta be to jump out of a perfectly good airplane."

True enough, thought Martha. Fitzpatrick had attempted to cajole her into a tandem jump earlier that afternoon and she had laughed in his face. She contented herself with remaining on the ground, just another whuffo observing plane after plane disgorge its cargo of jumpers. It was the landings that thrilled her the most, watching the jumpers hot-dogging, swooping down into graceful stand-ups or staggering forward, canopies trailing behind, if they flared too early or late. But no matter how rude the landing, they were always smiling. "Any jump you can walk away from is a good one," someone had told her. She couldn't fault that logic.

"I thought Jimmy was supposed to be here."

"I called him yesterday," Martha answered Price. "Left a message on his machine. He's still a little sore about Mac stealing his thunder, I think."

"Last time he got a 'little sore' at Mac he knocked his teeth in."

"What's he going to do when this is all over?"

Price saw Martha's eyes fixed on Mac. "Dunno. We haven't really talked about it. I doubt he knows. Truth to tell, I don't think he expected to live this long."

It took Martha a moment to register the implications of that casual reply. Price finally returned her questioning gaze, sensing her silent invitation for him to continue.

"Something you've gotta understand about Mac," he began. "He really took the Colonel's *samurai* code seriously. Not that the rest of us didn't, we all respected him, loved him in our own way. But bottom line, he was our CO. With Mac, the Colonel was *Sensei*. Mac grabbed on to *bushido* with both hands, like it was a life preserver."

"*Bushido?*"

"The way of the warrior. The *samurai* ethic. Probably would have worn his *gi* into the field, if he could." Price chuckled before turning sober once more. "It's like the Colonel said, at the funeral. 'The way of the warrior is in resolute acceptance of death.' We were all ready to die. You had to be, to do what we did, just like these guys, even," and Price waved his beer at the party. "But they don't want to die. Neither did we."

"You're saying Mac had a deathwish?"

"No, no," Price sighed thoughtfully. "Part of *bushido* is living in the moment. Not looking past what you're doing, to what might happen. You do that, make plans, you start to fear death. You start living your life — carefully. And that's when you get into trouble —"

"I don't understand," Martha interjected. "How can you not think about what you're doing? What's wrong with making plans?"

"Nothing. Unless you make your living being shot at."

"Yeah, but still . . . "

Martha trailed off as Price sat up straighter in his chair, leaning towards her. He spoke haltingly, choosing his words with care.

"When you're a soldier, when you do what we did, you have to do more than just recognize that you might die. You have to be ready to die. It's your *business*. You can't be afraid of it. You have to embrace it, to get past it. It's like, dipping your toe into a cold swimming pool. You can't ease yourself in, stand on the edge debating. You've gotta jump in and start swimming, take the shock and move through it. You turn into training and instinct, there's no time for debate 'cause if you hesitate for one split-second, you are dead. You take a big piece of your humanity and put it away somewhere so you can function. Survive."

Price's dark eyes glittered in the firelight. "You see? You have to become dead. In your mind. In your heart. There's no room for that piece of yourself that you've got locked off. After, that's when you go back to it, make it part of yourself again. Lots of folks who came back from the Pan-Am, they couldn't do it. Saw too much, changed too much. Some of 'em liked it too much, and I don't know which is worse."

"You're saying that's what happened to Mac."

Martha wasn't certain Price had heard her, he was silent for so long. When he finally spoke, she had to strain to hear his words.

"I saw him kill once. Bare-handed. I was up to my elbows in circuit boards and this guy hits the door from the outside, don't know where the hell he came from. We thought we'd fragged them all. My piece is leaning up against the console, Mac's about four, five feet from the entrance, he's reloading. Guy's got the dead drop on us both and I think, 'This is it, we're done.'

"Guy's here." Price raised his beer in his right hand, struck it lightly with his left and clasped it. "Mac's on him, I swear I still don't remember seeing him move. Hits him *irimi-nage*, inside throw, takes

193

the guy's piece as he drops. Snapped his neck, I guess, maybe crushed his trachea. I didn't check. Three seconds, tops, start to finish. And not a single sound except for the body hitting the floor."

He took a drink, held it in his mouth a long second before swallowing. "Twelve years I've known him. And I have never been afraid of Mac, except that one time. He didn't look at me. Didn't say anything, just went back and finished re-loading and then we were out. He's like a hole in the dark next to me, nothing coming off of him. Sitting in the pick-up car, there's his field code on his cammos, same place as on mine so I know it's Mac. But there's that black faceplate above it, I'm staring at it on the other side of the hold and the whole trip I'm waiting for him to take it off so I can make sure its really his face behind it."

Martha looked at Mac anew through the dancing flames and felt a chill come over her that the fire couldn't chase away. She thought of the man with whom she'd made love the night before, of the feelings the encounter had again stirred in that part of herself she'd locked away in the same way Price had described, just so she could function. She pulled her coat tighter around her arms as Price's voice came again.

"I didn't go Army to be a killer. Neither did Mac. Worst part of the job. But we all found our own way to that dead place so we could do it. Mac went deep, deeper than any of us. He turned into something else and I don't know what because I've never found it inside myself. If it hadn't been for the Colonel I don't think he would've come back to himself between drops at all. His life, pride, honor, sense of self — everything he was, was the 82nd. If the others had survived Stormcloud so there could have been some sort of formal closure, it would've been different. But it didn't happen like that.

"Mac never had the chance to reclaim that part of himself. It died with the *Reagan* and just like that, it was over. There was nothing to bring back. He went from being dead to being the last one left alive, only he wasn't, not in his heart. He's spent nine years since trying to find something that's just not there anymore."

"All of a sudden he's got to live," Martha finished, watching Mac. "And he doesn't know how." Mac turned and caught Martha's eye. He excused himself and started over.

"I'm still not convinced he wants to," Price finished, watching Mac move towards them. He looked over at Martha but she was ignoring him now, waiting for Mac. Price smiled. "But I think he might be having second thoughts."

Martha missed the last comment as she grinned up at Mac in welcome. "You look right at home."

"Yeah, but we should probably go," Mac replied. "Any idea what time it is?"

"Little after eight," Martha answered, glancing at her watch. "Big day tomorrow. I understand shuttle flights are a bitch with a hangover."

"Try combat drops," Price put in.

Mac turned to him. "Operation Sudden Thunder? Remember?"

Price was already nodding his head, grinning. He and Mac spoke in unison: "Operation Sudden Chunder!" They laughed. "Carr puked in his helmet at fifty-grand," Price explained to Martha. "All the way down, he's goin' . . . "

"'Help, I can't see, I can't see!'" Mac finished, comically groping the air before him. "We had to tell him when to pull, first thing he does when he touches down he rips his helmet off and his face is just *covered*. . . "

"Oh, thank you for sharing." Martha raised her beer to her lips, then decided against it in light of the mental image conjured by Mac's description. Price noticed and cut loose with a belly laugh, turning to Mac. His laughter died as he followed Mac's stern gaze back over his shoulder.

III

A battered pickup skidded to a halt on the DZ's gravel drive, rocking on bad shocks. The engine clattered loudly a few seconds then coughed to a halt, headlights still burning.

With a metallic groan, the driver's side door opened. A figure stepped out, stumbled, caught himself and walked unsteadily into the glare of the headlights, bottle of beer in his left hand, the baseball bat in his right revealed in silhouette.

Price turned his chair, squinted against the light, recognized the face. "Oh, this looks promising."

"Big party, huh? Big party for the hero."

"We were wondering where you were, Jimmy," Mac said calmly. The other jumpers were quiet now, everyone focused on Boykin standing rubber-legged in front of his truck.

Boykin spread his arms wide. "Here I am! Sorry, I only got your *message* this afternoon," he spat at Martha. "I don't check 'em that often since you don't need me anymore. Now that the *hero* is here!" He lifted his beer in Mac's direction, a cynical toast before draining the bottle and tossing it aside into the dark. He took another tottering step forward, his slurred drawl seething hatred. "Whatcha gonna do this time when you're in that dropsled, hm? Hm?"

"Hey, Jimmy. Lighten up."

"I ain't talkin' to you," Boykin snapped at Price, his eyes never leaving Mac. Price felt Mac move away to the left, drawing Boykin away from him and Martha. Boykin followed the motion like a bear tracking prey. He moved another step closer, stopping a yard away from Mac. "C'mon, hero! I wanna know! You gonna do your job, or you gonna go chicken shit again like when you left Tim to die . . . !"

On the last word, Boykin took a wild swing at Mac's head with the bat. Mac easily side-stepped the blow and Boykin fell to the ground. He pushed himself to his feet, staggering backwards against the grille of his truck.

"Jimmy!"

It was Fitzpatrick, moving towards Mac. He stopped as Price waved him back and shook his head 'no.' Attacking Mac was mistake enough, but Price knew Boykin was about to rue his choice of weapon.

"This is no good, Jimmy," Mac said, keeping his voice level and neutral. It was hard to see anything more than a hulking silhouette against the truck headlights. He took another sliding step left, trying to move out of the glare, careful not to take his eyes off of Boykin. The gravel crunched as the other man moved closer.

"It shoulda been you!" Boykin hissed. "I shoulda fuckin' killed you nine years ago when I had the chance!"

"C'mon, Jimmy," Mac began, but Boykin was already lunging at him, raising the bat above his head. Mac waited for the downswing, pivoted to the outside and grasped the bat just above Boykin's grip. He moved forward, blending with the blow, adding his own impetus to its downward arc.

Now it was Boykin who was clumsily hanging on to the weapon Mac had claimed as his own. The big man stumbled forward but managed to retain his grip on the bat. Mac pivoted left, still playing the arc: the momentum swung Boykin into Mac, who slid his right hand down to mid-length on the bat and drove the club end into Boykin's stomach. As Boykin bent double Mac ducked beneath his arms and slid his hands upwards, locking them onto Boykin's left wrist, cranking it in an excruciating *sankyo* lock. The bat fell from Boykin's fingers as he bellowed in pain.

Mac moved forward, cut downward and sent Boykin sprawling face-down on the gravel. He dropped swiftly to his knees, shifting the *sankyo* to an *ude-osae* submission, wrapping around Boykin's arm, locking out the shoulder while Boykin roared in drunken defiance, his right cheek grinding into the sharp gravel. Mac leaned in close, just a foot from Boykin's ear, from his purpled left eye.

"Where'd you get the shiner, huh Jimmy?" Mac snarled. "Wouldn't be when you were breaking in my house a couple nights ago, would it? Huh?"

Boykin roared again, struggling to free himself. Mac gave his anger its head, twisting his torso to the right, pulling the ligaments in Boykin's shoulder to the snapping point. Boykin's defiance became a howl of pain. He spoke through clenched teeth and spittle:

"He made me! Said he'd make it so I couldn't fly again if I didn't!"

"Conner?"

Boykin nodded, the motion grinding his face into the gravel even more. "Gave me the key, told me what to do. He made me! I had to, I didn't have a choice . . . !"

The tension suddenly drained from Boykin's body. Tears flowed from the big man's staring eyes. His mouth opened in an anguished moan, the words coming in a child's pleading cadence. "I was supposed to do it! I was gonna bring him home! I was gonna . . . oh God, I'm sor-ry . . . "

Boykin shuddered, his hoarse sobs the only sound other than the crackle of the fire.

Mac released Boykin's arm and stood. Everyone was looking at him, staring at him, Boykin's heaving body lying defeated at his feet.

"Somebody get him home," Mac mumbled. He turned on his heel and strode away from the fire, into the darkness.

* * *

Martha stopped walking, gave her eyes time to adjust to the sudden dark. After a few moments she spotted him, a darker shape standing in motionless profile a hundred feet distant, near the runway. She approached casually, giving him time to become aware of her presence. She halted a few feet away and still he hadn't moved.

"He's right," Mac said after a long moment.

"About what."

"I should've died with them."

"No, no you shouldn't," Martha urged. She recalled her conversation with Price moments earlier as she moved nearer to Mac. "Surviving isn't a crime. From where I'm standing you have nothing to feel guilty about."

Mac shook his head, not meeting her eye. Something was going on inside of him Martha could tell, but she couldn't fathom what. "The only life you're destroying is your own. I know what it's like to live with guilt, with, loss. Wondering if there was something you could have done differently. But you can't change what's already done, you have to go on living. It's hard, it's damn hard! But what else are you gonna do? Mac?"

She reached out and touched Mac's cheek, gently turning his head until he finally looked at her. "What else are you gonna do?"

Mac looked down at her, his haunted face softly lit by the distant fire. She moved closer, her hand still caressing his cheek, close enough to breathe his musk as her lips neared his. She closed her eyes as his head bent to her.

Martha opened her eyes at the light touch of Mac's hand on her chest. It might as well have been a slap. "I'm sorry," Mac muttered, seeing the pain on her face.

She laughed, a single, harsh syllable. "Oh, you're *sorry*. What does that mean, sorry about what, last night? The one before? We're supposed to act now like none of that happened?" Anger swelled in her voice. "What the hell are you afraid of, Mac? Huh? That you might actually wind up caring about somebody again and stop feeling sorry for yourself?"

Mac's head snapped around as the accusation struck home but Martha didn't flinch beneath his hard stare. "You're not the only person on this planet who's been hurt! It's been a rough stretch of road for me, too, but I haven't stopped feeling! I haven't forgotten how!"

"Maybe I have!" Mac shouted. "Maybe I did nine years ago, when everything I cared about blew to hell!"

He glared at Martha, daring her to contradict him, but she wasn't looking at him anymore. Her eyes were unfocused, her expression suddenly pensive. "Nine years ago," she murmured, lips barely moving.

She raised her eyes to Mac's once more. "Yesterday, in Mister Conner's office." Her anger was gone, her voice a near whisper. "Bobby said, 'remember what happened nine years ago. Remember your son —'"

But Mac was already moving. He grabbed Martha's hand and tugged him behind her, racing for the fire.

"Willie! Willie . . . !"

IV

Doctor Yamada bumped his car door closed with his hip and headed towards the main building. He navigated confidently from memory, studying the glowing screen of his e-pad, taking another bite of the wonderfully greasy fast-food hamburger he held in his right hand. God knows what his cholesterol was, he thought. If the stress of preparing for the drop and overseeing the reactor didn't kill him, his diet would.

He stopped walking as he caught a flicker of motion to his left, something moving through the pool of lamplight at the edge of the parking lot. Three figures hurried towards the same employee entrance that was his destination. He couldn't make out their faces, but there was only one person he knew who used a wheelchair.

"Lobby security."

"Hi Gene, it's Bobby Yamada."

"Evening, Doctor. What can I do for you?"

"This is going to sound silly, probably, but did anyone come through there in the last couple minutes?"

"Miss Reeves, Mister Harrison and Mister Price were in here just a moment ago. They took the private elevator up to the suite." He paused. "Doctor Yamada? Everything all right?"

"Uh, yes, fine. Thank you. G'night."

Yamada cradled the phone at his lab desk and glanced at his watch. It was just after nine. In less than twelve hours, Price and Harrison were scheduled to be on a jet to California. They should be home packing, sleeping, even Roger had taken the night off. Yet they were here. And then there was that queer business in the lab with Harrison the day before. Returning to his office after the reactor test, Yamada hadn't been able to shake the feeling that someone had been there. His crystal drive had sat exposed on his desk and he knew he hadn't used it in days, nor had any of his staff admitted to having been in his office. And he knew them, he realized, much better than he did Harrison.

He sat at his desk, staring at the phone. He polished off his burger, crumpled the wrapper, dropped it into the wastebasket to his left, and dialed Conner's home number.

V

Price emerged first from the elevator, into the darkened outer office. Mac and Martha followed right behind him.

"I can't do this."

"It's important, Martha," insisted Mac.

"Nobody's got to know," added Price.

Mac almost collided with her as Martha whirled on them both. "I'll know! Lights!" The room brightened, revealing her angry visage. "I've worked hard to earn his trust, and you're asking me to violate that trust on a hunch . . . "

"It's more than a hunch," Price interjected.

" . . . not to mention what you're accusing him of!" Martha finished, over Price's words.

"We're not accusing him of anything."

Martha glared at Mac. "You suspect. It's the same thing."

Mac and Price had brought her up to speed on their suspicions during the drive from the DZ to UniCom. Her reaction had gone from mild confusion to shocked disbelief, then stony anger as the full implications of what Price and Mac were suggesting sank in. It wasn't until they'd related the story of Boykin's sabotage two days earlier that Mac had seen the doubt begin to grow beneath her outrage.

The last ten minutes of the journey had ticked by in silence. When they'd arrived she'd remained in her seat. "You said Yamada mentioned Kevin," Mac had finally said, softly. He watched Martha stiffen at the mention of her dead fiancée. "Don't you want to know . . . "

"Don't!" Martha had turned on him, eyes flashing in warning. "Don't you dare use him to get what you want!" Mac and Price followed her out of the car but instead of walking to her Jeep she'd stood there, not looking at either of them, waiting for Price to unfold his chair and seat himself before making a beeline for the building.

Mac tried a new approach. "Look, there's a good chance there's nothing more in those files than what we know already."

"If you really believed that you wouldn't be asking me to do this, would you?" Neither man answered. She glared at Mac anew. "Is this why you agreed to the drop? So you could snoop around, spy on us? Is that what we're all about? Boy, when you decide to penetrate enemy territory you sure go all the way!"

"Jesus, Martha!"

And you!" She turned on Price. "You're worse than he is! You've been lying to me since the day we met! How do you think that makes me feel? Were you ever going to tell me?" Price looked away. "What if you had gotten what you've been digging for?" Martha pressed, hold them both in her livid gaze. "What were you two gonna do, just walk away from the promises you made, leave all of us to twist in the wind? Call the press, sit back and laugh while Mister Conner's life, my life blew up around us? Everyone here? Is that what you're both looking for? Revenge?" She shook her head in disgust. "You're up to your asses in felony computer espionage, I'm surprised Mister Conner didn't call the FBI —"

"So why didn't he?" Price put in. "You're right, he could've busted down our door and confiscated everything I've got. So how come he blackmailed Boykin into destroying it instead?"

Martha fell silent. Mac stepped over, standing before her, forcing her to look at him. "Martha. You and me — that's got nothing to do with this. Nothing. Can you believe that?"

"I don't know whether to believe anything you say anymore."

"I wouldn't ask anyone to risk their honor like this if I didn't think there was a damn good reason for it. I'm willing to stake everything I am on what Willie's told you." Her jaw was clenched tight with anger but Mac could see her inner struggle. "I can't make you do this.

You can leave now, with what you know you can hang me and Willie out to dry. We'll take that hit, if it comes to it. But I'm asking. Please."

Mac and Price watched expectantly as Martha walked briskly to her desk. She lifted the telephone handset, studied the touchface.

She cradled the handset. "Computer on."

She placed her thumb against the unseen monitor screen, tapped it thrice with her index finger. Conner's office doors unlocked with a soft *click*. With a final resentful glance at Mac and Price, she pushed open the doors and walked inside.

The only light came from outside, an ambient milky blue filtering through the glass wall, accented by the merest sliver of moon hanging high overhead. Mac realized as he entered Conner's office that it was the first time he'd been in the kingly sanctum without seeing Conner's bony frame seated on his throne behind that massive desk.

Martha sat there now, focused on the computer monitor rising out of the desktop. She ignored Price pulling his chair up to her right, Mac crossing around the far corner of the desk to stand at her left shoulder. The screen glowed to life and she executed the security protocol.

"Thank you," Mac offered as she worked.

"I'm not doing this for you," snapped Martha icily. "I'm going to prove you're wrong. Then you can both go to hell."

The security cycle ended. "Good evening, Miss Reeves," came the disembodied electronic tenor.

"Access personal directory, Roger Charles Conner."

"Password please."

"Hole four, dog-leg right, par three."

"Access granted."

Instantly, the now familiar graphic tree of Conner's personal directory was displayed.

"You know all the passwords?" It was Price.

"He trusts me. File search."

"Keywords, please."

Mac spoke up. "Stormcloud."

"Unauthorized user."

Martha sat, unmoving. Mac knew she was angry at him but beneath it there had to be fear, not only of discovering that Price's suspicions were on target but of uncovering the truth behind Yamada's cryptic statement about Kevin Conner. There were more ghosts in the room than those of the *Reagan* and her crew.

"Martha." Mac touched her shoulder. She jerked away. "Stormcloud!" she barked.

"Searching."

A moment later, the coveted files appeared on the screen.

"Of course he's got files on Stormcloud," Martha murmured distractedly. "UniCom was the chief contractor. He and Doctor Yamada testified before the investigative committee, they were up to their necks in it, why shouldn't he have, files."

A moment passed. "The flight recorder," Price softly prompted.

Martha swallowed. "File search. Subject, *D.S. Reagan* mission flight recorder. All files."

All of the files displayed on the screen blinked out, save for ten:

2-S-2
2-S-7
2-S-8
ComDat R066 .1
ComDat R066 .2
ComDat R066 .3
ComDat R066A .3
ComDat R066B .3
ComDat R066 .4
T001

"Willie," Mac breathed. Ten files, all of them containing information about the *Reagan's* MFR, the mission flight recorder that DoD swore was lost, never recovered. Six of them specifically referencing ComDat team, UniCom's combat data recovery unit.

He looked over at his friend — Price was mesmerized, leaning in, his face bathed in the light from the monitor. "It's gotta be here," he was muttering. "It's gotta be one of these." He pointed to the last file on the list. "Ask what this is."

"Identify file T-zero-zero-one," said Martha.

"*D.S. Reagan* mission flight recorder transcript. Multimedia available."

The room was so quiet, it seemed to Mac they stood in a vacuum. Martha. "Play file T-zero-zero-one, all media."

The monitor divided into four windows. Three displayed fish-eye views recorded by the *Reagan's* onboard cameras: the flight deck, mid-deck control center, and drop bay. The fourth window displayed systems operational data in a linear left-to-right crawl synched with the narrow time-code reference bar, which stretched the width of the screen at the bottom. The play indicator crept slowly right as the tinny hiss of unprocessed audio emanated from the computer's hidden speakers:

"Reagan, control. APU start is go. Confirm switch to onboard computer, over."

"Copy control. Confirm comp switch."

"T-minus five . . . four . . . we have main engine start . . . two . . . one . . . LRB ignition and liftoff . . . "

The images shivered, the vibration of the *Reagan's* launch engines shaking the cameras. It would be a half-hour before the ship was in drop position. Price scanned the time code bar, noted the event hash marks, located the time reference he sought. He pointed.

"Play from here."

Martha gave the order. The indicator leapt forward. The on-screen images pixilated and reassembled in an instant into fresh representations. The audio cut out, cut in. More conversation now, the voices overlapping:

"Stand-by for maneuver to retro-burn attitude." It was a woman's voice, cool, confident.

"Roger. APU start-up complete." A man, young but equally assured. *"Standing by for RCS maneuver burn. All hands, stand-by for maneuver to retro-burn attitude . . . "*

"Count." A steely voice intruded, the single world coming like a hammer blow.

"Rendezvous to target in four-thirty-nine," a new voice answered. *"Drop minus five-oh-nine, mark."*

"Status."

"Unchanged. Screens clear . . . "

"Countdown to maneuver in ten . . . nine . . . eight . . . "

"RCS nominal."

" . . . seven . . . six . . . "

"STEALTH sys nominal. Zero bounceback."

" . . . five . . . four . . . "

Mac, Price and Martha stared at the screen, their faces lit by the monitor's glow as the room filled with the voices of the long dead, the voices of Mac's nightmares.

VI

ONBOARD THE *D.S. REAGAN*
MARCH 11, 2013

" . . . three . . . two . . . one . . . mark."

"RCS firing."

The *D.S. Reagan* swam through the darkness. To any ground observer she simply was not there — a shallow nothing in the freezing vacuum ocean through which she moved, single-minded and silent, bent to her grim purpose.

There came from her starboard nose three simultaneous flashes of light, cobalt spurts of flame echoed by like fountains behind, her aft port RCS verniers firing in tandem. Losing none of her forward velocity, the *Reagan* gracefully pivoted on her vertical Y-axis, the pale radiance of the Earth below playing the shadows on her fuselage as she spun.

On the flight deck, Captain Mark Guthrie kept his eyes on the attitude indicator, left hand lightly grasping the stick, right hand hovering above the console. It descended, expertly playing the controls as he gently nudged the stick left. Through the flight deck windows, over the angled planes of the spacecraft's nose, he caught a glimpse of the port verniers firing, their starboard twins extinguishing, halting the big ship's inertia after exactly 180-degrees of spin. He knew with cool certainty that she was now flying tail-first along her orbital translation.

"Maneuver to burn attitude complete."

"Copy RCS burn."

Commander Amanda Ashdown sat to the left of Guthrie in the tight cockpit, her eyes flickering across her own instrumentation, confirming her pilot's diagnosis. "Stand-by for OMS retro-burn."

Guthrie played his console. "OMS engines armed. Standing by."

In seconds, Guthrie would activate the *Reagan's* massive rearward orbital maneuvering system, the main engines — 455,000 pounds of concentrated thrust at sea level, even more in orbit. The OMS burn would slow the *Reagan* until she exactly matched the rotation of the Earth, relying on the data fed from the control room below the flight deck to position the craft directly over the target.

Only 13 people aboard knew the *Reagan's* quarry — the eleven soldiers of the 82nd, Dropmaster Sergeant Rawlings and Lieutenant Eli Crowe, the navigator. Moments before launch, Crowe loaded the classified data into his nav station, which in turn relayed the coordinates to the flight deck computer which revealed the firing sequence to Guthrie and Ashdown. It once irked Guthrie that he wasn't trusted with the actual target information. It hadn't taken him long to dispense with that egotistical conceit, learning fast that he had enough things to worry about.

Ashdown's confident contralto came to Guthrie both across the few feet that separated them and through his helmet headset:

"Countdown to OMS burn in five . . . four . . . three . . . two . . . one."

"Ignition."

Outside the ship, the trio of OMEs blazed into life, eerily silent in the vacuum as they executed the deceleration burn, the ribbed nozzles gimbaling under the force of the sudden thrust. The *Reagan* began to slow, now less than two minutes away from target.

In the starboard nose of the ship, a light glowed. It was faint, indiscernible from the flight deck, from any angle other than dead-on. A red-orange fire, deep within the black ovoid exhaust of an RCS vernier engine.

Growing brighter.

"Burn complete. Velocity point-seven-five-nine KPS. Orbital translation good."

"Copy, confirm." Ashdown adjusted the com mic in front of her lips, switched channels. "Control, OMS retro-burn complete. Confirm status."

Mission Specialist Captain Bruce McEvoy sat at his station, one of four extending perpendicular from the walls of the *Reagan's* narrow mid-deck control center. At his back was the thick bulkhead and double hatch that separated the red-lit room from the much larger drop bay. Before him, manning Systems Operations, was Lieutenant David Waring. At McEvoy's right on the other side of room, Lt. Eli Crowe manned the nav station, while a few feet in front of Crowe Lt. Sonny Haeggstrom peered into the greenish glow of the STEALTH systems monitor at the Tactical Operations station.

All four men were strapped into their reclining acceleration chairs, asses glued there from launch to landing. The chairs faced to the fore, immovable, each compact console positioned over their laps. Over their heads was the flight deck, accessible via the ladder that climbed from the floor along the forward bulkhead to the sealed hatches that opened just behind the commander and pilot's chairs.

"Roger command, stand by," McEvoy replied. TacOps, confirm status."

"STEALTH systems nominal," Haeggstrom calmly answered. "Zero bounceback."

McEvoy breathed a mental sigh of relief. The *Reagan* was as stationary now as she'd get, relative to Earth, until she landed. An easy target if anyone was looking, and he knew that on this night enemy eyes were turned skyward. His quarry was a surface-to-space missile specifically designed to destroy orbital hardware. Though the *Reagan* hadn't existed when the Adriatic Confederation had reached across the Atlantic and tucked the weapon they sought into the deep concealing jungle, she was now its prize target. TacOps' confirmation that they hadn't been painted by any ground- or satellite-based detection system was music to McEvoy's ears. All that remained was to send the 82nd on their way, and get the hell out.

"STEALTH systems nominal, zero bounceback," McEvoy relayed to Ashdown. He scanned his own instrumentation. "All systems nominal."

"Copy that, Control. Stand-by for . . . "

McEvoy waited a moment. "Say again, Commander." A beat. "Control to flight deck. Say again, please."

"Stand-by."

"Roger."

McEvoy felt the hair on the back of his neck rise. For the first time ever, Ashdown had deviated from the script.

Something was wrong.

"Temperature warning, vernier F-3D," Guthrie repeated. He was already running a diagnostic, fingers swiftly tapping the console.

"Cause?"

Guthrie worked a moment more. "Looks like coolant valve failure."

"Compensate."

But Guthrie was shaking his head. "Negative response." Ashdown didn't miss the sudden tension in his voice. "Temperature still rising, now twenty-six percent of maximum."

"What?"

"Manifold pressure increasing, fifteen-percent of max . . . twenty —"

"Feather F-3D."

"Roger." Guthrie played the console, cutting power and fuel to the engine. He did it again.

"What's the problem?"

"I don't know," Guthrie murmured as he repeated the sequence a third time. "It won't . . . "

His hand froze above the controls.

"Uh-oh."

Through the starboard forward window, a sunburst flash of light flooded the flight deck.

Dropmaster Sergeant Otis Rawlings clutched the edges of his control podium as the *Reagan* lurched beneath him. If he'd encountered like turbulence on an airplane he wouldn't have bothered to look up from his book. Here, it sent every one of his body's alarms into full overdrive.

He glanced up out of habit to the drop rack, sealed into the battery bay before and above him. He keyed his helmet com: "Drop bay to flight deck. Status, over."

There was the merest squirt of static in his helmet com.

"Drop bay to flight deck," he repeated. "Status check." He tapped his helmet next to his ear, heard nothing but the hollow thump of his fingers. He touched the pedestal controls, switching to general intership.

"Drop bay to anyone. Com check, please."

"Anyone, please reply."

Guthrie frantically manipulated the controls, resisting panic. One by one, warning buzzers sounded, alarms flashed, klaxons bleated. He flicked a lightning glance out of the window, glimpsed a pale plume of coolant gas venting into space from the starboard nose of the *Reagan*. He raised his voice to be heard over the din: "We've lost the vernier!"

"Yes, I see that, thank you." Ashdown took in the impossible creep of disaster claiming her instrumentation. Her hands flew across the controls, confirming each failure: "ADI is out, HSI, Alpha/Mach — Christ, what the hell is this . . . "

Attitude direction and sister indicators were out. Guthrie looked out of the window, seeking the ship's orientation, saw the Earth tracking through his vision, left to right. The explosion had sent the *Reagan* into a spin.

"Translation compromised!"

"Compensate!"

The pilot clamped down on the fear in his gut and armed the port RCS. He eased the stick right. Pushed it further, then pushed it all the way.

"Negative! Forward RCS inoperative, aft — we've lost the whole damn system!"

"What?" Ashdown rearmed the engines and manipulated her own stick. It was as dead as its twin. "Check avionics!"

"Avionics are . . . " Guthrie looked up from the console, at Ashdown, his face strangely blank.

"Avionics are gone."

McEvoy ignored the harsh trumpet of the main warning klaxon, grappling with what confronted him on his console. He watched in shocked fascination as one-by-one, every monitored system winked out. "SysOps, status!"

"Massive systems failure!" shouted Waring, confirming McEvoy's fears. "I'm trying to pinpoint the origin —"

"Say again!"

"TACSAN inoperative!"

It was Crowe, opposite him at his station. McEvoy watched him stab at his console in frustration. "Translation unknown!"

"Say again!" McEvoy bellowed. He couldn't hear a goddamn thing but the blaring klaxon.

"TACSAN down! Translation unknown —"

"Copy, got it!" The *Reagan's* tactical space navigation system wasn't responding, the system that relayed ship's trajectory and drop coordinates to the flight deck. The *Reagan* was flying blind, with no way to control her except manually, from the flight deck.

"Control, flight deck! TACSAN is out! We're showing a chain failure in all primary systems!" McEvoy paused for the reply. "Control to flight deck, acknowledge!"

No reply. All at once it hit him: why the flight deck wasn't responding, why he was having difficulty hearing Waring and Crowe over the klaxon.

He shouted to the other three men: "Intership com is out!"

Less than two yards over McEvoy's head, Ashdown was shouting into her headset mic: "Control room, acknowledge! McEvoy, acknowledge! SysOps, acknowledge! Waring!"

She turned to Guthrie, bent over his instrumentation. A fountain of sparks erupted from the console, full in his face within the open helmet. He screamed, hands clawing his eyes. A fine mist of oily smoke quickly filled the cramped quarters, the console circuitry burning, tiny flames flickering through the charred aperture created by the detonation.

Ashdown yanked a fire extinguisher from its mooring over her head and jammed it into the firehole nearest the blaze, gave it a twist to activate it as it sank home. Coughing in the ozone haze, she reached over and pulled Guthrie's hands away from his eyes. He fought her grasp as he blinked wildly, disoriented, growling a steady dirge of pain.

"Mark! Mark, can you see? Goddammit, Mark!"

Guthrie turned to her. The flesh around his eyes was an angry red, his left eye squeezed completely shut, already blistered. He fought to focus on her with his right, blinking madly against the tearing. "Arm the OMS!" ordered Ashdown.

"No RCS, we can't maneuver —"

"Do it! Wait 'til the spin orients us nose-to-Earth!"

Guthrie nodded his understanding, breath hissing through his clenched teeth as he turned back to his console. The mission was over. There was no way to control the *Reagan* in space now, and the longer they remained where they were the greater the risk of being painted from the ground, if they hadn't been lit already. But with any luck, one good kick from the OMS would put them on a re-entry trajectory. Once they were in atmosphere, if they survived re-entry, there was a chance they could fly the *Reagan* like the glider she was and regain some control.

Ashdown turned her attention to the forward window, watching for the Earth to reappear. She put hands on the stick, ready to take over if Guthrie needed help. Any second now . . .

She was suddenly aware of a dull, rhythmic thumping from behind her. She heard a dim sound, like someone shouting.

She hammered the harness quick release at her chest and pulled herself around the chair, over to the floor hatch leading to the control room. Someone was banging on it, calling her name.

"McEvoy?"

"Mandy!"

She grabbed the chair frame and pulled her face close to the hatch, straining to catch his words as her lower body floated lazily behind her. "I can hear you! Can you hear me?"

"It's-frozen! The-hatch!"

She tried the control. Nothing. Two independently-operating parallel plates sealed the flight deck from the control room. The redundancy was a safety measure, mandated by the possibility of decompression if the *Reagan* was hit or in the event either crew had to abandon ship. The second hatch would prevent the control room personnel from blowing through the opening into space when the flight deck ejected. But some UniCom genius had made the hatches motorized instead of manual. The systems failures had locked them shut.

"Same here!" Ashdown confirmed. "RCS and avionics are gone! Do you have TACSAN?"

"Negative!" came McEvoy's faint reply. "No TACSAN, everything is out! We've —"

She waited. "Bruce?"

McEvoy's voice came again, louder, the single word terrifyingly clear in Ashdown's ear.

"Incoming!"

Haeggstrom was shouting. "We've been lit! Tracking incoming missile, impact in thirty-three seconds!"

McEvoy hung onto the ladder above and behind Haeggstrom's head. His lips were so close to the hatch he could feel his breath. "Impact in thirty-three seconds!"

"Launch countermeasures!" came Ashdown's faint order. "Fire control, target!"

McEvoy relayed the imperative to Haeggstrom. The man raced to comply. He shook his head angrily.

"Weapons and countermeasures inoperative! Impact in twenty-nine seconds!"

"Negative! Weapons and countermeasures are down! Everything is down!" McEvoy shouted at the hatch. "Mandy! We've got to get out!"

Rawlings was pounding on the drop bay hatch so hard he thought his hand would break. The damn thing was frozen shut, no one answered him on intership and they were less than a minute from drop, with eleven men locked in their sleds in the battery overhead. He thought he could hear a klaxon on the other side of the hatch. He didn't know what was happening but it sure as shit wasn't good.

He gave up on the door and turned back to the console. The red launch button stared back at him. All he had to do was press it and the sleds would fire from the ship, but there was no way he would do that until he knew what was happening. He tried intership one more time, then swore in disgust as he switched to the drop channel.

"This is Dropmaster. Com check, squad leaders confirm." No answer. He tried again — still nothing. Goddammit . . .

He whirled at the sound of pounding from the hatch. He yanked his grip boots from the deckplate and lunged over, banging on the hatch in reply as he shouted. "What the hell's going on?"

He heard a voice he thought might be Crowe's. Just two words.

Abandon ship.

Waring joined McEvoy in the center of the room. Together, they twisted the recessed toggle latches and hefted the aluminum plate, letting it float away in the zero-G. The single light inside the cramped escape pod flicked on. McEvoy said a silent prayer of thanks — the pod's power was self-contained, unaffected by the crescendo of madness around them, but he'd half-expected that to fail, too.

"Into the pod, go!" he shouted, pushing Waring before him. He anchored himself to the edge of the pod hatch with one hand and slapped his other onto Crowe's wrist as the man sailed towards him from the drop bay. Crowe pulled himself down and latched his free hand onto the hatch opening next to McEvoy's, gave him a nod.

McEvoy released Crowe's wrist. Haeggstrom was still at his station. McEvoy pushed himself over, catching himself on the back of the station chair. He grabbed Haeggstrom's shoulder and tugged, bracing one foot against the deckplate, the other against the wall. "Sonny, c'mon!"

Haeggstrom didn't budge, still belted into his harness. McEvoy reached over the man's shoulder and slapped the quick release. The harness straps burst open, the ends twisting crazily as they snaked away. McEvoy tugged again: "Now, Sonny! Let's go!"

Haeggstrom's gaze was transfixed on the tracking monitor, the sole operational system. The blinking bar of the missile was just a finger's-width away from center screen. From them.

His voice was a hoarse creak.

"Too late."

Ashdown fumbled with her harness, jamming the latches home. The OMS wouldn't burn, the nightmarish cascade of systems failures had claimed their last hope. With no way to maneuver the *Reagan* was dead, even without the missile streaking towards them. And unless they punched out now, they were dead, too.

She gave her harness a final tug to tighten it. "Mark?"

"Go, go!" Guthrie slapped his helmet faceplate down and grasped the arms of his chair.

Ashdown lowered her faceplate, reached up and clawed the safety cover off of the marked alcove directly over her head, closed her fingers around the yellow and black-striped ejection handle. She gritted her teeth and yanked with everything she had.

Rawlings again hammered his palm against the launch button. It was dead. Sweet Jesus, they were trapped, all of them.

He leaped onto the battery rack hydraulics, pulled himself close to the rack plate over his head. He removed his helmet and slammed it against the plate, knowing it was futile — there were so many layers of nanocarb, siliplas and metal between him and the 82nd he could have detonated a grenade in the drop bay and they'd never hear it.

He hammered the helmet against the plate, again and again, shouting as if somehow God would as his final blessing give his voice the strength to carry.

"Alpha override! All troops, punch out!"

Ashdown felt the flight deck tremble. She released the eject handle, grasped the arms of her chair. The floor lurched. There came a tearing groan. She felt her weight press into her chair as the deck began separation.

Rawlings' thumb cracked into the rack plate, caught between it and his helmet. The helmet fell from his broken grasp but still he screamed through his raw throat:

"Punch out! *Punch out . . . !*"

His heart leaped. He heard the distant *thunk* of an opening battery hatch, the faint, unmistakable whine of a sled engine firing.

McEvoy wrapped his arm around Haeggstrom's neck and pulled, resolved to drag him to the pod. The man started to rise, then jabbed his arm at the monitor: "Bravo bat one is away!" he yelped excitedly. "Bravo one is away! One is away!"

Rawlings gazed down at the broad yellow outline of the escape pod cover in the deckplate. He could be in it and away in less than ten seconds. He could survive. Two of them away, and ten dead. Or one away and eleven, if he remained.

He tucked, twisted and pushed off from the rack plate, sailing down head-first towards the pod. The outline disintegrated as the floor peeled open beneath him and for a final instant, suspended between the above and the below, he fancied he could see the Earth.

The shuddering deck nosed downward, then was still. They were moving away from the ship. They were going to make it. Ashdown braced herself for the jolt of the escape engine that would propel them from the *Reagan.*

Something slammed into the back of the deck. The bone-crushing impact flattened her in her chair, forced the air from her lungs. She labored to inhale. A malfunction with the escape engine, it had to be. The simulations were never like this . . .

The deck began tumbling. For a moment she saw the Earth, rising upwards out of sight through the forward windows before the orange-white glare filled the cockpit and she was staring straight into a billowing, roiling inferno.

She found her breath at last, her scream choked short by the hellish blast of fire as the windows blew inwards —

VII

The computer speakers hissed static, then abruptly silenced.

"End of file."

Martha stared at the monitor. The windows filled with snow, then abruptly switched to the *Reagan's* crew patiently waiting for liftoff, the player having returned by default to the beginning of the record. Eighteen people, already dead.

"Oh my God —" Her voice caught in her throat.

"Goddamn." It was Price. He wiped his eyes with the back of his thick hand. "Goddamn, they didn't have a chance."

He looked up to his left, past Martha to where Mac stood. His arms were wrapped around his chest, his callused knuckles white, the tendons on the back of his clenched hands standing out like cables. He stared straight ahead, rigid, eyes wide and unblinking.

"Mac?"

Price reached out. Mac spun violently away from his touch, careening into the glass wall behind him.

"Hey, Mac! Easy —"

"I couldn't hear him."

The words came like a midnight creak in a still house. Martha touched his arm. Again Mac lurched away, facing them both:

"I couldn't hear him!"

Comprehension struck Price. He moved in, seized Mac's elbows, stared up into his friend's contorted face.

"That's right! I heard it! He said punch out! Rawlings *ordered* you to *punch-out!"*

"I couldn't hear him."

"Nobody could, Mac. Nobody."

For long moments, there was nothing. Then, like a slowly deflating canopy, Mac sank to his knees before Price. His mouth moved as if silently testing the words. They came, the barest whisper —

"I did the right thing."

Price shifted his grip to Mac's shoulders, holding him hard. Mac met his gaze and this time the words came stronger, borne on wonder: "I did the right thing."

"You're the only one who did," whispered Price.

Mac's eyes closed tight. There were tears, his mouth opened into a sob but no sound came. Price held his hand gently behind Mac's head, bent forward until their foreheads touched, his own tears falling.

"Welcome back, my brother," he sighed.

Martha felt the power of Mac's catharsis, an invisible curtain of raw emotion pushing against her. She was bewildered, unsure what was transpiring, but certain this moment was not for her.

Price turned to her. She took his extended hand, let him tug her from her chair onto the floor next to Mac. She gingerly wrapped her arms around him, felt him momentarily stiffen against her embrace. Then he turned, burying his face into her shoulder. Martha stroked his hair and felt her own tears, not knowing from whence they came.

"Shh. It's alright," she purred, rocking him, feeling him quiet. "Shh."

Price slumped in his chair. He felt like an old towel, wrung out and ragged. It was dizzying, attempting to process the sudden deluge of information after so many years of building theories out of air.

He rubbed his face, forced himself into alertness. Took a mental step back, chased down the chain of events, held it tight. He played out the links, one by one.

The RCS burn before OMS retro burn. That was the pivitol event. Less than a minute after that routine maneuver they'd lost the vernier. F-3D RCS primary thruster, starboard nose. Coolant valve failure, he'd heard Gurthie say it. Not good, but not catastrophic. At least, not on paper.

He dredged up from familiar memory the *Reagan's* forward RCS specs. Pictured the vernier, traced it back to the injector, the manifold just behind the nozzle, the turbopump and the chamber coolant valve below it, the pre-mix coolant valve above it . . .

Martha felt Mac stir. She lifted her head, found him gazing at her, his eyes clear.

"You okay?"

He smiled in acknowledgement, a tired twist of his lips. "What's going on?" she gently pleaded.

"Son of a bitch!"

They both turned. Price's mouth was open, eyes wide. "Son of a *bitch!*" He slapped his palm atop Conner's desk, faced them. "The systems interface!"

Mac rose, helping Martha to her feet, his eyes glued on Price as the other man spoke excitedly. "Right between APU startup and the maneuver to retro-burn attitude, the F-3D coolant valve — pre-mix, probably, there's no way to know for sure, but you look at where it's located . . . "

Price stopped, seeing the confusion in Martha's face. He took a breath and began anew, leaning forward, hands working the air before him while he lectured.

"Right before every drop, you've got to slow the ship down. That's what the OMS retro-burn does, the orbital maneuvering system, the big engines in the back of the ship. But before you can burn them you've got to turn the ship around, a hundred-eighty degrees, so they fire against your forward velocity. It's like stopping your car by spinning it around backwards and then stomping the accelerator instead of the brake, right?" Martha nodded her understanding.

"Now, the forward RCS verniers, the reaction control system, they're these little thrusters on either side of the nose and tail that burn perpendicular to the ship — you wanna turn right, you burn the port forward and aft starboard verniers and vice-versa to stop. For some reason, one of the coolant valves on the F-3D starboard thruster failed during the maneuver burn, right before the vernier exploded. Guthrie said it, the data crawl confirmed it. I'm guessing it was the pre-mix, it could've been the chamber valve but I don't see how that would've caused it."

"Caused what?" Martha was following Price but she had no idea where he was leading.

"The interface." It was Mac, grim recognition in his voice.

Price nodded once in confirmation. "Yup. The primary systems interface, the one monitored by Waring at SysOps, McEvoy, too. Forward fuselage, mid-deck, right smack-dab between the port and starboard RCS. It would've been under Guthrie and Ashdown's feet, practically in their laps. It's heat shielded, but not by much. When F-3D blew out —"

" — the explosion burned through the insulation," Mac finished.

"And took half the shipboard systems with it." Price ticked them off on his fingers. "Avionics, primary intership com, fire control, tactical . . . "

He paused, fresh revelation showing on his face. "That's how she was targeted! STEALTH systems array runs through the same interface, when the vernier went it took STEALTH with it, probably right from the start. They were right on top of the fucking missile when it happened, with all the other systems gone they were sitting ducks!"

"Yeah, but they still had imaging at TacOps," Mac put in, as intense as Price. "Drop status, too, they were tracking the missile right to the end, saw me punch out."

"Just a matter of time before they would've gone, too," Price declared. "It was a chain failure. Initial blast took out flight systems, communications, access control to the hatches, who knows what else. I'll have to check the specs but I'll bet the datalink nodes for TacOps are on the port side of the interface."

"Fire just hadn't gotten to them yet."

"That's right. Hell, it's a wonder the fuel lines didn't blow. I'll bet they had gunnery and countermeasures right up until the second they needed them." His face turned ugly. "If they'd had just another few seconds of warning, Mac, just five seconds and they might still be here."

Price would never have believed it if he hadn't seen and heard the transcription. In his wildest musings he'd never imagined the cause of the *Reagan's* end would have been something so elementary, and so unforgivably stupid. The most sophisticated spacecraft ever built had been brought down by bad plumbing, by the horribly ill-timed failure of a mechanism he himself could have afforded to replace. And the ultimate irony: that the failure of that part had rendered the *Reagan's* multi-billion-dollar technology as useless as if she'd been made of pasteboard and twine, had allowed her to be destroyed by the very missile that had been their target.

He slammed his fists into his legs. "God-dammit! How!"

Now Martha spoke. "How, how wha —"

"How the hell do you miss something like that?" Price cried. "OMS, RCS, all that's supposed to be checked and re-checked, flushed and test-burned after every-single-drop! No way a cluster fuck this big wouldn't have shown up! How could they have *missed* it?"

"We didn't."

They turned towards the door. Conner stood there, leaning heavily on his cane, a skeletal silhouette in the brighter light of the outer office. Yamada nervously followed a few paces behind as the old man shuffled into the room, his parchment face slowly revealed in the soft illumination from the window. Martha was hardly able to say the words.

"You *knew?*"

"We had two weeks before Stormcloud," Conner croaked. He halted before the broad desk, the accused before his judges on the other side. "Two weeks to get the *Reagan* back to Vandenberg, check it, prep it for the drop, all the while the Pentagon breathing down our necks."

"You gave the go-ahead." It was Price, his voice hard. "You knew the *Reagan* wasn't fit to fly, but you gave the go-ahead anyway?"

"I was told it would be okay!" Conner pleaded. Yamada flinched at the words, but all eyes were on Conner. "I wanted to wait, I swear I told them we needed more time but they wouldn't listen! I had no choice!"

"Why didn't you say anything?" Martha asked, incredulous. "All these years — dear God, why didn't you tell someone?"

Conner laughed, a pained cough. "Who? The press? The secretary of defense himself told me if I said a word to anyone he'd cancel my lease on Vandenberg, hang me out to dry. Everything I've worked for, everything I had would have been destroyed —"

"You son of a bitch!"

Mac flashed out from behind the desk, lunging for Conner. The old man reared back, raising his hands before him as if expecting to be struck.

"Mac, no!"

Mac pulled up short of Conner at Martha's shouted warning. His face was twisted with rage. "You son of a bitch!" he spat. "You could have saved them!"

"I didn't have a choice!"

"You didn't have the *courage!*" Mac roared. "I lost my friends because you didn't have the balls to do the right thing!"

"*I lost my son!*"

He stared at Mac accusingly, his lined face transformed by his grief, his breaths coming in labored pants. He teetered unsteadily on his feet, fighting to remain erect, his whole weight resting on his cane.

Martha walked out from behind the desk in the lull, stopped between Conner and Mac. Conner didn't dare meet her eyes.

"He tried to stop me. Pleaded with me, to refuse, tell them no, for once. I told him that he, he didn't understand, how it was, what was at stake. Afterwards, he . . . " Conner moistened his lips. "I could see it, eating away at him. What he knew, the, the guilt . . . "

"No."

"I told him it wasn't his fault, it was my fault, not his! I cleared the launch! He wouldn't listen . . . "

"No," Martha said again, angrily, shaking her head in denial.

"I thought he could handle it!" Conner protested. "He had to know! He had to learn! I didn't know he, he would . . . "

His face sagged with the weight of his guilt. "My child is dead!" he moaned. "I killed my own son!"

Mac surged past Martha, hands clenching Conner's coat lapels. He half-pushed, half-dragged the old man up against the wall to the left of the desk, growling his rage. Conner's back slammed into the wall. His cane fell from his hand, clattered to the floor.

"Your own son!" Mac snarled into Conner's ashen face. "Seventeen men and women!" He cranked his fists tighter into the coat lapels, glaring into Conner's glassy eyes. "I ought to kill you right now."

Conner's mouth worked. The old man wheezed, struggling for breath. His right hand feebly clawed at his chest.

"Let go of him!"

Martha was there, brusquely elbowing Mac out of the way. Like a sack of twigs, Conner slid down the wall to the floor. His head lolled to the side, spittle trailing from the corner of his mouth, his breath rattling in his throat. Martha loosened his collar as Yamada rushed in, kneeling beside his longtime partner, his hands fluttering aimlessly over him.

VIII

Doctor Bid wore casual clothes beneath his white coat, at home when he'd gotten the call. He nodded greetings to Mac and Price, the only others in the ICU family lounge. He halted before the couch on which Martha sat.

"He's stable."

"Will he be all right?"

"It is too early to say. Doctor Mayhew performed an EKG, it showed some ischemia." He took a breath, remembering his audience.

"Damage to the heart muscle. This is not his first heart attack. He's had maybe two before, though none this severe. We will run an angiogram tomorrow, when he's stronger. Until then, the best we can do is monitor him, keep him sedated." Martha nodded dumbly. "You may see him, if you wish. Not too long."

It was several seconds before Martha rose. She exited, Doctor Bid following. Price took a sip of his coffee, glanced over to where Mac stood alone on the far side of the room.

Conner was breathing shallowly, an oxygen prong below his nose. His mouth hung open, gray tongue curled back. EKG pads dotted his hairless, exposed chest, transmitting their data to the chirping bedside unit.

Martha rested her hands on the cold aluminum railing. After a few moments his eyes opened, focused blearily on her.

"I'm sorry."

His unsteady hand rose, icy fingers brushing hers.

Martha turned and walked briskly from the room. Conner watched her go, hand falling to the mattress.

IX

He spied her standing not too far away, next to a grove of pines opposite the clinic side entrance. He walked the dozen paces over, stopping just short of her.

"You okay?"

She didn't turn. "Shouldn't you be celebrating now?"

Mac's intention to offer comfort vanished upon hearing the spite in her voice. "What's that supposed to mean?"

She made a sound, a harsh guffaw. Mac gave his anger full rein. "That bastard in there let seventeen dead soldiers take the rap for him while he lied to everyone! He used me, he used you — Christ, his own son! Kevin was the only one who at least tried to do the right thing and look where that got him!"

He felt the sharp sting of Martha's slap. She glared at him, tears glistening on her cheeks in the pink light from the clinic entrance. "Hurts, doesn't it?" Mac sneered. "Having your life torn to pieces, hurts like hell. Don't expect me to feel sorry for him, he never gave a shit about anyone but himself."

"Maybe he is responsible." Her level tone contradicted the flint in her eyes. "But you're just as guilty as he is of not facing the truth."

"I am *nothing* like him —"

"Oh bullshit, Mac!" Martha erupted. "You talk about your precious honor, how *he* lied, but did you ever tell the truth about what *you* did, to anyone? Do you really think Willie and Sensei wouldn't have forgiven you? But you didn't give them the chance, did you? No, you *ran*." Contempt coated her words. "Because you didn't have courage to face what you did, and if 'that bastard' you hate so much hadn't dragged you kicking and screaming from your safe little hole in the ground, you'd still be running!"

"It's not my fault!"

Martha shook her head in disbelief. "God, you still don't get it. Nobody forced you to punch out, Mac. You did that all by yourself. And all these years, you've been looking for somebody besides yourself to blame for that decision. Well, now you've found someone. Feel any better? Does it change anything?"

Mac was lost for a response. His usual defenses stripped by the night's revelations, Martha's broadside had found its target and blasted it to pieces.

"He should have told someone," he lamely countered. "Instead of, letting everyone think —"

"Go ahead, then!" Martha opened her arms wide. "Now you know the truth. Tell the whole world! Finish the job. Destroy him, destroy the company."

She dropped her arms, and with the motion her anger fell away, as spent as she was. "Your friends are still dead, Mac. Kevin is still dead, and maybe before the night's over his father will be, too. Then what will you do, fly back to Montana and gloat for another seven years?" She held Mac's eye, then shook her head once in disgust. "Boykin's right. You're no hero. You just chickened out."

X

"Sure wish I knew what I was feeling right now," Price mumbled. "One minute I feel like crying, next minute I'm mad, then I don't feel anything. Don't know whether to kill myself or go fishing."

It was after midnight. Mac lay on the couch in the living room, staring at the streetlight beyond the window. Price sat nearby, working on his second beer. They'd left Martha at the clinic at her stony insistence. Price's word were the first spoken since the ride back to the house.

"He'd write me." Mac adjusted his arm behind his head, the leather upholstery creaking. "Every year, on my birthday. I never wrote back. He must have thought I . . . "

"I know he missed you," Price offered into the ensuing silence. "I did, too."

"I'm sorry, Willie."

"You're sorry. Conner's sorry. Hell, I'm sorry and I don't even know what for. All I could think about for so long was finding out the truth, whatever it was. Like knowing one way or the other was gonna make a difference how I felt. It doesn't. They're still dead, and I still miss them. Miss them more."

He sat there in the dark room with the bottle between his hands, feeling the ghosts of the 82nd and the *Reagan's* crew press against his skin, the frantic din of their final words like a snatch of melancholy song he couldn't get out of his mind. He pushed them away and took another drink. "So. You made up your mind about today?"

It was the question they'd both been avoiding. This is what they'd wanted. This was the real reason he'd accepted Conner's dare, so he and Price could find out what had really happened during Operation Stormcloud. Yet they'd never planned for this moment, what they would do when it arrived. Maybe they'd never truly believed they would be successful. Now here they were, their mission accomplished beyond their wildest imaginings, and the shuttle for Moontown was still set to launch in just sixteen hours, they were still scheduled to be at RDU in less than eight, and everything still rested on him. The fate of UniCom, of Moontown. All on him.

"I wish he was here," Mac whispered. "I wish I could ask him what to do."

"That's easy," Price murmured. Mac turned his head to look at his best friend's shadowed face. "Same thing the Colonel always said. A warrior's greatest battle is fought inside himself. It's the only one you can't run away from. No matter where you go, it's always right there with you." He stroked the wheel of his chair with his free hand.

"Doesn't matter what it is. Sooner or later, you've got to turn and face it. Or it'll eat you alive."

He looked up, into Mac's attentive gaze. "That's the thing about the warrior's way, brother. It's never about winning or losing. It's about facing your demons and making your peace."

It was a beautifully clear night. Lying on his back on the roof, it wasn't hard to imagine he was reclining on the gentle slope of his property in Montana, staring up at the stars. There was *Orion*, the shining gem of *Betelgeuse* pinned at the hunter's right shoulder, *Rigel* bright on his left hip. *Eridanus* snaked its glittering way below the constellation while the twin stars *Castor* and *Pollux* defined nearby *Gemini*. He knew them all by sight, knew they would always be there for him, fixed for eternity in the heavens while countless lives passed in units too brief to win their notice, countless eyes beheld them in wonder, praying for the smallest measure of their constancy.

He sat up stiffly, elbows digging into the rough shingles. Price's words played in his mind. The warrior's way was all he had known his entire life, even as a child, even before he could put a name to the proud fire that had always been what he was. He hadn't wept when his father died, afraid that his innocent grief might somehow dishonor a man he'd never really known. Just a boy, then, thinking such thoughts; now a man, driven by the same demons, those of honor, of duty. The same demons which he now confronted after having run from them in fear for so, so long.

He wrapped his arms around his knees. If only he'd read the incident report. He would have seen the lies, just as Price had. He could have said something then, challenged the finding, worked to put things right . . .

No. That wasn't it at all. For the first time in nine years, he fully opened his heart to the truth.

He'd allowed the military to make him a hero, had obediently participated in the charade like the good soldier he'd been, until the guilt had become too much to bear. Then he'd fled to Montana, to the middle of nowhere, as far away from his celebrity as his meager funds could carry him. Yet the demons had traveled with him, demanding his attention his every waking moment, then even in his sleep. In his stumbling rush to flee the truth, he'd left behind his comrades and everything for which they'd stood. He had pretended to honor their memory even as he'd hidden behind it, brandishing their deaths like a talisman to ward off Conner, Martha, even Price's attempts to yank him out of his self-pity.

The world hadn't forgotten about the 82nd — he had. He'd purposely avoided reading the finding, avoided anything that might have forced him to confront his responsibility for his actions, any person or thing that might remind him of the lie he was living. This was his sin, and it was a burden as onerous as Conner's, just as Martha had said. The sacrifice of the *Reagan* and her crew was the coin that had purchased his celebrity. His years of self-righteous, abject denial, the only thanks he had shown.

No more. This was not who he was, not who he wanted to be.

He gazed at the sky. As if an omen summoned by his desire, a shooting star traced a line of white fire across the firmament, shaming its celestial kin with its radiance. Mac followed its path, feeling his long-forsaken honor swell new and hot in his heart.

In seconds, the meteor winked out. And in that time, all of Mac's doubts vanished, burned away by its proud incandescence.

It was time to settle the account. Time to stop running. Time for Major Mackinley Harrison face his demons and make his peace.

Part Three

Eight

I

Roger Conner lay in his hospital bed, listening to the steady chirp of the cardiac monitor, the sound of his mortality. Drops of fluid fell with metronome regularity from the hanging bag into the IV tube, glistening in the dimmed overhead light. The needle in his arm ached, it was all he could do not to yank the damn thing out. Instead, he lay still, feeling weak. Feeling old.

He inhaled as deeply as he could, ignoring the slowing cadence of the cardiac monitor. The tightness in his chest was gone. He exhaled slowly, then repeated the action a dozen times. When he finished his mind was clearer, purified by the oxygen that chased away the tag ends of his last dose of sedative. He resolved not to allow any more. If anyone argued, they would discover just how difficult a patient he could be.

The nurses in Vietnam had learned quickly enough. Two days after the surgeons at Tan Son Nhut had screwed together the remaining splinters of his hip he'd fought through his morphine haze to get out of bed. A passing orderly had barely managed to catch him as he slid from the metal cot, tearing the IV needle from his arm. They'd strapped him down after that. He'd ignored the shouted curses of the other wounded as he screamed for them to release him, screamed until the nurse emptied the syringe into the fresh IV tube.

It was another two days before he'd truly awakened, his hip throbbing with pain. He told the haggard-looking doctor who arrived a few minutes later that he felt fine, he didn't need more morphine. The doctor saw the pain in his face but honored his wish. After a few cursory

228

questions, he agreed to remove the restraints, with a promise to bind him anew if Conner didn't behave. The patient raised the middle finger of his hand beneath the sheet as he thanked his physician for his kindness.

It was a long convalescence. His hip had required complete reconstruction. A pin protruded like a nail from his betadine-stained flesh, heavy Frankenstein stitches puckering the flaking skin. They would come out in another week, he was told, the pin in two months, after he'd returned to the states. Congratulations, soldier. As soon as he was ambulatory, he was going home.

His CO visited once, soberly imparting the news of the deaths of Conner's squadmates. Conner's return fire as he parachuted into the jungle had miraculously taken out four VC, he was informed, though the bigger miracle to Conner was how the hell they could tell. Regardless, he would receive the Silver Star with his Purple Heart: the latter commendation for surviving; the former, he suspected, the Army's way of assuaging their own guilt. He knew their retaliatory air strike had probably killed more troops than the VC's bullets.

The days passed. He grimly endured the agony of physical therapy, consumed each day's edition of *Stars & Stripes*, the months-old back issues of *Life*. There were a few books, not counting the Bibles, classics lying neglected on the shelf beside dog-eared paperbacks of best-sellers: spy novels, crime, science-fiction. Escapist drivel, thought Conner as he scanned the covers dejectedly. He closed his eyes and extended his finger towards the shelf until he felt resistance, pulled the volume from the stack and wheeled himself outside to read.

He finished Arthur C. Clarke's <u>*2001: A Space Odyssey*</u> in two days. He loathed science-fiction, but this had been nothing like he'd expected, no hulking space monsters and zap guns. It was science, set in a future world where such science would logically exist, each invention confidently launched from a springboard securely affixed to reality. Little that was, but nothing that couldn't be.

He closed the book, stared at the cover. 2001 — he would be fifty, alive to see it if it happened. A future in which he could believe, a future within the grasp of present-day technology. Man had walked on the moon less than five years earlier. Anything was possible now.

He returned the volume to the shelf, disappointed when his eager search revealed nothing more by Clarke. A twenty dollar bill slipped to an orderly bought him three more paperback volumes from the base bookstore, the balance of the tender payment for his trouble. He devoured Clarke's hard science and later found the the same in the works of Isaac Asimov, Robert A. Heinlein, Ray Bradbury and others, more willing now to endure the elements of outright fantasy between the covers. What the authors had in common was humanity. The visionary science of their works wasn't the point; it was presented as a framework for the further advancement of mankind, a launching pad for tales as philosophical as they were fantastic. These were men with vision, a vision with which he could identify, a vision that had begun to stir something deep within himself.

Engrossed in his reading, Conner's convalescence flew by. Soon he was moving stiffly but resolutely about the hospital with the assistance of a walker. His doctors now argued with him not to push himself too hard. It was a wonder he was walking at all they said, though it was doubtful he'd ever be able to without assistance. Their words confirmed what Conner already knew in his bones but he refused to allow himself to indulge in self-pity. Self-pity was weakness, and he resolved never again to allow himself that selfish luxury. He would never accept defeat, not now, now that he had a plan.

At last the day of his discharge arrived. He stuffed his books into his tight duffel, yanking the straining zipper over them. He would go to college, get his degree. He would find money, somewhere, and a place to work. He would find people who possessed the technical skills he lacked, who shared his burgeoning vision.

Together, they would turn their eyes towards 2001.

He squirmed in bed against the hot ache in his hip. Fifty years it had been since his naïve epiphany. If he'd known then what it would cost him, in sweat and in soul, he doubted he would have undertaken the journey. How fitting that his dream should end as it had begun, with him lying in his sickbed — the terrified young boy praying his life was not over, the weary old man marking the days to his death.

Moontown had begun as a hobby, Conner collecting out of habit every scrap of data that might remotely be of use, shuffling the facts in his mind like index cards. Each new technology was factored into the equation, modifying or replacing existing variables until one day, Conner had realized his resources equaled technology's pace. All the pieces were there, like a jigsaw puzzle scattered across a global tabletop. All that was required to assemble them into a complete picture was money, and will.

Conner had both. In the decades since his military retirement he, with Bobby Yamada at his side, had built UniCom into a staggering entity. There were other companies that outshone UniCom in specific research specialties but none that were as far-reaching and flexible in the scope of their vision. With support for the national space program fast waning, Conner began carefully dropping a word here, an idea there, assaying the support a moonbase might expect. Had such an audacious vision come from anyone else, it would have been dismissed as laughable fantasy. But this was Roger Charles Conner.

Still, garnering support had been an arduous song-and-dance. Wall Street couldn't decide whether to worship or vilify him, while the press routinely attached the adjective *eccentric* to his name. No one could see a clear, commercial reason to build a base on the moon, not one as large as that which Conner described. He rattled off the usual research arguments, lent his supportive voice to the vociferous debate over whether a manned mission to Mars was necessary. Yet always his primary argument had been humanity's innate compulsion to push the boundaries of its existence, the poet Browning's call for mankind's reach to exceed its grasp, to finally close its fingers around Earth's pale sister and claim her as its own.

And all the while, he'd been lying through his teeth.

Yamada had been researching commercial fusion years before construction on Moontown had begun, using a spherical tokamak that was at the time the most widely-accepted platform, and it had been Yamada who had lobbied his old friend hard to abandon the unwieldy design in favor of the IEC reactor and helium-3. The first modest deuterium-^{3}He fusion reaction had been produced as early as 1949, using ^{3}He collected from nuclear fission. In 1978, the British Interplanetary Society's Daedalus project proposed using ^{3}He from space to power a reactor, although their plan had called for collecting it from the atmospheres of Jupiter and Saturn, a fanciful notion at best.

It wasn't until 1985 that scientists at the University of Wisconsin had reasoned that ^{3}He would be contained in the solar wind as a byproduct of solar fusion and further, that it would therefore be deposited on the moon. Incredibly, it was not until investigation of the hypothesis that the fusion community realized the crew of Apollo 11 had brought back to Earth samples of ^{3}He from that very source sixteen years earlier.

There was ^{3}He on the moon and ^{3}He fusion reactors on Earth, yet no one had bothered to proceed any farther than that. Yamada hadn't needed to press his argument. He'd given Conner the final piece that at last crystallized his vision.

Lunar Prospector's galvanizing evidence of possible ice hidden in the moon's polar regions had caused grave problems for awhile, with many of Conner's investors arguing for Moontown's relocation to take advantage of the unexpected vital resource. It had required every iota of Conner's persuasiveness to silence the voices without revealing the true necessity of Moontown's location, the stunning abundance of ^{3}He in *Mare Smythii.* He knew he was playing a dangerous game, inviting mammoth lawsuits should it be discovered he was using investor capital for his undisclosed purposes, but there was much more to be lost if someone talked. Once Moontown was up and running, once Yamada and his staff had mastered the ^{3}He IEC fusion process, then he would inform his investors. He doubted anyone then would rue the deception.

Pacifying his investors had soon ceased to be an issue. Moontown had narrowly avoided becoming another of the Pan-Am's casualties, funding choked to a trickle by the war effort. Conner had fought tooth and nail to rescue it from extinction, poured every bit of spare capital he could muster into simply keeping it alive. Ironically, the income from his own military contracts had saved Moontown, had enabled Yamada to crank fusion research into overdrive. Now fusion alone would save his dream. Or so it had appeared, until last night.

Conner sighed, a rattling wheeze. His stomach growled with hunger. He tried to remember the last time he'd eaten. A day at least, assuming it was now morning.

He began to tremble. How strange, he thought. He wasn't cold. He forced more shuddering breaths, to calm himself, refusing to acknowledge the emotions that gnawed now at the edges of his embattled conscience.

He had never considered himself ruthless, only single-minded. He'd had to be, to build his empire, to accomplish what he had, for without that empire the world would surely be a poorer place. The tree of progress, the blood of patriots, unwilling though they'd been. Surely it had been necessary.

His trembling worsened, his pulse drummed in his ears. He clenched the thin sheets with numb fingers, pulled them to his abdomen. He saw Beth on the Asheville property, marking the rooms of their unbuilt home by the flowers growing there, freckled shoulders bare to the sun. They'd made love in the grass, returned home not knowing their first child had just been conceived. Later they decided on Ashley, if it was a girl. Kevin if a boy, after Beth's grandfather.

Sweet God, Kevin.

Celestial providence alone had placed the moon at perigee on December 24th, 2022. Had it been otherwise, Conner would still have insisted on Christmas Eve. He would make that holy night once again cause for celebration, something other than the night his only child had killed himself. He had even managed to convince himself that Kevin would have wanted it that way. As if he'd ever known what had truly been in his son's heart.

Conner was stunned to feel water on his cheeks. When had he become this way? What moment had changed him so? He could blame it on Beth's death but that was so long ago now, more than half the span of his life. The years since were his, the sins on which he'd built his empire, the ruined lives. Now it was time to pay for his hubris. Harrison was probably on his way back to Montana, and soon he and Price would go public with their knowledge. It was over, and there was absolutely nothing he could do to stop it.

The self-pity he'd long ago forsworn swallowed him. Shuddering with the assault of his sins, he wept alone for the death of his dreams.

II

It was early, the neighborhood quiet, the air cold. Mac locked the front door behind him and walked the few paces in the foggy dawn to where the car waited in the driveway. He dropped his duffel atop Price's suitcase and computer case. A dog began barking somewhere, alerted by the hollow *thunk* of the trunk slamming closed. He walked to the driver's side, climbed in, pulled the door shut against the chill.

"You finally ready to go?" Price asked from the shotgun seat.

"If you hadn't taken so long in the bathroom we'd have been gone a half-hour ago."

"It's important to look pretty."

Mac started the car, cranking the heater wide open as the electric engine whined into life. He took the folded slip of paper Price offered, opened it, scanned the block-letter writing. "This everything?"

"Oughta do it. Lot of money, though."

"We're not paying for it." Mac reached into his shirt pocket, withdrew the UniCom cash card. "For 'expenses,' remember?"

Price chuckled. "Remind me to write Conner a thank-you note."

Mac dropped the card back into his pocket and shifted the car into reverse, backing onto the road. "I doubt he'll be in the mood to read it when he finds out what he bought."

The pounding came again, loud. Boykin kicked the twisted sheet from his legs and hauled himself erect, his head throbbing anew as he stood.

The pounding came a third time. "Christ, all right!" he bellowed, regretting it instantly. He shuffled out of his bedroom into the tiny living room, yanked open the door.

"What," he finally said.

"Truce, Jimmy."

After a moment's dull-eyed debate, Boykin turned and walked back into the apartment. Mac followed, closing the door behind him.

The big man dropped onto the sofa and Mac scanned the apartment. Small, minimal furnishings, but surprisingly neat. His host wore boxers and a sleeveless tee-shirt. He rubbed hard sleep from his face. "My shoulder hurts like hell," he said, not looking at Mac. "Oughta know better than to go after you with a stick."

"How's your head?"

Boykin dropped his hands. His cheek bore angry red scratches. "Fitzpatrick brought me home. From what I can remember."

"How much do you remember?"

"Enough." Still he didn't look up. "Seven years without a drink." He shook his head wearily. "Scared the shit outta me, you know. Thinkin' about it. Skydiving from the moon. I was really lookin' forward to it, though. Reckon I'm out of it altogether now."

"What makes you think that?" Now Boykin looked up, his bleary eyes revealing nothing. "Nobody knows what happened last night except whoever was there," Mac said. "Martha, Price and me are the only ones that matter, we haven't told anyone. No reason to."

"So, what, you're doin' me a favor now?"

"C'mon, Jimmy, let's give it a rest, all right? I didn't come here about what happened last night."

"So what are you doin' here? Shouldn't you be on a plane to Vandenberg?"

"Yeah, so I don't have much time." Mac considered sitting, remained standing. "Look, I didn't know Conner was using you but I know how he is. He's been doing it from the beginning, to get to me."

"No shit. Like he ever planned to let me do it."

Mac hid his surprise. "You already know, then."

Boykin guffawed. "I ain't as dumb as I might sound y'know, as everyone thinks I am. I'm a drunk. I know shit about skydiving. But I was too fired up about doin' it to think about why he asked me. Moment I saw you, I knew. Reckon I was good for something, though." He raised his hand towards Mac in mock presentment.

"You're still in this."

Boykin scratched his stomach, disinterested. "Yeah, flyin' escort. Like I got a choice."

"You've got more of a choice than you think. A lot's happened since last night. I can't tell you what, not yet."

"Ain't nobody told me shit from the beginning, why should that change now —"

"Look, man, you can sit here feeling sorry for yourself or you can listen to what I have to offer," Mac snapped. "I've got a plane to catch, all right?"

Anger surfaced on Boykin's face, and Mac saw the thick muscles of his shoulders tense. Nice job, he thought. Nothing more amenable than a pissed-off redneck. "Like I said, Conner's been using us both, Tim too, to get to me. I don't like it any more than you do. In fact, I'm ready to put a stop to it. You interested?"

Boykin glared, but Mac could tell his words had penetrated. He reached into his shirt pocket and withdrew Price's folded list, extended it to Boykin. The other man only looked at it. Mac dropped his arm, knowing it was going to take more.

He squatted, sitting back on his heels, level with Boykin. "You're right," he began, absently turning the list over in his hands. "I panicked. I chickened out." It was the first time the admission came free of guilt. Mac paused a moment to contemplate the new feeling, let it add its honest strength to the rest of his words. "But I didn't kill your brother. You know that, Jimmy, as well as I do. My only sin was surviving."

Boykin's head was down, so Mac couldn't see his face. His voice was husky. "Tim was a good soldier."

"Yes he was."

"I wish like hell he hadn't been."

His reddened eyes found Mac's. Now Mac recognized the source of Boykin's torment. That one wish, that his brother had done what Mac had done, that Tim Boykin had punched out, too. A new thought occurred to Mac then. He'd no idea if it was true, but he heard himself speaking even as it surfaced.

"You know, Jimmy, I bet he tried."

Mac held Boykin's eyes, waiting for the notion to fuse as he balanced it against the facts Price said were published in the public finding. "I bet they all tried to punch out. They all had to have seen the autodrop flash, just like me. Right?" They all had to have felt the bump of the exploding vernier, had to have realized the com was dead. "Tim could've been reaching for that button right when the missile hit. You know enough about what we did to know it was SOP." The last words were addressed as much to himself as Boykin. "I'll bet if we'd had just one or two more seconds, they'd all be here today."

Maybe it was nothing more than rationalization, but as he spoke Mac felt the last of his guilt lift. He'd panicked, but behind that impulse had been the sure notion that something was wrong. He'd watched the flight record, seen and heard Rawlings screaming for them to punch out, but he'd never really stopped to consider the silent voices that must have been shouting into their dead comlinks as he had, the other eyes glued to that autodrop button. There was no way to know how many sled engines might have been kicking into life behind his. True, it had been a mad sequence of events that had saved him after, but who could guess fortune's fancy?

He watched Boykin's grab hold of the idea. "You really believe that?"

Mac sighed, the thrill of inspiration fading as suddenly as it had arisen. "Truth? I don't know, man. I've been underneath this thing for so long. It's only been the last couple of days that I've really . . . " He left the thought unfinished. "I've missed Tim too, you know. Don't think I haven't wished a million times there was a way I could've traded places with him, with any of them. But I can't. And I'm done with apologizing for surviving."

Boykin held Mac's eye a few seconds more, then dropped his gaze to the list. Mac again extended the paper. Boykin leaned forward and took it, opened it, read it.

"When do you arrive at Vandenberg?" Mac asked.

"I leave tomorrow, get there around six PM, I reckon."

"Buy everything on that list exactly as it's written and bring it with you. Give it to Willie first thing, don't let anybody else touch it." Mac reached into his pocket and withdrew the UniCom cash card. He flipped it over to Boykin, who snagged it neatly out of the air. He raised the list in his other hand. "What's this stuff for?"

"We're gonna nail Conner." Mac grinned wolfishly. "Nail him so hard that wrinkled bastard won't be able to come after any of us ever again."

Boykin dropped the list and card beside him on the couch. For a moment Mac thought his entreaty had been in vain, but then Boykin reached down his shirt and pulled a chunky class ring out from beneath the wrinkled fabric. He held it in his hand, gazing at it.

"James B. Hunt High School, class of '96," he softly drawled. "It's his. He was wearing mine when he died. We were gonna give 'em back after the war. I knew I didn't have much chance of makin' it. Didn't matter. I was gonna bring Tim home, or die tryin'. Either way, I won."

"Let me bring him home for you, Jimmy. All of them. Help me make it right for both of us."

Mac stood as Boykin rose to his feet, lifting the chain over his head. He extended the precious token before him. Mac closed his fingers around the ring but Boykin held the chain tight.

"Don't fuck up this time," he warned. "I want that back."

III

The UniCom Shuttle *Sagan* stood tall atop the launch mount, tethered to the access tower at SLC-6, her ivory skin reflecting the light of the afternoon sun. She vented plumes of cold nitrogen gas which trailed down her flanks like waterfalls, the broad flyback booster wing extending beyond the platform to either side, patiently awaiting the command to roar skyward. Atop the access tower nearly three-hundred-feet aboveground, a launch tech in a hard hat paused to gaze out over the complex and beyond, to the dark olive swells of the Pacific Ocean.

Space Launch Complex Six — *Slick 6* — was what the old-timers still called the UniCom Commercial Space Launch Facility. Originally built for NASA's Manned Orbiting Laboratory program, construction had begun in 1966 but was halted in June of '69, when the program was mothballed. It wasn't until almost ten years later, in January of 1979, that SLC-6 had been reactivated and modified for the infant Space Transportation System program, the existing facility demolished and rebuilt to the required specifications to launch NASA's space shuttles into orbit.

Though fully operational, SLC-6 had rarely seen a shuttle launch. Its sister facility at Kennedy Space Center on the Atlantic handled that duty well enough that Vandenberg was consigned to boosting satellites into orbit and testing payload delivery systems. Not until the turn of the century, almost forty years after the first foundation was laid, was SLC-6 finally called into service for that purpose for which it had been originally intended, when it saw the UniCom Shuttle *Kitty Hawk* and its crew of engineers off on their journey to the moon. Since then it had seen dozens of manned and unmanned launches, both for UniCom and the military, including eleven wartime missions by the 82nd Special Airborne, traveling aboard the *D.S. Reagan*.

There was a monument to the *Reagan* at SLC-6 now, a burnished aluminum plate affixed to the side entrance of the massive Shuttle Assembly Building that, with the open-faced Mobile Service Tower, bracketed the Access Tower. A larger twin was placed outside the entrance to the Launch Control Center, set into an otherwise unadorned granite block, each monument bearing the engraved image of the *Reagan* in flight and the names of those who had perished on her final voyage.

Mac peered over the shoulder of the driver and through the windshield, watching the *Sagan* grow steadily larger. He rode in the back of the van that carried him to the Access Tower, wore the standard blue UniCom flight suit, his modest kit resting on the floor beside his feet. The vehicle that had carried the 82nd to the *Reagan* had been windowless and isolated from the cab, so he'd never been able to see the ship from any angle other than straight up when they exited the vehicle at the Access Tower base.

Davis was with Mac now inside the van, sitting beside Martha on the bench seat behind the one on which Mac and Price sat. Mac had met him at UniCom as planned, and there had been a phalanx of reporters waiting at RDU outside the gate that opened onto UniCom's private hangar when they'd arrived an hour later. Davis had taken five minutes to deliver a cursory statement and answer a few questions. Martha had filled him in on Conner's heart attack, Mac learned, information Davis had insisted be kept confidential. All Martha would say, when she said anything to Mac, was that Conner remained in ICU.

Davis was still jabbering into Mac's ear. "Don't forget the press conference, first thing when you get there."

"I know, Tracy Johnson, she'll meet me."

"Short hair, about my height —"

"I know."

"She'll be wearing a nametag so you should be able to spot her pretty easy."

"Will you relax?" Mac craned his neck to glower at Davis. The young man's frenetic energy was jacking his own stress level higher. "I've got it covered."

"Sorry, I'm sorry. Just, wanna make sure everything's covered."

Price chuckled. "Don't worry, Steve. It'll be fine."

"Right. You're right." He paused. "Did I tell you about . . . "

And so on. A handful of launch personnel were waiting when they arrived at the Access Tower, opening the van's sliding door even as the vehicle rolled to a halt. Mac stepped out first, grateful of escaping Davis' frenzied inquisition. Davis and Martha followed but Price remained where he was. "You're not coming out?" Mac asked.

"Just have to climb right back in."

Mac stepped back inside, sat next to Price, waited. Price shook his head, smiling wanly. "Just can't help thinking, the last time any of them stood here. Can you feel it?"

Mac looked out at the *Sagan*. He did feel it — a shift in his perception, the familiar sounds and scents of the SLC transporting him back a decade. He and Price standing close to this very spot, body armor and weaponry weighing heavy on their flesh, boots tramping on the concrete as Alpha and Bravo companies marched in twin columns to the tower elevator in the warm California dusk. For a moment he was there once more, the old emotions briefly stirring in his gut. The expectation, the hard resolve, the fear.

"Major Harrison?"

Mac opened his eyes, nodded to the launch tech. "I never asked you what changed your mind," said Price.

"You did. Last night."

"Oh no, don't you hang this on me, I'm the one who got you into this mess in the first place!" He tried to keep it light, but Mac could see it was all Price could do hold his emotions in check.

They embraced. "Don't embarrass me, now," said Price.

"See you in a couple days."

Price scowled at the impatient launch tech. "He's coming! Go on, get out of here before he drags you out," he finished to Mac, giving him a push towards the door.

Davis shook Mac's hand energetically after he stepped out. "Good luck. Not that you'll need it."

"I'll take it anyway."

Davis stepped back, and Mac faced Martha.

"Well." She forced a smile. "Like Steve said. Good luck."

"Look, about what you said last night —"

Martha shook her head quickly. "You're here. That's enough."

Mac unzipped a leg pocket in his flight suit, withdrew a small gift-wrapped box. Martha hesitated before taking it from his outstretched hand. "What's this?"

"Merry Christmas. You can open it later."

"Major." Mac lifted his hand in acknowledgement to the tech. Martha extended her hand to shake. Mac took it, leaned in and kissed her softly. He felt her momentarily stiffen, felt her hand pull against his in surprise, then felt her respond, her grip softening as she lightly brushed his chest with the other. It lasted only a second or two, long enough.

They separated. Mac turned and followed the tech to the tower elevator. Martha watched his receding back, the gift clutched in her hand.

It was on all the networks, every goddamn one of them. Conner used the remote to flip through the channels, watching the television he'd demanded be brought into ICU as soon as he'd gotten the call from Yamada. Mac was on the plane. He was going to Vandenberg. He was going to do it.

Doctor Bid entered the room as the countdown neared finality. He watched with Conner as the *Sagan* roared from the pad, watched the cameras pan across the thousands gathered in the observation area miles away, cheering the shuttle rising on its billowing fountain of orange flame. Conner's heart beat faster as ground control called for throttle-up at T+01:09, watched the twin liquid rocket boosters peel away from the main tank at T+02:11 and swing gracefully back to Vandenberg, guided by remote control, leaving behind the *Sagan*, now a hazy, rapidly-shrinking blur, soon to be lost from sight.

Conner sank back into his pillows, feeling like a man brought back on the wings of angels from the brink of annihilation. He didn't know what had changed Mac's mind, nor did he care. There would be time later to puzzle out his motivation. For the moment, it was enough to celebrate the rebirth of his dream.

"Raj," he said, muting the television audio. "You think I could get something to eat?"

Nine

I

Tracy Johnson sat at her desk terminal, reviewing the day's work. She sipped tea, her second cup — Indian Assam, brewed in her office. Strong as coffee if you let it steep long enough, strong enough almost to kill the taste of the water.

The mass driver generator repair was nearing completion. Fortunately, the damage hadn't been as severe as they'd feared on first inspection; amazingly, they had the replacement parts in stock. Repairs were on track to be finished by the time of Harrison's arrival the next day. Hell, they might even have time to test it.

The assignment of personnel to stand 'round-the-clock guard at key drop stations had effectively broadcast the fact that the 'accident' was anything but. Rumors were sweeping through the base at quantum speed, and any attempt by her or Soos to address them publicly would only fuel the idea of a cover-up. She could think of no practical firewall other than work, of which there was plenty. She'd have to trust her people's professionalism to keep speculation in check. Other than the generator, the dropsled was her chief concern, the prime target for sabotage. It would arrive on the *Sagan* with Harrison; Soos had vowed to off-load it himself and never let it leave his sight until Harrison was inside and on his way. And God help anyone who crossed Mendoza.

Johnson had sent a priority flash to Yamada to check Torgerson and Redding's mail, while Soos had handled the legwork. Al Buckmore had returned from *Talbot* earlier in the day, had confirmed Torgerson had been with him for the run's duration, though he'd showed up at the last minute, saying he'd overslept. There was no record of his having gone outside until just before his shift, though he might have deduced a way to bypass the airlock safety protocol. Unlikely, but possible. He was still suspect.

Redding had been servicing the solar array in the hours prior to the generator overload. He'd been the last to finish his work, about twenty minutes overdue returning; just enough time, given his job location, to make it to the power plant and back. No one had seen him leave his station but SPA techs worked sometimes a quarter-mile apart on the massive array; given the restricted range of vision imposed by P-suit buckets he could easily have gone AWOL and returned without having been spotted.

She rubbed her eyes. They were right back where they'd begun; suspicions, but no proof. One thing she'd done that morning. As extra insurance, she'd instructed the bubble crew to monitor the surface airlocks around the clock and let her know immediately if anyone went outside off-shift. Their quarry would be stupid to call attention to himself that way but given the dire results of his last attempt, better safe than doubly sorry.

At least they now knew for certain how the saboteur had gained access to the power plant. The only door, the same through which Osborne had been pulled to his death, faced the track and took a almost a full minute to cycle open and closed. It would have been near impossible to enter the bunker through it without someone noticing. Instead, the saboteur had created a back door.

The thick parallel power conduits leading from the SPA into the plant proper ran aboveground, shielded from damage and temperature by a hard insulating casing. Raised on supports about three inches above the surface, they entered the building at ground level. The original plant specs called for secondary conduit connected to a remote back-up SPA but they'd never been installed, another victim of Conner's merciless schedule. What resulted was an opening in the rear of the building which was twice as wide as it needed to be, leaving just enough space for an average-sized person, even in a pressure suit, to shimmy through. Remove the bolts that held the outer pressure-seal plate fast over the redundant opening, then use a standard-issue laser torch to cut through the much thinner inner plate, and voila. The building wasn't pressurized when not in use so there would have been no interior pressure to overcome, nor would a depres alarm have showed in the bubble. Once inside, five minutes, tops, to disconnect the limiters, a few backside spot welds to reaffix the interior plate, a few minutes more to bolt the outer plate back on, and you were done.

Since the conduit entered the generator in the rear, the damage to the inner cover hadn't been visible until they'd gone back there and looked while disassembling the machine. There were fresh torque wrench scores in the exterior bolts and clear signs in the dust that someone had been there, but no footprints anywhere. A mystery, until Mendoza had leapt atop the conduit, using it as an elevated road to walk all the way to the SPA, then a few yards along the ground-level step plate which jutted from the bottom of the array. He hopped off, landing amidst a jumble of tracks left by others. There were footprint traces of maria on the conduit, proof of his theory. More evidence, utterly useless.

Johnson called up the suspect's faces on her monitor. Both had the skills necessary to effect the sabotage, but it had taken real stones to break into the power plant like that, mass driver techs just a hundred yards away. Whichever one it was, he was desperate to make certain the moondrop didn't happen. And he had two more days to do his worst.

II

It was just after eight o'clock. Price was lying in bed in his hotel room watching a retrospective on the 82nd some cable network had cobbled together out of old DoD and press footage, punctuated by interviews with retired military personnel, none of whom he'd ever met. Evidently there was evidence from unnamed sources that Mac had actually been doing covert work for the Army during his retirement. He'd have to remember to tell him.

There came a knock at the door. Price called for the party to wait while he swung himself off the bed and into his chair, making the door a few seconds later. Boykin stood on the other side, arms laden with boxes. Price moved aside to allow him to enter, closing and locking the door before moving over to the bed where Boykin deposited his load.

"Sorry I'm late." Boykin stretched his biceps. "Fog delay at RDU, everything was pushed back two hours —"

"Anyone see you come in?"

"What, here? No one I recognized." He frowned. "Does it matter if anyone saw me?"

"Probably not," Price admitted. "Just paranoid." He turned his attention to the boxes.

"Everything on the list, brand names an' all," said Boykin. "Took me all day yesterday to find the stuff. What the hell's a virtual drive shadow stacker?"

"How much do you know about computers?"

Boykin scowled. He dug the cash card out of his jacket pocket and handed it to Price. "Don't know if it matters but some of the stuff was on sale, saved a few hundred."

"No, it doesn't, but thanks anyway. And for doing this."

"Yeah." He debated a moment. "Harrison wouldn't tell me what any of this was for, 'cept that it was gonna nail Conner."

"I can't tell you, man. And not because it's you who's asking. But Mac was right. We're gonna make sure Conner can't touch any of us ever again, and that includes you."

"You're gonna make sure. With this stuff."

"That's the plan."

"I'm two doors down on the left if you need any help."

Price grinned. "You're not the only one who wants to kick the shit out of him."

"There's a bulletin." Boykin glanced at his watch. "Gotta check in at the base. Got an F-120 with my name on it." He headed for the door. "Might even let me take a spin in the 120-A. Never flown one of those before."

"From what I've heard there's not much you can't fly."

"Who told you that?"

"Your brother." Boykin stopped, turned as Price spoke again. "He was a good friend. Good soldier."

"He was the best," Boykin flatly declared.

Price shook his head. "He didn't think so. He always told me there was somebody better."

Boykin cleared his throat. "Look, I know Harrison is your friend an' all."

"He wasn't talking about Mac. He was talking about you."

A moment passed. "Timmy said that?"

"Only thing I ever lie about is my fishing."

Boykin swallowed thickly. "All right then."

He left the room, walking taller than when he'd entered. Price locked the door and began unpacking the boxes.

Ten

I

It was exhilarating, after so many hours of relative motionlessness, the sense of speed Mac enjoyed as the *Sagan* sailed across the lunar surface. It had been a peculiar reunion, traveling aboard a shuttle after so many years. He'd had but one bow-to-stern tour of the *Reagan*, never seeing anything after but the drop bay. The *Sagan* was similar enough in design to be eerily familiar, yet still she was utterly different from the dark and spartan warfighter. The *Reagan* hadn't even had a toilet, though after his first adventure with the contraption Mac knew he hadn't missed a thing.

He sat taller in the payload specialist's seat as the *Sagan* traversed *Mare Tranquillitatus*. The pilot pointed out the spot where Neil Armstrong had taken his giant leap for mankind fifty years past, but Mac couldn't make out anything on the gray plain other than boulders. They left the Sea of Tranquility behind, skimmed the southern edge of the smaller *Mare Fecunditatus*, flew onward over a field of rubble dotted by massive craters and then, there it was, directly ahead. Moontown.

The model in Conner's outer office hadn't prepared Mac for what he now beheld. Nothing could. It rose out of the level plain of *Mare Smythii* — a smooth, ivory scarab, powerful arc lights painting its curved surface. Mac knew it was nearly a quarter-mile in diameter but at his present distance the base was dwarfed by the surrounding terrain. The curved solar power arrays ringing the lonely outpost made it seem as it if was the center of a shining bulls-eye, a pearl at the bottom of a bowl. As they flew closer he could make out tiny dots on the surface around the dome, a few smaller constructs and vehicles, details slowly coming into crisp focus. And beyond, perpendicular to the shuttle's final approach path, was that for which he'd been searching.

The mass driver stretched into the far distance, toothpick-thin from his distant perspective and faint in the lunar evening. Had it not been for the floodlights illuminating the base and the regularly-spaced dots of light twinkling along its surface, crowding one another as they raced towards the horizon, he would have missed it entirely. He searched his gut for some emotion as he studied it but it was still too unreal. The closest base of reference he had was a combat drop, and he doubted tomorrow's ride would be anything like that.

The *Sagan* slowed as she neared the brightly-lit landing pad, until her nose obscured all but the farthest quadrants of the base. The commander's voice sounded in Mac's headset.

"Smythii Station, this is shuttle *Sagan*, requesting final landing clearance, over."

"*Sagan*, Smythii Control. Confirm approach at two-six-five, you are cleared for manual L&D on pad one. Major Harrison, welcome to Moontown."

Mac stepped over the threshold of the landing pad airlock and into organized chaos.

The industrious energy inside the main dome was a stark contrast to the serenity of the shuttle ride. The narrow, low-ceilinged corridor was flowing with people clad in the now-familiar blue UniCom coverall, hurrying about with long, loping strides in the microgravity. Some wore baseball caps with the Moontown logo stitched above the brim which reminded Mac of the caps worn by shipboard naval personnel. *Welcome to Mare Smythii Commercial Lunar Research Facility* read the sign set into the wall directly opposite him, the UniCom logo proudly displayed below the words. Below that was a smaller framed placard — *No Shirt, No Shoes — No Service!* — and another message, scribbled in black on the placard's plexi cover. Mac chuckled as he read it: *Thou who smelled it, dealt it.*

Mac saw no one around fitting Johnson's description. He adjusted the duffel strap over his right shoulder, waited for a break in the traffic and then stepped into the corridor — straight into the far wall. He felt a steadying hand on his arm, smiled sheepishly at his rescuer before she moved on down the hall to his left.

He'd been warned by the *Sagan's* crew about micro-G — at just under 200 pounds, Mac's body mass was exerting about forty pounds of downward force. He felt as if he was trying to walk on the bottom of a filled swimming pool, his feet not quite contacting the floor. He hadn't had to deal much with micro-G onboard the *Reagan* but he'd assumed that experience would service him here. It was obvious now that wouldn't be the case.

"Don't move."

It was a woman's voice, coming from his right. She was maybe five-nine, Mac guessed, pushing forty, solidly-built with broad hips and wide shoulders. The chestnut hair that showed beneath her ball cap was curly and just starting to gray, framing her pale, scrubbed face. She moved towards Mac with the same easy, minimal gliding stride as the other personnel he'd seen. She tugged an odd-looking pair of sandals from a thigh pocket and handed them to Mac.

"Put these on before you hurt yourself."

Mac took them, recognized them as grip slippers. He let his duffel fall to the floor and pulled them on over his boots while she offered her forearm as purchase. "I'm Tracy Johnson," she said as Mac worked.

"Mac Harrison."

"What?"

"I'm Mac Harrison —"

"No, nineteen thirty, not oh-nine-thirty! Who told you oh-nine-thirty?"

Mac looked up. Johnson was speaking into her headset, ignoring him. He finished with his right foot and set to work on the other, shifting his grip on Johnson's arm. "Well, you tell them I said next time check the schedule themselves," she finished. She looked down at Mac. "You really don't need the grippers to move around, but they help. You won't be here long enough to get used to it."

"Try not to sound so disappointed."

"We're servicing the number two LUNOX plant, the entire ME extraction system's been taken off-line . . . !"

Mac stood and tested his new footwear while Johnson argued with her unseen party. Now he felt as if he was glued to the floor. He tugged his left foot free and bumped his right shoulder into the wall, the momentum overbalancing him. He re-planted the foot and peeled it away from the deck, heel-first, pitching his weight slightly forward.

It was better, though he could tell that his instep and shins would soon be aching. Like Johnson had said, he wouldn't be there long enough to worry about it.

"Oh, bullshit he didn't know," Johnson groused. "It's been posted for three cycles. If he's that ticked off about it tell him he can haul his skinny ass over there and help them blow the lines. Yeah, I know. Nothing personal."

Mac shouldered his duffel and turned back to Johnson. She was staring at him expectantly, the slender headset mic pulled away from her mouth. He realized her last comment had been directed to him. "No problem."

"It's just that for the longest time, it felt like everyone had forgotten we were up here at all." She moved aside to let another worker pass. "Now they won't leave us alone."

"I've heard. Double shifts."

"If you're lucky. We're getting it done but we'll all be glad when this is over."

"How's it going? Any problems?"

"No," Johnson answered, looking him in the eye. "None worth mentioning. Sled's being off-loaded as we speak. Jesus Mendoza's handling it, he's the mass driver and drop crew chief. Best I've got, more time up here than anyone except the man in the moon. We'll get you home tomorrow, Major."

"Never a doubt in my mind."

She guffawed, a flicker of humor showing in her eyes. She reached behind her and pulled a crew cap out of her belt, handed it to Mac. "Welcome to Moontown. I'll take you to your digs. You'll be sleeping in my bunk tonight." She moved back the way she came, towards a ladder than emerged from an opening in the floor and up through one in the ceiling. Mac followed, sticky-footed.

"Where will you sleep?"

"None of your business." She swiveled the mic in front of her mouth, climbing the ladder one-handed, leaping easily past the first two rungs. "Yes, he's here, he's with me right now! Tell Davis if he bothers me one more time I'll tell everyone the real reason he wears glasses!"

Mac donned his cap and followed Johnson up the ladder.

II

The dropsled rested on shock-absorbing supports atop the squat, treaded crawler that would carry it to the mass driver. The siliplas cowling was off, suspended above the gleaming black torpedo. A jumble of wires and fiber optic leads rose from the front interior like multicolored weeds, the instrument panel itself lying exposed on a workbench across the room where one of Mendoza's crew bent over it, giving it a once-over before final installation.

Mendoza sat in mass driver control, an independently pressurized narrow room that ran the length of the bunker opposite the workbench. It was here that he would oversee the next day's sled launch, along with Johnson stationed in the dome bubble. He studied the control panel, e-pad held in one hand displaying text and schematics, a stopwatch in the other, reviewing the power-up and launch procedures for the third time since he'd begun, working to commit them to memory. Occasionally he glanced up at Ski working outside — Ski was easier to manage than Lichodziejewski — but resisted the urge to check on him. He knew his job.

He reset his stopwatch and began his review for the fourth time.

Johnson was on her way out of her office when the com alert chimed. She swore, executed an aerial pirouette and pushed off the wall, making it back to her desk in a single stride, catching the call just after the second chime. "Johnson."

"Chief, it's Tag."

Johnson recognized the voice: Claire Taggart, up in the bubble. "I'm just on my way up. Can it wait?"

"Well, you said to let you know if anyone went outside off-shift."

Johnson felt the hair on the back of her neck stand up. "What've you got?" she asked, staying calm.

"About ten minutes ago. He's not scheduled to go out for another cycle. I had to use the head, then I got some coffee, so I didn't see it right away —"

Johnson cut her off. "Tag, who?"

"Umm . . . " A second passed. "SysTech3 Redding. Kyle Redding?"

Ski looked up from his work at the sound of the personnel airlock cycling, next to the larger crawler door. No one was expected until a couple hours before launch, still a full two cycles away, and no one had called to say they were coming.

He glanced over his shoulder to Mendoza, engrossed in his work. He'd told Ski to alert him if anyone came by. He lay the circuit tester on the bench and started across the room towards his boss just as the inner airlock door opened.

He didn't recognize the perspiring face revealed as the bucket came off but as soon as he saw it, his suspicion gave way to concern. The man looked ill, unsteady as he shucked his gauntlets and wiped his pale brow. He was too far away for Ski to make out the name on his left breast.

"Can I help you?"

The other man startled at the question. He nervously scanned the room as he spoke. "I, um, I was working on the, the array." He waved his hand vaguely before him. "I suddenly felt, um, I don't know, I just had to get . . . " He trailed off, swallowing.

"You okay?"

"Yes, fine." He sucked air through his nose. "Could I just have a moment to catch my breath?"

Ski considered a moment, glancing again at Mendoza, who was unaware of the visitor.

"Yeah, sure. Don't touch anything, all right?"

"Right, I won't." He smiled wan gratitude. Ski smiled reassuringly in answer and turned back to his work.

Redding stood where he was, stuffing his gauntlets into his helmet, waited until the other man took up a circuit tester and re-focused on his task. He tucked his helmet beneath his left arm and took a casual step towards the sled crawler, detaching a chunky black device from his work belt as he moved. Two more steps and he was standing atop the crawler, beside the open dropsled.

He glanced once more at the workbench, raised the device and focused it into the two-inch-wide cowling seal channel that ringed the sled opening. He gave the protruding end of the device a twist and depressed the yellow button set into the grip. A needle-thin beam of red light flashed silently from the tip into the channel, scoring the indentation. He braced the tip against his trembling forearm and re-aimed the beam into one of several regularly-spaced darker depressions set laterally into the outer channel wall. There was a faint sizzle, a puff of smoke.

He released the button, checked the workbench. He moved the device a few inches left and pressed the button again.

Mendoza was exactly forty-six seconds away from completing the run-through when the com light blinked on his console. He sighed and clicked the stopwatch off.

He listened as Johnson spoke. He snapped his head to the right, peering through the clear partition into the main room. He was out of his chair and into the room like a flash.

"Redding!"

Ski jumped where he stood, spinning in time to see Redding back away from the dropsled, panic writ plainly on his sallow face. His right hand jerked behind his back. "What the hell are you doing, I told you to stay away from that!" Ski barked.

"I was just having a look," Redding protested. "I didn't touch anything!"

Mendoza moved into the room, eyes fixed on Redding. "What's that in your hand?" Redding didn't answer. He hopped clumsily off the crawler, backed away towards the vehicle's broad access door. "C'mon, Kyle. It's over."

"I'm sure I don't know what you mean."

"Bullshit, Kyle," Mendoza flatly declared. He kept on advancing, slow, sliding steps towards Redding, driving him away from the dropsled between them. Redding cast about the room — Mendoza before him, Ski to his left, nothing but wall behind. Trapped.

Mendoza worked his way left, around the crawler. Redding whipped his hand out from behind his back, brandishing the laser torch before him. Mendoza didn't even slow down.

"C'mon, Kyle, you know that won't reach this far." He continued his approach, forcing Redding to turn towards him so his back was half-facing Ski. The tech took Mendoza's lead and moved stealthily right, measuring inches with each step, working his way behind Redding.

"I know you didn't mean to kill Osborne," Mendoza calmly continued, holding Redding's attention as Ski moved. "All you wanted to do was disable the generator, I know that. But it's over. There's nowhere to go, man. Time to give it up."

Redding licked his lips, blinked against the sweat running into his eyes. He was panting, fighting the dizziness, the sick nausea. A scuffling sound penetrated the ringing in his ears. He spun left just in time to catch Ski rushing him from behind, hands reaching for the laser torch. The tech grabbed Redding's wrist just as the tool fired. He yelped as the scarlet lance cut through his P-suit like a scalpel, tracing a line of white-hot fire across his belly. He reflexively grabbed his stomach, allowing Redding to twist his wrist free of his grasp.

In that moment Mendoza was on him, his powerful hands clamping onto Redding's, the hand that held the torch, driving the arm upwards, holding Redding's thumb pressed against the button. Redding's helmet fell to the floor, the laser tracing crazy patterns on the ceiling as they struggled, too weak even at that short range to do any damage.

Mendoza set his weight and heaved upwards, lifting Redding off his feet, carrying him backwards in the micro-G until he slammed into the wall to the left of the main door. Redding's hand banged against the surface, feet scrambling for purchase, his wrist bending inexorably backwards. The pinprick dot of the torch's fire crawled down the wall, the beam shortening, smoke now rising from the black trench it burned until its barrel was pressed flush against the door's control panel.

Mendoza saw what was happening and yanked Redding's hand away — too late.

The warning klaxon blared. There was a deep, mechanical *thud*. The crawler door began rising.

Mendoza dropped Redding onto his feet, fighting now to pull his opponent away from the opening, but Redding was held too fast in the grip of his panic to comprehend what was happening. He squirmed madly, yanking his wrist free. Mendoza's momentum carried him sprawling backwards onto his buttocks, bouncing up against the sled crawler.

Ski moved towards the panel, forgetting his injury. Mendoza waved him away.

"The override! The booth!"

Ski understood at once. He bounded across the room, ears popping as he entered the room and sealed the door behind him. Mendoza surged to his feet, shouting at Redding: "Get away from the door!"

Redding saw Mendoza's mouth moving but all he could hear was the maddening screech in his ears. He dropped the torch and covered them with his hands, gut heaving.

Something tugged at the back of his legs. He staggered to his left, turning, tripped over his own feet and fell onto his back. Only then did he see the opening door, did he dimly realize the tug on his legs was the room's decompression.

He felt friction against his buttocks. The opening moved a few inches closer. He slapped his hands onto the cold floor, skin abrading from his fingertips dragging against the surface. He tried to scream but for some reason he couldn't catch his breath.

Mendoza was at the workbench, bracing himself with his knees against the metal legs. He rammed Ski's helmet over his head, locked the neck ring into place. He donned the gauntlets, acutely aware of the increasing, insistent pull on his body. The technical manual Ski had been using leaped from the bench, pages flapping as it spun out of sight towards the door.

Mendoza clicked the last wrist clip into place and relaxed his legs, twisting his body left and shoving off like a swimmer diving into current. The door was one-quarter open, Redding's toes already digging into the dirt outside. Mendoza landed on his belly a yard away, pushed off with his knees and slapped his hand onto Redding's outstretched wrist. He crabbed left, pulling against the force that dragged Redding outside, braced his left foot against the wall next to the door.

Redding managed to twist to his right, onto his belly. His eyes locked onto Mendoza's — glassy, bulging, already showing the red dots of depres hemorrhage.

The door stopped, began lowering.

"Hang on!" Mendoza yelled through his effort, even though he knew couldn't be heard through the helmet. Blood now trickled from Redding's nose, into his gasping mouth, his distended tongue curling back into his throat. His legs began kicking madly, devoid of control, his body's most primal survival instincts now frantically engaged.

Mendoza felt his grip weaken as Redding struggled. The wrist slipped away. The palm. The fingers.

The last thing Mendoza saw was the gout of pink froth boil up in Redding's throat, droplets flowering from his mouth into the micro-G like the splash of a stone in water. Blood and fluid burst from his ruined eye sockets.

The door dropped in front of him. The klaxon abruptly silenced.

Mendoza fell onto his back, sucking the stale air of his suit. He couldn't catch his breath. No oxygen, he hadn't had time to open the cock.

He gasped, light-headed, hot breath fogging against the helmet faceplate. He reached for his hip, fingers closing around the small knob.

" . . . Soos?"

Mendoza came to, still lying on his back. His helmet was off, Tracy Johnson's worried face bent close to his. He took a deep breath, coughed, greedily took another.

Johnson leaned back onto her heels as Mendoza pushed himself up on his elbows. He felt hands on his shoulders; Ski was there, helping him sit up. There was a smear of blood on the fabric of his P-suit, below the slash bisecting his torso. "You okay?" Ski asked. Mendoza nodded, pointed at the injury. The tech waved his hand dismissively. "Nice thing about lasers, they cauterize when they cut. Didn't get me bad enough to do any real damage." He turned serious. "I closed the door as fast as I could."

Mendoza nodded again, turned to Johnson. "It was Redding."

"I know. They're taking his body back to the dome now. How do you feel?"

"I tried to save him . . . "

Johnson leaned in and kissed him hard. Mendoza sank his gloved fingers into her curls, holding her to him. She caressed his bronze cheek as he withdrew.

At once, they remembered they had an audience. They looked to Ski. He smirked.

"Oh, like no one knows."

III

"It looks all right so far but we can't be positive there's no damage without a more thorough checkout."

Conner frowned. "How long will that take?"

"To do it right, twenty-four hours," Johnson replied. "Minimum."

Conner looked over to Doctor Yamada. The engineer pecked at his e-pad. "Moon is at perigee in less than that. Next time it'll be as close . . . January 20th." He looked up. "Twenty-seven days."

"Stand-by, Tracy." Conner touched the desk monitor. Johnson's face blinked away, replaced by the rotating UniCom logo.

"We could go a day late," Yamada offered, hopeful. "It's only an extra seven-hundred miles or so distance. I could do the math tonight, re-align the mass driver, move the landing site to Edwards."

"The press is already set up at Vandenberg."

"Never mind the press, Roger!"

Conner folded his hands across his belly, elbows resting on the arms of his wheelchair. He felt naked without his cane. "None of this means anything unless the whole world sees it," he growled. "We change the schedule now, people will think something's wrong."

"Something *is* wrong!"

"Tracy said they didn't find anything."

"Which doesn't mean there's nothing there!" Yamada insisted. "We don't know what Redding was trying to do. There could be microscopic damage, the smallest current arc at the wrong time could be disastrous."

"I'm willing to take that risk."

"You're not going to be in that dropsled." Yamada stared at Conner's stony expression. "Roger! We're talking about a man's life! What if something does happen? What if Mac dies, with the whole world watching? You will have proved nothing!"

"*We* will have proved that the mass driver works," Conner replied evenly. "The blame for the failure will fall where it belongs."

"On us!"

"No. Leslie checked Redding's e-mail traffic. He was working for Helios, for Innes. I've got copies of his last two transmissions, encrypted instructions to stop the drop, at any cost."

"That changes nothing, Roger."

"It changes everything," Conner countered. "Innes is finished. He so much as says the word 'fusion' in public and I'll be on him like white on rice, every goddamn reporter in the world will be camped outside that antique rathole he works in. Our nearest competition other than him is years behind us." He grinned. "We're there, Bobby. No one can stop us now."

Yamada couldn't believe what he was hearing. "You're willing to let Mac die, just so you can, can win?" He spat the last word like a rotten morsel of food. "After everything that happened, the *Reagan*? Seventeen people died then because we wouldn't wait, we didn't take the time to do it right! Can't you see this is the same thing? With Innes out of the picture, there's no reason to rush anymore!" He held his hands before him, pleading. "Twenty-four hours, Roger. One day, that's all. The press won't go away."

Conner knew Yamada was right, but that acknowledgement sat at the edge of his cognizance, just another variable to be factored into the grand equation. Before his brush with death three days before he doubted Yamada's protestations would have carried any weight at all. But this was different. He couldn't afford — the moondrop couldn't afford to sacrifice the momentum it had generated thus far. Still, Yamada's request was reasonable.

He unclasped his hands, tucking his cold fingers beneath his armpits. "All right. You get eight hours."

"It's not enough."

"It's what you've got."

Yamada stood his ground, locked in a staredown with Conner. Finally: "I'm not going to be a part of this."

"Meaning what?"

"I'm going to tell Tracy to take all the time she needs."

"You'll do no such thing," Conner snapped. "I've made my decision, Bobby. Eight hours, and you don't need to be wasting it arguing with me."

"What are you going to do if I say no? I'll be just as responsible as you if anything happens."

"I'm glad you finally chose to realize that."

There was a long silence. Conner stared at his knees. "We go back a long way. From the beginning. You've always been the one man I've counted on to give it to me straight. The one man whose judgment I trust above all others."

Now he looked up. "Nine years ago, in this very office. Remember? Who was it, Bobby, that told me the *Reagan* was fit to launch?" Yamada's face went suddenly ashen. "How'd you put it? 'I'd fly the damn thing myself, if I knew how?'"

"And I'm telling you now, Roger," Yamada urged. "Let's not repeat the same mistake we —"

"Make sure you don't, then," Conner pronounced, cutting him off. "I took a bullet for you, Bobby, I could have hung you out to dry. I don't need to tell you what it cost." He looked hard at Yamada. "You owe me."

Eleven

I

Yamada rubbed his tired eyes, replaced his glasses. He stood at his flight director console in the SLC-6 Launch Control Center at Vandenberg. He'd arrived with Conner that morning just before six-thirty. Most thought Conner was still flat on his back in the clinic. He'd made Yamada promise to keep his arrival mum, wanting it to be a surprise. Yamada had no problem with that. After the previous night's altercation, the less he thought about Conner, the better.

He donned his headset, looked out over the flight control room. The basic design hadn't much changed since the days of NASA's Mercury launches almost three-quarters of a century before. The FCR, or 'ficker,' was UniCom's exclusive domain, custom-built. Gently scalloped like an amphitheater, its shallow terraces descended to the front of the room, where the monitor array that dominated the forward wall showed assorted views of the mass driver base and terminus. Upon each terrace was a curved control console, twenty-one standard stations in all, each controlling an equally vital mission aspect: the CAPCOM primary communications tech, the designation another holdover from the days of space capsules; flight dynamics officer; guidance procedures officer; data processing system engineer; surgeon, and so on.

He checked the count chronometer: a few minutes before noon, four hours to launch. Jesus Mendoza and Moontown's senior engineers had stayed up all night poring over the dropsled millimeter by millimeter. The only obvious damage they'd discovered was some laser torch scoring in the cowling sink channel, obviously Redding's work. MRI and ultrasound imaging had revealed nothing overtly suspicious within, although the only way to determine for certain whether there was significant damage was to open the sled body, impossible even if they'd been granted the time. The siliplas-coated skin was of single-piece construction, seamless. They'd have to cut it open to examine the interior and that would be the end of the sled, and the drop.

"He would've been better off just bashing the damn thing with a hammer," Mendoza had told Yamada when last they'd spoken that morning. "He could've whacked the nose antenna off and scrubbed the launch right there. Hell, he could've fallen on it and done the same thing, claimed it was an accident, still be alive. Part of me wants to say he was so berkers he overlooked the obvious, but the CDP-1000 has been declassified for years, it's pretty simple technology. Anyone goes after it with a laser torch, I've gotta think they had something specific in mind."

"Like what?" Yamada had asked.

"Like something he didn't want to show up until it was too late. Given the scoring in the sink channel, my guess is the jettison bolts. They don't blow when they're supposed to, Harrison's a spot in the dirt."

"But you haven't found anything, no evidence —"

"Doc, I'm saying I don't know," Mendoza wearily huffed. "If you're asking me if I think the sled is fit to launch, all I can tell you is that judging from what I've seen so far it appears that way. But I haven't seen everything, and unless I can hold every damn one of those bolts in my hand, stick 'em under a microwave spectrometer, I'm not about to give an unqualified go for launch. Not really my decision anyway, is it?"

Yamada knew he was referring to Conner. They'd talked a few moments more before Yamada signed off, feeling no less worried than the night before.

Davis entered, leading a gaggle of VIPs, laminated passes dangling from their necks as they gawked. Yamada ran his hands through his hair and straightened his tie as Davis caught his eye and led his charges over. Everything's going just fine, he recited to himself, rehearsing his pitch. No problems at all.

II

Mac tightened the laces on his boots and stood, ducking involuntarily as he rose. He'd already bumped his head against the low ceiling several times in the micro-G. If he wasn't careful he'd give himself a concussion.

Johnson's quarters were small, though she'd told him they were the most spacious on base. The only homey touch was a framed photographic print affixed to the ceiling directly over the bunk, a lush meadow awash in flowers of every color. It was the last thing he'd seen before sleep and the first when he'd awakened, making him think, just for a moment, that he was back on Earth. There was an alarm on the bedside table that could be set to emit various sounds, from the flat hiss of white noise to gentle rain. Mac had awakened to chirping birds and a rooster's crowing. Johnson had been away from home a long time.

He stuffed his dirty clothes into his duffel. He'd already bathed and shaved, eaten a light meal the night before which had completed its natural course shortly after he'd risen. He wouldn't take anything other than liquid nourishment for the next sixty-three hours. He'd shuck his UniCom coverall and boots when he donned his drop P-suit, after they'd shaved and sanded his chest and glued the medical monitor tabs to his raw skin. He hadn't had to tolerate them during the war except during training drops. This would be the first time in fifteen years, and the last forever.

He touched the lump of Boykin's ring beneath his tee-shirt. The formal portrait of the 82nd slid out of its frame. He stared at it a moment, tucked it inside the coverall, tugged the zipper closed over his drumming heart.

Johnson was waiting for him in the hall. He obediently handed her his duffel; it would be returned to him when the *Sagan* departed for Earth a week later. He appreciated that she didn't say anything, didn't try to force the moment into something other than what it was. She offered Mac a smile, a nod which he returned. For a moment he thought of Mandy Ashdown, the *Reagan's* commander. She would've been about Johnson's age now.

He followed the chief down the corridor.

III

"If there's even the slightest deviation from nominal, don't wait for me, hold the count."

"Copy that."

Yamada gulped coffee as Johnson confirmed his order. His stomach was in knots, the caffeine unhelpful. Price and Martha were in the room now. Davis had been there too, but had left a few minutes earlier after receiving a call on his portable phone.

He checked the count chronometer. Less than an hour to go. Harrison should be suited up by now.

"Launch control, this is UniCom. Status, over."

"UniCom, launch. Primary and auxiliary systems nominal. Standby for sled status." Johnson switched channels. "Soos, where're we at with Harrison?"

Mendoza looked into the main room from his command station. Mac was in his drop P-suit, gauntlets on, the helmet resting on the corner of the sled crawler. One of the two techs assisting him was holding his parachute.

"He's about to put on the parachute. Another few minutes."

"How's he look?"

Mendoza shook his head admiringly, watching Mac speak calmly to the tech holding the rig. "Cool as a cucumber."

"I want to repack the canopy."

"There's no time, sir."

"Ten minutes. I never jump a rig I haven't packed myself."

"It's been test-jumped. It's brand-new."

"So was the *Titanic*."

The young man tossed a worried glance in Mendoza's direction, saw him watching. He turned back to Mac, clearly uncomfortable. "We don't have ten minutes, Major, you've gotta be in the driver in fifteen."

Mac watched the tech's youthful face color beneath his scrutiny. He read the name stitched over the left breast. "You a jumper, Gershon?"

"Yessir. That's why they picked me for this."

"What do you usually do?"

"Service the heads."

Mac bit back a comment. "Let me do a pin check, at least."

Gershon shifted the black package in his arms, glad to be off the hook. Mac lifted the flap and checked the rig. "Seven-cell reinforced combat main and reserve, pull-out main deploy, two point cutaway," Gershon recited. "Hook knife's here," and he pointed to the bright yellow handle of the razor held in its elastic loop against the chest strap. "Digital AAD, pre-set to two grand."

Mac pressed the flap shut and turned his back to the tech, shrugging on the rig. He tapped the face of the compact altimeter affixed to the left inner wrist of his P-suit. A pinlight in the center blinked active, but nothing read on its face. "What's wrong with the altimeter?"

"Nothing." Gershon walked around Mac, latched the chest and belly straps and pulled them tight. "It's set to activate after re-entry. It was zeroed at Vandenberg, right in the peas." He turned his attention to the leg straps, yanking them snug.

Mac jumped at the touch on his right thigh. The second tech sat back on his heels, held up a silvered canister about ten inches long and two in diameter. "It's just the helium-3."

Mac relaxed, watched the tech stuff the canister into the tight nylon tube sewn to his suit. "No chance that'll, explode or anything, is there?"

The tech didn't look up. "Not unless you dive-bomb the sun."

He finished, rose and moved to the crawler as Gershon stepped back. Mac inhaled, ribs pressing against the chest strap. He raised each leg, allowing the the straps to nestle safely around his groin. "They're tight, I know," Gershon admitted. "Don't tell anyone I said so, but loosen them if you want once you're underway, it's not like you're gonna need 'em tight until re-entry anyway. But not too much, and of course make sure you snug them up before you bail. Good?"

Mac nodded. Gershon fetched the helmet from the crawler. The room lights dimmed as the polarized faceplate descended before Mac's eyes. He felt a moment of vertiginous disorientation: he was back onboard the *Reagan*, waiting in the drop bay for Rawlings' order to enter his sled. Then Gershon's face moved into his vision, clicking the neck ring home. He turned to his right, mouth moving, voice muffled. Mac heard a static pop and then Mendoza's voice: "Com check. Can you hear me, Major?"

Mac turned and gave him a thumbs-up. "Roger com check," he said, his voice loud inside the helmet.

"T-minus twenty-five. It's time."

Mac moved carefully forward. Johnson had been right — he still hadn't gotten his 'moon legs.' Gershon bounded atop the low crawler platform in a single easy hop. Mac took his outstretched hand. In two steps he was standing atop the crawler, staring down past the suspended cowling into the open dropsled.

At first glance it appeared identical to the sleds he'd jumped during the war, but there were subtle differences. The form-fitted interior padding was a lighter Ascot gray, and the instrumentation was set flush into the matte black console, though the pistol grips were identical to those he remembered.

The biggest change, however, was the addition of life support and rations. Two capped tubes extended from the starboard side of the console: one for water, the other for the protein and carbohydrate slurry that'd serve as Mac's nutrition for the trip. He'd sampled it back at UniCom — sweet mushroom soup was the closest description. The thin medical datalead protruded from sled left; it would mate with the medical port at the left waist of his P-suit, transmitting data on his vital stats to the flight surgeon at Vandenberg.

The backup oxygen tube snaked up portside from the tail. He'd breathe from it during launch, then switch to on-board after the sled pressurized. In the event he irretrievably lost life support he'd breathe again from the back-up while the *Sagan* was dispatched to capture the sled in flight. Pure oxygen, fifteen hours of life if he remained calm. He'd done the math the night before. No matter how he figured it, he came up with a give-or-take safety window of twenty-four hours from sled launch to when he'd pass beyond the *Sagan's* ability to reach him in time. Nobody had mentioned a plan for hour twenty-five and beyond.

He'd already noticed that there was no booster engine affixed to the sled's exterior tail, unnecessary as it was for the mass driver launch. Emblazoned on both sides of the sled was the UniCom logo, next to the company crest of the 82nd. Mac hadn't expected the latter to be there. The cynic within him wrote it off to Conner's showman's touch. The warrior noted it with approval.

"Major." It was Gershon's voice. Mac realized he'd unconsciously been waiting for Rawlings' gruff order to enter.

He waved off Gershon's offer of assistance. Absent the *Reagan's* zero-G, Mac climbed in as gracefully as he could. Grasping the steering levers to brace himself, he worked his body from side to side, settling into the molded depressions. There was more room than he remembered. No body armor, no powergun barrel jutting over his right shoulder, no spare mags and grenades pressing into his belly and hips.

Mac felt hands on his body, Gershon connecting the medical lead and oxygen hose. The air hissed, flowing into his suit. Both would automatically pull free when he exited the sled.

The oblong siliplas cowling descended over and around him, blanketing the sled interior in dusk. He heard the rubbery *crump* even through his helmet as it settled into the sink channel, then the solid unison thump of the explosive bolts shooting into place. Lights to either side of the console winked on, the instrumentation simultaneously glowing to life.

He was sealed into the sled now. There was no way out other than to activate the manual cowling jettison. He eyed the control and then realized there was one last difference he'd missed. There was no punch-out button. No need for one, not now. Not anymore.

"Com check."

"Confirm com check," Mac answered Mendoza, keeping his voice steady against the thumping of his heart. "Cowling seal confirmed, on-board systems active."

"Copy all." There was a brief pause. "We're off the public channel now, Major," Mendoza said. "This'll be the last time I speak to you directly. Thought you'd like to know we all took a poll this morning. Results were unanimous that you're nuts."

Mac chuckled despite his nervousness. "I thought the word was berkers."

"Berkers is when you lose it completely."

"It's early yet."

It was Mendoza's turn to laugh. "You won't be alone, Major," he said, soberly now.

Mac felt Boykin's talisman pressing into his chest, the photo flat against his bare skin. "I know."

"Good luck, and Godspeed."

Through the dark tint of the cowling Mac saw the now fully- suited tech step behind the crawler's drive pedestal. Gershon hopped off the vehicle, heading for the control room.

"This is drop control. All personnel, clear the crawler track," Mendoza ordered. "All personnel clear the track. Door coming open."

Light strobed across the cowling. With a lurch, the crawler moved forward.

IV

Price watched the monitor in UniCom Control: the drop shack door rising, the treaded crawler creeping forward towards the mass driver base, the gleaming black missile of dropsled atop it. Martha stood to his right, beside him on the topmost level, Yamada at his console to the left.

Martha was wound tighter than Price had ever seen her. He knew she must be wrestling with more than the worry they all felt for Mac's safety, but any comfort he might offer presumed an insight into her relationship with Mac that risked offense. He'd settled for what he hoped were reassuring smiles whenever their eyes met.

"Hope I haven't missed anything!"

Price turned towards the familiar growl. Conner was heading towards them, beaming, his wheelchair pushed by Davis.

Martha looked stunned. "When did you . . . "

"If you thought I'd be content to witness this spectacle on a hospital television then you don't know me at all, dear." He stopped next to her, Davis positioning the chair so that it faced the front of the room.

Martha forced a smile. "I'm glad you're feeling better."

"Thank you. I am."

She turned back to the monitors. Conner watched her a moment, something near to sadness showing on the aged face. It vanished when he turned towards Price, nodded a neutral greeting.

Price nodded back. "Nice chair."

The crawler had reached the mass driver base. The pilot manipulated his pedestal controls. The sled rose from the crawler on scissored hydraulic arms, stopped when it was dead level with the load platform fifteen feet above the surface.

After a moment, the sled moved forward onto the platform, nudged by slowly telescoping arms set into either side of the scissors lift. One of the two techs there raised his arm when the sled was resting fully on the platform, and the scissors lift retracted. Price expected the sled to move into the driver tube automatically. Instead, the techs physically pushed it into the broad, dark opening, as if loading an enormous shell into a cannon.

Mendoza confirmed sled carriage lock, gave the go to close the access hatch and for all personnel to assume their launch stations. The techs climbed nimbly down the ladder and bounded for the drop shack, where the crawler was already berthed.

Twin red lights ignited atop the driver base, strobing as the thick hatch slowly descended into place. It came to rest, sealing the opening.

Mac peered forward over the glowing console, through the tinted cowling. He knew the driver tube stretched open before him for miles but there was no impression of depth in the flat darkness, no lights to plumb its reach. It was as if he was waiting in the sled battery on the *Reagan*, wide open eyes fixed on the battery hatch he could not see but knew was there, waiting for it to open.

Now it began in earnest. His pulse throbbed at his temples, kicked at his chest like a hostage pounding a prison door. He breathed, relaxed his clamped jaw, lowered his head until the helmet rested against the acceleration pad.

Let it come, this one last time. Open yourself to its final visit, your journey's fell companion that is as much a part of your history as the memory of souls you carry in your heart.

Breathe. The way of the warrior is resolute acceptance of death . . .

Mendoza's voice sounded again: "This is drop control. We are go for launch. Repeat, we are go for launch."

Conner had moved during the load procedure. He sat now beside Yamada, eyes shining as he watched the monitors.

"This is it, Bobby. This-is-it. You feel like I do right now?"

Yamada didn't take his eyes from his console. "You have to throw up, too?"

"All launch personnel, this is Smythii control. We are ready for launch. Commencing full power-up in five . . . four . . . three . . . two . . . "

" . . . one . . . mark. Go power-up."

"Roger, control. Power-up now."

Johnson watched the power indicator climb. Even though the post-sabotage prelims had gone flawlessly, Osborne's death was an albatross whose weight she'd not yet shaken. She flicked her eyes to the wide view of the mass driver. It gleamed in the lunar dawn, the mammoth reach fully revealed for the first time in over two weeks; a sunlit arrow racing for the horizon, narrowing to an indiscernible point before disappearing entirely.

She returned her attention to the indicator, the power plant tech confirming what she saw: "Power at eighty percent . . . ninety percent . . . power at one-hundred percent. We are at full power and holding steady."

Johnson fancied she could feel others in the room with her relax as she exhaled. "Roger full power-up. All systems go for launch in T-minus twenty seconds. UniCom, confirm no-hold."

"No-hold confirmed," Yamada's voice answered. "Go for launch."

Johnson turned the key, flipped the clear protective cover from the launch button, held her hand poised over the raised, lighted square. Mendoza would be doing the same at his station.

"Drop control, we are at T-minus fifteen. Confirm you are go for launch."

"That's affirmative. Waiting for your mark."

Johnson watched the count chronometer. "T-minus twelve . . . eleven . . . "

She counted off the seconds, knowing her voice was being heard all over the base, all over the world.

" . . . six . . . five . . . four . . . three . . . two . . . one . . . mark."

She mashed her thumb hard against the launch button on the last word, watched it change to green as it sank flush with the console.

"Acceleration sequence initiated."

There was no jolt, no hard thump of the booster engine firing. Just a sudden sense of smooth forward movement.

He gripped the locked steering levers more tightly as his body was pressed rearward. His feet flattened against the brace plate. He kept his head down, knowing that in seconds the acceleration would make it impossible for him to lift it. Had his sight been able to penetrate the bottom of the sled he would have seen tiny flashes of bluish light sparking along the carriage as the driver coils powered on and off in split-second sequence, pulling the sled inexorably forward, faster . . .

Faster . . .

The pressure on his body increased. His feet mashed harder against the brace plate, his helmet bearing against the P-suit's shoulder pads as Johnson's voice sounded in his ears:

269

"Velocity point-one-five KPS and climbing."

His heart pounded harder. He sucked air through his nose, fighting the urge to pant.

"Velocity point-nine-seven KPS and climbing."

Inhale . . . exhale . . . inhale . . .

"Velocity now one-point-six-three KPS and climbing. Escape velocity in ten seconds."

The pressure grew, a massive invisible foot crushing his head, his shoulders, his spine. His every muscle was locked rigid against the force that labored to bulldoze him into the foot of the sled like a crumpled aluminum can.

"Eight . . . seven . . . "

He was grunting now with every exhalation, eyes squeezed shut, straining against the swelling G-force.

"Six . . . five . . . "

The sled vibrated, a low-level oscillation which flowed into his body like an electrical charge, melding his flesh with the sled so that he no longer could feel where one ended and the other began.

"Four . . . three . . . "

He struggled to breathe, managed a half-lungful of air. White dots swam before his eyes, his world reduced to the struggle to remain focused, remain conscious . . .

"Two . . . one."

The velocity indicator on Johnson's console reached 2 .38 KPS.

"We have escape velocity! Carriage sep in four . . . three . . . two . . . one . . . mark!"

On the giant monitor at UniCom flight control a raven bolt of lightning spurted from the mass driver terminus, too fast for the eye to fully register. The screen immediately blinked to a wider view, barely in time to catch sight of the sled as it sailed above the lunar surface, arcing upwards, sunlight glinting off its dark skin as it sailed over the horizon, into space.

Johnson's voice boomed over the PA: "Confirm carriage sep! OTV is away! Repeat, the sled is away!"

Davis opened his mouth to cheer, then clapped it shut. No one else in the ficker had moved. He glanced over at Doctor Yamada. He was staring raptly at the monitor, the sled now lost from view.

"UniCom control to dropsled. Do you read, over."

Silent moments passed. Price gripped the arms of his chair. Martha clasped her hands beneath her chin. Everyone waited.

"This is UniCom control to dropsled. Major Harrison, do you read? Over."

Another moment passed. Then:

"Roger, UniCom. That was one hell of a ride."

The room exploded into joyful clamor. Davis joined in gleefully, pumping his fists into the air. Conner slapped Yamada on the back so hard that the grinning engineer winced. Price reached up and clasped Martha's hand as she bent over and wrapped her arms around his neck, kissing his bald pate. For the first time all day she was grinning.

Conner motioned for Yamada to give him his headset. Yamada switched to the private channel at his nod. "Tracy!"

"Yes, sir."

"Excellent job! Well done, all of you! Well done! First round's on me!"

"Thank you sir. Tell Bobby he can handle it from here. Smythii Station, signing off."

In the bubble over two-hundred thousand miles away, Johnson cut the comlink to UniCom. "Soos, you hear that? Old man Conner actually said thank you."

"Glad you heard it, too. Thought I was hallucinating there for a minute."

"See you when you get in."

She tugged her headset from her curls, tossed it on the console and slumped back in her chair. There had been no celebration in the room. Johnson surveyed the faces one-by-one, holding their eyes, seeing in them the same slow flood of relief she felt, like runners winding down after a grueling marathon. Glad it was over, but too winded just yet to revel in their victory.

She smirked, acknowledging the mood, saw the answering smiles. "You heard Conner. Who's gonna get the beer?"

V

It was late. Martha had intended to head back to the hotel following her token appearance at the celebratory LCC Christmas party but instead she'd found herself strolling the launch complex in the cooling ocean breeze, watching the rich autumn colors of the sunset play on the massive buildings. She didn't know how long she'd wandered but she ultimately found herself standing once again before the LCC monument to the *Reagan*.

It was different reading the crew roster now. Dropmaster Sergeant Otis Clarence Rawlings, Commander Amanda Leigh Ashdown, Captain Mark Francis Guthrie — they weren't just names anymore. There were voices to go with them. She felt some kinship to them, like a minister who had heard their last confession in the moments before their deaths, secret knowledge she was forbidden to voice to anyone. She could not imagine anyone having watched that captured nightmare play to its dreadful, predestined end and not feeling as she did. Not even Conner. How he had been able to deny for so long this horrid sickness of heart bespoke of a depth of arrogance to which even she had been blind, a repellent pollution of soul. Yet he had continued in silence for nearly a decade, even after the same knowledge had consumed his only child.

She turned away from the squat marker, hugged herself against the growing chill. She recalled her brief California visit years before. She'd forgotten how cold the seaside evenings could get.

She didn't startle when Conner drew up beside her. He extended to her the wool overcoat folded in his lap.

"You'll catch cold," she said.

"I brought it for you."

She relented and draped the heavy garment over her shoulders. Together they gazed out across the SLC.

"I just spoke with Bobby," said Conner after a time. "He says everything's running like clockwork, no problems at all."

"That's good."

"Yes, it is." A moment. "We haven't had a chance to talk."

"About what?"

Conner paused again, hearing the distance in her reply. "I'm not asking you to condone what I did. Or forgive. No one can I suppose except God, and I'll find out what He thinks soon enough. But I hope you understand why I did it."

"I accept it. How I might feel about it won't change anything. But how could you ask Mac to help you now? Or Boykin, or Price? How can you even look them in the eye, knowing what your decision cost them?" She faced Conner, seeing him as if for the first time, speaking to him as she'd never before dared. "Weren't you even the least bit ashamed? I know what kind of man you can be but God almighty, when did you turn into the kind of man who can do that!"

"That's enough." Martha stared at him. "I'm sorry," Conner gruffly apologized. "Those are all fair questions."

Martha was astounded by the understatement. "'Fair questions'," she echoed. "But you're not going to answer them."

"The war is over. The dead buried. Tell me what purpose the truth would serve now."

"Oh, it's more basic than that," Martha flatly countered. "The lie serves you. The truth doesn't. You've got more to lose than anyone. The truth is the last thing in the world you want known."

Conner was silent a long while. "The day before he died, Kevin and I argued." He tucked his fingers beneath his armpits, clamped them tightly against the cold. "He didn't believe the defense secretary would cancel our lease here if we went public with the truth about Stormcloud. He said we could agree beforehand to take the blame publicly, ask DoD for whatever I wanted under the table in exchange. All they wanted was a scapegoat, he said. Morton Thiokol survived the blame for *Challenger* back in '86. He said we could take the hit for the *Reagan*."

It was the first time Conner had told Martha about Kevin's entreaty. She took some comfort in knowing he'd stood up to his father. "He was right," she declared.

"You don't know what I was up against. Neither did he. DoD had the war all tied up in a nice, neat little bow. They had absolutely no interest in telling the public anything more than bare minimum. I tried to explain it to him but Kevin insisted, threatened to leak to the press." Conner swallowed, his mouth dry. "I told him if he did, I couldn't be responsible for what Washington might do."

He looked at Martha now, keeping his voice even with difficulty. "All I'd meant was that they'd come after us both. After the business. He stared at me, for the longest time, and then he left. It wasn't until after he'd . . . " Conner still couldn't bring himself to say it out loud. "It wasn't until later that I realized how it must have sounded to him. That I was saying I wouldn't defend him, wouldn't be there for him. I was not the best father I could have been. But I loved my son. And I would *never* have let —"

His voice caught. It took every bit of control he had to maintain his composure. "I lost Beth a long time ago and I couldn't do anything to stop that. Kevin was all I had left of her. When he died, it was like I'd lost the last piece I had of his mother. My family was gone, and sometimes it's hard to remember that I ever had one. Work was all I had left, all I thought I had left. It's not true."

He paused, waited for the silence to turn Martha's face to him. "I always felt I had a daughter, in you. Please don't tell me I've lost that, too."

Martha fought to keep her emotions at bay. "I stood beside you at Kevin's funeral," she managed. "We went through his things together. I asked 'Why?' so many times and all you ever said was, 'I don't know.' But you did, even then. You have no idea how much I've trusted you, how much I believe in what you're doing."

"I know you do."

"But you don't trust me. No, not enough to tell me the truth," she insisted, cutting off Conner's protest. "If I mean so much to you, you should have told me. You couldn't have been afraid of what I would think. Not you. I would have been angry but I could have understood it a lot easier then. And all the conversations we've had about Kevin since . . . Tell me how I can trust you now the way I did before."

Conner didn't answer. Martha held his eye long enough to give him the chance then looked away, back out over the SLC. She thrust her hands into her jacket pockets and felt Mac's gift there. She absently withdrew it.

"What's that?"

"Christmas present."

Conner smiled, grateful for the change of topic. "For whom?"

"For me. From Mac."

She turned back to Conner, took in the smile now frozen on his thin lips, his eyes fixed on the small package in her hands.

He abruptly stirred, shifting in his chair. "Oh. I had no idea that you and Mac were, um . . . "

He left the thought unfinished. Martha held him in her gaze. She didn't know what he saw in her face that made him stop but she found herself resentful now of even that modest probing into her personal life. Any claim to intimacy Roger Conner might have enjoyed before was gone forever.

"I'll tell *you* something now that you never knew about your son," she began, looking down on him, feeling Kevin's presence suddenly strong beside her. "He used to say to me that he wished you would find someone. Someone new to love."

She continued without pause even as Conner looked away. "Maybe he never would have said that if he'd known his mother, had loved her more than as a memory, he was aware of that. And that's why he never said it to you. He didn't feel he had the right. But that's what frightened him the most about one day taking over for you. That he'd get so wrapped up in it that he'd forget about us, forget about everything but UniCom. That he'd wind up like you."

The words struck Conner in the belly like a sledge. His body felt leaden, the chill breeze stung his eyes unblinking eyes. That his son had been frightened of him was something he had recognized since before Kevin's death. But he had not known that the son had pitied his father.

Martha saw only Conner's expressionless face. "I don't say this to hurt you. It's been seven years since Kevin died, almost to the hour. All I've done since is work, just like you, anything to keep from thinking about what I lost. I felt I had to, that in refusing my own life I was somehow paying for what I thought was my part in his death. My own selfishness."

And yet Kevin had never shared with her his pain. He had been that much his father's son, keeping the family secret even from his lover while it drove him into his grave. How much more selfish could one be, even though it be born of grief, to abandon her so.

She raised her eyes to the night sky. Somewhere, in a far greater darkness, the tiny dropsled was making its way home. Mac had spent just as much time as she beating himself up, and just a few nights before, in that ghost-filled office, he at last discovered his truth. He hadn't said why he'd changed his mind about the moondrop, but Martha knew. And now she, too, was free.

She raised Mac's gift, peeled away the tape from one end. From out of the wrapping slid out a dark velvet jewelry box. She lifted the lid, the light from the LCC behind her sparkling against the delicate gold within.

Martha gazed at the *ki* pendant, stunned by the quiet power of the elegant talisman. So much history, so much love revealed in the graceful curves she traced with her finger. But it was the giving of it that moved her, knowing it had never before seen separation from its owner. She would never have guessed Mac would have parted with it, would actually have left the planet without it. She laughed at the last idea even as she blinked back tears.

Martha lifted the glittering pendant from its resting place, tucked the box into her jacket pocket. With a graceful flick of her head she swung her hair off of the back of her neck and fastened the chain's tiny clasp. It settled cool against her breast. Sensei's gift of love to Mac, now Mac's gift to her.

She removed Conner's coat from her shoulders, draped it across the arm of his chair. "Don't get too cold."

She walked back to the LCC, leaving him behind.

Only when Martha's footsteps had faded completely did Conner slowly pull the heavy overcoat to him. Its weight settled onto his thighs, the scratchy fabric atop his frozen hands.

He loved his son. Conner tried to hold the idea in his mind but it refused to obey, defined as it had been for so long by his guilt over Kevin's death. Defined, as was everything, by his desires alone.

"That he'd wind up like you."

Kevin Conner's ghost rose into the night, carrying with it a further piece of his father's bartered soul, sighing farewell to his former betrothed as she embraced another man's love. The man Conner may have already condemned to die.

From somewhere in the shadowed maze of the SLC there came a faint groan of metal. Just the wind, the old man's rational mind told him. In his heart, the gates of Hell made ready for his arrival.

VI

Mac yawned. The sled chronometer displayed 23:52 hours, eight minutes before midnight Pacific time, Vandenberg time. He'd been in the sled seven hours. Without the chronometer, he would have had no sense at all of time's passage.

Not long after launch he'd taken Gershon's advice and loosened the rig straps, luxuriating in the few extra inches of freedom it afforded him. Yamada had assured him that he could move freely in the sled without fear of altering its trajectory. Still, Mac had waited as long as he could before finally squirming over onto his back for a time, moving gingerly as he stretched, careful not even to touch the cowling.

He yawned again, gazed into the inky blackness surrounding the sled. It was true evening, the sun obscured now by the Earth. The siliplas tint was too dark to allow him to see anything but the brightest stars, and his home planet. It hung before him in the far distance, he could discern its stately rotation if he stared long enough. It was the only true reference point he had.

His eyes closed, head nodding. He'd been up, what was it now, seventeen hours? There was nothing for him to do anyway. Nothing but lie there, listen to the soporific white noise hiss of life support, feel his warm breath against his lips as his head settled against the padding . . .

Something made him look up. He blinked sleepily, peered through the forward cowling.

At first he couldn't be certain it was there. Just a black dot against the Earth, so close now that it filled his vision. It moved across the radiant orb from left to right, like a solitary bird traversing the sky. Mac observed it with an odd sense of detached curiosity, not knowing what it was, yet finding its presence unremarkable.

He blinked again. Like the click of a camera shutter, his eyes opened to a more immediate view. He could see now that the object was spinning slowly, light glinting dully off of its angled surfaces.

It wasn't a bird. It was something man-made. Even though it was still moving laterally it somehow managed to remain directly before him, close enough now that he could make out more detail. Its skin undulated in shallow swells like wind on a dark lake, presenting alternating layers of opacity and translucence. There were faces inside, faces he recognized, faces which turned now as one towards him, hideously contorted, mouths moving without making any sound he could hear. But now he could feel their helpless terror, a psychic wave rolling over him, piercing his heart with icicles of dread.

And then he saw it.

The missile smashed into the belly of the *Reagan*. The warhead detonated in stages, first a flash of white, now a gout of bloody flame which poured out of the topmost stage and boiled through the ship. Whipping tendrils of plasma splashed against the fuselage, burning away the outer skin from within, lancing open white-edged wounds through which the screams exploded. They detonated in Mac's ears like grenades, each one more deafening atop the other, escalating steel-on-slate screeches rending his sanity. He flailed madly, hammering his fists against the sled padding, the cowling, fighting to escape the agony.

The *Reagan* exploded. The conflagration swelled, the encircling corona bleaching away the darkness before it, trailing white fire. It raced through space, its sizzling, malevolent hiss drowning out the screams as it embraced the edges of Mac's vision and pulled him into the inferno at its heart . . .

"UniCom, dropsled."

Mac jolted awake with a gasp. He was trapped, sealed inside some sort of dark box redolent with the stink of sweat —

"Dropsled, this is UniCom control. Answer please, over."

He knew that voice. The recognition pulled him fully from his nightmare. Before him was the Earth, still a distant marble as it should be. Of course that's where it should be.

"UniCom control to —"

"I read you, Doc." Mac glanced at the chronometer. Barely three minutes had passed. "Must have dozed off."

"Are you all right? We're reading your pulse at — well, slowing now."

"Yeah, I'm fine. What's up?"

"Just a moment."

A few seconds passed. "Hello, Mac."

His heart lifted at the sound of her voice. "Martha. Hi."

"Bobby says you were scaring the flight surgeon. You okay?"

"Yeah, I'm, I'm good. Still can't get used to going to the bathroom in my pants, though."

She laughed lightly. "Just pretend you're a kid again."

Yamada discreetly moved away, busying himself with some task to her left. Martha touched the *ki* pendant. "I opened your gift. Thank you."

"You're welcome."

"Why did you give it to me?"

"Because you liked it. Because you understand."

"I know how much it meant to you."

She didn't know what she was hoping he would say but Mac's silence disappointed her. "Well. Thank you again."

"You're welcome."

She dropped her hand. "So, tell me what it's like up there. Can you see us yet?"

She'd meant it as a joke, but Mac's reply was somber. "It's so beautiful. So small. I never had the time to appreciate it before. I can hold it in my hand."

Mac stared at the Earth, shadowed still. "When I look at it, it never seems to get any bigger, like I'm just hanging here. Then I'll look away for awhile and when I look back, it is bigger. But it never feels any closer. Still so far away, and I'm just, heading towards nothing. I'll just keep on going, pass it by, so close, but just out of reach. No one will know."

Mac was whispering now, disembodied words surfacing through the hiss of the line compression that strove to boost their volume. Martha strained to hear:

" . . . lonely . . . never been this lonely . . . "

"We're all thinking about you, Mac." She breathed comfort across the cold miles. "There's not a person on this planet who doesn't know you're there, who isn't praying for you. We're all waiting for you to come home."

"I want you there when I get back, Martha. I need you to be there."

It was close enough. Her hand found the *ki* pendant. "I will. I'll be right there waiting, I promise." The main chronometer on the forward wall ticked over. "It's midnight. It's Christmas."

Warm light washed over the sled console. He looked up in time to see the sunrise, a dazzling radiance cresting the northern hemisphere, golden rays lengthening across the Earth. His spirits soared as he beheld the dawn.

"Merry Christmas, Mac."

"Merry Christmas, Martha."

Twelve

I

Price had assembled his presents from Conner early Christmas morning. He ceased lamenting the loss of his old system as soon as he'd booted up the new one. After sixty minutes of testing and tweaking, he was in love. He felt like a composer of chamber pieces, now presented with a symphony orchestra. Time to make grand and beautiful music.

He had begged off Conner's Christmas Day press conference and dinner the night before, and no one had tried to cajole him into changing his mind. Nine years in a chair had taught him that the able-bodied rarely pressed the disabled about sociability. Sometimes it pissed him off. Today, it gave him the privacy he needed to tackle the virus.

Isolate, identify and innoculate. That was his task. The first step had been partially accomplished without him — he had the disk Boykin had left behind, containing a pristine copy of the virus. Sacrificing a reconfigured e-pad to safeguard his system, he'd copied the bug onto crystal and locked it into the drive, then partitioned and configured the medium to create layers of virtual data cores, like isolating biological virus samples in sealed petri dishes stacked one atop the other, each loaded with a rudimentary BIOS and a few shell programs as culture. In this way, Price could watch the virus do its worst while holding his primary system safely out of the loop. With a stand-alone monitor completing the circuit, he had his voyeur's window into the virus's secrets.

Identifying the virus was more problematic. Price simply had never seen anything like it, not even on the most hostile battlefield systems. Typically there was was a signature flair to even the most malevolent viruses, an egotistical conceit of their creators, but this one was as without personality as it was lethal. It simply ate everything in its path, including other viruses. It mercilessly fragmented the data core, replicated itself on every byte of data there and then consumed it, leaving nothing behind but itself. But most frightening of all, the damn thing mutated, just like a true virus. It constantly modified its configuration to defeat and then consume every ephemeral anti-viral application with which Price attacked it. Arduously, he modified anti-vees on his main system, copied them onto fresh crystal, offered them via a new drive provided by Conner, watched them fail. It hadn't taken Price long to recognize he was hunting bear. And that the bear might very well win.

He hadn't moved in hours. The door was locked, *Do Not Disturb* caution displayed, curtains drawn. The only light came from the twin monitors, an isolated bubble of ghostly luminescence within which he worked. Price immersed himself in his task with the same religious ferocity that Mac brought to his martial study. He made himself an empty vessel, devoid of expectation, his mind an organic data core inside which the virus now replicated, synapses crackling with electric fire, becoming one with the digital toxin. It was no longer frightening. It was mesmerizing. Existential. Beautiful.

From within, Price saw the key. Just as the virus tolerated his cognizance, so too did it lay dormant within UniCom's netframe, co-existing with terabytes of data, the same way a biological virus could dwell within an immune host. Only when the virus infected a new host did it awaken. Ergo, there had to be a digital antigen resident in the UniCom netframe which rendered that system immune, but which did not accompany the virus when it infected a fresh host.

The antigen obviously wasn't keyed to passwords. If it were, he would have been able to read the Stormcloud files downloaded from Yamada's terminal. He doubted as well that it was a dongle, since the hardware keys were too damn easy to steal. Simple was always best, which meant that the antigen was probably a registry, one or more files which were separately loaded onto remote systems before a netframe connect was ever attempted. Open an infected file, and the virus first searched for the registry, like a sentry challenging 'friend or foe' in the night. If it found the registry, it went back to sleep.

That registry was the innoculant Price needed in order to read the Stormcloud files. And all he needed was a spaceship to travel to Mars.

He rubbed his eyes beneath his glasses, yawning. Where the hell was he going to find a registry he could isolate and copy? Steal Davis' laptop, Yamada's ever-present e-pad? Download their contents entire to his system and he still couldn't be certain the registry would tag along. He needed that registry all by its lonesome, to satisfy the virus that he was no threat. That he had business there. Cleared for access. Howdy, pardner. Come on in.

The recognition detonated in the back of his brain like a door suddenly opened.

Exactly like that.

He pushed back from the table, weariness evaporating. He crossed the room, opened the closet, bent over double as he rummaged through his suitcase until he found what he sought.

He tucked his prize beneath his thigh and returned to the table. He eagerly rummaged through the jumble of hardware in his travel toolkit. C'mon, it has to be here, he thought. Don't tell me I left the damn thing back home . . .

Yes! He lifted the bizy card. Not much larger or thicker than its hoary paper version, the business e-card was designed to accept data-coded smart cards. Slide one into the bizy frame and the viewer displayed its contents, which could be saved for future reference or uploaded to other platforms, just like a trusty e-pad. Which is exactly why the bizy card had quickly gone from the Next Big Thing to the Latest Big Bust.

Price set the bizy card aside. He reached beneath his thigh and withdrew his UniCom passcard.

Price and Mac had been issued the smartcard keys the day they'd signed on for the moondrop; they were required to gain entry to employee entrances and secure inner doors. Price wasn't certain how wide an access his particular card granted him, but the answer was unimportant. One thing only mattered.

If, as he assumed, the virus was resident on all UniCom data, no matter how pedestrian, then it was possible that both the virus *and* the registry had been copied onto the tiny chips inside the passcard as a matter of routine. That thin plastic wafer was the lean, lonesome, netframe-approved system he needed. Even as he committed to the hypothesis he recognized its weaknesses, but it was the only shot he had. His passcard could, in the most literal sense, be the key he needed to unlock the Stormcloud files.

He booted up his laptop, unwilling to risk anything more. Ran a quick diagnostic, satisfied himself all important data were safely backed up elsewhere.

Now to test the bizy card. He held it next to the laptop's upload port and pressed *Xmit*.

Nothing.

His heart sank, until he saw the bizy card's low battery warning light. He cursed, once more rummaged through his tool kit and scared up a fresh cell. He replaced the battery and tried it again. This time it worked, old files scrolling down the card's tiny viewer until the upload light flashed completion of the task, the laptop application opening and echoing the confirmation. Everything working.

He took a moment to purge the bizy card's datacore. He wanted no files there to distract the virus. Task complete, he slid the UniCom passcard into the frame. Crossed his fingers, and pressed *Read*.

Instantly, the viewer displayed his UniCom ID photo, retinal scan, personal stats and clearance codes. He allowed himself a fleeting moment of elation. The bizy card could read his passcard. So far the hypothesis held, modest though the victory.

He held the bizy card once more next to the laptop port, thumb resting lightly on the *Xmit* button. If this didn't work, the laptop would be all he'd lose, if the virus was on the passcard. He'd be right back where he started, but . . .

Screw it. He mashed *Xmit*.

The laptop chirped. There he was on the monitor, in all his bald, middle-aged glory. He kissed the bizy card and put it aside, thanking God for making him a gadget freak. Now for the true proof. If the virus was on the passcard, it was now on his laptop. And since the laptop wasn't curently shuddering in its death throes, the registry was there, too. Only one way to find out for certain.

He knew from the day's explorations where the virus first set up shop. There he looked, and there it was, sleeping like a baby — the now-familiar viral signature.

He slapped the table triumphantly, so hard the laptop jumped.

Isolate, identify, inoculate — done, done and fucking done. He had the registry, had a safe system. He'd isolate the registry itself later, wherever it had installed itself. Only one thing now left to do.

He hooked the new crystal drive to the laptop, loaded the ball containing the Stormcloud files he'd downloaded in Yamada's office.

The upload completed. Price tapped the keypad.

He slumped in his chair, staring at the monitor. His head fell back, his delighted laughter shaking the very walls. "Yes! Don't you *mess* with me!" he crowed. "You see what happens when you mess with me!"

He beheld the laptop screen in wonder, the neat, crisp, beautiful columns of files. He eagerly scrolled through the data, stopping once he saw the MFR transcription. "We've got his ass in a sling now, Mac," he chuckled. "Nothing left but the cryin'."

He attacked the laptop with renewed zeal. Much work still remained but by the time he called it a day, he'd be able to load and read the files on his main system. Then he'd make copies, two of which would be transmitted first thing in the morning to waiting parties in Charleston, along with very specific instructions.

He giggled like a child as he worked. It was turning into his best Christmas ever.

Thirteen

December 26, 2022
Monday

I

L-04:27:00

Roger Conner made his way through the clot of reporters gathered around the SLC main gate, escorted by Martha, Price and Davis. He swung his cane jauntily, elated to be out of that damned chair. He waved at the press, answered their shouted questions with only an indulgent smile. They were running a bit late, their departure from the hotel delayed by Price, something about having to call his shop in Charleston to check in. Normally it would have irritated Conner, but not today. He felt on top of the world.

They entered the waiting van, which took them to the LCC. Davis departed immediately upon their arrival; a group of VIPs would be arriving soon, invited by Conner personally to watch Mac's landing at the temporary DZ set up northwest of the SLC. Potential investors all, though none was aware of the true reason for their summons. That would become clear at the press conference immediately following Mac's return. Conner had spent most of the night before with Davis, putting the finishing touches on the prepared statement tucked in his inner coat pocket. In just a few hours, he was going to knock the world on its collective ass.

The ficker was buzzing, Mac's arrival now less than five hours away. Conner cheerfully greeted Doctor Yamada:

"Afternoon, Bobby! How are we doing?"

"We are doing nominally."

Conner chuckled. "Nominal? Why don't you just admit everything's going splendidly? What's wrong with 'great? Everything's going great?'"

Dark circles hung below Yamada's eyes. He covered his headset mic with his hand. "When that cowling jettisons and Mac is on the ground in one piece, then I'll say everything's great."

Conner casually glanced about, confirming no one was within earshot. "I thought we covered this, Bobby."

"Just because you choose to ignore what happened up there doesn't mean —"

"Any indication so far that there's a problem?"

"No," Yamada grudgingly admitted. "We ran a remote diagnostic first thing this morning."

"Well, then." Conner held his eye, daring him to say more.

Yamada didn't back down. "We should tell him," he urged. "No one has more of a right to know."

"Bobby. There's nothing to tell." He turned to face the main monitor, showing an image of the cloudless blue sky.

II

L-03:41:00

Davis stood aside as the VIPs disembarked from the shuttle bus. They'd just finished a tour of the SLC, including an audience with Conner and Yamada in the LCC. They'd been flown to Vandenberg on the UniCom tab the night before, wined and dined at a private banquet and presented with drop briefing booklets and laminated passes that morning. These weren't easy people to impress but even to Davis' cynical eye, so far it appeared as if they were succeeding.

The last of the bigwigs filed into the viewing tent, where two rows of chairs were arranged on a bi-level carpeted bleacher. There were portable air conditioners, but the weather so far was balmy. He moved to the front of the tent, where a video monitor had been erected, for now obscuring their view of the far distant windsock marking Mac's precisely calculated landing site, give or take a mile. There were a few vehicles there, tiny against the sandy, scrub-dotted terrain — UniCom camera crews setting up to record the event, plus a fire truck and two ambulances, just in case. Davis couldn't imagine why they might need a fire truck.

He turned to his guests as they settled in. "Ladies and gentlemen. I suppose you're all wondering why we've invited you out here today." It was an old line but it won a more laughs than he'd expected, a good sign. He cranked the charm full-on while he delivered his brief preamble, his jaded audience hanging on every word; no degree of calculated cool could diminish the event's wonder. They would be able to say they were there, Davis declared. That they saw they sky, felt the wind, heard the sonic boom. They shook Major Mackinley Harrison's hand.

He wrapped his comments to warm applause and nodded to the technician manning the console off to the side. The video screen blinked to life, the thundering tympanis and regal brass of Aaron Copeland's *Fanfare for the Common Man* filled the air. Davis had scripted the half-hour presentation himself, a summary of the labors which had brought them to this day. Let the engineers fret over the drop. This was showbiz, baby.

He moved discreetly out of the tent, took in the solid wall of press lining the other side of the fencing a half-mile away. The sun glinted off of a forest of vehicles, antennae, microwave dishes and cameras. He felt proud. He'd done his job. Everyone was there, watching, and waiting.

He turned and gazed at the drop zone, then lifted his eyes to the sky.

III

L-00:54:00

Had Price been watching on television, things would've appeared no different than in the hours preceding. But inside the ficker, the mood was electric. As soon as the count clock had tripped over the one-hour mark the rise in the tension level had been immediate and palpable. Martha had left the ficker a few minutes earlier, arranging her and Price's transportation to the DZ — they'd agreed that they'd depart together following Mac's re-entry, to be there when he touched down. Conner was now absent from the room as well. On the odd occasion that they'd caught one another's eye, Price had only nodded and smiled. He'd pick his own time to drop his bombshell. After the press conference, perhaps, when the smug bastard was basking in his triumph. Someplace where it could be just the two of them, and Mac. Hell, he might even invite Boykin.

He made his way over to Yamada. The engineer glanced over as Price pulled up. "Good timing. We're about to radio Major Harrison for the last pre-entry check."

"May I talk to him?"

"As soon as we're done, certainly." He nodded to the CAPCOM officer, who returned the gesture. "Dropsled, UniCom."

Mac sipped water from the tube, rinsing the last of the sweet protein soup from his mouth. He swallowed. "Roger, UniCom, I read you."

"T-minus twenty-nine minutes to atmospheric re-entry. L-minus-fifty-one, confirm."

Mac checked his console chronometer, ticking away in synch with the UniCom master. "Roger that, Doc." He lifted his eyes. The Earth filled the entirely of his vision now, the way he remembered it from his combat drops. "All systems read normal. Looks like the folks in Colorado are in for some snow. Tell everyone I said to wax their skis, will ya?"

"Roger that," Yamada replied, voice grave as always. "Stand-by, please."

Mac waited a moment. Then:

"UniCom to crazy fool. Come in, crazy fool."

Mac grinned. "Willie! How's the weather down there?"

"Nothing but sunshine. Thought I might do a little surfing before you show up. How's the weather up there?"

"I keep reminding myself there won't be anyone shooting at me this time."

"Hey, if it'll make you feel any better I'll head on out to the DZ with a powergun and lob a few tracers up at ya."

"You'd do that for me?"

"Pshaw, just say the word! I'll be out there anyway when you get here."

"You will, huh."

"Yes, her too," Price playfully added. "There's a lot of people waiting on you down here, brother." His voice was solemn now. "Waiting on all of you."

"We're on our way."

"Roger that. D-minus-forty-nine. Alpha leader out."

"Bravo leader acknowledge and out."

That was it. It wasn't Conner's drop anymore. Price had just officially claimed it for the 82nd. The Shooting Stars were nearing the end of their final mission.

IV

L-00:41:00

Boykin strode onto the flightline where his F-120 Goshawk waited, fueled and ready to go. It felt good to wear the flight suit after so long. His two days in the air getting reacquainted with the Goshawk had been like returning to a former lover's forgiving embrace. In her arms he had rediscovered himself, had found no judgment. She and no other accepted him for what he was now, and that mirror had enabled him to finally do the same. He didn't need the weight of captain's bars on his shoulders to be a man again. Only her.

He took a moment to run his hand across the aircraft's sun-warmed skin, a fond moment of wordless thanks.

"Beautiful, isn't she?"

Boykin nodded affirmatively to the young flight tech ducking under the nose of the warfighter, just finishing his pre-flight check. "Don't know why they bothered with the 120A. Not a thing in the world wrong with this one."

"Yeah, that's what my old man says," the boy responded. "He used to fly 'em during the war."

Boykin scowled and climbed the ladder up to the cockpit.

Davis pocketed his phone. "I've just received word that Captain James Boykin is in the air," he announced, drawing an excited murmur from his guests. "We should be able to see him any minute now."

The still-active video monitor had been moved to one side, allowing an unobstructed view of the DZ. Davis caught his assistant's eye; he activated the motor that cranked back the forward fabric of the tent roof. The VIPs shielded their eyes from the sudden flood of sunlight as they looked up.

A finger stabbed skyward, a scant second before the doppler-shifting scream of a jet engine floated down upon them. Davis looked up in time to see Boykin's aircraft streak by overhead, climbing fast to his rendezvous.

V

L-00:31:00

"Dropsled, UniCom. Sixty seconds to entry interface, stand-by for LOS, over."

"Copy, UniCom. Standing-by for entry. Next communication at L-minus-twelve, over."

"Affirmative. UniCom out."

The Earth lay open before him, the angular sense of approach gone. He was a diver now, plunging head-first into invisible layers of atmosphere. It was all so familiar, and yet so new, this journey which had always before been bound by design to death. That fatalism was absent now, gone forever. The Earth shone, and Mac felt strong.

He gave his parachute rig straps a final tug and lowered his helmet faceplate. He was already surrounded by the thermosphere. In less than a minute he would penetrate the outer layer of the thick mesosphere, and the sled would be engulfed in flame. That's where loss of signal would peak, the total communications blackout caused by electrical interference as the intense heat ionized the atmosphere around the sled. LOS would end when he emerged into the stratosphere, after which he'd blow the cowling and hit the peas.

And just like that, it would be over.

The sled began to vibrate. Mac gripped the steering levers and snugged himself down into the padding. A ripple of heat like sheeting rain painted the cowling nose warm orange, then fiery yellow.

Mac lowered his head and hung on.

"Velocity eighteen-thousand KPH and slowing." The guidance officer relayed the data. "Pressure at fourteen PSI, temperature at nine-hundred forty degrees Celsius and rising."

CAPCOM spoke on his heels: "LOS in five . . . four . . . three . . . two . . . one. Confirm LOS. Next communication in twelve minutes."

Yamada stared at the monitor, showing only blue sky. Nothing to do now but wait.

The sled was shaking violently now. Mac squeezed his eyes closed against the warm sweat sheathing his face, dripping off his nose onto the helmet faceplate. The heat, he'd forgotten how hot it got, even with the thick siliplas protecting him.

He gritted his teeth against the increasing violence of his passage, all sense of time gone, all sense of rational perspective stripped away.

His entire world was compressed into this moment, his history, his solitary, penitent years. The hellish crucible burned away the last vestiges of his guilt, cleansed the impurities from his warrior's soul.

The images of his fallen comrades flashed before him. At last he was able to confront them on equal footing, to stand with them once more as they made their final journey home, the journey they'd been denied by lies and honor forsaken. Mac reclaimed that honor now, holding each of their faces in his mind, formally acknowledging their presence; reunited now, sisters and brothers. Price, too, Boykin and even Martha. Mac carried them all in his heart, bearing them through the fire. He wasn't dead, not this time. His duty now was to live.

From deep in his memory a snatch of bawdy verse arose, called forth by his homecoming. He'd thought he'd forgotten it, but now Nick Kaligolos' hale baritone filled his mind. He smiled through the strain and thought of Davis as he sang through gritted teeth:

Call your mama, soldier
Your fightin' days have passed
I'm locked and loaded, comin' for ya
With a rocket up my ass . . .

The sled attained terminal velocity, a bright flaming meteor streaking Earthward.

Oh the clouds will part with a mighty fart
From the rocket up my ass . . .

A faint, rumbling peal of thunder echoed across the flat landscape. A sonic boom.

Davis searched, stopped, stabbed his extended finger at the sky: "There! There it is!"

Boykin pulled the stick back and right, roaring through the burning blue towards the scorched black dot above him.

"UniCom, this is chase. I have visual on the dropsled. Moving to intercept."

* * *

291

Price moved forward, staring at the monitor where the hazy image of the tiny dropsled hung suspended in the powder haze. There were a few cheers in the room. Yamada's hand flew to his headset mic.

"Dropsled, UniCom. Confirm AQS, over."

"Roger, UniCom, I hear you." Mac's voice was strong. "All systems read nominal. Deploying stabilizers, standing by for manual cowling jettison. Acknowledge."

Yamada cast a quick glance over at Conner, standing next to him. "Roger that. Standing by."

Price didn't miss the concern on Yamada's face. "Something wrong?"

"No a thing," Conner replied, eyes not leaving the monitor.

"Altitude one-hundred-thousand feet," a voice called. "Velocity Mach-plus-one and decelerating. L-minus ten-minutes-thirty-seconds, counting."

Mac pulled back on the steering levers, felt the sled slowing, felt it belly out against the resistance. The sunlight shone on his upturned face. It felt right, everything felt right.

He snapped the safetys in place, locking the levers into position, ran a final swift systems check. His wrist altimeter was active now, just as Guthrie had promised. The P-seal on his flight suit was holding — comforting to know his blood wouldn't boil when he ejected. The pressure would decrease automatically as he descended, air escaping through the bleeder cock set to read barometric pressure, just like during the Pan-Am.

Everything was set.

He thumbed the cover back from the jettison control.

"Jettison in three . . . two . . . one . . . mark!"

He took a steeling breath and mashed the button.

Staccato thuds sounded as the explosive bolts fired. Mac immediately lowered his head and tucked his elbows in tight against his ribs against the blast of wind to come . . .

At once the sled rocked, pitching violently right. Mac's left shoulder slammed into the padding, his helmet banging against the lip of the sled.

He raised his head in alarm — the sled was spinning, tumbling tail-over-nose. Only the left edge of the cowling had separated. The right was still held fast, providing the resistance that had just destroyed the sled's carefully-plotted trajectory.

He shouted to be heard over the roar of the windrush: "UniCom, we've got a problem!"

"No!" Conner lunged forward, banging his cane into the floor. "No!"

The data processing systems engineer half-rose out of his seat: "Jettison failure! The cowling has not jettisoned! Repeat, the cowling has not jettisoned —"

"Copy!" Yamada shouted. "FIDO, status!"

"Altitude ninety-two-thousand-feet! L-minus five-minutes, thirty-seconds."

Martha watched the monitor in horror. The sled was tumbling through the air like a missile deprived of power. "Oh no," she murmured, unable to believe what she was seeing. "Oh no . . . "

"This is chase," came Boykin's voice over the PA. "Somebody there wanna fill me in? Over."

"Bobby, do something!"

Yamada whirled on Conner, furious despite his near-panic. "You see? Do you see?"

"See what?" Price demanded.

Conner glared at Yamada warningly. Price looked to one man, then the other. Neither answered.

He surged forward and slammed his hand into Yamada's chest, grabbing a handful of the surprised engineer's shirt. He pulled Yamada down to his level, digging the thick fingers of his free hand into Yamada's throat, pinching the larynx until his eyes bulged. He held his face inches from Yamada's.

"I don't need my legs to kick your ass! You tell me what the fuck's going on!"

"The sled!" Yamada gurgled, face contorted. "Sabotaged, before the launch! The cowling . . . "

Price pushed him away and spun on Conner. The old man backed hastily away as Price advanced on him. "You did it again! Didn't you? You did it again you son of a bitch!"

"Hello? Is anyone still listening to me?"

Mac's shout seized everyone's attention. Price yanked away Yamada's headset. "You copy all this, Mac? You hear this bullshit?"

"Jimmy, you out there?"

Boykin flew the F-120 in a tight corkscrew, keeping roughly parallel with the dropsled.

"Roger, Mac, right with ya."

"Can you still fly that thing like you used to?"

"Whatcha got in mind?"

"Ram me!"

There was sudden silence in the control room, disturbed only by Boykin's voice.

"Say again?"

"Aim for the cowling! The impact should knock it loose!"

"I thought that thing had a parachute —"

"Sled's too heavy with me in it, it'd tangle to hell the way this thing's moving, anyway! You've gotta hit the cowling, Jimmy!"

Conner was staring, shaking his head vehemently. "That's crazy. It'll never work —"

"You listen to me," Price said, moving closer. Conner took another step back. "You remember back in your office? I've got copies of every single one of those files."

"That's imposs —"

"Including the MFR! If Mac dies, before this day is over every goddamn reporter here will have a copy of it, too! You copy *that?*"

Conner could only stare. Yamada watched him a moment then reclaimed his headset from Price, held it to his ear:

"Chase, this is UniCom. Do what Mac says. Now!"

Jesus.

Boykin swallowed his suddenly pounding heart. He craned his neck, peering over the leading edge of his starboard wing, studying the sled's movement. It was set in a pattern now, spinning in a barrel roll to the right as it tumbled. The cowling presented itself every three seconds, sunlight strobing off it when it flashed past.

No way. The window wasn't long enough. It just wasn't possible, no pilot could thread that needle, least of all a recovering drunk flying his first warfighter in ten years . . .

"Jimmy! You want that ring back?"

Tim's face flashed through Boykin's mind. He snugged his oxygen mask, flexed his fingers on the stick.

"Roger that, Major. Coming topside."

He zeroed the stick and pulled back, peeled out of his spiral pattern and climbed, putting a half-mile of blue between him and the sled in seconds. He pushed the stick left in a hard bank, swooping down on the sled like the Goshawk's namesake. The seat pressed against him as he kicked the belly fans into life, slowing his descent until he precisely matched that of the sled, hovering just above and to the right of it.

It wasn't going to work. He could barely see the sled now, and he'd have to time his impact precisely. He wasn't going to be able to come in from above.

He eased the jet around, metal groaning against the strain, the craft bucking beneath him. It wasn't designed to fly like this. He was in a controlled freefall, the nose held down just enough to prevent full stall.

He retracted the wings as much as he could, narrowing the jet's ventral silhouette, compensated for the lessened resistance by gunning the belly fans into full-throated thrust. It helped, though he still had to work hard to keep the jet level with Mac, taxing every bit of the F-120's celebrated combat maneuverability. As it was, the best he could manage was a surging rise and fall relative to the careening sled, but he was close enough now to glimpse Mac through the dark cowling. The oblong bubble was vibrating violently, Mac's body alternately slamming into it and falling away as the sled tumbled.

"Mac! Can you hold yourself away from the cowling?"

"Not for long! Tell me when!"

Boykin focused on the sled's somersaulting descent, silently timing the revolutions, counting the seconds between the flashes of cowling, gauging the distance between it and the nose of the jet. He couldn't hit it head-on without demolishing the sled and killing Mac. It would have to be a glancing blow, the merest skip of the Goshawk's belly across the cowling.

The irony of his situation flitted through his mind. Just days before, he would have celebrated Mac's death. Now he was praying he could summon the skill to save his life.

"Altitude forty-one-thousand feet . . . "

"Somebody shut him up!"

Boykin shouted at the nameless voice. He switched the stick to his left hand, lightly rested the heel of his right against the main throttle, counting silently.

Steady now . . .

Steady . . .

"Mac! Brace yourself!"

The cowling disappeared from view. Boykin counted one-one-thousand. Two-one-thousand.

He gritted his teeth and pushed the throttle full open.

Mac pulled himself into the padding and kicked his feet hard against the aft braceplate. He had a split-second impression of an enormous shadow blocking the sun before something smashed into the cowling. The sled bucked insanely in concert with the impact, tearing free his death grip on the steering levers. His head snapped back, slammed into the cowling, forcing a cry from between his clenched teeth as the scream of the jet's engines exploded in his ears.

He caught a glimpse of the aircraft's belly as it roared away and then his head went light . . .

" . . . over! Mac, do you copy?"

Yamada's urgent words pulled Mac out of his daze. He'd been knocked briefly unconscious by the impact of the jet. His ears were still ringing from the blow. He tasted salt, felt moisture running from his nose onto his top lip. Must have hit the helmet faceplate . . .

"Mac!"

"Yeah, I'm still here!" Mac barked, spitting blood.

"Did it work?"

He was lying sideways in the sled now, his back to the free edge of the rattling cowling. The siliplas was starred, spiderweb cracks spreading from the point of impact. The cowling had been bent back a few inches in the starboard sink channel but it was still held fast.

"Negative, negative! Jimmy, hit it again!"

* * *

Boykin had both hands on the stick, fighting to keep the jet nose-up and level. He attempted to re-extend the wings to full flight. They responded sluggishly.

A shrill beeping sounded inside the cockpit. His eyes flashed across the instruments, locked on the blinking warning light. The hydraulic pressure was dropping rapidly. He was losing fluid. As it was, he had to keep the throttle full open to remain airborne. He'd never be able to land at that speed, without the wings in full spread. And with the plane bleeding to death, he soon wouldn't be able to do much of anything at all.

"We've lost signal! Last altitude thirty-thousand feet!"
Yamada shouted into his headset. "Chase! Can you see anything?"
"Stand-by, UniCom . . . "
"Jimmy!" It was Mac. "Did you hear me? Hit it again!"
No response.
Yamada watched the monitors. The dropsled filled the main screen, close enough now that it seemed to be spinning directly for them. A secondary screen tracked Boykin's jet. It was nosing downward, venting a faint spray from beneath the port wing.
"Chase! Do you copy? Chase!"

Boykin wrestled with the dying craft. Memories of the Pan-Am flashed through his mind, of that singular battle over the Adriatic, the one that had defined him as a pilot and as a man, ending with his plunge into the icy waters. Nothing but desert below him now, rushing up to claim him.

Good luck, Mac. I did what I could.

The labored engine whine grew louder as the ground raced closer. Boykin slapped his helmet faceplate down, tucked in his elbows and reached between his knees.

Davis watched the sky, eyes darting back and forth between the dropsled and Boykin's jet as it nosed more sharply downward, then began tumbling end-over-end. Seconds later the scream of the engines reached his ears and then he saw the black-orange fireball as the F-120 plowed into the ground a mile away. The explosion echoed across the terrain.

He stared open-mouthed, ignoring the startled cries of his guests. The fire truck and one of the ambulances raced towards the pillar of black smoke.

"Oh, this sucks."

"We've lost contact with chase!"

"No shit!"

Price shouted, seeing the fireball on the monitor, hoping Boykin had been able to eject in time. He re-focused on the main monitor, unable to determine if Boykin's efforts had done any good.

It couldn't end this way, no just God would let it end this way. He prayed with everything he had.

"C'mon, Mac, get out of there!"

They'd lost contact with Boykin, Mac had heard the frantic announcement. He didn't know what had happened to Boykin but it was clear he was now on his own, with precious little time left.

He squirmed in the cramped space, trying to face the cowling. Something arrested his movement, something tugging at his left hip. He reached down and felt the oxygen feed and medical lead. He yanked the latter away from his suit, but the tube was stuck. He twisted his body harder, trying to yank it free of the tether, knowing it was designed to pull free when he ejected. It obstinately refused to budge. He felt a sudden wave of desperation . . .

His hand darted to his chest, fingers closing around the hook knife Gershon had pointed out back in the drop shack. The U-shaped plastic was lined with a razor, designed to capture and cut tangled shroud lines.

He yanked the knife free of its elastic chest strap and swiped viciously at the oxygen tube. He felt the pressure at his hip vanish as the razor clove it in two.

He dropped the knife as he twisted onto his back, bracing his elbows against the sled's sides to keep from being further jostled. With the cowling partially freed, there was just enough room for him to plant his feet against the cracked siliplas now directly before his eyes.

He brought his knees into his chest and pushed. The clamshell rose a precious few inches, more daylight now showing to his right. He slid his right foot along the concave surface, knees grinding together, trying to sneak his toe beneath the lip. He had to release the pressure against the cowling to do it. It settled an inch. It wasn't going to work.

He re-planted the foot next to his left and pushed anew, straining. The cowling gave once again. He kept pushing, finding new strength as he heard the stressed metal groan by his left ear.

He released his grip on the sides of the sled and quickly grabbed his knees, bracing his elbows against his ribs, locking them beneath his legs like pillars, straining, refusing to give up.

There was no way he was going to die like this. Not now.

Sensei, he prayed. Father.

Help me.

One last time.

His body tingled as that familiar thrumming vibration filled his head, blotting out the sounds of the windrush, the rattling sled, the approach of death. He inhaled, ignoring the clotting blood in his nose, pulling the air deep into his one-point, feeding the furnace of his *ki*. His tired muscles swelled with new resolve, with the strength of those invisible who walked the Path by his side. Placing their hands on his in answer to his prayer, pouring their *ki* into his heart.

Summoning every burning ember of his warrior's spirit, Mac kicked against the cowling with his entire being. His thighs burned with the effort, triceps trembling as he dug his hands into his knees. His defiant *kiai* rumbled up from deep within him, exploded from his throat like a physical force. The roar filled the sled, detonating like a cannon shell against the obstinate lid of his coffin.

The cowling groaned a final time and then all resistance disappeared. The windrush clasped his legs and pulled him into empty space.

He was free.

There was pandemonium in the control room. Every person was on their feet; jumping, cheering, embracing as the glorious sight of Mac flying free of the dropsled filled the monitor.

"Yes! My man Mac!"

Price screamed with joy, pumping his fists into the air. He felt Martha's hands around his neck and returned her embrace. Conner looked as if he didn't know whether to cheer or weep. Price jabbed his finger into the old man's chest.

"Eat that!"

He grabbed Martha's hand and sped for the door, to the waiting jeep. Conner sagged as Yamada stared at him, hands splayed on his console, drained.

Mac tugged his helmet off, reveling in the cold blast of air on his sweat-slick face. He flung the helmet from his fingers and threw himself into an arch, stretching every fiber in his body, letting the wind resistance toss him about in the air like a falling leaf.

He glanced at his altimeter: eleven-thousand feet. Damn near a whole two miles to play.

He tucked, somersaulting, arched again and spun in pinwheel circles, exulting in the joy of being free of the sled, of being alive. The sky was a beautiful cloudless blue-white and stretched into infinity all around him. Below he could see Slick Six, anchoring the chain of SLCs stretching to the north, up to the shining dots of cars making their slow way along the highway at the south end of the main base. He spun again and faced the ocean, dark and glittering in the sun. Beautiful, all so beautiful . . .

Boykin! He scanned the sky full circle, searching for the jet. Then he saw it, far below, to his right, the plume of black smoke.

His heart fell. No, it couldn't be. Not now . . .

He felt hands close around his ankles. He twisted — there was that broad hillbilly face, grinning at him through his open helmet faceplate. Boykin released his hold and tucked in his elbows as Mac turned towards him, flying in close. Mac reached out and slapped his hands on Boykin's outstretched wrists. Together they flew, laughing, the redneck crowing a long, high whoop of delight.

Mac released his right hand and reached down into the broad neck opening of his pressure suit. He fumbled beneath the fabric until he felt it through his glove.

He yanked, snapping the chain, held out Timothy Boykin's class ring. Boykin sobered, reached out and carefully accepted the talisman, his to carry the final distance home. His fingers closed tightly around it as the thin gold links streamed from the top of his fist in the wind. He released his other hand and drifted away, raising his free hand in a final salute.

Mac checked his altimeter again, reached behind him and tugged the pilot 'chute free from its mooring, let it catch air and rise from his hand. In seconds he felt the hard yank as the main rag deployed, jerking him upright. He reached up to unstow his brakes and beheld the company crest of the 82nd Special Airborne, revealed as the parachute billowed open, the UniCom logo riding next to it: Conner's final theatrical touch.

Mac grabbed the front risers and pulled. The canopy nosed downward, speeding him home.

Far below, the sled crashed into the ground. It bounced. Bounced again, flipping end-over-end as it skipped across the surface, kicking up explosions of sand before finally stabbing nose-first into the ground like a blunt dagger, a thousand feet from the point of impact.

With a groan it slowly toppled over, coming to final rest topside-down, rocking gently before it was still. After a moment, the recovery pilot 'chute popped out of the ruined tail and floated gently to the ground.

Martha brought the borrowed jeep to a sliding halt two-hundred feet from the windsock, where the ambulance and camera crew waited. Everyone's eyes were raised skyward, following Mac's descent.

Price unfolded his chair in record time and strove to push himself forward. The narrow wheels spun in the sand. Martha tried her best to help, pushing from behind.

"Go, go!" Price waved her away with a grin.

Martha trotted forward, face uplifted. Mac was close enough now that she could hear the flapping of his slider. He banked the canopy hard in her direction, released the front risers and yanked down on the back ones. The parachute flared a foot above the ground and Mac touched down ten feet away. A perfect stand-up landing.

The canopy collapsed behind him as Mac strode forward, taking Martha into his arms. She tasted the sweat and blood on his mouth as they kissed, ignoring the rough beard stubble against her face. He held her hard, drinking her, leaving no doubt now about his love. She responded in kind, pulling his head down to hers, affirming her love in kind.

They parted. Mac reached out and laid his finger against the *ki* pendant resting atop her blouse.

"Looks good on you."

"What do you think Sensei would say?"

"He'd say it's about time I came back home."

Over her shoulder, Mac saw Price, waiting next to the jeep. He tore open the front seal on his pressure suit as he strode over, pulled out the photo of the 82nd. He knelt beside his friend, holding it where both could see. It was wrinkled, damp with sweat. They stared at the faces in reverent silence.

"Looks like they made it home after all," Price finally said.

They embraced, brothers.

Mac looked up and behind him as the sound of a slider filtered in. Boykin touched down a few yards away, taking a few hard steps to recover from his late flare. He turned and yanked his risers, collapsing the canopy as Mac approached.

"You punched out, you know." Mac raised his chin towards the far-off wreck of the Goshawk.

Boykin pulled off his helmet and looked over, squinting. "Yep. Reckon I did." He dropped the helmet to the sand at his feet and stripped off his gloves, shrugging. "Didn't much feel like dying today."

"You saved my life."

Boykin looked back at him. He upended a glove and his brother's class ring dropped into his hand. He held it up between them.

"Call it even," he said, grinning. They shook hands, another circle closed.

"Outstanding!"

Mac turned. Conner was making his way towards him, past Martha and Price. He was ebullient, playing his munificent role to the hilt as the cameras tracked him. Mac grinned, rubbing blood from his lip as he walked over to meet him.

"Incredible, Major! The sheer courage! Thank God you're all right, that's all I can say! Well done, my boy, well do —"

Conner bit off his last word as Mac took his outstretched hand and twisted. He gasped, staring at Mac in shock as pain lanced through his thin wrist. Mac held his grin, barely moving his lips as he spoke.

"You were gonna let me die, you wrinkled heap 'o shit."

"No . . . "

Conner gasped again, knees buckling as Mac twisted harder. "Careful," Mac murmured. "The whole world is watching."

Conner forced himself to remain erect, screwing on a comical smiling grimace through the pain. Mac raised the photo of the 82nd.

"I didn't do this for you. I did it for them. For Sensei. For Boykin. For Martha, and for me."

He held Conner's eye. "You go to hell."

Mac released Conner's hand. He tucked the photo beneath his arm as he slid the helium-3 canister from its thigh pouch. They both turned towards the camera. Conner draped his arm around Mac's shoulders and held out his left hand, then winced as Mac slapped the metal cylinder hard into his palm and the cameras recorded it all for posterity.

Mac looked to his right, where Boykin stood, out of range of the cameras. He motioned him over and the three of them stood together, a very nervous-looking Conner sandwiched between the two much larger men.

After a few moments the director called clear. Conner moved away without saying a word, heading for the vehicle that would take him back to the SLC and the press conference. He didn't feel nearly as pleased as he had minutes before. This was supposed to have been his moment, but now he felt as if it had slipped beyond his control.

His fingers tightened around the smooth metal of the helium-3 canister. That was real. That's what it had been about all along, and it was his at last.

His spirits lifted as he gripped the prize. Bobby would find some way to explain away the jettison malfunction and the sheer drama of Mac's arrival would have his guest's expectations at a fever pitch, ready for his grand announcement.

He walked taller as he neared his ride. Things were working out splendidly after all.

He drew up as Price moved into his path.

"You remember our little talk? Back at the ficker?"

"Yes," answered Conner brusquely.

"My lawyer has a copy. *His* lawyer has a copy. Half-a-dozen people you will never meet have copies."

"Don't bluff me, Mister Price. The GRID-E virus ensures —"

"Oh, is that what it's called?" Price cut in, bemused. "I took care of that yesterday."

He reached into his pocket and tossed a CD to Conner. The old man fumbled to catch it. "I figured you wouldn't believe me so I copied a few of the more interesting files on that. Flight recorder's there too. You can verify it at your leisure." Price smiled affably. "I know you've got things to do."

Conner regarded the disk a moment before tucking it into his suit coat pocket. He studied Price's face.

"What do you want."

"Not a damn thing," Price answered, stone-faced. "Nothing you can give me that'll bring people back from the dead." He leaned in. "But you listen to me, old man. I don't like you. And I know exactly what you're capable of. If anything happens to me, or to Mac, or Martha, or Boykin, if any one of us so much as bounces a check or catches cold, *ever*. . . "

He waggled his finger in Conner's face. "You better watch your ass."

Conner swallowed, refusing to release Price's hard, triumphant gaze. There was nothing he could do. For the rest of his life, there would be someone out there with the knowledge to ruin him, utterly.

He turned — Mac and Martha were standing to his left, listening. And for the first time, Roger Conner saw something in Martha's face he'd never before seen. Pity.

The photographer called for everyone to assemble for a group photo. Mac moved behind Price and pushed, helping him through the deep sand towards the cameras, leaving Martha and Conner alone.

Conner again searched Martha's face, looking for alliance. She held his eye a moment, then glanced down at the helium-3 canister.

"Well. You got what you wanted," she said.

"What *we* wanted. There's a lot of work ahead of us now."

She only smiled as she moved forward and softly kissed his cheek, like a daughter kissing her father goodbye. She walked away to where Mac stood waiting for her.

Epilogue

The parcel had sat on Innes' desk since its arrival via overnight service that morning.

He gazed at it from his chair, as he'd been doing for hours. It was perhaps two foot square, wrapped in ordinary brown paper, and bore a U.S.A. return address. He recognized that address, knew it by heart, but it had taken him a moment to recognize the name of the sender. When he had, his heart had almost stopped as his nagging question had finally been answered.

He hadn't heard from Redding in over a week, not since his final communiqué before the moondrop. Obviously he had failed to stop the event, though Innes didn't know if Harrison's brush with disaster after re-entry had been Redding's handiwork. Redding's silence had troubled him, but he'd had too many other things to worry about.

He'd personally addressed his senior research staff, told them UniCom's fusion triumph was only a minor obstacle. Their spheromak was still on target. The massive publicity Conner was receiving would actually help them, by re-igniting interest in fusion in general. Those who didn't wish to play by Conner's rules would find Innes waiting with open arms. They were still a player. In his more optimistic moments, Innes almost believed it. He hoped his shareholders would.

He rose, walked to the wet bar across the office and poured himself a stout whiskey, downed it in one gulp. He poured another and carried the tumbler with him to the desk, setting it down next to the parcel as he once more read the name above the UniCom address. Mavis Chatham, Redding's imaginary lady love. Mavis had been Innes' mother's name, a private joke. It didn't seem at all amusing now.

He peeled the paper away, used his letter opener to cut the tape sealing the cardboard box beneath. He drank down half the whiskey in the tumbler before he lifted the lid.

His face flushed hot as he saw what rested below the crumpled packing paper. He lifted a clear siliplas pyramid from the box, a flake of ilmenite and tiny canister of helium-three suspended within, the aluminum plate affixed to the base bearing Conner and Harrison's engraved signatures and the date of Harrison's landing. He'd seen the commemorative trophy often enough on television to know what it was, knew Conner was mocking him.

He resisted an impulse to fling the object across the room. He instead placed it carefully next to his drink and lifted the large legal envelope from the box, the last of its contents. There was nothing on its clean white surface to indicate what it held.

He tore open the gummed flap, set the box on the floor and upended the envelope over his desk. A plastic card fell out, and a single photograph almost as large as the envelope. It dropped face-down onto the desk surface.

Innes let the envelope fall to the floor as he lifted Redding's identity card in his fingers. Why would Conner bother sending it? He'd already made it abundantly clear that he'd caught the spy. Rubbing his face in it even more, Innes realized. His anger returned as he tossed the card atop the desk and brusquely flipped over the photo.

All he could do for long moments was stare at the color image in shock. Liquid sloshed over his fingers as he clumsily grabbed the tumbler and finished off the whiskey, at last looking away from the photograph. Without the ID, Innes would never have recognized the swollen, bloodied face. Dear God, the eyes. It looked as if the eyes had exploded.

He lifted Redding's ID card in his unsteady hand. He hadn't noticed before. Someone had crossed out Redding's last name in black ink and written another above it in neat block letters.

Who on Earth was Berkeley?

Inspiration and Sources

Shooting Stars was from its inception intended to be one thing: an entertaining adventure. The central idea – that of a 'skydive' from the moon – came first, born of an all too brief foray into that exhilarating sport, during which I first learned of the existence of HALO jumping. My highest jump was from a modest 10,500 feet, just shy of two miles. Why stop there, I mused? Why not orbital jumps?

Why not higher?

Why indeed? Why would orbital skydiving become necessary? How would it be achieved? What prize would be worth spending the fortune necessary to stage UniCom's 'moondrop'? Library card in hand, modem at the ready, I searched for the answers which would provide the factual foundation for *Shooting Stars*.

Anticipating that I would be obliged to invent much of the foundation I required, I was startled to discover that everything I needed already existed. Each successive discovery as I explored both bolstered the central idea and expanded it, ultimately laying a foundation of real science which both supported and propelled the narrative, one more solid than ever I imagined it would be.

Resigned to invent, I now found myself pressed to keep pace with the real as new advances and discoveries rendered the science of earlier drafts old news. NASA's Lunar Prospector returned data suggesting the existence of lunar polar ice, dropping the gauntlet before UniCom's LUNOX-reliant technologies. Computer speed progressed from megahertz to gigahertz, gigabytes of data to terabytes, silicon processors to molecular. I saw a functional aircar. Had I the cash, I could *buy* the damn thing.

The challenge thus presented was not to find what I needed to support the story, but deciding what to leave out – when to stop trying to keep pace with this rapid technological development, where to plant that foundation of real science and begin building the fiction upon it.

That science which survived this winnowing to be sketched upon these pages is indeed real. The 82nd's Non-Recoverable Glide Vehicle dropsleds, space shuttle flyback boosters, mass drivers, LUNOX extraction, IEC ^{3}He fusion and more – all of it either already exists or is the subject of active research. But while I wanted the story to be as technically accurate as possible, when all was said and done, I wanted *Shooting Stars* to be that entertaining adventure I envisioned from the start. And so, while I hope you found *Shooting Stars* to be such, at the end of this journey I hope as well that you found *Shooting Stars* the modest scientific treatise, intriguing.

Concerning the latter prospect, what follows is a partial list of sources upon which I drew during my research, their inclusion here dictated by what I thought you might find interesting. I encourage you to explore these sources and hope you will find them as fascinating and stimulating as I did.

Thanks for reading my stuff.

Christopher Watson

March, 2000

Internet addresses were current at the time of first publication. Neither the author nor publisher assume any responsibility for their possible absence or alteration.

MARE SMYTHII COMMERCIAL LUNAR RESEARCH FACILITY (MOONTOWN)

"Moon Outpost Debated," *Ad Astra*, June 1991, p. 49.

"U.S. Draws Blueprints For First Lunar Base," *Aviation Week & Space Technology*, August 31, 1992, pp. 47-49, 51.

"Gas and Go on the Moon, *Ad Astra*, May/June 1994, pp. 31–35.

"Moon's Resources Key to Man's Return," *Aviation Week & Space Technology*, July 18, 1994, pp. 60-62.

"Early Lunar Resource Utilization: A Key to Human Exploration," B. Kent Joosten and Lisa A. Guerra: http://www sn.jsc.nasa.gov/ explore/Data/Lib/EICWord/ eic034w.doc
"Lunar Oxygen – Ground Truth and Predictions," Carl Allen; http://www-sn.jsc.nasa.gov/explore/Data/LEONews/ leo195/ lunox.htm
The Artemis Project homepage: http://www.asi.org/

ELECTROMAGNETIC MASS DRIVER

"U.S. Draws . . . " *Aviation Week & Space Technology, op.cit.*
"Gas and Go . . . " *Ad Astra, op.cit.*
Numerical Aerospace Simulation Facility at NASA Ames Research Center homepage: http://www.nas.nasa.gov
PERMANENT homepage: http://www.permanent.com

FUSION AND ³HE

"Mining the Moon's Gold," *Ad Astra*, May/June 1994, pp. 36–39.
"History of Research on ³He Fusion," G.L. Kulcinski; from "Second Wisconsin Symposium on Helium-3 and Fusion Power", John F. Santarius, compiler; Wisconsin Center for Space Automation and Robotics, report number WCSAR-TR-AR3-9307-3, July 1993
"Near Term Commercial Opportunities from Long Range Fusion Research," G.L. Kulcinski; *Fusion Technology*, Vol. 30, Dec. 1996.
"Reducing the Barriers to Fusion Electric Power," G.L. Kulcinski and J.F. Santarius; Fusion Technology Institute, University of Wisconsin-Madison, August, 1997.
Princeton Plasma Physics Laboratory homepage: http://www. pppl.gov University of Wisconsin NEEP 602/Geology 376 – Resources from Space Course Notes: http://silver.neep.wisc.edu/ ~neep602/ neep602.html
University of Wisconsin-Madison Fusion Technology Institute Homepage: http://fti.neep.wisc.edu/FTI/fti.html
Berkeley Department of Nuclear Engineering homepage: http://www.Nuc.Berkeley.EDU/

DROP SHIP REAGAN AND VANDENBERG

"Recoverable Glide Vehicle Tests Avionics Systems," *Aviation Week & Space Technology*, August 31, 1992, p. 60.

Guardians of the High Frontier, Internal Information Division, Headquarters Air Force Space Command Office of Public Affairs, Peterson AFB, Colorado.

The Space Shuttle Operator's Manual, Kerry Mark Joels, Gregory P. Kennedy and David Larkin; Ballantine Books, © 1992, Joels, et.al.

History of NASA – America's Voyage to the Stars, E. John and Nancy DeWaard; Exeter Books, © 1984, Bison Books Corp.

The Encyclopedia of U.S. Spacecraft, Bille Yenne; Exeter Books, © 1985, Bison Books Corp.

Vandenberg Air Force Base/30th Space Wing homepage: http://www .30sw.vafb.af.mil/

SPACE POLITICS

"A Space Program for the Rest of Us," *Ad Astra*, May/June 1994, pp. 21-25.

"Return of the Moon Treaty," *Ad Astra*, May/June 1994, pp. 27-29.

"Mining the Moon's Gold," Ad Astra, *op.cit.*

"U.S. Draws . . . ", *Aviation Week & Space Technology, op.cit.*

Astrobusiness – A Guide to the Commerce and Law of Outer Space, Edward Ridley Finch, Jr., and Amanda Lee Moore; Praeger Publishers, © 1984, Finch, Jr. and Moore.

MISCELLANEOUS

Carolina Sky Sports homepage: http://www.carolinaskysports.com/

United States Parachute Association homepage: http://www.uspa.org/

Moller International (aircars): http://www.moller.com

Biography

Christopher Watson

Christopher Watson was born into an Air Force family and grew up traveling the world, residing in eight states and two foreign countries before high school graduation. He worked his way through college as a radio disc jockey, farm hand, dishwasher and musical theater performer. Upon earning his BFA in Theater Arts he embarked upon an award-winning career as a writer and producer of original radio comedy. An avid martial artist, Mr. Watson is a contributor to the "Journal of Asian Martial Arts" and is co-author, with Roy Suenaka Sensei, of *Complete Aikido*. His past and present leisure pursuits include skydiving, scuba diving, fencing, chess, armchair physics, and perfecting his recipe for guacamole.

Printed in the United Kingdom
by Lightning Source UK Ltd.
101254UKS00002B/45